SHADOWS
DO NOT DIE

Solomon Nyx, Book One

JUSTIN LAMPERT

LAMPERT & SONS PUBLISHING

Copyright © 2026 by Justin Lampert

Published in the United States by Lampert & Sons Publishing.

Library of Congress Cataloging-in-Publication Data

Names: Lampert, Justin, author.
Title: Shadows do not die : a novel / Justin Lampert.
Series: Solomon Nyx ; book 1
Description: First edition. | Lampert & Sons Publishing, 2026.

ISBN 978-1-969709-49-4 (hardcover)
ISBN 978-1-969709-48-7 (paperback)

Cover design by Lampert & Sons Design

FIRST EDITION

For everyone who keeps fighting
even when the shadows don't behave.

"The spirit does not die.
What we give to others continues
even when we are gone."

—Kofi Asante

PART ONE

THE AWAKENING

CHAPTER ONE

Threads

The man across from Solomon Nyx was going to die in six days.

Solomon knew this the way you know when a glass is about to fall off a table—not logically, not visually, but with a certainty that settled in the chest before the mind could argue. The knowledge arrived complete, fully formed, unwanted. It didn't ask permission. It never did.

The man wore a gray business suit worn soft at the shoulders, the fabric bunched where weight had shifted over years of desk work and train rides. The collar had yellowed at the edges from sweat and repetition. He smelled faintly of cigarette smoke and citrus cleaner—addiction and shame, the combination that came from smoking in places you weren't supposed to and trying to hide the evidence. His knuckles were white against the handle of his briefcase, his eyes unfocused as the Tokyo subway rattled beneath them.

Six days.

Not from the smoking. Not from the stress visibly eating him alive. Something sudden. Solomon could see the thread now—a filament of deeper darkness running from the center of the man's chest upward, vanishing into a distance that had nothing to do with physical location. The thread was taut, humming with a vibration too low to hear but impossible to ignore.

If Solomon focused—really focused—he could almost trace the pattern of its ending. But that way lay madness. Literal madness, the sort that fractured your sense of what was real. He'd learned that lesson the hard way.

And lately, when he traced the threads too far, he sensed something else at the other end. Not death itself—death was simple, just an ending, a destination all threads eventually reached. This was something before death, something underneath it. An awareness so immeasurable and primordial that catching even a glimpse of it made his lungs forget how to breathe. The first time he'd felt it, three weeks ago on a crowded train platform, he'd stumbled off the train and vomited into a trash can, spent the rest of the night unable to sleep.

He hadn't traced a thread that far since.

Solomon looked away.

He wasn't supposed to stare.

That was rule number one, even if he'd never written the rules down. Staring made it worse. Staring made the threads sharpen, multiply, become a web of futures branching and collapsing around every person in his field of vision. Staring turned the subway car into a map of inevitable endings.

The threads were always there. Solomon had learned to blur them, to push them to the peripheral edges of his perception where they became noise rather than information. But looking directly at someone was like adjusting the focus on a camera—suddenly the soft blur resolved into sharp lines, and he couldn't unsee what the threads told him.

The train lurched through a tunnel, fluorescent lights flickering overhead. Solomon watched the reflection of the car ripple across the dark window—faces stretching, compressing, becoming something else for a half-second before snapping back into place.

That happened more often lately. The reflections not matching. The shadows not behaving.

He pressed his thumb into the scar on his palm, grounding himself. Chicago habit. Pain kept the world real. The scar was a raised line running from the base of his thumb to the center of his palm—a kitchen accident, officially, from when he was twelve and learning to cook because someone had to feed him when Naomi was at work.

Unofficially, it was where he'd cut himself during the first flash of death-sense, before he understood what was happening. He'd been sitting in English class when Mr. Harrison's thread snapped into focus—three months, maybe less, something in his chest already growing—and Solomon had grabbed the scissors without thinking, desperate to cut the image out of his own hand.

It hadn't helped. Mr. Harrison died right on schedule. But the scar remained, and now Solomon used it like a touchstone.

Something solid in a world of whispers and warnings.

Across the aisle, a woman laughed softly at something on her phone. The sound was bright, genuine—someone she loved had sent her something worth smiling about late on a Wednesday night. Above her shoulder, faint as smoke, a thin black filament trembled.

Long. Her thread was long, stretching upward in lazy spirals rather than the tight, urgent lines of imminent death. Decades, probably. Relief flickered through him, immediately followed by shame. He shouldn't be relieved about strangers' lifespans. Caring was just another way the threads wormed into your head and made themselves at home.

He swallowed.

Don't count, he told himself. Don't measure. Don't decide.

Those were the other rules—developed over months of accidental knowledge, of walking through crowds and trying not to calculate the collective remaining years of everyone he passed. Counting was addictive. Measuring led to comparison. And deciding what to do with the information—whether to warn or ignore or despair—that was the trap that would swallow you whole.

He hadn't always seen it.

Back then, death had been loud. Sirens. Shouting. The heavy stillness of a body that didn't answer anymore.

Naomi's body.

The memory hit like it always did—sudden, visceral, refusing to be filed away. The phone call at three in the morning. The walk to the hospital that was like swimming through concrete. The sterile room where they'd put her, covered by a sheet someone had chosen specifically for covering the dead. The wrongness of knowing such sheets existed, that someone manufactured them and shipped them and invoiced for them like towels or curtains.

He'd lifted the sheet.

He wished he hadn't.

The train screeched to a stop, metal shrieking against metal.

Doors slid open with a pneumatic hiss. People surged in and out—controlled chaos Tokyo performed better than any city in the world. Every body knew its place in the choreography.

Solomon stepped onto the platform at Shinjuku Station and immediately felt it.

Pressure.

Not emotional—spatial. The air had weight.

Shinjuku Station at midnight was a different creature than Shinjuku Station at rush hour. The crowds were thinner, more deliberate—people with reasons to be moving this late. The fluorescents buzzed at a lower frequency, casting shadows that pooled in corners and spread along walls like slow water.

Underneath it all, something coiled. A tension threaded through the concrete, the rails, the ceiling above his head. Tokyo was layered—everyone knew that. Centuries of history built on top of each other. But this was different. This existed in the spaces between things, in the gaps where normal attention didn't reach.

It tugged at him.

Not pulling—recognizing.

The sensation was hard to describe. Not hostile, exactly. More like a familiar room that leaned toward you when you entered it after being away—walls adjusting, air accommodating your presence.

Except this was a whole city responding to something in him that he didn't understand.

He'd felt hints of it in Chicago, in the months before Naomi died, when shadows occasionally thickened for no reason and certain corners made him uneasy. But Tokyo amplified whatever was happening to him. Whispers became conversations. Hints became statements.

And deep beneath the city—so far down that Solomon shouldn't have been able to feel it at all—something stirred. Not waking. Just... noticing. The way a sleeper notices a sound that isn't loud enough to wake them, incorporates it into dreams, and keeps sleeping.

Tokyo knew what he was, even if Solomon didn't.

And something beneath Tokyo knew too.

He adjusted the strap of his backpack—cheap canvas, second-hand, heavy with everything he owned that fit—and moved with the crowd. Head down. Shoulders hunched. Chicago had taught him how to disappear. You learned fast which posture invited attention and which deflected it. You learned to make yourself small without looking scared, to move with purpose without looking hurried.

Tokyo refined it. Here, invisibility was an art form. The salarymen, the students, the late-night wanderers—they all practiced their own versions of it, retreating into private worlds of phones and earbuds and carefully cultivated disinterest. Solomon had adopted their style. Earbuds in, even when nothing was playing. Eyes fixed on middle distance. Walk that said I know where I'm going, don't interrupt.

Most of the time, it worked.

A janitor mopped near a pillar plastered with advertisements—a pop idol whose duplicated smile grew more desperate the longer you looked. For a moment, Solomon saw the man's shadow detach from his feet and lag behind, reluctant to follow.

Solomon stopped walking.

The shadow snapped back into place.

No one else reacted. The late-night passengers continued their parallel journeys, faces illuminated by phone screens, bodies on autopilot. The janitor kept mopping, oblivious.

Solomon's heart hammered. His hands trembled. He shoved them in his jacket pockets and forced himself to breathe.

It's nothing. Just exhaustion. The city messing with you.

Except it wasn't nothing. These moments were happening more frequently—reality hiccupping, the rules governing light and shadow briefly forgetting themselves. In the beginning, he'd convinced himself he was imagining it. Stress and grief did strange things to perception. Sleep deprivation made the world shimmer at the edges. But imagination didn't explain why the shadows always moved the same way. Why they always moved toward him.

He exhaled slowly, counting steps as he climbed the stairs into the city's neon spill. Night swallowed him—signs blazing in Japanese and English and pure color, voices overlapping, music bleeding from bars and arcades and restaurants serving drunk salarymen their post-midnight ramen.

Alive. Loud. Beautiful.

And threaded.

The death-sense was easier to ignore up here, in Shinjuku's chaos. Too many people, too many competing stimuli. The threads blurred into background radiation, a constant hum of mortality he could push beneath the louder frequencies of neon and noise.

Solomon stood at the top of the stairs, staring out at the crossing crowds, and understood something that made his stomach tighten. The threads weren't random.

They were *listening*.

He walked for hours.

Not wandering—Tokyo didn't allow for wandering. Its streets were designed for purpose, for movement, for the relentless efficiency of a city that had rebuilt itself so many times it had forgotten how to be surprised by destruction. Every path led somewhere. Every corner connected to somewhere else.

But Solomon walked anyway, letting his feet trace patterns that had nothing to do with destinations. Past the neon temples of Kabukicho, where the night never ended and everyone was selling something. Through the quieter streets of Yoyogi, where old houses huddled together like conspirators. Along the edges of Meiji Shrine, where trees older than the surrounding buildings breathed differently, where the shadows fell naturally and the pressure in his chest briefly eased.

He didn't know what he was looking for.

That was a lie.

He was looking for her. Not Naomi—not in any literal sense. But for the shape she'd left behind, the negative space where his sister had been. Some part of him was convinced that if he walked far enough, searched long enough, he'd find traces of what had happened. Clues that would explain why she'd died, who had killed her, what any of it meant.

The police had called it random violence. Wrong place, wrong time. A mugging gone bad in a neighborhood she'd had no reason to be in.

Solomon didn't believe that.

He'd never believed that.

Even before the threads had started appearing, before shadows developed opinions, before Tokyo began recognizing him like an old friend—even then, he'd known the official story was wrong. Naomi had been too careful, too aware, too shaped by survival to put herself in danger without reason.

She'd been in that neighborhood for a purpose.

And someone had killed her before she could achieve it.

The thought circled back, same as it always did. The familiar loop of grief and fury that kept him company through the long nights when sleep wouldn't come. He'd followed that loop from Chicago to Tokyo, across an ocean and a language and a culture, and found it waiting for him wherever he arrived.

Who? Why? What were you doing, Naomi? What did you find that was worth dying for?

No answers. There were never any answers. Just questions that multiplied like the threads, spawning new questions with every attempt at resolution.

Solomon caught himself standing at the edge of a narrow alleyway, the sort that existed between buildings rather than because of them—a gap in the urban fabric where two structures hadn't touched. A vending machine glowed at the far end, its light painting the concrete in white and blue, offering canned coffee and green tea to an audience of no one.

He went in anyway.

Alleyways didn't judge. They didn't pretend. The shadows here were honest about what they were—darkness filling the spaces where light didn't reach. At least, that's what Solomon told himself. A stray cat watched him from a stack of wooden crates, its eyes reflecting the distant glow of the vending machine. Thin, gray and white, a communal stray that Tokyo neighborhoods adopted collectively. As Solomon passed, its shadow didn't match its movements exactly—a step behind, deciding whether to follow.

He stopped.

The cat blinked.

The shadow snapped into place.

Solomon laughed under his breath, a brittle sound. "Yeah," he murmured. "Me too."

The cat yawned, unimpressed, then went back to staring at whatever cats stared at in the small hours of the night. Its eyes caught the light strangely—for just a moment, they seemed to look past Solomon rather than at him, focused on something behind him that wasn't there.

Wasn't there.

Solomon didn't turn around.

But he felt it anyway. The attention. The vast, patient awareness that had been growing stronger ever since he'd arrived in Tokyo. It wasn't watching him in any normal sense—it was too big for watching, too ancient for anything so simple as observation. It was more like... gravity. Like the pull of something so massive that light itself bent around it.

The feeling passed.

The cat went back to being a normal cat.

Solomon leaned against the cool brick wall and let his head rest there. The city hummed around him, distant but constant. He could almost pretend he was another foreign kid killing time between shifts, counting yen, missing home.

Chicago came to him anyway.

Naomi's voice—low, warm, hoarse from too many late nights.

She used to sing when she was cleaning, old songs their grandmother had taught her, and sometimes Solomon would pretend to be annoyed but he loved the sound, loved the way it made their cramped apartment feel like somewhere rather than just anywhere.

Naomi's laugh—sudden, loud, completely unself-conscious. She laughed like she meant it, every time, as if joy was something you committed to rather than something that happened to you.

The way she used to stand between him and the world like she could block everything just by being there.

His fingers curled reflexively, nails biting into skin.

You should've told me, he thought, for the thousandth time. You should've run.

She'd known something was wrong, at the end. He was sure of it now, looking back with the clarity of loss. She'd been nervous in those final weeks. Checking her phone too often. Looking over her shoulder. Coming home late with excuses that didn't add up.

He'd asked her once if something was wrong.

She'd smiled—her real smile, the one that reached her eyes—and said she was just tired. Just stressed.

He'd believed her because he'd wanted to believe her.

And then she was dead, and no one could explain why she'd been in that part of the city at that time of night, and the official story was wrong place, wrong time, like it always was when the truth was too complicated or too dangerous to tell.

The pressure returned all at once—heavier now, focused.

Solomon straightened.

Someone was behind him.

Still distant, but approaching. Footsteps echoing softly against concrete— deliberate, unhurried, the type that knew exactly where they were going. Not the stagger of a drunk or the hurry of someone late. Not the distracted shuffle of someone on their phone. Purposeful. Intentional. Interested.

Solomon didn't turn around.

The threads in the air tightened, vibrating in unison, like a warning hum building toward a note he didn't want to hear. He felt them converging, pointing toward something just behind his field of vision. The shadows in the alley deepened, leaned inward, took notice.

Whatever was coming wasn't random.

It wasn't passing through.

It was moving *toward him.*

And somewhere deep inside Solomon Nyx—beneath grief, beneath fear, beneath the part of him that wanted to believe this was all in his head—something primordial stirred.

Not awake. Not fully.

But aware.

His shadow stretched across the alley wall, cast by the distant glow of the vending machine. For just a moment, it was too sharp. Too dark. Too present, like it was something separate from him rather than an absence of light.

The footsteps continued.

Solomon's hand found the scar on his palm.

And the night, which had been holding its breath for hours, exhaled.

The presence behind him didn't feel human.

That was the wrong way to phrase it. It probably was human—most things that moved through cities at night were. But there was a quality to the attention focused on him that didn't match casual curiosity or predatory calculation.

This was recognition.

He forced his breathing to stay steady. Forced his feet to stay planted. Running would acknowledge there was something to run from, and acknowledgment was a kind of invitation. He'd learned that in the months since the death-sense awakened. The strange things in the world responded to attention. They fed on acknowledgment. The less you admitted to seeing them, the less solid they became.

But this presence wasn't going away.

The footsteps continued—measured, patient, close enough now that Solomon could hear the specific quality of shoe leather against concrete. Something heavier than sneakers, older than cheap dress shoes. More deliberate.

"You're going to have to turn around eventually."

The voice was unexpected. Female. Calm. Japanese, but with an accent Solomon couldn't place—each syllable too precise for a native speaker.

He turned.

The woman was younger than he'd expected—mid-twenties, maybe, though her eyes suggested someone older. Dark clothes, practical, the type that didn't attract attention or impede movement. Short hair, efficient cut. Her posture held the stillness of someone who knew exactly what her body could do and was choosing not to demonstrate.

But that wasn't what Solomon noticed first.

What he noticed first was her thread.

Or rather, the absence of one.

He stared at the space above her head, at the place where the filament should have been—that thin dark line connecting every living person to their eventual ending. Every human he'd ever seen had one. Some short, some long, some trembling with imminent arrival, others stretching into decades.

This woman had nothing.

No thread at all.

The space above her head was simply empty.

"Ah," she said, watching his face. "You can see it."

Solomon's mouth was dry. "Who are you?"

"Someone who's been watching you for a long time, Solomon Nyx."

His name in her mouth was a blade unsheathing. He hadn't told anyone his full name since arriving in Tokyo. He'd been careful—using only his first name, paying in cash, staying in places that didn't require identification.

This woman knew him anyway.

"I'm not here to hurt you," she continued. "If I wanted to hurt you, I would have done it weeks ago."

"Weeks?"

"We've been aware of you since Chicago." Her eyes were dark, steady, revealing nothing. "Since your sister."

The mention of Naomi was a physical blow. His hands clenched, felt the scar on his palm pulse with remembered pain. The shadows in the alley deepened around him, leaning inward, and the woman's expression flickered, not fear, exactly, but attention. Like a scientist observing a particularly interesting reaction. "Don't," Solomon said, his voice hoarse.

"Don't what?"

"Don't talk about her."

The woman inclined her head slightly—an acknowledgment that felt like respect. "Very well. But you should know—what happened to her wasn't random. And neither is what's happening to you."

"I don't know what you're talking about."

It was a lie, and they both knew it. But Solomon needed her to say it first, to confirm what he'd spent months trying not to believe. To give shape to the shapeless dread that had been building since Naomi died and the shadows first started speaking.

The woman smiled—a mechanical expression, all mouth and no warmth. "The threads you see. The shadows that lean toward you. The sense that something's watching from the spaces between things."

She stepped closer, and Solomon resisted the urge to step back. "You've been pretending it's grief. Trauma. The side effects of loss. But it's not, is it?"

He didn't answer.

"It's real," she said. "All of it. And it's only going to get worse unless you learn what you are."

"And what am I?"

The question came out before he could stop it—the need to know overriding the caution that had kept him alive and invisible for months. The woman's smile widened slightly, but there was no warmth in it.

"Come with me," she said. "There are people who can explain it better than I can."

"I'm not going anywhere with—" The shadows moved.

Not slowly. Not subtly. The darkness pooled at the edges of the alley surged inward like a tide, swallowing the distant glow of the vending machine, blocking the exit to the street. For a moment, Solomon couldn't see anything—just black, pure and absolute, and the sensation of something boundless and unhurried pressing against his skin. Then the darkness receded, settling back into normal shapes.

The alley was empty.

The woman was gone.

Solomon stood alone in the narrow space between buildings, heart pounding, breath coming in short gasps. His hands were shaking. The scar on his palm burned like it had been touched with ice.

On the wall beside him, painted in darkness that gleamed wetly like fresh ink, were two words: FIND HER He didn't know who had written them, or when, or how—the paint hadn't been there a moment ago. But he knew what they meant. Knew it the way he knew the threads, the way he knew the deaths. Naomi.

Not gone. Not entirely—not yet.

Solomon stared at the words until the darkness stopped gleaming and became ordinary paint, until his heartbeat slowed and his breath steadied and the night around him felt merely dark rather than alive. Then he walked out of the alley and into the neon glow of Tokyo, the threads trembling around him like the strings of an instrument being tuned.

The next movement was about to begin.

And somewhere beneath the city—beneath the concrete and the rails and the accumulated weight of human history—something shifted in its long sleep.

Still sleeping, but dreaming more vividly now, its dreams shaped by the presence of the one it had been waiting for.

Three hundred years it had waited. Three hundred years since it had last felt a resonance like this—a consciousness that touched the threads the way it touched them, that existed in the spaces between life and death where it made its home. The others had been pale shadows of what it needed, flickering candles that guttered out before they could illuminate anything.

But this one was different.

This one saw.

The entity that had no name—that had forgotten its name so long ago the forgetting itself had become ancient—stirred in the dark places where forgotten things collected. It couldn't reach the surface, not yet. The bindings that held it were old and strong, woven by hands that had understood what they contained even if they hadn't understood why it mattered.

But bindings could be loosened. Patience could accomplish what force could not.

And the Reaper's vessel—the one who saw the threads, who spoke to shadows, who carried death like a second heartbeat—was finally beginning to wake.

The entity settled back into its dreams, satisfied.

Soon, soon, the waiting would end.

And then...

Then it would show the Reaper what waited at the other end of all those threads. What had been waiting since before human memory, since before the first cities rose and fell, since before anything with a name had walked beneath the sun.

Not to consume or destroy—to connect.

It had been alone for so very, very long.

But not much longer now.

Not much longer at all.

CHAPTER TWO

The Shape of Protection

Four years earlier Chicago — South Side The radiator was dying again.

Solomon could tell by the sound—a wet, metallic cough that started around midnight and continued until someone kicked it hard enough to remind it of its job. The building super had promised to fix it three times already. The building super promised a lot of things. He'd been promising to fix the stairwell light for four months. Promising to address the mold in the bathroom since before Solomon was old enough to notice it.

That was life in this building. Promises without follow-through. Hope deferred so long it stopped feeling like hope. You learned to work around the broken things instead of waiting for repair.

He pulled the blanket tighter around his shoulders and stared at the notebook in front of him. Geometry homework. Proofs. The teacher wanted him to prove that two triangles were congruent, as if the universe cared whether shapes matched, as if math could protect you from anything that actually mattered.

Mrs. Chen would give him a disappointed look if he showed up without it done. She'd started giving him those looks a lot lately—I know you're smarter than this and I know something's wrong—without ever actually asking what. Teachers learned not to ask too many questions in this neighborhood. The answers rarely made anyone feel better.

The apartment was cold enough to see his breath if he exhaled hard. Through the thin wall, he could hear Mrs. Patterson's television—some late-night preacher promising salvation to anyone who called the number on screen. His grandmother had loved those programs before she died, had sent money they couldn't afford to men who promised miracles that never came. Below that, the baseline thump of someone's stereo three floors down. And underneath all of it, the constant whisper of the city: sirens, traffic, the particular frequency of a neighborhood that never slept because sleeping meant missing something.

Missing the sound of trouble coming.

Solomon was fifteen years old, and he hadn't slept properly in weeks.

Not since he'd started noticing the shadows.

It was nothing he could point to and say this is wrong. Just a feeling, sometimes, when he walked home from school. A sense that the darkness in doorways was paying attention. That the space between streetlights held its breath when he passed.

His mother would have told him he was being dramatic. His mother told everyone they were being dramatic, when she was sober enough to form opinions about anything. She'd been living with her boyfriend for six months now, coming back to the apartment just often enough to collect mail and remind Solomon and Naomi that she technically existed.

Three days ago, walking home from the corner store where he'd bought bread and peanut butter with money Naomi had left on the counter, he'd passed an alley he'd passed a thousand times before. But that day the shadows inside had seemed deeper—not darker, exactly, but fuller, like they had weight and substance his eyes couldn't register. They hung in the space between dumpsters and brick walls like something solid, like curtains drawn across a stage.

He'd stopped walking without meaning to. Had stood on the sidewalk staring into that alley while people brushed past him, annoyed at the kid blocking the flow of traffic. An old man with a shopping cart full of cans muttered something about kids these days. A woman on her phone nearly walked into him.

Solomon hadn't noticed any of them.

Because something in there had noticed him staring.

He couldn't explain how he knew. No sound, no movement, no eyes reflecting streetlight. Just a sudden certainty that attention had shifted in his direction, that something in the dark had opened an eye that didn't exist and looked at him. The prickle at the back of your neck that tells you you're being watched.

Except this felt older. Deeper. Like being watched by something that had been watching for a long time.

Solomon had run home.

He'd dropped the bread somewhere on the way—had to go back for it the next morning, found it torn open and scattered by dogs or rats or the homeless guy who slept behind the laundromat. He'd told himself it was the cold. The stress. The not-sleeping making him see things. He was a teenager whose mother had essentially abandoned him, whose sister was working herself to death trying to keep them afloat. Stress did things to your brain. Made you paranoid. Made you see threats that didn't exist.

But that night he'd dreamed of the alley, and in the dream the shadows had spoken to him in a voice that was somehow his own voice, and when he woke up his pillow was wet with tears he didn't remember crying.

He'd tried to draw it once—the feeling, the shape of what he almost-saw—and ended up with a page full of spirals that made his eyes hurt to look at. The pencil had moved almost on its own, like automatic writing, like something was guiding his hand toward shapes it wanted him to see. He'd thrown the page away before Naomi could find it. Before she could ask questions he didn't have answers for. Before she could look at him the way their mother looked at people who started talking about conspiracies and signs and messages only they could see.

The front door opened.

Solomon straightened immediately, the geometry homework forgotten. His hand found the baseball bat he kept beside the desk—not because he'd ever used it, but because holding something solid made the world feel more manageable. The bat was aluminum, dented from when Marcus Thompson had thrown it against a fence during a pickup game last summer, but it was heavy enough to matter.

"It's me," Naomi's voice called from the hallway. "Put down whatever weapon you're holding."

He released the bat, heat rising to his cheeks even though she couldn't see him. She always knew. Annoying and comforting in equal measure.

Naomi appeared in his doorway a moment later, wearing her work uniform—navy polo shirt, khaki pants, a name tag that said NAOMI in cheerful letters above the grocery store logo. Her hair was pulled back in the braids she wore when she didn't have time for anything else, and there were shadows under her eyes that hadn't been there a year ago. She'd lost weight too. The uniform that used to fit snugly now hung loose around her shoulders.

Twenty years old. Working two jobs. Taking night classes at the community college. Raising a teenage brother because someone had to and their mother had stopped being someone a long time ago. She looked exhausted.

She also looked like the only good thing in Solomon's entire world.

"Why are you up?" she asked.

"Homework."

Naomi crossed to his desk and glanced at the notebook. Her eyes moved over the half-finished proofs with the practiced assessment of someone who'd been doing her own homework until two in the morning for years. "Geometry."

"Proofs."

"You hate proofs."

"Everyone hates proofs."

She smiled at that—small, tired, but real. It transformed her face, reminded Solomon of the sister who used to make up stories for him when they were kids, who could turn their cramped apartment into a castle or a spaceship just by believing it hard enough. She'd been a better mother to him than their actual mother ever had. Changed his diapers, taught him to read, held him when he cried. All before she was old enough to have any of that expected of her.

That was before. Before their father left. Before their mother started disappearing into bottles and then into the apartment of whatever man promised to make things better. Before Naomi had to become something harder than a storyteller.

"You eat?" she asked.

"There's leftover rice."

"That's not an answer."

"Yes," Solomon lied. "I ate."

Naomi's eyes narrowed. She'd inherited their mother's face—high cheekbones, full lips, eyes that seemed to look through you—but she used it differently. Their mother looked through people to avoid seeing them. Naomi looked through people to find what they were hiding. She'd always been able to read Solomon like a book she'd memorized by heart.

"There's leftover rice," she said flatly. "Which means you didn't eat the leftover rice."

"I wasn't hungry."

"Solomon."

"I'm fine."

"You're fifteen and you're shrinking." She moved to the door, already done with the argument. "Come on. I'm making eggs."

"It's almost one in the morning."

"Then it's almost breakfast time. Move."

Solomon considered arguing. Naomi was tired. She had an eight AM shift at her other job, the one at the dry cleaner that paid better and treated her worse. She should be sleeping, not cooking for a brother who could feed himself if he remembered to want things like food.

But Naomi was already walking toward the kitchen, and Solomon had learned years ago that arguing with her was like arguing with weather. You could complain all you wanted. It wasn't going to change.

He followed.

The kitchen was barely big enough for one person, let alone two. Naomi moved through it with the efficiency of someone who'd memorized every inch, pulling eggs from the refrigerator, oil from the cabinet, a pan from the stack of dishes that never made it back to their proper homes. She'd been cooking in this kitchen since she was twelve years old, had burned a lot of eggs before she figured out the right temperature, had nearly set the apartment on fire once trying to make fried chicken for Solomon's birthday.

Solomon sat at the small table wedged into the corner and watched her work. The overhead light buzzed with that particular fluorescent whine that made everything look yellow, sickly. Through the window, he could see the building across the alley—dark windows mostly, except for one on the third floor where a blue television glow flickered.

His eyes caught on the alley below. Even from here, the darkness down there looked wrong. Too solid. Too patient. Like it was waiting.

He looked away quickly, stomach tightening.

"How was work?" he asked.

"Long." Naomi cracked eggs into the pan with one hand, a skill Solomon had never mastered. The eggs sizzled, the sound almost aggressive in the quiet apartment. "Some guy tried to return a watermelon he'd already eaten half of. Said it was 'underripe.'"

"Was it?"

"It was half-eaten, Sol. The ripeness was no longer the relevant factor."

He almost laughed. Almost. The sound caught somewhere in his chest and stayed there, stuck behind the worry and exhaustion and the persistent feeling that something was about to go wrong.

Naomi glanced over her shoulder, reading him the way she always did. Her eyes moved over his face with that particular attention that said she was cataloging everything. The circles under his eyes, the way he was hunched into himself, the tension in his shoulders.

"What's wrong?" she asked.

"Nothing."

"Try again."

"I'm just tired."

"You're always tired lately." She turned back to the eggs, stirring them with a wooden spatula that had survived three apartments and two decades of use. Their grandmother had bought that spatula at a garage sale when their mother was young. It had outlasted the grandmother, outlasted the mother's sobriety, outlasted everything except Naomi's stubbornness. "You sleeping?"

"Sometimes."

"Nightmares?"

Solomon hesitated. "Not exactly."

Naomi didn't push—one of her few mercies. She let silence do the work instead, filling the kitchen with the sizzle of eggs and the hum of the refrigerator and the distant sound of Mrs. Patterson's preacher finding new ways to demand money from people who didn't have it.

Finally, Solomon spoke.

"Do you ever feel like something's watching you?"

Naomi's spatula paused mid-stir. "Watching me how?"

"I don't know. Like…" He struggled for words that wouldn't make him sound crazy. That wouldn't make her look at him the way people looked at their mother during one of her spirals. "Like the city pays attention sometimes. To specific people."

She was quiet for a long moment. When she spoke, her voice was careful, measured—the voice she used when she was thinking hard about something.

"This is Chicago," she said. "Something's always watching.

That's why you keep your head down and your feet moving."

"That's not what I mean."

"Then what do you mean?"

Solomon looked at his hands—long fingers, ashy knuckles, nails he kept forgetting to trim. His father's hands, everyone said. He'd never met his father, so he had to take their word for it.

"I saw something," he said quietly. "Three days ago. Near the corner store."

Naomi's stirring stopped completely. "Saw what?"

"Shadows. In the alley. They were…" He couldn't find the right words. "They were watching me. I know how that sounds. But they were."

He expected her to dismiss him. To tell him he was overtired, stressed, imagining things. That's what their mother would have said. That's what teachers said. That's what normal people said when you started talking about shadows that watched.

But Naomi didn't dismiss him.

She turned off the stove and came to sit across from him, her expression unreadable but intent. The eggs sat in the pan behind her, cooling, forgotten.

"The corner store alley," she said. "By the shoe repair place."

Solomon nodded.

Naomi was quiet for a long moment, her fingers interlaced on the table, her eyes fixed on something Solomon couldn't see. When she spoke, her voice was low, almost reluctant—the voice of someone admitting something they'd rather keep hidden.

"I felt something there too," she said. "About a month ago.

Walking home late from the library. I crossed to the other side of the street without thinking—just this instinct that said don't go near that."

She shook her head. "I told myself I was being paranoid. Tired, jumpy from working too much. But my body knew better. My body knew to stay away."

"But you weren't paranoid."

"I don't know what I was. I don't know what you saw." She met his eyes. "What I know is that this city has places that feel wrong. Places you avoid without understanding why. Maybe it's trauma bleeding through the concrete—all the violence this neighborhood has seen, all the pain soaked into these streets. Maybe it's just bad energy accumulated over years of bad things happening. But it's real, even if it's not real the way geometry is real."

"That doesn't help."

"I know." She reached across the table and squeezed his hand.

Her fingers were warm from the pan, calloused from work, real in a way that pushed back against the unreality of everything else. "Here's what helps: you trust your instincts. If something feels wrong, you don't go near it. You don't try to understand it. You don't be a hero. You just move."

"And if it follows me?"

The question came out raw and frightened in a way that embarrassed him. He was fifteen. Too old for monsters under the bed. Too grown for fears without rational explanations.

Naomi's grip tightened.

"Then I'll be there," she said simply. "Between you and whatever it is. That's not negotiable."

They ate their eggs in comfortable silence. The food was good—Naomi always cooked with too much pepper and not enough salt, but that was familiar, and familiar was its own comfort. Solomon found he was hungrier than he'd realized, had cleaned his plate before Naomi was halfway through hers.

She noticed. She always noticed.

"See?" she said, her mouth twitching. "You were hungry."

"I was distracted."

"By triangles."

"Proofs are hard."

Naomi laughed—a real laugh, tired but genuine, transforming her face from exhausted twenty-year-old to something younger and freer. Solomon realized he couldn't remember the last time he'd heard her laugh. It had been months, maybe. Since before their mother left for good.

"I got my paper back," Solomon said eventually. "English. The one about Morrison."

"And?"

"B-plus."

Naomi's face split into a grin—real, bright enough to push back the fluorescent gloom. "Solomon. That's amazing."

"It's not an A."

"It's a B-plus on a paper about Beloved. That book is impossible. Mrs. Carter probably cried reading it."

"She did leave a note that said 'emotionally resonant.'"

"See?" Naomi reached across the table and squeezed his hand again. "You're brilliant. Don't let anyone tell you different. Especially yourself."

Solomon looked at their joined hands. His skin was darker than hers—he'd gotten their father's complexion, apparently, along with the hands—but the shape was similar. The same long fingers. The same knobby knuckles.

"Naomi," he said quietly. "Do you ever think about leaving?"

Her grip tightened almost imperceptibly. "Leaving what?"

"Chicago. This neighborhood. Everything."

She was silent for a moment. When she answered, her voice was soft, and Solomon heard in it all the dreams she'd set aside to raise him.

"Every day," she said. "But leaving costs money. And money means time. And time…" She shrugged, a gesture that carried years of deferred dreams, years of sacrifice no one had asked her to make but that she'd made anyway. "Maybe after I finish my degree. Maybe after you graduate. We'll go somewhere warm. Somewhere that doesn't try to freeze you to death six months out of the year."

"Like where?"

"I don't know. California? Arizona?" She smiled, but it didn't reach her eyes. "Somewhere the radiators work."

Solomon wanted to believe her. Wanted to believe in California, in Arizona, in a future that didn't look exactly like the present but colder and more tired. He wanted to believe that Naomi would get her degree and they'd pack up and drive west, windows down, radio up, leaving Chicago in the rearview mirror like a bad dream.

But he'd seen the bills stacked on the kitchen counter. He'd watched Naomi fall asleep over her textbooks at three in the morning, only to wake up four hours later for another shift. He understood, the way children understood even when no one explained it, that some futures were just stories you told to make the present survivable. Some promises were just prayers in disguise.

"I love you," he said.

The words came out raw and sudden and embarrassing. He and Naomi didn't say things like that. They showed it in cooked eggs and covered shifts and the way she always checked his homework even when she was exhausted beyond reason. Saying it out loud felt like breaking a rule.

Naomi's eyes glistened.

"I love you too, Sol." Her voice cracked on his name. "More than anything. You know that, right?"

He nodded, not trusting himself to speak.

"Whatever happens," she continued, "whatever comes—I'm going to keep you safe. That's not a promise. That's just how it is. Like gravity. Like the sun coming up. It's not something I choose. It's just what I am."

"You can't promise that."

"Watch me."

She squeezed his hand once more, then released it and stood, gathering their plates with practiced efficiency. Her movements were quick, businesslike, hiding whatever emotion had flickered across her face.

"Bed," she said. "Both of us. The triangles will be congruent tomorrow."

Solomon almost smiled. "That's not how proofs work."

"Everything's a proof if you're stubborn enough. Go."

He went.

The morning came too soon, gray light filtering through windows that needed cleaning. Solomon woke to the smell of coffee and the sound of Naomi moving through the apartment with the particular urgency of someone already late.

"You're up," she said, appearing in his doorway already dressed in her dry cleaner uniform—different logo, same exhaustion. "Good. I need you to pick up groceries after school. There's money on the counter."

"I have homework."

"You have time." She was already moving toward the front door, grabbing her jacket, checking her bag. "And don't cut through the alley by the corner store."

Solomon sat up, instantly awake. "What?"

Naomi paused, hand on the doorknob. She looked back at him with an expression he couldn't read—something between concern and something older, something that had nothing to do with mothering and everything to do with recognition. Like she was looking at someone who understood something few people understood.

"I walked past it this morning," she said. "On my way to the bus. The shadows there were wrong. Darker than they should be for that time of day."

"You believe me."

"I believe something." She held his gaze. "Stay away from it.

Promise me."

"I promise."

Naomi nodded once, her expression softening slightly. Then she was gone, the apartment door clicking shut behind her with the finality of all departures.

Solomon lay in bed for a long moment, listening to her footsteps fade down the stairs. Outside his window, Chicago was waking up—car engines, voices, the distant rumble of the L train that never stopped no matter what time it was. The city had its own heartbeat, its own rhythms, its own way of moving that had nothing to do with the people living in it.

He thought about the alley. About the shadows that watched.

About Naomi walking past them in the early morning darkness, feeling what he felt, seeing what he almost-saw.

He should have felt validated. Instead, he felt afraid.

If Naomi could see them too, then they were real.

And real things could hurt you.

Naomi didn't go straight to the bus.

She walked past it—let the doors hiss shut on a morning full of tired people who couldn't afford to be late for jobs that couldn't afford to keep them. She told herself she'd catch the next one. She told herself she had time. Neither was true, but she'd learned years ago that there were some decisions you made with the parts of yourself that didn't keep a schedule.

The alley was four blocks east.

The air had that particular quality it got just before the sun came up properly—not dark, not light, a gray that belonged to neither. Delivery trucks idled at the back of the bodega. A man in a stocking cap pushed a handcart across the intersection, coffee breath visible. The shoe repair place's steel shutter was still down.

The alley was between the shoe repair place and the laundromat.

Naomi stopped on the sidewalk across the street. Didn't stare. Just... let her attention drift that way, the way she'd taught herself to do when her mother had started bringing strange men home, when you had to read a room without looking at it.

The alley was dark.

Obviously. It was a north-facing alley at six in the morning in March. Dark was what it was supposed to be.

But there was dark, and there was *dark*, and what she was looking at now wasn't the kind her eyes had adjusted for. There was a weight to it. A density. Like the air in there had chosen not to move, and the shadows had chosen not to retreat, and something was waiting without waiting—patient in a way that meant it had plans.

She'd crossed the street to avoid it a month ago and told herself she was being paranoid. Last night, when Solomon said *they were watching me*, she'd felt something drop in her chest the way a word drops when you realize you've been hearing it wrong your whole life.

She hadn't told him everything.

She hadn't told him about the man at the grocery store two weeks ago—the one who'd come through her register with nothing in his basket but a bottle of water, who had looked at her name tag and said "Naomi" in a voice that wasn't a question and wasn't a greeting and wasn't anything she could put a name to. She hadn't told him about the car that had parked outside the building three mornings in a row last week, or the way her work schedule had started getting changed without her asking—extra shifts, odd hours, always placing her in the store at specific times that someone, somewhere, seemed to want her there.

She hadn't told him because telling him would mean admitting she'd noticed. And admitting she'd noticed would mean doing something about it.

And doing something about it would mean he'd be the one standing alone at the kitchen table at one in the morning, wondering where she was.

She stood there on the sidewalk across from the alley and let herself look for ten full seconds. Not into it. Just near it—the way you looked near a fire to feel its edge without letting it touch your eyes.

The shadow at the alley's mouth moved.

Not wind. Not traffic. Not a rat or a stray cat or a trick of the gray hour. It shifted the way something shifts when it turns its head to see who's watching it.

Naomi looked away.

Kept her face loose. Kept her pace ordinary. Walked to the corner and waited for the light like a woman who hadn't noticed anything, who had somewhere to be, who was just another South Side shift worker trying to make a bus she was already going to miss.

At the back of her neck, she could feel it still looking.

When the light changed she crossed with a cluster of other people—a woman with grocery bags, a man in a suit that didn't fit him, a kid in a hoodie too light for the weather. She chose the woman. Walked half a step behind her like they were together, like anyone looking would have to untangle which of them was which. It was a trick she'd picked up from their mother, back before their mother had stopped being someone they could learn from.

She didn't look back until she was on the bus.

She sat in the second-to-last row, the spot where she could see the doors and the driver and the street sliding past, and she put her hands flat on her thighs and breathed slow until the tremor in them stopped.

Then she took out the small spiral notebook she'd started carrying a week ago—drugstore, ninety-nine cents—and she wrote, in the handwriting she used for grocery lists so that nothing would look out of place if someone else opened it: *Alley, 6:14 AM. It saw me. It's been there at least a month. Sol saw it three days ago. He is fifteen years old and he saw it and he knew what he was seeing. Something is wrong. Something has been wrong for a long time. I'm just the last one paying attention.* She looked at what she'd written. Then she underlined the last line.

Then she turned the page, wrote a single sentence at the top of a fresh sheet, and stared at it as the bus pulled onto Stony Island. *Don't let them do it to anyone else.* She didn't know yet who *they* were. She didn't know yet what *it* was. She didn't know yet that she had six months left, or that the notebook in her hands would outlive her, or that her brother would someday sit on the floor of a bookshop in Tokyo and read these words and understand.

She only knew that she'd finally stopped looking away.

And that would have to be enough to start with.

Later, in his narrow bed with the blanket pulled up to his chin, Solomon listened to the building settle. The radiator had finally given up for the night, surrendering to the cold with one last metallic sigh. Through the thin walls, Mrs. Patterson's television had gone silent. The stereo three floors down had found a gentler tempo, something with bass but no urgency.

He closed his eyes and tried to sleep.

Behind his eyelids, he saw spirals.

Not threatening. Not even particularly strange. Just spirals, turning slowly in the dark, getting deeper the longer he looked at them. Like a staircase going down. Like a hole with no bottom. Like something waiting for him to take the first step.

He'd read once that the human brain invented patterns to make sense of chaos. That pareidolia—the tendency to see faces in clouds, messages in static—

was just evolution's way of keeping you alert for threats that might or might not be there.

Maybe that's all this was.

His brain, tired and hungry and stressed about geometry, inventing shadows that watched and spirals that descended and a sister who promised to keep him safe like she could control the universe through sheer determination.

Maybe tomorrow he'd wake up and everything would be normal.

He held onto that thought as sleep finally pulled him under.

He didn't notice the shadow in the corner of his room. The one that didn't match the shape of anything that could cast it.

He didn't see it lean forward, almost imperceptibly, as his breathing deepened.

He didn't feel it watching.

Not yet.

Two years later, Naomi would walk into a convenience store at the wrong moment.

She would be buying milk and orange juice and the particular brand of cereal Solomon had liked since he was a child. She would be thinking about a paper due for her English composition class, about the rent that was due in three days, about whether she could afford to take a Saturday off for the first time in months.

She wouldn't see the man with the gun until it was too late.

She wouldn't have time to be afraid.

Two years later, Solomon would identify her body in a morgue that smelled like chemicals and bureaucracy.

He would stand there looking at her face—so peaceful, so wrong, so much like the sister who had made him eggs at one in the morning and promised to keep him safe—and he would feel something inside him crack.

Not break. Not yet.

Crack.

Two years later, the spirals behind his eyes would stop being metaphors and start being something else entirely. The shadows would stop watching and start speaking. The darkness would stop feeling like a threat and start feeling like a home.

But that night—that last good night, when the eggs were too peppery and the radiator was dying and the future was something you could lie about— Solomon Nyx slept, and dreamed of nothing he could remember, and was safe.

It was the last time he would be safe for years.

CHAPTER THREE

Afterlight

The bookstore closed an hour later than it should have.

Solomon noticed only because Akari glanced at the clock—an old analog face mounted between shelves of poetry and philosophy—and sighed. Not frustration. Recalibration. A person adjusting a mental schedule that had organized her life into predictable segments.

She flipped the sign to Closed without ceremony and drew the curtains halfway, leaving the lamp on. Light pooled where it always had—soft, patient, refusing to spill beyond its territory. Not the harsh fluorescence of convenience stores or the gaudy neon of Shinjuku's streets. This was light with boundaries. Light that knew its place. The shop smelled like old paper, dust, and something faintly herbal—tea, maybe, or incense burned so long ago that only its memory lingered. Shelves lined every wall, floor to ceiling, crammed with books in multiple languages. Japanese titles mixed with English, French with German, religious texts beside detective novels beside academic journals on subjects Solomon couldn't pronounce.

It should have felt chaotic. Instead, it felt curated. Like everything here had chosen to be together.

"Sit," Akari said. Not asking.

Solomon did.

The chair creaked—old wood protesting sudden weight, then settling with a sound that suggested it had heard worse. His body finally remembered it was a body: knees aching from concrete, wrists sore from catching his fall, shoulders burning with effort he couldn't recall.

What had he done in that alley? The specifics blurred when he focused on them, like dreams fading in daylight. He remembered the men. The knife. The girl. Shadows surging around him like loyal animals responding to a whistle he hadn't known he could make. And then... nothing. Just movement and darkness and the sensation of being used by something that lived inside him but wasn't entirely him.

His hands trembled.

Akari noticed. She always noticed—Solomon was beginning to understand that about her. Attention that moved through a room like water finding every crack. Not surveillance. Something gentler but equally thorough.

She filled a basin with warm water from a kettle on the hot plate—chipped ceramic, probably older than Solomon, steam catching lamplight and turning briefly golden. Then she returned with bandages that looked older than the shop. Clean. Carefully folded. Worn from use but maintained with religious attention.

"Palm," she said.

He hesitated, then opened his hand.

The cut was shallow now, edges already knitting in a way that made no sense. Not healed—deciding to heal. The skin around it looked tired, like it had done too much too fast. A faint darkness traced the wound's lines, not blood but something else—shadow, maybe, or residue of whatever had passed through him in the alley. Akari washed it gently, her touch precise and unafraid. Her fingers were calloused in unexpected places—thumbpad, palm-sides—calluses from work Solomon couldn't identify. When she wrapped the bandage, the room seemed to exhale. He hadn't realized he'd been holding his breath.

"That shouldn't do that," he said quietly, nodding at his palm.

"No," Akari agreed. "It shouldn't."

She didn't say but. She didn't say why. She didn't reach for explanations like tools to pry him open. In Solomon's experience, people always needed to explain—to categorize and rationalize, fit strange things into familiar boxes. Akari let the strangeness exist without demanding justification.

She sat across from him, hands folded, eyes steady. In the low light she looked different, not younger or older, but more present, like the lamp was revealing layers that fluorescence would have hidden.

"What happened tonight?"

Solomon stared at the shelves behind her—paperbacks with cracked spines, hardcovers worn smooth by years of hands. Stories that had survived their authors. Stories quiet long enough to be trusted.

"I don't know," he said, and meant it. "I didn't plan anything. I was just trying to get home."

Home felt strange in his mouth. He didn't have a home, not really. A capsule hotel paid by the week. A storage locker with his few possessions. A city that tolerated his presence without welcoming it.

Akari nodded. "And then?"

"And then the alley stopped making noise."

That made her pause.

A fractional hesitation, a slight tightening around her eyes—it hit like a shift in atmospheric pressure. He'd said something significant. Something that changed her assessment.

She leaned back, studying him with new focus—not fear, not awe. Care. The attention she might give to a valuable but damaged book requiring careful handling.

"When did you first notice the threads?"

The question hit a target he hadn't known was exposed.

"You know about that?"

"I know about pressure," she said. "Places that feel too tight around the future. People who carry the end of things in their wake."

She tilted her head. "I didn't know it was you. Not until you walked in."

A ripple passed through him. The threads—usually so insistent—were quiet here, like they respected the space. Like whatever made this bookstore what it was had politely asked them to lower their voices.

"Chicago," he said. The word came out before he decided to say it, pulled by the safety of this place, by Akari's calm, by the exhaustion of carrying secrets alone. "That's when it started. After my sister."

Akari didn't interrupt.

There was power in that silence. In someone willing to wait without demanding. Solomon had talked to therapists, counselors, case workers—all leaning forward with professional curiosity, taking notes, asking follow-up questions that felt like surgical instruments. Akari just listened. Let words come at their own pace.

"She died," he continued, voice flat. "Wrong place. Wrong time. That's what they said. After that, I started noticing patterns. Not like this. Smaller. Glitches. I thought it was grief."

Grief did strange things. Everyone had told him that. Made you see things. Made you paranoid. Made you assign meaning to coincidences and patterns to chaos. He'd spent months believing his therapist's explanation: that his traumatized mind was trying to regain control by predicting future losses, that the "death-sense" was just hypervigilance dressed in supernatural clothing.

But hypervigilance didn't explain threads that grew clearer every month. Didn't explain shadows leaning toward him in alleyways. Didn't explain tonight.

"And Tokyo?" Akari asked.

"Tokyo made it louder."

She smiled faintly—knowing. "Tokyo does that."

Silence settled between them. Not awkward. Not heavy. A working silence—the kind found in places that repair things: mechanics' shops and hospitals and churches where people come broken and leave at least partially mended.

Outside, a siren wailed and faded. Solomon flinched anyway, the sound hitting deep-buried instinct.

Akari turned the lamp down a notch. Shadows shifted but didn't surge. They behaved. Solomon wondered if that was her—some quality she carried that made darkness docile—or if this place was special in its own right.

"That thing you felt," she said carefully, "the sense of being noticed—it wasn't wrong."

His stomach tightened.

He'd wanted her to tell him he was imagining things. That the presence in the alley was adrenaline, that the woman with no death-thread was a trick of exhausted perception, that the words painted on the wall were graffiti that had been there all along. He'd wanted normalcy offered like a gift.

Akari wasn't offering that.

"There are people who pay attention to anomalies," she continued. "Not gods. Not monsters. People. They prefer things predictable. They don't like when the future starts improvising."

Silence stretched.

Akari's voice cut through it. "You're not in danger. Not immediately. But you've been noticed. And people who get noticed have two choices: learn to control what they carry, or be controlled by those who fear it."

Solomon stared at his bandaged palm. "What am I carrying?"

Akari considered him for a long moment.

"There's a term," she said at last. "Myth-seed. It's old—older than any language spoken. The idea is that certain archetypes exist at the foundation of human consciousness. Death. Light. Chaos. Order. Stories so old they became part of how the universe processes itself."

She leaned forward. "Sometimes those archetypes fragment.

Pieces of them lodge in human souls, passed down through generations, dormant until trauma or choice or fate wakes them up."

Solomon thought of the alley. The way shadows had responded to his grief like instruments to a conductor. The threads that measured mortality, visible only to him.

"You're saying I have… a piece of Death inside me?"

"I'm saying you carry something that resonates with endings,"

Akari replied. "Whether that's Death or something adjacent to it, I can't say yet. But your abilities—the threads, the shadow manipulation, the death-sense—they all point to the same archetype."

"The Reaper," Solomon said, and the word felt right in a way that terrified him.

Akari nodded. "That's one name for it."

Solomon must have slept eventually.

He didn't remember deciding to, but at some point the conversation had faded and the exhaustion had won, and he'd realized he was stretched out on a narrow cot behind the shelves, staring at a ceiling that didn't exist in the alley but somehow felt familiar. When he woke, gray light filtered through the high windows and Akari was making porridge on the hot plate.

"You slept," she said without turning around.

"A little."

"That's more than I expected."

She ladled rice porridge into two bowls and set one before him. Simple—rice, a soft-boiled egg, pickled vegetables on the side—but the smell made Solomon realize how long it had been since he'd eaten anything that wasn't convenience-store food.

"Thank you," he said. The words felt inadequate.

Akari waved dismissively. "You need to be fed. What happens next will take energy."

Solomon ate slowly, letting warmth spread through him. The porridge was perfect—soft but not mushy, seasoned with something that brought out the rice's natural sweetness.

"What does happen next?"

Akari sat across from him with her own bowl. "That depends on several things."

"Such as?"

"How quickly the Fate-Weavers move. How much attention last night attracted. Whether you're willing to learn."

Solomon set down his chopsticks. "The woman in the alley—the one with no thread—she wasn't a Fate-Weaver, was she?"

Akari's expression flickered—surprise, then respect. "No. She wasn't."

"Then who was she?"

"I don't know. Not specifically." Akari ate a bite of porridge, taking her time. "But I know what she is. Or what she isn't. People without threads are rare. It usually means they're no longer entirely human."

"No longer?"

"There are levels of transformation," Akari said carefully. "Some people carry myth-seeds without awakening them—they live ordinary lives, feel ordinary emotions, die ordinary deaths. Others awaken partially, like you, and gain abilities but keep their essential humanity. And some…"

"Become something else entirely," Solomon finished.

"Yes. The threads measure mortality. Absence of a thread means mortality no longer applies."

Solomon thought about the woman's eyes—dark and knowing, filled with patience that suggested decades, maybe centuries. "She knew about Naomi. She said what happened to her wasn't random."

Akari set down her own chopsticks. "Tell me about your sister."

Not a request. Not a demand. Something in between—an invitation with weight.

Solomon found himself talking.

He talked about Naomi's laugh, her protective fierceness, how she'd stood between him and the world. He talked about her death—the official story, the parts that didn't add up, the investigation that went nowhere because no one seemed interested in answers. He talked about shadows that started moving in his peripheral vision afterward, threads that gradually became visible, the sense that something in him had cracked open and let in darkness that had been waiting all along.

He talked about leaving Chicago, the strange woman who'd approached him at the bus station with a one-way ticket to Tokyo and a warning that staying wasn't safe. About months of hiding in capsule hotels and day-labor jobs, trying to be invisible while the threads grew clearer and the shadows grew bolder.

He talked until the porridge was cold and morning light had shifted from gray to gold.

Akari listened without interrupting.

When he finally finished, she was quiet for a long moment.

"Your sister," she said, after a moment. "Do you remember if she ever mentioned knowing things? Sensing things before they happened?"

Solomon frowned. "What do you mean?"

"Small things. Knowing who was calling before she answered.

Finishing people's sentences. Being in the right place at the right time too often for coincidence."

He thought back. The memories were painful to examine—each one a reminder of loss—but he made himself look.

"She always seemed to know when I was in trouble," he said slowly. "Even before I told her. She'd just… show up. At the right moment."

Akari nodded as if this confirmed something. "The myth-seeds run in families. It's not always the same seed—not always the same abilities—but the potential passes through blood. If Naomi had a dormant seed, if she was starting to manifest without fully awakening…"

"Someone would have noticed her," Solomon realized. "Before they noticed me."

"Yes."

The implication settled into his chest like a stone.

They killed her because of what she might become.

The shadows in the shop's corners stirred, responding to his emotional state. Akari's eyes tracked them, but she didn't flinch. "The people who came last night," Solomon said. "The Fate-Weavers. Did they kill her?"

"I don't know," Akari admitted. "But I intend to find out."

She stood and carried their bowls to the small sink. As she washed them, she spoke without turning.

"You have choices now, Solomon. You could try to go back to hiding— though I doubt it would work for long. You could accept the Fate-Weavers' offer—training and suppression, in exchange for serving their purposes. Or…"

"Or?"

She turned, drying her hands. "Or you could learn to control what you carry. Not suppress it. Not serve others with it. Control it. Master it. Use it to find the truth about your sister."

"Can you teach me that?"

Akari smiled. The same small, genuine smile from last night. "I can teach you some things. For the rest, we'll need to find others. People who understand different pieces of this puzzle."

Solomon looked at his healed palm, at the shadows that had settled back into their corners, at the bookstore that had somehow become the first safe place he'd known since Naomi died.

"When do we start?"

Akari's smile widened slightly. "We already have."

Outside, the city churned with its million small dramas—commuters rushing to trains, shopkeepers opening doors, the endless cycle of Tokyo's daily life. None of them knew that in a bookstore in Shimokitazawa, a young man had just agreed to become something he didn't yet understand.

And somewhere in the city's depths, in offices that didn't appear on any map, the Fate-Weavers reviewed their reports and adjusted their plans.

The ledger had been updated.

But the story was far from written.

CHAPTER FOUR

Observers

Solomon didn't sleep.

Not really. The cot held his body, exhaustion dragged at his mind, but every time he drifted, something pulled him back—a sound from the street, a shift in the shadows, the persistent certainty he was being watched even here, even in this space that was supposed to be safe.

The ceiling above him was old and dark, wooden beams barely visible in the thin light creeping between shelves. He traced the patterns without seeing them, his mind circling back to the alley, to the way the shadows had moved, to Naomi's voice in a memory he couldn't reach.

He lay listening to the bookstore breathe. Old buildings had rhythms—pipes ticking as water cooled, wood settling into positions learned over decades, distant vibrations threading through foundations like remembered footsteps. This one felt steadier than most. Like it knew its purpose.

The threads were quieter here.

Not gone. Never gone. But dampened, as if the room absorbed excess possibility and filed it away in the same system that organized the books. When Solomon closed his eyes, images drifted up and dissolved before hardening into visions—fragments of death-threads, whispers of futures, faces of people he'd passed on the street without knowing he was cataloguing their endings.

That alone felt like mercy.

He raised his arm and looked at where the knife had cut him.

The wound was fully closed, not scarred, not even pink, just smooth skin that looked newer than the flesh around it. He pressed his thumb against it and felt nothing. No tenderness. No memory of pain. As if the injury had happened to someone else and he'd simply inherited the aftermath.

What am I?

The word Akari hadn't quite said surfaced anyway.

Reaper.

It felt right in a way that made his stomach turn. Reapers harvested. Reapers ended things. Reapers were the final punctuation at the end of every sentence.

But he hadn't ended the knife man.

He'd interrupted him. Held the thread, felt it like a wounded bird cradled between his palms, and then let go—let it reform on its own, find its own new path, connect the man to a different ending than the one he'd been heading toward.

Was that power? Was that violence? Was that mercy?

He turned onto his side and stared at the gap between two bookcases where lamplight cut through. Akari moved softly in the front of the shop, straightening things that didn't need straightening, locking cabinets already locked, checking the same corners twice. Not anxious—methodical. Vigilance practiced until it became indistinguishable from routine.

Prepared.

The thought tightened something behind his ribs. Prepared for him? Or prepared for whatever came next? He wondered how many people like him had passed through this shop, how many had lain on this same cot listening to the same building breathe.

He wondered how many of them had survived.

Solomon sat up slowly, careful not to let the shadows stretch too far. They responded to intention now. Not commands—expectations. He expected them to stay close, and they did. He expected them not to surge toward the light, and they obeyed. Like learning a language he'd always spoken but never consciously heard—discovering that darkness had been listening for years, waiting for him to realize he could speak back.

The thought should have terrified him. Instead, it felt almost natural.

That was what terrified him.

Akari glanced back, her attention a physical thing that touched him without crossing the distance. "You can come out. You're not interrupting."

Solomon padded forward, the floor cool under bare feet. Wood old and smooth, worn by generations into a surface that felt almost alive. Books loomed on either side, spines catching lamplight, titles in languages he couldn't read—Japanese, English, German, Sanskrit. The collection felt deliberate, organized by some system he couldn't decipher.

"I don't want to be a problem," he said.

"You already are," Akari replied, without cruelty. Then she smiled, small but genuine. "That doesn't mean you're unwelcome."

She poured two cups of tea—ceramic pot, hand-thrown, lopsided in a way that suggested artistry rather than error. Steam rose in thin lines that didn't waver, as if even the air here knew how to behave. "Drink. It helps with the aftereffects."

"Aftereffects of what?"

"Of having something move through you that isn't entirely yours."

Solomon picked up the cup, let heat seep into his palms. The tea smelled of herbs he couldn't identify, not bitter exactly, but complex, layered. The taste grounded him when he drank—earthy and ancient. The pressure behind his eyes eased a fraction, the death-sense quieting further.

"How do you know all this?"

Akari leaned back against the counter, her own cup warming her hands. In the lamplight she looked tired but alert—someone who had long ago learned to function in spaces between sleep.

"Because I've spent my life repairing things that burn out."

Solomon frowned. "Lanterns."

"Lanterns. And people who stand too close to them."

The phrasing was deliberate. She was offering information without explanation, letting him decide how much to press. The same technique he'd used in Chicago when he didn't want to talk about Naomi.

"Is that what I am? Someone who got too close to something?"

Akari studied him, her gaze weighing things he couldn't see.

"You're not the first to walk into this shop carrying something dangerous. You're the first carrying that."

The shadows stirred at his feet, offended by the characterization. They didn't like being called dangerous. They thought of themselves as something else—protective, maybe, or simply his.

"Sorry," Akari added. "Not dangerous like a weapon. Dangerous like a truth that doesn't want to stay hidden."

"And the lanterns? They're not dangerous?"

Her smile flickered with something old. "Everything that illuminates is dangerous. Light reveals. People don't always want to see what's there."

She moved to a cabinet near the back wall—older than the others, wood darker and more worn. When she opened it, Solomon glimpsed objects he couldn't identify: a cracked mirror wrapped in cloth, a bundle of old shrine paper marked with inked symbols, and a lantern with blackened glass.

"These are repairs that couldn't be finished," Akari said. "Things that burned too bright or too long. Things that couldn't be made safe again."

"Why keep them?"

"Because forgetting what light costs is more dangerous than the light itself."

Outside, a car passed slowly. Too slowly. Headlights moved across the curtained windows like searchlights, and Solomon tracked their progress with the part of his mind that never stopped watching. The death-sense prickled—not alarmed, but attentive.

Akari's gaze flicked to the window. The lamplight dimmed—not flickered, just lowered, like the room was holding its breath. Subtle. Easy to dismiss. But Solomon saw it. He was learning to see everything now.

The pressure returned. Different from the alley, or from when the shadows had first responded to his fear. This pressure was cleaner. Organized. Something that approached the world systematically rather than instinctively. It felt like being measured—not for clothing, but for a coffin.

"They're here," he said.

"Yes. They were always going to be."

"You knew they'd come tonight?"

Akari closed the cabinet and turned to face the door, her stance shifting almost imperceptibly. "The alley wasn't quiet. Events like that create ripples. They can feel the ripples."

"They?"

"You'll understand in a moment."

The bell over the door chimed once.

No one entered.

The sound echoed longer than it should have. Just a bell, brass striking brass—but the resonance hung in the air, spreading through the room, touching the books on their shelves and the shadows in their corners. It passed through him like a tuning fork finding the frequency of his bones.

"That wasn't normal," he said.

"No."

The bell chimed again.

This time the door opened.

A man stepped inside wearing a city worker's jacket and sensible shoes. Mid-forties. Face so unremarkable it slipped from memory even while you looked at it. He looked like he belonged anywhere people waited in lines and filled out forms—forgettable by design, invisible by practice.

His shadow behaved perfectly.

Too perfectly.

"Evening," the man said pleasantly, inclining his head. "Sorry to disturb you so late."

Akari returned the bow. Polite. Distant. "We're closed."

"Yes. I know. I won't take long."

His eyes moved, not scanning the shop, but measuring it. The lamp. The shelves. The space between moments. Solomon felt the attention like a weight, pressing down on possibilities, narrowing futures to approved channels.

Then those eyes settled on him.

The threads snapped tight.

Not vibrating. Locked.

Every death-thread in Solomon's awareness froze in place, held by some external force that didn't ask permission. The death-sense went silent—not dampened like before, but suspended, as if someone had pressed pause on a recording and left him staring at a frame of mortality.

Cold certainty slid into place.

This man could see him.

Not the way Akari did.

The man smiled. "Solomon Nyx."

Hearing his name spoken like that—precise, confirmed, clinical—sent a chill down his spine. He hadn't introduced himself. He hadn't needed to.

"You have me at a disadvantage," Solomon said.

The man's smile didn't waver. "That won't last."

Akari's fingers tightened on her teacup. A warning. Let me handle this.

"What do you want?" she asked.

"To ensure containment," the man said mildly. "To confirm classification. To prevent escalation."

Solomon laughed once, sharp. "That sounds like control."

The man's smile thinned. "It sounds like survival."

He stepped forward. The room seemed to resist him, light bending away. He paused, assessed, then adjusted—like someone changing tactics mid-game.

"You experienced a Manifestation event tonight," he continued. "Localized. Minimal exposure. Acceptable collateral. But it crossed a threshold."

Solomon's jaw clenched. "I saved someone."

"Yes. And you were seen."

Silence stretched.

Akari's voice cut through it. "You don't own him."

The man looked at her fully now. His expression changed—respect, edged with caution.

"A Light-Bearer," he said softly. "That complicates things."

Akari didn't deny it.

The man sighed, genuine annoyance creeping in. "You know the rules."

"I know your rules. They aren't the same."

Something passed between them—old negotiations, old compromises. A history Solomon couldn't read but could feel pressing against the conversation. These two had dealt with each other before. Or at least, their kinds had.

"The rules exist for reasons," the man said. "Centuries of reasons. Hard lessons."

"The protocols are the problem."

For a moment, the pleasant mask slipped entirely. Frustration, certainly, but also something like regret. This man wasn't evil. He believed in what he was doing. He thought he was protecting something important.

That made him more dangerous, not less.

The man turned back to Solomon. "We can help you. Training. Suppression. Guidance. You don't have to stumble through this blind."

"And if I say no?"

The threads trembled—their first movement since they'd locked. Something in the system was uncertain, calculating branches it didn't like.

The man considered him with those measuring eyes. "Then we adapt."

Adapt. The word sat heavily. It could mean anything. Patience. Persistence. The kind of adaptation that ended with someone disappearing into a system designed to contain things that didn't fit. Solomon had grown up in Chicago. He'd seen what happened to people who became inconvenient to power.

Akari stepped between them, light warming the space without flaring. "He stays. Tonight."

The man met her gaze for a long moment. Whatever calculation he was running, it produced a result he could accept. Not because he was defeated. Because he was patient.

Finally, he inclined his head.

"Tonight," he agreed. "But understand this, Solomon Nyx."

The threads tightened one last time, then released—pressure breaking like a wave that had crested and passed. The death-sense returned to its normal hum, individual threads becoming visible again. The world unstuck.

"You've been added to the ledger."

He turned and left. The bell chimed once more—ordinary this time, brass on brass, simple physics. Just a bell. Just a door. Just a man walking away into the night.

Solomon exhaled shakily. His hands trembled. The shadows at his feet were coiled tight, ready to strike at something already gone. "That was…"

"Fate-Weavers," Akari said. "Or something close enough. They have other names in other places, but the function is the same. They watch for awakening

41

myth-seeds. They contain the ones they consider dangerous. They... edit... the ones that can't be contained."

"Edit. What does that mean?"

Akari's expression flickered with something dark. "It means they make sure certain stories never get told. Certain people never become what they might become. They're not evil, not exactly. They genuinely believe they're protecting the world from chaos. But they're ruthless. Efficient. They've been doing this for a long time."

"How long?"

"Centuries. Maybe longer. They were old when my grandmother first encountered them."

Solomon thought about the man's shadow—that perfect, unnatural stillness. About the way the threads had locked rather than vibrated.

"They'll come back."

"Yes."

"When?"

"Soon. And next time, they won't just observe."

Akari walked to the window and pulled the curtain aside, looking at the street where the car had passed—gone now, leaving nothing behind but the memory of too-slow headlights.

"They'll test you," she said. "They always do, with new awakenings. They'll create situations designed to provoke responses, measure your limits, identify your weaknesses. They'll try to determine whether you can be trained, controlled, or if you need to be..."

"Edited."

"Yes."

Something settled in his chest—not peace, but resolution. He'd been running since Chicago, fleeing from Naomi's memory, from truth he'd glimpsed and couldn't face. Now there was nowhere left to run. The thing inside him had awakened, and people who spent centuries managing such awakenings knew his name.

The only way forward was through.

"Then I'd better learn fast," he said.

Akari's smile was small but real. "That is exactly what I was hoping you'd say."

She said it again as the first gray touched the eastern sky, and this time her voice carried something harder.

"There's more. I didn't want to say it while he was still close enough to hear."

Solomon turned from the window. "Say it."

"When my sources heard about the alley, they pulled every record they could reach. Yours. Your family's. What brought you to Tokyo in the first place." She set her teacup down with careful precision. "The cultural exchange program you came through—the one that got you a visa, the one that paid your first month's rent—it doesn't exist. Not officially. The paperwork was filed, the fees were paid, the sponsor on record is a foundation that's been dormant since 1994. Someone wanted you here, Solomon. Someone arranged it."

The words landed like a stone in still water. Every assumption he'd made about the last eighteen months was suddenly available for rereading.

"A Fate-Weaver."

"Possibly. Or someone intercepting you before they could reach you." She didn't blink. "There's something else. The report your sister filed with the police before she died—the complaint about being followed. It was recorded. It was filed. And then somebody reclassified it, archived it, made it effectively invisible. That kind of reach isn't street crime."

"Naomi knew something."

"Naomi knew something. Or she was noticing things she wasn't supposed to be able to notice."

He stood very still. "You think she had a seed."

"I think it's possible. Seeds run in families. Not like genetics—more like a pattern that keeps looking for somewhere to land. Siblings awakening to related seeds isn't unheard of." Akari watched him carefully. "If she carried one—even a small one, even one that never fully woke—then the things she noticed weren't paranoia. And what happened to her wasn't random."

He sat down because his legs had stopped deciding to hold him. The seed inside him stirred, the way it did whenever Naomi's name was spoken in the wrong light.

"Then her death was—" "I don't know. I don't want to say it until we know. But yes.

That's the possibility we're standing next to."

"How do we find out?"

"There are people who keep records. Track awakenings.

Document patterns the world doesn't see." She hesitated. "Going to them means exposing you. Letting the Weavers know you're not just awakening, you're asking questions. That's a different kind of dangerous."

"More dangerous than what we're already facing?"

"Considerably."

He thought about Naomi. About the way she'd stood between him and every bad thing since he was old enough to remember. About the scar on his palm that had started the day Mr. Harrison's thread first clicked into focus. About all the things she'd carried for him without ever naming them.

"She kept me safe my entire life," he said. "If someone killed her because of what she was, or what I might become, then I need to know. Whatever it costs."

Akari studied him for a long moment. Then she nodded once, a decision made.

"All right. Then we start looking. Carefully. Quietly. And we hope we find answers before the Fate-Weavers decide what to do about you."

Before they left the shop, she made him practice.

"Sit here," she said, positioning him on a cushion near the shop's front window. Morning light was filtering through the glass, and through it the first commuters passing on the street outside. "Don't close your eyes. Watch the people."

"Watch them how?"

"Without reading them."

Solomon frowned. "I'm not sure I understand."

"You're seeing threads now even when you're not trying to."

Akari knelt beside him, her voice patient but precise. "They're always there, at the edge of your awareness. The death-sense is part of you—you can't turn it off completely. But you can learn to… not engage with it."

"Like peripheral vision."

"Exactly. You don't have to focus on everything you can see.

You can let things exist without giving them your attention." She gestured toward the window. "Watch the people walking by. See them. But don't read them."

Solomon tried.

A man in a blue jacket passed the window, phone pressed to his ear, hurrying somewhere with the desperate urgency of the chronically late. Solomon saw the thread immediately—a faint line extending from the man's chest, stretching forward into a future that ended in— "No," Akari said quietly. "Don't follow it."

"I wasn't—" "You were. I could see your eyes change." She touched his shoulder gently. "Try again. See the man. See that he's wearing blue, that he's on his phone, that he's moving fast. But don't see where he's going. Don't see where he ends."

Solomon breathed out slowly and tried to soften his focus. The next person who passed was a woman with a red umbrella, closed against the dry morning, swinging from her wrist like a pendulum. He saw the umbrella. Saw the way she walked, slightly favoring her right leg. Saw the— No.

He pulled back before the thread could fully form in his vision. It was like trying not to read words you could see clearly, but he managed it, just barely— keeping his attention on the surface of the woman rather than the depths that lay beneath.

"Better," Akari said. "Again."

They practiced for nearly an hour. By the end of it, Solomon's head was throbbing with a strange new kind of headache—not pain exactly, but strain, the muscles of his attention aching from unfamiliar exercise. But he could do it now. He could look at people without automatically cataloging their endings.

"Why does this matter?" he asked when Akari finally let him stop.

"Because if you walk around reading every thread you see, you'll go mad within a week." Her voice was matter-of-fact. "The death-sense isn't a gift. It's a burden. Some Reapers throughout history have broken completely— overwhelmed by the knowledge of how everyone around them will die, unable to connect with anyone because they can't stop seeing their endings."

"That sounds exhausting."

"It is." She met his eyes. "But the alternative is worse."

The training session that came later went badly.

Solomon sat on the floor of the under-room, back against the wall, trying to slow his breathing. His shadow had surged out of control again—responding to his frustration, his fear, his desperate need to master something that refused to be mastered. The walls bore scorch marks where darkness had touched them, shadows so intense they'd left physical traces.

Akari knelt a few feet away, her light dimmed to almost nothing. She'd used it to pull him back from the edge, to gentle his shadow the way you might gentle a panicking horse. It had worked. But the effort had cost her something—he could see the exhaustion in the set of her shoulders, the careful way she held herself.

"I'm sorry," he said.

"Don't be." Akari's voice was soft but firm. "Control takes time. The fact that you're struggling means you're actually trying."

"I almost hurt you."

"You didn't." She shifted, moving to sit beside him against the wall. Close enough that he could feel the warmth of her, the faint glow that lived just beneath her skin. "Your shadow responds to your emotions. That's not unusual—most myth-seeds work that way. The challenge is learning to feel things without letting them control you."

Solomon laughed bitterly. "I've never been good at that."

"Neither was I, at first." Akari pulled her knees to her chest, wrapping her arms around them. In the dim light, with her defenses lowered, she looked younger than usual. More vulnerable. "When my seed awakened, I burned down my family's house."

Solomon turned to look at her.

"I didn't mean to," she continued. "I was sixteen. A boy I liked had said something cruel, the way teenagers do. I felt humiliated. Angry. And my light just—" She made a gesture, fingers spreading like an explosion. "Everything I touched caught fire. My room. The hallway. My mother's garden."

"Was anyone hurt?"

"My sister. Burns on her arms and face. She has the scars."

Akari's voice was steady, but Solomon heard the weight beneath it. "She doesn't speak to me anymore. Can't look at me without seeing the flames."

"I'm sorry."

"Don't be sorry. Just understand." Akari turned to face him, her eyes meeting his in the dim light. "You're not the only one who's hurt people without meaning to. You're not the only one who's afraid of what you carry. The difference is that I've had years to learn control. You've had hours."

Solomon held her gaze. Something passed between them—recognition, maybe. The particular understanding that exists between people who have both touched darkness and survived.

"How did you learn?" he asked. "To control it?"

"A teacher found me. Someone like us, older, who had already walked this path." Akari smiled faintly. "She was patient. Kind. She told me something I didn't believe at first, but have come to understand was true."

"What?"

"That the power isn't separate from who you are. It's not a curse or a gift— it's just you, expressed in a way you didn't know was possible." Akari's hand moved, almost unconsciously, to rest near his. Not touching. "Your shadow responds to your emotions because it is your emotions. Learning to control it means learning to accept all the parts of yourself you've been afraid of."

Solomon looked down at her hand, so close to his.

"That sounds terrifying."

"It is." Akari's smile widened slightly. "But it's also the only way forward. Trust me—I've tried the alternatives. They don't work."

The under-room was quiet around them. The shadows had settled, docile now, behaving the way shadows should. Solomon's heartbeat had slowed. His breathing had steadied.

"Thank you," he said.

"For what?"

"For not giving up on me. For sitting here in the dark with someone who almost hurt you, and telling me it's going to be okay."

Akari was quiet for a moment.

"It's not entirely selfless," she said. "I've been alone for a long time, Solomon. Running, hiding, keeping everyone at arm's length because I was afraid of what might happen if I let someone close. You're the first person in years who's made me think maybe that wasn't the right choice."

Solomon didn't know what to say.

So he reached out, slowly, and let his hand rest on hers.

Akari didn't pull away.

They sat like that for a long time, two people learning to trust each other in the spaces between words.

After a while, when the silence had settled into something comfortable instead of careful, Akari stood.

"Wait here."

She came back with a cloth bundle and set it on the floor between them. When she unfolded it, there was a notebook inside—spiral-bound, drugstore ordinary, its cover bent from use.

Naomi's handwriting on the first page. His throat closed up before he'd read a single word.

"A friend sent this to me," Akari said quietly. "Before you arrived in Tokyo. Someone who keeps records the world prefers to lose. Your sister left it with her as insurance—something to reach you if the rest of what she was building didn't." Akari sat back on her heels. "I've been holding it until you were ready to read it without setting fire to anything you'd regret. I think today is that day."

Solomon didn't trust his voice. He turned the first page. Then the next. His sister's careful, cramped handwriting filled every line— but not research, not yet. Something more personal. A record of what she'd been feeling in those final weeks. Fragments she couldn't say out loud to anyone, least of all to him. She had been investigating something; that much was obvious. But this notebook wasn't the investigation itself. It was the journal of a woman who knew she was running out of time.

At the back, in handwriting that shook slightly, a note dated the day before she died: *If something happens to me, Solomon needs to know the truth.

Not because it will help him—it probably won't. But because he deserves to know why. And because the people who did this shouldn't get to keep their secrets. *Below that, underlined twice:* Don't let them do it to anyone else.* He read the line three times. Then he closed the notebook and held it against his chest, and for a long moment he couldn't do anything else.

Akari didn't speak. She just sat with him.

And far away, across the city—and the world—other threads tightened in response.

The ledger had been updated.

A new name had been added.

The hunt had begun.

CHAPTER FIVE

What Naomi Saw

Later, reading her notebook for the first time, Solomon would piece together the story of her final weeks. Her handwriting would become her voice, and her voice would carry him through the days he hadn't been there to witness.

This is what she saw.

Chicago — Three Weeks Before The man had been following her for six blocks.

Naomi didn't look back to confirm it. Looking back was amateur hour—told the follower you'd noticed, gave them information, forced confrontation before you were ready. Instead, she watched reflections. Store windows. Chrome trim on parked cars. The dark glass of the coffee shop she'd just passed.

He was good. Kept distance. Varied his pace. Stopped to check his phone at natural intervals.

But Naomi was better.

She'd learned to notice things before she'd learned to name what she was doing. Her mother had called it intuition. Her teachers had called it hypervigilance. The school counselor Solomon didn't know about had called it a trauma response that might benefit from professional support.

Naomi called it staying alive.

The South Side had taught her that lesson early. She remembered being seven years old, walking home from school with her mother, when a man had stepped out of an alley with something in his hand. Her mother had pulled her close, said something quiet and calm, and they'd crossed the street without running, without panicking, without looking back.

Later, Naomi had asked what the man wanted.

"Nothing good. That's why we left."

"How did you know?"

Her mother had been quiet for a long moment. "You learn to see the shape of trouble before it finds you. The way someone stands.

The way they look at you—or don't look at you. The spaces where things don't fit right."

Naomi had learned. By twelve, she could walk through any neighborhood and know within seconds which corners to avoid, which strangers to smile at and which to ignore, which routes were safe at what hours. Not magic. Pattern recognition refined by necessity.

The man following her now fit a pattern she'd never seen before. She turned left at the next intersection, heading away from the apartment, away from Solomon, toward busier streets where witnesses accumulated like insurance policies. The man turned left too, fifteen seconds later, his reflection sliding across the window of a laundromat where an old woman was folding sheets.

Interesting.

He wasn't trying to catch her. If he'd wanted to close the distance, he could have. He was content to follow, to observe, to gather information without confrontation.

Almost worse.

Street criminals wanted something immediate—money, property, opportunity. They closed distance because delay meant risk. This man was patient in a way that suggested time. Resources. A plan that didn't require hurrying.

Naomi catalogued what she'd observed. Mid-thirties, maybe older. Dark suit that fit too well for the neighborhood—tailoring that cost more than most people here made in a month. No visible weapon, but he moved like someone who knew how to use one. And his shoes—dress shoes, leather, polished—were wrong for the cracked sidewalks and uncertain weather.

Everything about him was wrong for this place.

Which meant he wasn't from here.

Which meant someone had sent him.

Naomi ducked into a convenience store, not the one near their apartment, a different one, three blocks further into the commercial strip. The clerk barely looked up, too focused on his phone. She walked the aisles without seeing them, positioning herself near the back where refrigerators hummed and the security mirror gave her a distorted view of the entrance.

The man didn't follow her in.

She waited five minutes. Bought a bottle of water she didn't want. Made small talk with the clerk—asked about his day, mentioned the weather, established herself as a memorable presence in case she needed witnesses later.

She stepped back onto the street and scanned.

Gone.

Or better at hiding than she'd estimated.

Naomi walked home the long way, doubling back twice, checking reflections and shadows with paranoid precision. She mapped escape routes as she walked. Noted which businesses were open, which had cameras, which had back exits she could use if necessary.

By the time she reached the apartment, her hands were steady but her heart was pounding.

The building loomed against the evening sky—five stories of aging brick and fire escapes that probably violated code. Home for eight years, ever since their mother had moved them here after the eviction, after the boyfriend, after the disasters that had stripped away everything except what mattered.

Solomon.

Everything Naomi did was for Solomon.

She climbed the stairs to the third floor, key already in hand, senses tuned for anything out of place. The hallway smelled like fried food and cleaning products and the particular staleness of buildings that had been around too long. Normal. Familiar.

Solomon was at the kitchen table, hunched over homework he'd probably finish in twenty minutes and then pretend had taken two hours. The lamp beside him cast a warm circle that made him look younger than seventeen, more like the little boy she used to carry on her hip when their mother worked double shifts.

He looked up when she came in, and she saw how his eyes tracked to her face, reading her the way he read everyone—too closely, too carefully, noticing things he shouldn't be able to notice. "You okay?" he asked.

"Fine." She set the water bottle on the counter, keeping her voice light. "Long day."

"You're home late."

"Worked overtime." The lie came easily. Lies always came easily when they were for his protection. "Mrs. Patterson needs help with her groceries tomorrow. I told her you'd carry the heavy stuff."

"Sure." Solomon turned back to his homework, but she caught the flicker of doubt—the sense that he knew she wasn't telling him everything, he was choosing not to push.

That was the deal they'd made without ever discussing it. He didn't ask about the things she didn't explain, and she didn't ask about the drawings he thought she hadn't seen.

The spirals.

The dark shapes that looked like people but weren't quite.

The sketches he'd started making six months ago and then abruptly stopped, shoving them deep in his closet as if he could hide them from himself.

Naomi knew about the drawings. She'd found them two months ago while putting away his laundry, a stack of papers hidden under old t-shirts. The images had made her skin crawl—not because they were violent, but because they felt true in a way art wasn't supposed to feel. Like he wasn't imagining what he drew, but recording it.

She knew about how Solomon sometimes stared at people too long, eyes focused on something above their shoulders that no one else could see. She knew about the nightmares he didn't mention, the way he'd started avoiding crowds, the gradual retreat from a world that seemed to be showing him something he didn't want to look at. She didn't know what any of it meant.

But she was starting to suspect it connected to the man who'd been following her, to the questions she'd started asking at work, to the pattern she'd been noticing for weeks now without being able to name what she was seeing.

"I'm going to shower," she said. "Don't stay up too late."

Solomon nodded without looking up.

Naomi walked to the bathroom, locked the door, and stood at the sink with hands braced on the porcelain, staring at her own reflection. Same face. Same tired eyes. Same tension in the jaw that never relaxed. Twenty-two years old and she looked thirty—the kind of premature aging that came from responsibility carried too young. She'd been raising Solomon since she was twelve and their mother had checked out emotionally, since she was fourteen and their mother had checked out physically, leaving them with a signed lease and a promise to send money that arrived some months and not others. But something behind the reflection felt different tonight.

Deeper. As if the glass wasn't just showing her what was there, but hinting at what might be underneath.

You're losing it. Seeing patterns that aren't there. Letting the paranoia win.

But Naomi had survived this long by trusting her instincts, and her instincts were screaming that something was wrong—with the man following her, with the things she'd noticed at work, with the feeling that had been building for weeks like pressure before a storm. She turned on the shower and let the sound cover the silence.

Tomorrow, she would find answers.

Tonight, she would pretend everything was fine.

The job was nothing special.

Data entry at an insurance company in the Loop, the kind of work that paid just enough to keep them housed and fed without ever threatening to become a career. Naomi typed numbers and forms and claims into systems she didn't understand, and she watched.

She always watched.

Three weeks ago, she'd noticed Marcus Webb.

He was middle management—neither high enough to matter nor low enough to ignore. What caught her attention wasn't his position but his patterns. He arrived early. Stayed late. Took lunch alone at his desk while studying files that weren't on his official project list. And he asked questions. About procedures. About security protocols. About what happened to claims that fell into certain categories.

Questions that didn't match his role.

Naomi knew how to be invisible. She'd learned that skill the same way she'd learned everything else—by necessity, by observation, by making herself small enough to be overlooked while keeping her eyes open. She let Marcus think she was just another drone, just another temporary worker who wouldn't remember his face in six months.

She watched him for two weeks.

She documented everything.

And when she finally had enough information to be useful, she did something she'd never done before: she made herself visible. "Mr. Webb?" She caught him in the break room, coffee cup in hand, during the afternoon lull when most people were too drowsy to notice conversations. "I think we might have similar interests."

He went still. "I'm not sure what you mean."

"I think you're looking for something. Something the company doesn't want people to find." She kept her voice low, her posture casual, just two coworkers having a normal conversation. "I've been looking too."

"Looking for what?"

"Patterns. Discrepancies. Places where the numbers don't add up and no one asks why."

Marcus studied her for a long moment. His face was impossible to read—trained, she realized, the same way hers was trained.

Someone had taught him to hide what he was thinking.

"This isn't a safe conversation to have," he said after a beat. "I know."

"Then why are you having it?"

Naomi thought about Solomon, about the drawings, about the feeling that had been building for weeks. "Because I need to understand something. And I think you might be able to help me."

Marcus didn't trust her. That was obvious from the way he kept distance, the careful vetting he conducted over the following days. He asked questions that seemed innocent but weren't. He tested her knowledge in ways designed to expose lies or gaps in her story. Naomi passed every test because she wasn't lying. She genuinely had noticed the patterns he was investigating—the claims that disappeared, the files that got flagged for "special handling," the employees who asked too many questions and then stopped showing up.

A week after their first conversation, he finally opened up.

"There are people," he said quietly, "who believe the world works differently than most of us think. That there are... elements. Powers. Things that don't fit into normal categories."

"Myth-seeds," Naomi said, testing the word she'd found in her research.

Marcus went pale. "Where did you hear that term?"

"I've been doing my own research. There's not much available, but there's enough to know the concept exists."

He was quiet for a long moment. "You need to be careful with that knowledge. There are organizations—factions—that take serious interest in anyone who knows too much about this subject."

"Like the organization you work for?"

Marcus laughed shortly. "I don't work for them. I'm investigating them. There's a difference."

"But you know who they are. What they do."

"I know some of it." He leaned forward, lowering his voice further. "They call themselves the Fate-Weavers. They believe they're protecting the world from chaos—from people whose... seeds... might awaken and cause damage. They've been operating for centuries. Maybe longer."

"What kind of damage?"

"The records aren't clear. The organization is good at erasing evidence. But there are references to incidents—catastrophes that got attributed to natural causes or random violence but were actually caused by uncontrolled awakenings."

Naomi thought about Solomon's drawings. About the way he stared at things no one else could see.

"What happens when someone awakens?" she asked.

Marcus hesitated. "It depends on the type of seed. Some are relatively benign—enhanced perception, minor abilities, things that can be hidden. Others are…" He trailed off.

"Others are what?"

"Dangerous. Powerful. The kind of thing that, if uncontrolled, could…" He shook his head. "Let's just say the Fate-Weavers have reasons for what they do, even if their methods are horrific."

The silver-haired woman found Naomi two days later.

She was waiting outside the apartment building when Naomi came home from work—tall, angular, dressed in clothes that somehow managed to look both expensive and understated. Her eyes were a gray so pale they seemed almost colorless, and when she spoke, her voice carried the faint accent of somewhere else, somewhere older.

"Miss Nyx," she said. "We should talk."

Naomi's instincts screamed to run, to get to Solomon, to grab the emergency bag she kept hidden in her closet and disappear. But something in the woman's posture suggested that running wouldn't help—that whatever conversation was coming would happen whether Naomi wanted it to or not.

"Talk about what?" she asked.

"Your brother. What he is. What he's becoming."

Ice spread through Naomi's chest. "I don't know what you mean."

The woman smiled. "I think you do. You've been researching. Asking questions. Noticing patterns that most people miss." She tilted her head, studying Naomi with an intensity that felt almost physical. "You have some of it yourself, you know. Not a full seed—not yet—but the potential. That's how you notice things."

"Who are you?"

"Someone who wants to help your brother. Someone who represents an alternative to the people who've been watching him."

"The Fate-Weavers."

The woman's expression flickered—surprise, quickly hidden.

"You've been busy."

"What do you want?"

"To offer you a choice." The woman produced a small notebook, leather-bound and old-looking. "The Fate-Weavers will find your brother eventually. When they do, they'll give him two options: join them, or be… managed. Neither outcome is good for him."

"And your alternative?"

"We can protect him. Train him. Help him understand what he's becoming without crushing who he is in the process." The woman held out the notebook. "Everything you need to know is in here. Read it. Consider it. When you're ready to talk again, you'll know how to find us."

Naomi took the notebook. It felt heavier than it should have.

"Why me?" she asked. "Why tell me instead of approaching him directly?"

The woman's smile was sad. "Because he trusts you more than he'll ever trust a stranger. And because you're going to have to make this choice for him—at least initially. That's what older sisters do, isn't it? Protect their brothers from the hardest parts of the world?"

She turned and walked away, dissolving into the evening crowd with a speed that shouldn't have been possible.

Naomi stood on the sidewalk, holding a notebook full of secrets, and felt the weight of a decision she wasn't ready to make.

The Fate-Weavers came three days later.

They didn't knock. They didn't announce themselves. One moment Naomi was alone in the apartment, reviewing the silver-haired woman's notes for the hundredth time, and the next moment there were two men standing in her living room as if they'd always been there.

"Miss Nyx," one of them said. "We need to discuss your brother."

They looked human. They wore human clothes, spoke with human voices, moved with human gestures. But something was wrong with them—a fundamental wrongness that made Naomi's skin crawl.

Their shadows didn't match their movements.

It was subtle—most people would never notice. But Naomi had spent her life noticing things, and she saw the way their shadows lagged behind, the way they bent toward the light instead of away from it, the way they seemed to belong to something other than the bodies casting them.

"Who are you?" she demanded.

"Representatives of an organization that has humanity's best interests at heart."

"The Fate-Weavers."

The man smiled, but it didn't reach his eyes. "You've been busy, Miss Nyx. Asking questions. Making contacts. Learning things you weren't meant to learn."

"What do you want?"

"The same thing our competitors want—access to your brother.

But unlike them, we're offering something in return."

"Which is?"

"Your safety. His safety. A controlled environment where his awakening can be managed without risk to himself or others."

Naomi felt her hands clench. "And if I refuse?"

The man's smile widened. "Miss Nyx, you don't seem to understand the situation. This isn't a negotiation. We're offering you a choice only because we prefer cooperation to coercion. But make no mistake—your brother will be managed, one way or another. The only question is whether you're part of the process or not."

Naomi stood still.

Not because she was surrendering. Because she was calculating. These weren't street criminals. They weren't even human, not entirely—she could see that now, in the way they moved, in the wrongness of their presence. They'd walked through locked doors. They spoke with borrowed voices. They existed outside the normal rules.

But they wanted something from her. That meant negotiation was possible.

"And if I don't cooperate?"

"Then his awakening will be unguided. Chaotic. Potentially fatal." The man smiled, and it was the most terrible thing Naomi had ever seen—a human expression performed by something that had studied humans without ever understanding them. "You've protected him his whole life. Surely you want to continue protecting him."

"You're threatening my brother."

"We're offering you a choice. Cooperate, and he lives. Refuse, and we can make no guarantees about what happens when his seed tears its way out of him."

Naomi thought about the notebook under her mattress. About the silver-haired woman and her explanations. About the patterns she'd been noticing her whole life, the awareness that had kept her alive and led her to this moment.

She thought about her brother, hunched over homework, drawing spirals he thought she hadn't seen, staring at something above people's shoulders that no one else could see.

"I need time," she said.

"You have one week. After that, we'll assume your answer is no."

They left the same way they'd arrived, not through the door, not through any visible exit, just fading from the room as if they'd been holograms someone had switched off.

Naomi stood in the empty apartment and tried to stop shaking.

One week.

One week to decide whether to sell out to people who terrified her, or to risk her brother's life on the hope that the silver-haired woman's people could protect him instead.

One week to figure out which set of monsters was less monstrous.

One week to find another option.

Chicago—The Night Before She found another option.

Not a good option. Not a safe option. But the only one that didn't require trusting people who had proven themselves untrustworthy. She would run.

Not immediately—running required preparation, resources, a destination that wouldn't be obvious. But she could do it. She'd been preparing for something like this her whole life, squirreling away money in accounts nobody knew about, keeping documents updated, maintaining contacts in places where questions weren't asked.

She could take Solomon and disappear. Head south, maybe, or west. Find a city where they could blend in. Keep moving until his seed awakened on its own terms, and then figure out how to help him from there.

It wasn't a plan. It was barely a hope.

But it was better than surrendering to either faction of monsters who wanted to control her brother.

She spent the day making preparations. Withdrew cash in small increments from three different ATMs—never more than the reporting threshold, never in a pattern that would trigger flags. Bought burner phones at a corner store where the clerk didn't ask for ID. Mapped routes that avoided cameras and checkpoints and obvious paths anyone tracking them would expect.

By evening, she had almost everything in place.

She just needed one more day.

One more day to gather the last resources.

One more day to figure out how to tell Solomon they were leaving.

One more day.

The hardest part would be the conversation. Solomon would ask questions—where they were going, why they had to leave, what she wasn't telling him. He would look at her with those eyes that saw too much, and she would have to decide how much truth he could handle. She went to the convenience store to buy supplies for the trip—energy bars, water, things that wouldn't spoil. The store was three blocks from the apartment, the same one she always used, the safest route she knew.

The evening air was cold enough to see her breath. Streetlights buzzed overhead, some working, some flickering, some dark entirely. The neighborhood was quiet in the way it got between dinner and the late-night activity—families eating, televisions murmuring, the lull before whatever happened after dark.

Naomi didn't see the car until it was too late.

Black sedan. Tinted windows. No plates.

She didn't see the men inside until they were already opening the doors.

She didn't see anything after the first shot, except Solomon's face in her memory—her little brother, hunched over homework, drawing spirals, staring at something above people's shoulders that no one else could see.

I'm sorry, she thought, as the world went dark.

I tried.

Take care of yourself, Sol. I love you.

I love you.

I— Solomon woke up screaming.

He didn't remember falling asleep, didn't remember dreaming, didn't remember anything except the sudden certainty that something terrible had happened—not to him, but to someone he loved.

The apartment was dark and quiet.

Naomi wasn't home.

Solomon sat in the darkness, hand pressed to his chest where something had just torn itself open, and felt the first thread appear in the air before him—thin, dark, stretching from his own body up toward a ceiling he couldn't see.

His own thread.

Connected to his own ending.

And far away—impossibly far, in a place that had nothing to do with distance—he felt a second thread snap, and knew without knowing that his sister was gone.

The drawings he'd hidden hadn't been imagination.

The things he'd seen above people's shoulders hadn't been hallucinations.

And the world he'd been pretending not to notice had just reached out and taken the only person who had ever truly known him. Solomon Nyx sat alone in the dark, watching his own death-thread shimmer in the air, and understood what he was becoming.

A burden, not a gift.

A door that had been waiting his whole life to open.

And now that it had, there was no closing it again.

CHAPTER SIX

The Man Who Knew Her Name

Marcus Webb found him first.

That was the thing Solomon would remember later, when he had time to think about how badly he'd miscalculated. He'd spent three days studying Naomi's notebook, mapping the names and locations she'd documented, building a picture of the network that had killed her. He'd felt like a hunter tracking prey through unfamiliar territory. He hadn't considered that the prey might be tracking him back. The notebook had consumed him. He'd read it a dozen times, memorizing every entry, every name, every fragment of pattern Naomi had noticed. He'd created his own notes, cross-referencing her observations with what he now knew about the myth-seed underground, trying to build connections she'd never had time to complete. Late at night, when the bookshop was quiet and Akari was resting, he'd sit in the back room with the notebook open on his lap, running his fingers over the indentations her pen had left in the paper. He'd felt clever. Focused. Dangerous.

He'd felt like he was finally doing something instead of just surviving.

The approach happened on a Tuesday evening, in the liminal hour between the end of the workday and the beginning of night. Solomon was walking through Shibuya, threading through crowds that moved with the particular purpose of people heading somewhere specific, when he felt it.

A thread.

Not ahead of him or behind him—beside him, matching his pace exactly, close enough to touch.

The sensation was unlike anything he'd experienced before.

Threads normally existed in his peripheral awareness—present but not pressing. This one insisted on being noticed. It pushed against his consciousness like a finger tapping his shoulder, patient and persistent. Something deliberate about its presence, as if whoever carried it was allowing Solomon to sense them, making themselves known by choice rather than accident.

Solomon stopped.

The crowd flowed around him, a current parting around an unexpected stone. Thousands of people moving through the famous scramble crossing, each one carrying their own thread, their own future, their own ignorance of the invisible world. None of them noticed the young man frozen in their midst. None of them saw the shadows at his feet beginning to twist.

He turned his head slowly, the way Akari had taught him to move when he sensed something that demanded attention.

A man stood three feet away, watching with an expression of mild curiosity.

Tall. Black. Well-dressed in a way that suggested money but not flashiness—Italian cut suit, dark gray, shoes with the soft shine of leather cared for by someone who understood that good shoes were worth maintaining. He had the kind of face that looked trustworthy, the kind that made you want to believe whatever he said, which immediately made Solomon's stomach clench.

There was something else about him—a stillness that seemed deliberate, a way of holding himself that spoke of training. His hands hung loose at his sides, visible and empty, the posture of a man who wanted to appear non-threatening while being ready for anything. Marcus Webb, Naomi's notebook had said. Field agent. The one who offered me a choice.

The words had been squeezed into the margins: Approached me in the parking garage. Knows too much. Offered to explain. Can't decide if he's dangerous or desperate. Something in his eyes—like he's tired of carrying a weight he never wanted but can't put down. What does it cost them to do this work?

Both, Solomon thought now. He's both.

"Mr. Nyx," Marcus said. His voice was calm, measured, the voice of someone who had learned how to seem harmless while being anything but. A trace of an accent Solomon couldn't place—something Southern, softened by years abroad. "I was hoping we might talk."

Solomon's shadow stirred at his feet, responding to the spike of adrenaline. The darkness pooled and stretched, reaching toward Marcus like a dog straining against a leash. Solomon forced himself to breathe, to stay calm, to not do anything stupid in the middle of a crowd of thousands.

"You knew my sister," he said.

"Yes." No denial. No deflection. Something flickered across his face—too fast to read. "I approached her three weeks before her death. I offered her recruitment. She declined."

"And then you killed her."

Marcus's expression shifted—regret, might have been calculation. For just a moment, Solomon saw something crack in that careful facade—a wince, perhaps, or the ghost of an old pain.

"I didn't kill her," he said. "I filed reports. Made recommendations. The decision to terminate was made by people above my authority." He paused. "That's not an excuse. It's context."

Something cold settled into his chest. Context. They called murdering his sister context.

"What do you want?"

"To talk. Somewhere less public." Marcus glanced at the crowds flowing around them. His eyes moved constantly—the automatic vigilance of someone who never stopped watching for threats. "There are things you should know. Things that might change how you understand what happened to Naomi."

"Why would you tell me anything?"

"Because the people I work for have decided you're too valuable to eliminate." Marcus's voice was flat, honest in a way that felt more dangerous than any lie. "And because I've spent eighteen months watching you stumble through an awakening that could have been guided, could have been controlled, could have been so much less painful."

Something in his voice when he said the last words—a bitter edge that didn't match the careful neutrality of his demeanor. "Painful for who?"

"For you." Marcus met his eyes. "And for me."

Solomon studied the man who had helped kill his sister. The thread above Marcus's shoulder was strange—not short, not long, but muted, as if something was interfering with Solomon's ability to read it. It flickered and shifted, refusing to resolve into the clear line that every other thread presented.

"You're shielded," Solomon said.

"Yes. Standard procedure for field operatives." Marcus didn't seem surprised. "It makes us harder to track, harder to read. It also makes us harder to interrupt. The technology is old. Older than the organization itself. Some say it was developed from fragments of myth-seeds harvested centuries ago—residue of abilities that no longer exist in living form."

He knew. Of course he knew—the Fate-Weavers had been watching Solomon since before he was born. They would have documented his awakening, analyzed what he'd done to the knife man, filed reports about his new ability to stand at the threshold and pause the passage.

"I could try anyway," Solomon said quietly.

"You could." Marcus's expression didn't change. "You might even succeed. But you'd learn nothing, and I'd be replaced by someone less interested in conversation."

"Why are you interested in conversation?"

Marcus was quiet for a moment. The crowds continued to flow around them, the crossing light changing, thousands of lives carried through space that felt too small.

When he spoke, his voice was lower, more careful. There was a rawness to it now, something less rehearsed.

"Because I knew Naomi," he said. "Not well. Not long. But I knew her. We spoke for nearly an hour that first time, in a parking garage that smelled like exhaust and old concrete. She had questions I couldn't answer. Suspicions I couldn't confirm. And she had a way of looking at you that made you feel like she could see exactly what you were trying to hide." He paused, and the weight of grief flickered across his face. "She deserved better than what happened to her."

Solomon's hands clenched at his sides. His shadow writhed, eager and angry. The darkness wanted to surge forward, to wrap itself around this man who had played a role in Naomi's death.

"You don't get to say that," he said. "You don't get to pretend you cared about her."

"I'm not pretending." Marcus reached slowly into his jacket—showing his movements, keeping things visible—and withdrew a small card. "I'm offering you the same thing I offered her. Information. Context. A chance to understand what you're involved in."

He held out the card.

Solomon didn't take it.

"She took the card," Marcus said. "She listened. She made her choice. And when she chose to run instead of cooperate, she knew the risks." He paused. "She thought she could protect you. She thought running was the only way."

"Was she wrong?"

"I don't know." For the first time, genuine uncertainty crossed Marcus's face. It looked foreign there, like an emotion he'd forgotten how to wear. "I've been doing this for a long time. Twenty-three years. I've seen seeds awakened and guided successfully. I've seen them destroyed before they could become dangerous. I've seen them…" He stopped, his careful composure cracking entirely. His eyes went distant, focusing on something Solomon couldn't see. "I've seen a lot of things."

"But you've never seen someone like me."

"No." Marcus lowered the card but didn't put it away. "What you did in that alley—interrupting a thread without severing it, allowing it to reform on a different path—that's not supposed to be possible. The Reapers in the old stories could cut threads. They could end things. They couldn't pause them. They couldn't give death a chance to reconsider."

"So I'm special."

"You're unprecedented. And unprecedented things make the people I work for nervous."

"Nervous enough to kill me?"

"Some of them. Others think you could be useful." Marcus finally pocketed the card. "I'm here because I was ordered to make contact. To evaluate your state of mind. To determine whether you're a threat that needs to be contained or an asset that can be cultivated."

"And what have you determined?"

Marcus studied him for a long moment. His eyes were the color of coffee left too long on a burner—dark, deep, holding heat that didn't show on the surface.

"That you're angry," he said. "That you loved your sister. That you're going to keep looking for answers whether I help you or not."

He paused. "And that you're already more powerful than you realize."

The truth of those words settled into him. He thought of the knife man's thread reforming, of the infinite branching paths he'd glimpsed in that moment of contact, of the terrible weight of holding someone's entire existence in his hands.

"If you want to find answers," Marcus continued, "there's a place you should go. A person you should meet. Someone who knew Naomi better than I did—someone who tried to warn her about what was coming."

"The silver-haired woman."

Marcus's expression shifted—surprise, quickly masked. "You know about her."

"Naomi mentioned her in her notebook. She never wrote down a name."

"Her name is Iris. She runs a network of… let's call them dissidents. People who believe the Fate-Weavers have lost their way. Who think the harvesting has become more about control than protection." Marcus glanced around, checking the crowds with automatic vigilance. "I can tell you where to find her. What you do with that information is your choice."

"Why would you help me?"

"Because I'm tired." The words came out flat, exhausted, carrying weight that surprised Solomon. "Because I've spent twenty years serving an organization that claims to protect the world but mostly just protects itself. Because I watched your sister die for asking questions that deserved answers."

He reached into his jacket again and withdrew a folded piece of paper.

"Iris operates out of Kyoto. This is an address, not her address, but a place where you can make contact. Tell them Marcus sent you. Tell them you want to know what happened to Naomi Nyx."

Solomon took the paper before he could stop himself.

"Why should I trust you?"

"You shouldn't." Marcus smiled without humor. "You should verify everything I've told you. Assume I'm manipulating you.

Assume this is another layer of control." He paused. "And then go anyway, because you don't have any better options and you know it."

Solomon looked down at the paper. An address in Kyoto. A name. A thread leading somewhere he couldn't see.

When he looked up, Marcus had stepped back.

"One more thing," Marcus said. "The shielding I mentioned—it's not perfect. If you wanted to read my thread, you could probably push through it. But I'd recommend against it."

"Why?"

"Because what you'd see wouldn't help you." Marcus's face was unreadable, but his voice held something that might have been warning. "And because some knowledge changes people in ways they don't expect. Naomi learned that the hard way."

He turned and walked away, disappearing into the Shibuya crowds with the ease of someone who had learned how to become invisible long ago. One moment he was there; the next he had dissolved into the current of bodies, just another stranger in a city of twelve million.

Solomon stood alone, holding a piece of paper that might be a trap or might be a lifeline.

His shadow had gone still.

Waiting.

Akari was furious.

"You talked to him," she said, pacing the length of the bookshop with energy Solomon had never seen from her. Her usual calm was gone, replaced by something sharp and bright that made the shadows in the shop recoil. Light gathered around her in unstable patterns. "A Fate-Weaver operative approached you in public and you talked to him."

"He had information."

"He had bait." Akari stopped pacing and faced him, light gathering around her in ways that made the darkness shrink toward the corners. "Everything he told you could be a lie. The address. The name. The whole story about being tired of the organization. Do you understand what they do? They manipulate. They control. They've spent centuries learning how to make people do exactly what they want while believing it was their own idea."

"I know."

"Then why did you take the paper?"

Solomon set it on the counter between them. The address stared up at them both.

"Because he was right," Solomon said. "I don't have better options."

Akari stared at him. The light around her flickered, unstable. She was afraid, Solomon realized. Not for herself—for him.

"You're going to go," she said. "To Kyoto. To meet this Iris person."

"Yes."

"Even though it's probably a trap."

"Yes."

"Even though the Fate-Weavers could be waiting for you—" "Kill me?" Solomon shook his head. "They had eighteen months to kill me. Countless opportunities. If they wanted me dead, I'd be dead."

"That's not comforting."

"It's not meant to be." He picked up the paper, folding it carefully, tucking it into his pocket. "Marcus said something I haven't been able to stop thinking about. He said some of them want me contained, and some of them think I could be useful."

"And you believe him?"

"I believe that's how organizations like this work. Factions. Disagreements. People with different agendas pushing in different directions." Solomon met Akari's eyes. "The Fate-Weavers aren't a monolith. They're a collection of people who happen to work together. And if some of them are tired—if some of them think the organization has lost its way—then maybe I can use that."

Akari was quiet for a long moment. The light around her slowly dimmed. The fear was there, but something else was overriding it—respect, maybe, or resignation.

"You're not the same person who walked into my shop a month ago," she said finally.

"No."

"That person was drowning. Lost. Looking for someone to explain what was happening to him."

"I know."

"This person—" She gestured at him, at his steady hands and calm eyes and the shadow that lay quiet at his feet. "This person is dangerous."

She turned away, busying herself with something on the shelf.

Solomon had learned to read her evasions—when she straightened books that didn't need straightening, when she cleaned surfaces that were already clean. Akari organized things when she was trying not to feel.

"What is it?" he asked.

"Nothing."

"Akari."

She stopped. Her hands went still on the shelf. When she spoke, her voice was smaller than he'd ever heard it.

"The last person I trained got killed. Before you. A Light-Bearer in Osaka. Seventeen years old. I spent three months teaching her control, and then the Fate-Weavers found her and I wasn't there." Akari didn't turn around. "I told myself I wouldn't do this again. Get invested. Start caring about whether someone makes it."

"And?"

"And then you walked into my shop bleeding from an alley fight, and here we are." She turned back, expression composed again—but Solomon had seen what was underneath. "So yes. This person is dangerous. Try not to get yourself killed."

Solomon considered the word. It had meant something different before—a threat to himself, a burden he couldn't control, a curse slowly driving him mad.

Now it meant something else.

"Good," he said. "I want them to think I'm dangerous. I want them to look at me and see something they can't predict, can't control, can't file away in their reports and protocols."

"And if that gets you killed?"

"Then at least I died trying to find out the truth." He thought of Naomi, writing her final entry in the notebook she knew might be her last words. "At least I didn't let them keep their secrets."

Akari sighed—a long, resigned sound that carried exhaustion and fear and something that might have been respect.

"I'm coming with you," she said.

"You don't have to."

"I know." She moved to the counter and began gathering things—objects Solomon didn't recognize, tools of a trade he was only beginning to understand. Small pouches of herbs, strips of paper covered in shimmering characters, crystals that glowed with their own light. "But someone needs to make sure you don't get yourself killed before you finish whatever it is you're starting."

"What am I starting?"

Akari looked at him, her expression unguarded—worry and wonder and the weight of someone watching something they couldn't stop.

"I don't know," she said. "But I don't think the Fate-Weavers know either. And that might be the only advantage we have."

They took the Shinkansen to Kyoto the next morning.

Solomon sat by the window, watching the landscape blur past at speeds that made the world look temporary. Rice paddies and industrial zones and mountains that appeared and vanished before he could register their shapes.

The bullet train moved at nearly 300 kilometers per hour, but it felt impossibly smooth—no vibration, no jolt. Just the landscape streaming past like a film being fast-forwarded, reality reduced to impressions rather than details.

Akari sat beside him, reading from a book in a language Solomon didn't recognize. The characters looked like Japanese but weren't quite. She hadn't spoken much since they'd boarded. Her face was calm, but he could see the tension in the way she held the book—too carefully, as if afraid it might slip away.

Solomon watched the threads.

They were everywhere on the train—passengers sleeping, working, staring at phones. Each one carried their thread above their shoulder, stretching toward futures Solomon could glimpse but not change.

Not without touching them.

Not without interrupting.

He thought about Marcus's words: You're already more powerful than you realize.

Was that true? He'd only used his ability once—in the alley, on instinct. He didn't know the limits of what he could do. Didn't know the costs.

The knife man had survived. His thread had reformed, found a new path.

But what if that future was worse?

What if interrupting someone's ending just delayed it, redirected it, transformed it into something darker?

He closed his eyes and tried not to think about the possibilities. But the threads were there, visible even through his closed eyelids—a web of light connecting every passenger to their future. He was beginning to understand that the world was far more interconnected than he'd ever imagined. That every life touched every other life, in ways too subtle to track.

And that somewhere in that vast web, Naomi's death had been just one thread among millions. Important to him. Meaningful to him. But to the Fate-Weavers, just another variable in an equation too large for any single person to comprehend.

Kyoto was different from Tokyo.

Not quieter—no major city was truly quiet—but slower. The streets breathed with a rhythm that felt older, more deliberate. Temples rose between modern buildings, their wooden gates and stone paths insisting on history in the face of change.

Where Tokyo felt like a city racing toward the future, Kyoto felt like a city that had made peace with its past. The streets were narrower, the buildings lower, the atmosphere less frantic. The air smelled different—less exhaust and steel, more incense and old wood and fallen leaves.

The address Marcus had given them led to a neighborhood in the eastern part of the city, near mountains that loomed green and patient against the sky. Traditional architecture dominated—machiya townhouses with distinctive facades, narrow alleys that looked like they hadn't changed in centuries. The modern world existed here too—power lines and vending machines—but it felt like an overlay, a temporary addition to something permanent.

"There," Akari said, pointing.

A tea house.

Nothing remarkable about it—just a small establishment with a wooden sign and paper lanterns, the kind of place tourists walked past without noticing. But Solomon felt something as they approached, a subtle shift in the air that reminded him of the bookshop's quiet. A sense of threshold.

This place knew how to keep secrets.

They stepped inside.

The interior was dim, lit by candles that flickered without apparent airflow. The walls were paper screens, casting soft shadows that seemed to move with life. Jasmine filled the space, mixing with tatami mats and the faint acrid hint of incense.

An older woman stood behind a small counter, her hair silver and long, her eyes the color of rain on old glass. She was dressed simply, in a dark kimono that seemed to absorb the candlelight. Her hands were folded in front of her, perfectly still, her face holding patient amusement—as if she'd been waiting for this moment for a long time.

She looked at them both—first at Akari, a brief nod of recognition, and then at Solomon, a longer gaze that seemed to see far more than the surface.

She smiled.

"Solomon Nyx," she said. Her voice was low and musical, carrying an accent Solomon couldn't place. "I've been waiting for you."

CHAPTER SEVEN

The Dissident

The tea house existed in a fold of Kyoto that tourists never found. Solomon felt the difference the moment they turned off the main street—a subtle wrongness in how the air moved, like stepping through a curtain into a room that had been waiting. The narrow alley should have been unremarkable, but his shadow stirred with recognition, responding to something in the stones themselves. "This place is old," Akari murmured. "Really old."

Old wasn't the right word. The buildings wore their centuries lightly—wooden facades weathered silver-gray, tile roofs slumped with patient weight, moss claiming the gaps between paving stones. But the tea house at the alley's end felt older than architecture. It felt like something that had been here before the city built itself around it. A single lantern hung above the entrance, its light too steady for flame. Paper screens glowed from within, casting shadows that didn't match the shapes that should have made them.

Solomon stopped three steps from the door.

"What is it?" Akari asked.

"She's watching us." Attention pressed against him like warm breath on the back of his neck. Not hostile. Curious. Assessing. "She's been watching since we entered the alley."

The door slid open before either of them could knock.

The woman who stood there was silver-haired and calm in ways that had nothing to do with age. Her face carried lines that spoke of decades spent outdoors, decisions made under pressure, consequences absorbed without complaint. She wore a simple kimono in dark blue, unadorned—the kind of garment that suggested either poverty or wealth so complete it didn't need announcement. But it was her eyes that stopped Solomon cold.

They were the eyes of someone who had been looking at the world's ugliness for so long that nothing could surprise her anymore—and who had chosen to keep looking anyway.

"Solomon Nyx," she said. "You look like your sister."

The words hit harder than any blow.

"You knew her."

"I did." Her eyes moved to the bag at Solomon's side, and something in her expression softened for a moment before closing again. "And I see she reached you. That's good. That means we can skip the part where I convince you she was someone worth listening to." She stepped aside, gesturing them in. "My name is Iris. Please—we have much to discuss, and not as much time as I'd like."

Inside, the tea house was smaller than Solomon expected—a single room with a low table, paper walls, tatami mats worn smooth by generations of use. Incense burned somewhere, a scent that shifted depending on which direction he turned his head. Candles provided the only light, their flames steady despite drafts that crept through unseen gaps.

Akari had gone quiet since they'd entered, her usual presence somehow muted. Solomon didn't know if that was strategy or instinct—a Light-Bearer's recognition of something that deserved respect.

They sat where Iris indicated. She moved to a small brazier and began preparing tea with unhurried hands—methodical, treating the ritual as something important rather than a delay.

Solomon watched, and felt his shadow settle, responding to the room's particular quiet. Whatever protections this place held, they extended even to him.

"Marcus sent you," Iris said without looking up. It wasn't a question.

"Yes."

"And you came because you want to know about your sister."

"I came because I want to understand what she died for."

That earned him a glance—sharp, appraising.

"Better," Iris said. "Understanding is more useful than knowing."

She finished with the tea and set cups before them, the liquid dark and steaming in ways that had nothing to do with heat. "Drink. It will help with what comes next."

The tea tasted like smoke and something floral Solomon couldn't identify. It spread warmth through his chest that went deeper than temperature, settling into places he hadn't known were cold.

Iris sat across from them and lifted her own cup.

"I met Naomi four times," she said. "The first time, she found me. The second time, I found her. The third time, we argued for three hours about whether anyone could be trusted. The fourth time, I tried to convince her to run."

Solomon's chest tightened. "She didn't listen."

"She listened. She always listened—that was one of her gifts."

Iris set her cup down with careful precision. "She just didn't agree. She thought running would put you in more danger. She thought if she disappeared, they'd come for you directly instead of using her as leverage."

"Was she right?"

"I don't know." Her voice carried the weight of someone who had stopped pretending to have easy answers. "I've spent forty years opposing the Fate-Weavers, and I don't understand all the ways they think. They're not evil—that would be simpler. They're convinced. They believe they're protecting the world from something terrible, and that belief justifies everything they do."

"What do they think they're protecting the world from?"

Iris glanced at Akari, then back at Solomon. Something passed between the two women—recognition, maybe, or the particular acknowledgment that exists between people who have seen the same darkness.

"They think they're protecting it from you," Iris said. "From people like you. From what happens when myth-seeds awaken fully and become something more than human."

Solomon's shadow stirred despite his efforts to keep it still. The candle flames wavered as if a wind had passed through the room. "Apotheosis," Akari said quietly. Her first word since they'd sat down.

"The ascension of a human consciousness into something divine." Iris nodded. "The Fate-Weavers have records going back thousands of years—events they attribute to myth-seeds reaching their full potential. Cities destroyed. Civilizations collapsed. Reality itself torn and rewritten by beings who used to be people."

She paused, letting the weight settle.

"The Pompeii eruption. The Bronze Age Collapse. The fall of the Khmer Empire." Her voice stayed steady, clinical. "History records natural disasters, political upheaval, mysterious decline. The Weavers know differently. They know what happens when a seed awakens fully—when a human being becomes something that no longer operates by human rules."

"And they think I could do that?" Solomon asked.

"They think you're the first Reaper-class awakening in three centuries." Iris's eyes stayed steady, unblinking. "The last one was a woman named Elena Voss. She lived in Prague. She had a gift for seeing how things ended—deaths, relationships, empires. She used it to advise kings and merchants, to predict wars and famines, to shape outcomes according to her own design."

"What happened to her?"

"She stopped being satisfied with seeing endings." Iris's voice went quiet. "She started causing them. Not out of malice—out of certainty. She became convinced she could see the perfect future, and that any deaths along the way were acceptable costs. By the time the Weavers managed to stop her, she had killed fourteen thousand people in a single night."

The number hung in the air like smoke.

Fourteen thousand.

Solomon tried to imagine it—fourteen thousand threads severed at once, fourteen thousand futures collapsing into nothing. His stomach turned.

"I'm not going to do that," he said.

"No?" Iris tilted her head. "How do you know?"

"Because I—" He stopped. Because he what? Because he was a good person? Because he loved his sister? Because he couldn't imagine becoming a monster?

Elena Voss had probably thought the same things once.

"The Weavers don't think you'll do it on purpose," Iris continued. "They think you'll do it by accident. Reaper-class seeds are volatile—connected to death in ways that make them unpredictable. Under enough stress, enough trauma, enough pressure, even well-intentioned people break. And when a Reaper breaks…"

She didn't finish.

She didn't need to.

Akari set her tea down carefully, her hands betraying a slight tremor. "You said you've been opposing them for forty years," she said. "How?"

Iris smiled—thin, humorless.

"I was one of them, once. A Light-Bearer, like you, recruited young and trained to believe that what we did was necessary. I helped identify awakenings. I helped evaluate threats. I helped—" She paused, and an ache that resembled pain crossed her face. "I helped process people who were designated for extraction."

"Process," Solomon repeated flatly.

"Take them from their lives. Transport them to facilities. Prepare them for what came next." Iris's voice had gone hollow. "I was good at it. I believed what they told me—that we were protecting the world, that the sacrifices were necessary, that the people we processed were dangerous."

"What changed?"

"I found a file. My own file." She laughed softly, without amusement. "I discovered that I was scheduled for processing myself. My seed had stabilized—I was no longer developing toward anything the Weavers could use. So I had been reclassified from 'asset' to 'resource.' They were going to harvest me the same way I had helped harvest hundreds of others."

The candle flames flickered.

"And that's when you ran."

"That's when I realized the truth." Iris met Solomon's gaze. "The Fate-Weavers don't serve humanity. They don't even serve their own kind. They serve an idea. The idea that certain people have the right to decide who lives, who dies, and who gets fed to the machine. Once you're inside that system, you're either useful or you're fuel. There's no third option."

"So you escaped."

"I disappeared. Spent years in hiding, learning what they were, building connections with others who had survived. Some were like me—former assets who had outlived their usefulness. Others were people whose families had been taken, whose communities had been disrupted, whose lives had been shattered by the Weavers'
interventions."

"And Naomi found you."

"Your sister was brilliant." Iris's voice softened. "She came to me with questions I hadn't heard in decades. She had tracked patterns, followed money, analyzed disappearances. She had mapped more of the Weaver infrastructure in two years than I had uncovered in twenty."

Pride and grief swelled in him simultaneously.

"What did she find?"

"Would you like me to tell you?" Iris rose and walked to a cabinet against the far wall. "Or would you prefer to see for yourself?"

She withdrew a worn leather folder and brought it to the table. "Your sister built two records of what she was doing. One was for you—so you'd know why, if it came to it. The other was the case itself." Iris laid a hand on the folder. "The evidence. The maps. The names. Everything she'd gathered before they killed her. She sent this to me a week before she died. Insurance, she called it. A way to make sure the information survived even if she didn't."

Solomon reached for the folder, his fingers trembling.

"Why didn't you give this to me before?"

"Because you weren't ready." Iris sat back down. "Because grief makes people reckless. Because I needed to know you could hear the truth without burning yourself down trying to avenge her."

"And now?"

Iris smiled faintly. "Now I've seen your eyes. You're angry—anyone would be. But you're also thinking. Planning. That's your sister in you."

Solomon opened the folder.

The papers inside were organized with the meticulous care that characterized everything Naomi had ever done. Maps marked with symbols Solomon didn't recognize. Names connected by lines indicating relationships—professional, familial, hostile. Financial records tracing flows of money through shell companies and offshore accounts.

And at the center: photographs.

Facilities hidden in plain sight—clinics, research centers, private hospitals. Their official purposes ranged from pharmaceutical testing to advanced medical care. Their actual purposes, according to Naomi's annotations, were something else entirely.

The Prometheus Initiative, she had written across one photograph of a concrete building nestled in forested mountains.

Primary processing hub for Northeast Asia. Estimated capacity: 200-300 subjects. Current status: ACTIVE.

"Processing," Solomon said, the word tasting like ash.

"Harvesting," Iris corrected quietly. "They extract the seed from the person. Sometimes the person survives, broken but alive. Usually they don't."

"And the seeds?"

"Refined. Concentrated. Stored." Iris's voice was clinical, distanced. "The Weavers have discovered that myth-seed energy can be transferred—partially, imperfectly—to other hosts. They use it to enhance their agents, to power their operations, to maintain their grip on the world's invisible machinery."

Solomon turned pages, reading Naomi's careful handwriting.

The extraction process requires the subject to be alive but suppressed—awake enough to maintain the seed's connection to their consciousness, sedated enough to prevent resistance.

Success rates vary by classification: Light-Bearers (73%), Shadow-Touched (61%), Storm-Born (44%), Reaper-Class (unknown—no successful extractions recorded).

The failures don't die quietly. They collapse inward, taking everything around them with them. The last Reaper extraction attempt destroyed a facility in Siberia in 1987. Official records blame a nuclear accident.

Solomon looked up sharply.

"Chernobyl?"

Iris nodded once.

"The reactor explosion was real, but it wasn't what killed most of the people. The Weavers had a facility hidden nearby—they thought the radiation would mask their activities. When they tried to extract a Reaper-class awakening…" She shook her head. "The death toll was much higher than the public ever knew."

Solomon stared at the folder, trying to process what he was reading.

His sister had known all of this. She had gathered this evidence, documented these horrors, traced these connections—and she had never told him. She had carried this weight alone, trying to protect him from a truth that had eventually killed her.

Near the back of the folder, he found a note in Naomi's handwriting. Personal, hurried, the letters cramped as if she'd been writing in a moving vehicle or trying to fit too many thoughts onto too small a page.

They've been tracking him since birth. They know what he is.

They've been waiting for his awakening.

But they're not planning to cultivate him.

They're planning to EXTRACT him.

Reaper-class seeds are too valuable to waste on a person. The Prometheus Initiative wants what's inside him—not the human, just the power.

I have to get him out before they move. I have to— The note ended there.

Unfinished.

Like everything else.

Solomon set the folder down carefully.

His hands weren't shaking. His shadow was still. Something had gone quiet inside him—not calm, not peace, but a kind of clarity that came from finally understanding the shape of the thing he was fighting.

They hadn't killed Naomi just to trigger his awakening.

They'd killed her because she was going to save him from being harvested.

"Priority extraction," he said, his voice flat.

"Reaper-class seeds are rare," Iris said quietly. "Rarer than any other classification. In three centuries, you're only the fifth one to awaken. The others were all lost—destroyed during containment or extraction, driven to the kind of catastrophe Elena Voss became."

"So they want to be more careful with me."

"They want to succeed this time." Iris's eyes stayed steady.

"Whatever they extract from seeds, whatever power they're harvesting—a Reaper-class seed would provide more than anything they've ever captured. You're not just valuable to them, Solomon. You're unprecedented."

Akari made a sound—somewhere between a gasp and a sob that she caught before it fully escaped.

"The people who want him dead," she said, "and the people who want him alive—" "Both see him as a resource." Iris nodded. "The ones who want him dead think extraction is too risky—that a Reaper-class awakening can't be harvested safely. The ones who want him alive think he's too valuable to waste."

"And no one," Solomon said slowly, "thinks I'm a person."

The candle flames wavered.

Iris was quiet for a long moment.

"Your sister did," Iris said at last. "That's why she died. She saw you as her brother, not as a seed or a threat or a resource. She loved you, and that love made her dangerous—to the Weavers, to their plans, to the entire system they've built."

Solomon closed his eyes.

He felt Naomi's presence in the folder—her determination, her intelligence, her stubborn refusal to accept the world as it was. She had spent months gathering this evidence, knowing she was being watched, knowing the risks. She had kept going anyway.

Because she loved him.

Because she believed he was worth saving.

"What do you want from me?" he asked, opening his eyes.

"Nothing, yet." Iris smiled faintly. "Take the folder. Read what your sister found. Understand the full scope of what you're facing. And when you're ready— when you know enough to make a real choice—come back. We'll talk about what comes next."

"And if I decide not to come back?"

"Then you'll have made a choice." Iris rose to clear the tea cups. "That's all I ask—that you choose, instead of letting them choose for you."

She paused at the cabinet, her back to them.

"Your sister chose. She chose to investigate instead of ignore. She chose to fight instead of run. She chose to die trying to save you instead of living by letting them have you." Her voice was quiet but carried absolute conviction. "The Weavers want to take that ability from you—the ability to choose your own path. They want to reduce you to a resource, something to be used and discarded. Whatever you decide to do with what you've learned tonight, don't let them take that from you."

They left the tea house as evening deepened over Kyoto.

The narrow alley felt different now—less strange, more weighted with significance. Solomon walked beside Akari in silence, the folder heavy under his arm, his mind churning with everything Iris had revealed.

The city was quieter than Tokyo—older rhythms, longer shadows, history pressing up through the pavement. Somewhere, temple bells rang the hour. The sound was beautiful and lonely and utterly indifferent to human concerns.

Akari's hair caught the last of the evening light, and Solomon found himself watching the way she tilted her head when she was thinking—slightly left, eyes narrowed, lips pressed together.

He'd seen her do it a hundred times. He didn't know when he'd started noticing.

He looked away before she could catch him.

"Do you believe her?" Akari asked finally.

"I believe Naomi." Solomon stopped walking and turned to face her. "Everything in this folder—the maps, the names, the evidence—it's her work. Her handwriting. Her mind. Whatever Iris might be, whatever agenda she might have, this is real."

"The Prometheus Initiative."

"The harvesting operation." He touched the folder's worn cover. "People being sorted and processed like crops. Seeds being cultivated and extracted. A system that's been running for centuries, hidden behind secrecy and noble-sounding justifications."

Akari was quiet for a moment.

"There's a facility in Naomi's notes. The closest one to Tokyo—in the mountains west of the city."

"I saw it." Solomon had memorized those pages already—the location, the layout, the questions Naomi had been planning to answer. "She was going to investigate. Try to get inside, find proof of what they were actually doing."

"And now?"

Solomon looked down at the folder, then up at the darkening sky.

"Now I'm going to finish what she started."

Akari didn't argue. She didn't try to talk him out of it, didn't list the reasons it was dangerous or stupid or likely to get them both killed.

She just nodded.

"When?"

"Soon." Solomon started walking again, and Akari fell into step beside him. "But first I need to read everything. Understand every piece of what Naomi found. Know exactly what I'm walking into."

"And then?"

"Then I see it for myself." His shadow stretched before him, longer than the fading light could explain. "Not what Iris says, not what Marcus implies, not what anyone else claims. The truth.

Whatever that turns out to be."

They walked back toward the station, two figures against the evening, carrying secrets that could change everything.

Above their heads, invisible to the crowds around them, the threads stretched toward futures that were less certain than they'd been that morning.

And in the tea house behind them, Iris poured herself another cup of tea and sat alone in the candlelight.

She had been waiting for a long time.

She had learned to be patient.

But something in Solomon Nyx's eyes had reminded her of his sister—the same fierce determination, the same refusal to accept what couldn't be changed.

That kind of fire could illuminate the world.

Or it could burn everything down.

Iris had seen both outcomes before.

She hoped—genuinely, painfully hoped—that this time would be different.

But hope, she had learned, was not the same as belief.

So she waited, and watched, and prepared for whatever came next.

Iris set down her tea.

"You want to understand what Reapers can become? Let me tell you about Lisbon."

Solomon listened.

"1755. November first. All Saints' Day, when the churches were full." Iris's voice was quiet, matter-of-fact. The tone of someone recounting history rather than horror. "There was a woman named Isabella Vasconcelos. A merchant's daughter. She'd manifested a Reaper-class seed six months earlier, after watching her entire family die of plague."

"Another Reaper."

"One of the earliest fully documented cases. The Fate-Weavers—they used different names then—had been watching her. Debating whether to intervene. She seemed stable, they told themselves. Learning to control her abilities on her own. They decided to observe rather than act."

Iris paused.

"They were wrong."

"What happened?"

80

"We don't know exactly what triggered it. A religious procession passed her house—something about the bells, the chanting, the crowds of people celebrating faith while she carried death inside her. Her shadow expanded. Not attacking anyone, not at first. Just… reaching. Looking for connection."

His own shadow stirred in uneasy recognition.

"The earthquake hit at 9:40 in the morning. Three massive shocks in ten minutes. But it wasn't the shaking that killed most people. It was what came after." Iris's eyes were distant. "Isabella's shadow had touched something deep. Awakened something. The earth cracked open and released fissures of fire. The ocean pulled back and then returned as a tsunami thirty feet tall. And the fires—the fires burned for five days."

"How many?"

"The official count is around thirty thousand. The real number is probably twice that." Iris met his eyes. "Isabella herself survived. She walked through the devastation like a ghost, untouched by flames that consumed everyone around her. By the time the Weavers reached her, she wasn't human anymore. She'd become something else entirely."

"What happened to her?"

"She simply… stopped. Sat down in the middle of the destruction she'd caused and refused to move. She spent the next three days communing with her own shadow, trying to understand what she'd done. On the fourth day, she willed herself to die. Her seed dissolved into nothing. Whatever she'd become couldn't continue, and she knew it."

Solomon absorbed this.

"You're telling me this could happen to me."

"I'm telling you it happens to Reapers who don't find balance. Who let grief consume them. Who reach for connection without understanding what they're touching." Iris picked up her tea again. "You're stronger than Isabella was. Better trained. But the potential is the same. Never forget that."

CHAPTER EIGHT

What She Found

Solomon read through the night.

Akari had offered to stay, but he'd asked her to leave—not unkindly, but firmly. This was between him and Naomi now. The journal she'd left him, the evidence file Iris had kept safe, all of it spread across the floor in stacks that grew and shrank as he rearranged them, trying to piece together a single coherent picture from two halves of a record his sister had split for safety.

He needed to meet her alone.

The bookshop was quiet around him, the under-room's presence a gentle weight at the edges of his awareness. He sat on the floor with the folder open, papers arranged in careful stacks, and let his sister's final gift unfold.

She'd been methodical. That was the first thing he noticed—the precision of her organization, the way each piece of evidence connected to the next in a chain of logic that built inexorably toward conclusions no sane person would want to reach. Naomi had never been the academic one; that had been Solomon, the kid who disappeared into books while she worked two jobs to keep them fed. But this research was meticulous in ways that humbled him.

She'd learned to think like this for him.

She'd become someone new—a researcher, an investigator, a hunter of secrets—because she'd known something was wrong with the world her brother was about to enter, and she'd refused to let him face it blind.

Solomon touched the edge of a photograph—Naomi's handwriting on the back, a date from eighteen months ago. Before everything. Before the death that wasn't an accident, before the awakening that wasn't chance.

She knew, he thought. She knew she was being watched. She knew the risks.

And she built her case anyway.

The earliest documents were from her job at the logistics company—shipping manifests that didn't match invoices, routing schedules that made no geographic sense. Containers marked THREAD PRIORITY traveling between cities on three continents, always to the same handful of destinations.

They're moving something, she'd written in the margins. Or someone. The weight classifications don't match standard cargo. The handling instructions are medical-grade—temperature control, vibration isolation, orientation requirements. You don't ship machine parts this carefully.

You ship bodies.

Solomon spread the manifests across the floor, tracing the routes Naomi had highlighted. Rotterdam. São Paulo. Osaka. A dozen smaller locations in between—transfer points, holding facilities, waypoints in a network that spanned the globe.

She'd started mapping the patterns, cross-referencing shipment dates with news reports, looking for anomalies. And she'd found them.

A young artist in Buenos Aires who had shown strange abilities—paintings that predicted events before they happened—who had "relocated" to pursue her career abroad. A retired professor in Lagos whose students reported he could see connections no one else noticed, who had "accepted a research position" at an institution no one could locate. A teenage boy in Jakarta who had survived a car accident that should have killed him, who had been "transferred to a specialized recovery facility" and never heard from again.

Names. Dates. Photographs. Fragments of lives quietly removed from the world.

They take people, Naomi had written. They identify seeds—people with potential, people who are starting to awaken—and they take them. The families get stories about opportunities, relocations, treatments. The records get altered. The people themselves just… vanish.

Where do they go?

The middle section was denser, harder to parse. Financial records. Property transfers. Corporate registrations in jurisdictions that specialized in secrecy. Naomi had been teaching herself forensic accounting, following money through systems designed to make following impossible.

Solomon found notes in the margins where she'd worked through complex transactions, arrows connecting shell companies to parent organizations to investment vehicles that led, eventually, to a single source.

The Prometheus Initiative.

Headquartered in Geneva. Founded in 1847—a date that seemed impossible until Solomon remembered how long the Fate-Weavers had been operating. Board members whose names appeared in no other public records. Charitable mission statement about "advancing human potential" that read like satire once you knew what they were actually doing.

They're funding everything, Naomi had written. The facilities, the transportation, the personnel, the research. Billions of dollars flowing through channels designed to be untraceable. This isn't a side project. This is an industry.

They're harvesting people at industrial scale.

Solomon found a page where Naomi had tried to estimate the numbers—calculations based on shipping volume, facility capacity, operational frequency. Her math was rough, hedged with question marks and margin-of-error notes.

But the low-end estimate was horrifying enough.

At minimum, several hundred people per year. Possibly more.

For over a century.

Where are they? What happens to them? What are they being used for?

The next section contained interview notes—conversations Naomi had conducted with anyone who might know something, contacts she'd cultivated through months of careful work, sources who had given her fragments without always understanding what they meant. A former security guard who'd worked at the Rotterdam warehouse. He'd signed an NDA and taken a generous severance, but three beers into their conversation he'd admitted that the "cargo" he'd been guarding sometimes made sounds.

"Like crying," Naomi had quoted him. "Muffled, like through insulation. The first time I heard it, I reported it to my supervisor. He told me some cargo is temperature-sensitive and the cooling systems make noise. I knew that was bullshit. But the pay was good and the work was easy, so I stopped asking questions."

When I pushed him on details, he shut down. Said he didn't remember anything else. But he was scared, not of me. Of something that happened there that he won't talk about.

A shipping clerk who'd noticed strange cargo crossing her desk. She'd tried to research the destinations once, out of curiosity, and her computer had frozen. When the IT department fixed it, all her search history was gone and she'd received a polite but firm warning about "accessing restricted systems."

"After that, I just processed the paperwork," she'd told Naomi. "But I kept copies. I don't know why. I just felt like someone should know."

A nurse dismissed from the Osaka facility for asking too many questions about patients who never recovered but never died either. She'd described rooms full of people in what looked like suspended animation—breathing, alive, but absent in ways that made her skin crawl.

"Their eyes were open sometimes," she'd said. "But there was nothing behind them. Whatever made them who they were—it was gone. Harvested.

That's what the doctors called it when they thought no one was listening. The harvest."

Solomon read that passage three times.

Harvested.

The clinical language made his stomach turn. These weren't crops being gathered. These were people—people like him, people who had awakened to something strange and beautiful and terrifying, people whose only crime was becoming something the world couldn't control.

And they were being processed like raw materials in a factory. The final section was the hardest to read.

Lists.

Names and dates and classifications, organized in columns that Naomi had recreated from documents she'd photographed or memorized or stolen. Hundreds of entries spanning decades, each one representing a person who had been processed through the Fate-Weaver system.

AWAKENING STATUS: PARTIAL SEED CLASSIFICATION: MINOR DISPOSITION: TRANSFER TO FACILITY 7 OUTCOME: COMPLETE EXTRACTION - 94% YIELD AWAKENING STATUS: SIGNIFICANT SEED CLASSIFICATION: MODERATE DISPOSITION: TRANSFER TO FACILITY 3 OUTCOME: PARTIAL EXTRACTION - 67% YIELD - SUBJECT TERMINATED AWAKENING STATUS: COMPLETE SEED CLASSIFICATION: MAJOR DISPOSITION: PRIORITY EXTRACTION OUTCOME: COMPLETE EXTRACTION - 99% YIELD - EXCEEDED PROJECTIONS Solomon read the entries with growing horror.

These weren't threats being neutralized. These weren't dangerous awakenings being prevented.

These were people being sorted. Categorized. Processed like inventory in a warehouse. And at the end of each entry—the outcome. The yield. The clinical assessment of how much had been successfully extracted before the subject was "terminated" or simply ceased to exist as a person.

What are they extracting? Naomi had written at the bottom of one page. What do you get when you harvest a myth-seed? Power? Knowledge? Something else entirely?

And what are they using it for?

She hadn't found the answers.

But she'd found something else.

On the last pages, in handwriting that shook slightly—written quickly, probably the night before she died—Naomi had added her final notes.

I found Solomon's file.

Solomon's breath caught.

They've been watching him since he was born. Since BEFORE he was born—they had Mom under observation during the pregnancy. They knew what he was going to become. They've known all along.

His classification is listed as REAPER-CLASS POTENTIAL.

Priority extraction if awakening is achieved. They're not planning to kill him. They're planning to HARVEST him.

The file mentions something called the "Prometheus Protocol"—a specialized extraction method for high-value subjects. It's only been attempted twice before. Both times failed. Both times caused massive collateral damage.

They're willing to risk that for what's inside him.

I can't let them have him. I won't.

Solomon set the folder down carefully, hands trembling.

His whole life.

They'd been watching his whole life—measuring, tracking, waiting. Every moment of normalcy had been an illusion, a carefully maintained fiction while the Fate-Weavers positioned their pieces. And Naomi had discovered it. She'd found his file, seen what they planned, and made her choice.

Not to run.

Not to hide.

To fight.

And it had killed her.

Dawn came slowly, gray light seeping through the bookshop's windows as Solomon sat amid his sister's legacy. The folder lay open before him, its contents spread across the floor like a map of everything wrong with the world.

Akari found him there when she arrived.

She didn't speak at first—just stood in the doorway, taking in the scene. The stacks of paper. The photographs. The quiet devastation on Solomon's face.

"You read it all," she said finally.

"Every word." His voice came out rough, scraped raw by hours of silence. "She knew everything. She knew about the network, the facilities, the harvesting. She knew about me—what I was, what they planned to do. She'd been building this for months."

Akari crossed the room and knelt beside him.

"And?"

Solomon picked up the final pages—Naomi's last notes, the ones she'd written the night before she died.

"She found a facility," he said. "In the mountains west of Tokyo. The closest one to the city, probably the one they would have taken me to. She was planning to investigate. Get inside, find proof of what they were actually doing."

"She never got the chance."

"No." He set the pages down. "But I'm going to finish what she started."

Akari was quiet for a long moment.

"You know this could be a trap," she said. "The folder, the information, the convenient facility within reach. It could all be designed to lead you exactly where they want you."

"I know."

"And you're going anyway."

"Yes."

She studied him—the steadiness of his hands, the quiet in his eyes, the shadow that lay obedient at his feet.

"When?"

"Tomorrow night." Solomon had been thinking about this through the long hours of reading. "The facility is isolated—no public transportation, no nearby towns. We'll need to approach on foot, at night, when there's less chance of being seen."

"We?"

"You don't have to come."

Akari laughed softly—a tired sound, resigned but not defeated. "You're going to infiltrate a Fate-Weaver facility, alone, with powers you barely understand, on evidence that might be designed to get you killed." She shook her head. "I'm coming."

"Why?"

"Because someone has to make sure you don't get yourself harvested before you finish whatever it is you're starting." She met his eyes, her light steady. "And because I've spent years staying neutral, staying safe, staying out of the larger conflicts. Your sister didn't have that luxury. She saw something wrong and she fought it, even knowing it would kill her."

Her voice softened.

"I think I've been hiding long enough."

They planned until evening.

Akari's contacts had provided satellite imagery of the facility—recent, detailed. It showed a compound in a mountain valley, accessible by a single road that wound through dense forest. Multiple buildings arranged around a central structure. Fenced perimeter with guard posts at regular intervals. A helipad on the eastern edge, suggesting the facility received VIP visitors who didn't want to be seen using public roads.

"Security is professional but not military," Akari said, tracing routes on the printed images. "They're not expecting assault. They're expecting secrecy to be sufficient protection."

"Can we get in?"

"There's a service entrance on the north side—supplies come in twice a week, according to Naomi's delivery schedules. The fence there is older, probably less monitored." She traced a path through the forest. "If we approach from this ridge, stay off the main trails, we can reach the perimeter without being seen."

"And once we're inside?"

"That's where it gets complicated." Akari looked up. "I don't know what we'll find. I don't know how many people are there, what security measures they have internally, whether they have awakened individuals working as guards. We'll have to adapt."

"No plans survive contact with the enemy."

"Something like that." She gathered the images. "We go in, we observe, we get out. We don't engage unless we have to. We don't try to shut anything down or rescue anyone or play hero. Information only."

"Agreed."

"And if we find something we can't handle—if there are too many guards, too much security—we leave. We come back with better plans, better resources."

"Agreed."

Akari held his gaze for a moment longer, searching for something—certainty, maybe, or the particular determination that made people do things like this.

Whatever she found satisfied her.

"Tomorrow night," she said. "We leave at sunset."

That night, Solomon sat alone in the under-room.

He hadn't asked to come here—hadn't known he could, without Akari's guidance. But the shop had opened for him anyway, recognizing something he hadn't known he possessed. The shelves stretched into impossible distances. The shadows watched without malice. The silence held him.

He thought about Naomi.

About the months she'd spent gathering evidence, knowing she was being watched. About the late nights working through documents, the careful conversations with sources who could have betrayed her. About the night she'd given her folder to Iris and gone home to pack bags she'd never finish filling.

About the choice she'd made—to run instead of cooperate, to bet everything on getting her brother to safety, to refuse the world's cruelty even when refusal meant death.

She'd lost that bet.

But she'd left him something better than safety.

She'd left him the truth—and one simple instruction, the one that had cost her everything to put on the page.

Her dying wish had not been vengeance, though she would have understood that impulse. It had not been survival, though she'd wanted that for him more than anything.

It had been a request. One he intended to keep.

Tomorrow, he would start.

Solomon closed his eyes and let the under-room's quiet settle over him. His shadow stretched out, relaxed, no longer fighting for control. Whatever he was becoming—Reaper, monster, something new—it was his to shape now.

The Fate-Weavers thought they knew what he was.

They thought they could harvest him like all the others.

They were wrong.

He was done being studied, tracked, manipulated, guided toward outcomes that served everyone's purposes but his own. He was done letting other people's plans determine the shape of his life.

Tomorrow, he would start writing his own story.

And the Fate-Weavers would learn that some threads couldn't be cut, couldn't be harvested, couldn't be controlled.

Some threads could only be reckoned with.

Tomorrow never came the way he'd planned.

Akari's contacts reached her before dawn, and what they told her changed everything. The Tokyo mountain facility Naomi had mapped was being evacuated — reassigned to some emergency protocol none of her sources could name. Whatever Solomon and Akari had hoped to find there would be gone by nightfall. But another door had opened. Helena Vance herself had surfaced — and Helena was willing to talk.

Akari knew people. That was the first thing Solomon learned about her network—not its size, but its depth. She made calls on burner phones, sent messages through encrypted channels he couldn't begin to understand, and slowly assembled the resources they would need. "Geneva is suicide," Marcus said when they met him at a ramen shop in Shibuya. He'd arrived without warning, sliding into the booth across from them with the same contained stillness Solomon had noticed the first time — the stillness of a man who had been trained to take up less space than he needed, and who had never stopped doing it even when there was no longer a reason. His Southern vowels were barely audible now, smoothed by years away, but they surfaced on certain words. *Suicide* was one of them. The ease of someone who had been avoiding detection for years. "Helena Vance doesn't make mistakes. She doesn't leave openings. And the facility—" He shook his head. "It's not like the processing centers. It's her fortress."

"We're not trying to assault it," Solomon said. "We're trying to negotiate."

Marcus stared at him. "Negotiate. With the woman who approved your sister's death."

"With the woman who has information I need." Solomon kept his voice steady, even as Naomi's face surfaced in his memory. "Helena Vance knows things about Reaper awakenings that no one else does. About what I might become. About how to prevent it."

"And you think she'll just... share that?"

"I think she'll want to study me." His shadow stirred beneath the table, responding to the truth of the statement. "Iris said I'm unprecedented. Helena will want to understand why. That gives me leverage."

"That gives you a one-way ticket to an extraction table."

"Maybe." Solomon met Marcus's eyes. "But staying here, hiding, waiting for them to find me—that's not a life. That's just a slower death."

Marcus was quiet for a long moment.

"There's a man," Marcus said, choosing each word. He turned a chopstick between his fingers while he spoke — not fidgeting. Marcus did not fidget. He moved a small object to mark his speech the way some people used their hands. "Inside Prometheus. Someone who owes me a debt. He can get you into the facility—not through the front door, but through channels they don't watch as closely."

"Why would he help us?"

"Because I helped him once, when he needed it." Marcus's expression was unreadable. "And because he's been having doubts about what Prometheus has become. He won't act against them directly—he's not that brave. But he might be willing to look the other way."

Akari leaned forward. "Can he get a message to Helena? Let her know we're coming?"

"He can do better than that." Marcus pulled a phone from his pocket— different from the one he'd used before, older, a flip phone that belonged to a previous decade. "He can arrange a meeting. Somewhere neutral. Somewhere she'll feel safe enough to listen."

"Why would Helena agree to that?"

"Because she's curious." Marcus's smile was thin. "I've known Helena for fifteen years. She's ruthless, but she's also a scientist. If you tell her you can show her something she's never seen—something that contradicts everything she thinks she knows about Reapers—she won't be able to resist."

Solomon looked at Akari.

She nodded.

"Make the call," Solomon said.

The days that followed were a blur of preparation and waiting. Akari drilled him on what to expect. The facility's layout, based on intelligence gathered over years of careful observation. The personnel they might encounter—scientists, administrators, security forces with training that went far beyond conventional military. The man with no thread, whom she called Silas, a weapon that Prometheus had created or discovered or summoned from somewhere else entirely.

"He's not human," she said flatly. "I don't know what he is, but he's not like us. Your abilities won't work on him the way they work on others."

"I noticed."

"So don't try to fight him. Don't try to manipulate him. If you encounter Silas, you run."

"And if I can't run?"

Akari was quiet for a moment.

"Then you hope he's been ordered to bring you in alive."

On the second night, Solomon practiced.

Not the combat applications of his power—those required an enemy, and the bookshop's under-room was too peaceful for violence. Instead, he focused on perception. On seeing the threads more clearly, tracing them further, understanding the patterns they formed.

The Dreamer stirred at the edges of his awareness.

He felt it now whenever he reached too far—that vast presence lurking at the other end of all the threads, watching his progress with something that felt disturbingly like hope. It didn't speak. It didn't interfere. It simply attended, the way a parent might watch a child learning to walk.

The comparison made Solomon's skin crawl.

But he couldn't deny that his powers were growing. Each day, he could see a little further. Feel a little more. The threads that had once been whispers were becoming conversations, and the conversations were revealing patterns he hadn't noticed before.

Everything was connected.

That was the secret hiding in plain sight. Every thread touched every other thread, directly or indirectly, forming a web that encompassed all of human existence. Deaths cascaded into lives which cascaded into more deaths, an endless cycle of endings and beginnings that stretched back to the first consciousness and forward to the last.

And at the center of the web, holding it all together, something ancient waited.

"You're reaching too far."

Akari's voice pulled him back. She stood in the doorway of the under-room, her light casting warm shadows across the walls.

"I can feel it," Solomon said. "The thing beneath everything. It's real, isn't it? Not just a story the Fate-Weavers tell themselves."

"It's real." Akari crossed to sit beside him. "I felt it once, when I was younger. When my seed first awakened and I didn't know how to control it. I reached too far, saw too much, and…" She shuddered. "It noticed me. Just for a moment. But that moment was enough."

"What did it feel like?"

"Lonely." The word came out soft, almost a whisper. "Old and vast and terribly, terribly lonely. Like something that had been alone so long it had forgotten any other way to exist."

Solomon thought about the presence he'd felt. The attention that wasn't hostile but wasn't safe either. The sense of something reaching back toward him whenever he reached toward it.

"Do you think it wants to hurt us?"

"I don't think it knows how to do anything else." Akari's eyes were distant. "The Light-Bearers have stories about it. We call it the Dreamer. They say it existed before the first seeds awakened, before humans had any concept of the supernatural. It's been sleeping for so long that waking up might destroy everything."

"And Prometheus knows about it?"

"Prometheus has been trying to keep it asleep for three centuries." Akari met his eyes. "That's the real reason they harvest seeds. Not for power. Not for knowledge. To feed the Dreamer just enough to keep it dreaming. To prevent it from waking up and consuming everything in its path."

Solomon absorbed this.

"So they're not just monsters."

"They're monsters and they might be the only thing standing between humanity and something worse." Akari's laugh was bitter. "Welcome to the real world, Solomon. Where the villains sometimes have a point, and doing the right thing might end civilization."

On the third morning, Marcus called.

"It's arranged," he said. "Helena will meet you at a research annex in the mountains. Neutral ground—or as neutral as you'll get when dealing with Prometheus."

"When?"

"Three days. That gives you time to travel, to prepare, to decide if you actually want to go through with this."

Solomon looked at Akari, who was listening from across the room.

"We'll be there," he said.

PART TWO

THE HARVESTING

CHAPTER NINE

The Facility

Solomon had never flown before.

The realization hit him as the plane lifted off from Narita, the pressure pushing him back into his seat, the city lights tilting away beneath him until Tokyo became a scattered constellation swallowed by cloud. Nineteen years old, and this was his first time leaving the ground.

Beside him, Akari sat with her eyes closed, hands folded in her lap, her light barely visible, just a faint warmth that kept the recycled cabin air from feeling so stale. She'd slept on planes before. Probably many times. Another reminder of how different their lives had been.

Solomon watched the darkness outside his window and tried not to think about everything he was leaving behind.

Tokyo had never been home. Not really. It had been refuge, hiding place, the city where he'd stumbled into a new life without asking for it. But somewhere in the last weeks, it had become something else. The bookstore with its careful quiet. The training spaces where Akari had taught him to miss. The streets where his shadow had learned to behave.

He might never see any of it again.

"You're thinking too loud," Akari murmured without opening her eyes.

"Sorry."

"Don't be sorry. Just try to rest. We have eighteen hours before Geneva, and you'll need your strength."

Geneva. The word felt unreal. A city he'd only seen in photographs, home to organizations that operated in the spaces between nations, now destination for a mission that felt like walking into the dragon's mouth.

"Tell me about her," Solomon said quietly. "The woman we're going to find."

Akari was silent for a moment. When she spoke, her voice was careful—measuring what to share.

"Helena Vance. She's been with Prometheus for over twenty years. Started as a field operative, worked her way up. Now she runs their European operations."

"What kind of person is she?"

"The kind who believes she's doing the right thing." Akari opened her eyes and looked at him. "That makes her dangerous, Solomon. More dangerous than someone who knows they're evil and does it anyway. Helena genuinely thinks Prometheus is protecting the world. She'll sacrifice anything—anyone—to maintain that belief."

"You've met her."

"Once. Years ago. Before I understood what they were." Akari's expression flickered—old pain, carefully controlled. "She seemed kind. Reasonable. The sort of person you'd trust with a secret."

"And now?"

"Now I know that kindness is just another tool. She'll be kind right up until the moment she decides you're a threat. Then she'll do whatever's necessary with the same calm she uses to order coffee."

Solomon filed that away. Helena Vance. A true believer. The worst kind of enemy.

"What does she know about us?"

"That we exist. That you're Reaper-class. That I've been training you outside their network." Akari paused. "She'll have questions. She'll want to understand why we're coming to her instead of hiding."

"And what do we tell her?"

Akari's smile was thin. "We tell her the truth. That you've discovered something in their network that they missed. Something that's growing. Something that might destroy everything they've built."

"Will she believe us?"

"She'll believe her own observations. When you show her what you can do—what you can see—she won't be able to deny it." Akari closed her eyes again. "Whether she acts on that belief or tries to contain you anyway... that's what we're gambling on."

The plane hummed through darkness, carrying them toward a confrontation that would determine everything.

He didn't sleep.

The mountains swallowed sound.

Solomon noticed it first as they left the car behind—the way the forest closed around them, muffling everything except their footsteps and breath. They'd landed in Geneva that morning, spent hours in safe houses and borrowed cars, and now stood at the edge of a wilderness that felt older than the nation surrounding it.

No traffic noise reached this far. No planes overhead. Just wind moving through pine branches and the occasional call of birds settling into night.

Akari moved ahead, her steps careful on the uneven terrain.

She'd changed before they left Tokyo—dark clothing, practical boots, her hair pulled back tight. She looked like someone who had done this before.

Maybe she had.

Solomon followed her lead, trying to match her silence. His shadow behaved itself, staying close and contained, but he could feel it paying attention—alert in ways it hadn't been in the city.

They'd parked two kilometers from the facility's perimeter. The hike took over an hour—treacherous ground, roots hidden under fallen needles, stones that shifted when you put weight on them. By the time they reached the ridgeline overlooking the valley, full dark had settled. Solomon crouched beside Akari at the edge of the trees and looked down at what Naomi had died trying to expose. The facility looked almost normal.

That was the worst part.

From above, it could have been a corporate retreat or a research campus— clean lines, well-maintained buildings, landscaping that suggested significant investment. Lights glowed in windows. A parking lot held a dozen vehicles. Somewhere, a generator hummed the steady bass note of infrastructure.

"Smaller than I expected," Solomon said.

"The important parts will be underground." Akari studied the compound through a small scope. "Surface structures for administration, housing, logistics. Everything else hidden."

They watched for another twenty minutes, tracking patrol patterns. Two guards made regular circuits of the perimeter—not military, like Akari had said, but professional. They carried flashlights rather than weapons, which suggested confidence in the facility's isolation.

Or other forms of security they couldn't see.

"The north fence," Akari said after a moment. "There's a gap in the patrol— maybe three minutes between passes. We can make it to the service entrance."

"And inside?"

"We improvise."

She was still lowering the scope when Solomon felt it.

Something was wrong.

He sensed it before he could articulate it—a pressure in the air, a tightness in the threads around them. His shadow stirred uneasily, pressing against his skin like an animal sensing a predator.

"Wait," he whispered.

Akari froze beside him.

The forest behind them was too quiet. No birds settling for the night, no small animals rustling through underbrush, no ordinary sounds of life doing what life did when darkness fell. Just silence, thick and complete and wrong.

"We're not alone," Solomon said.

"The patrols are supposed to stay near the facility."

"This isn't a patrol." He let his senses extend, feeling for the threads that should have been there. People, animals, anything alive within the radius of his perception. "There's something in the forest with us. Something that doesn't have a thread."

Akari went still. Whatever she was about to say, she swallowed it. His shadow wanted to spread, to scout, to identify the threat. He held it back, afraid that extending his power would make them more visible rather than less.

"Can you tell where?"

He tried. Reached out with the death-sense, mapped the negative space where threads should have been. The absence was moving—slowly, deliberately, circling toward their position from the northwest. Closing.

"We go now," Akari said. "Before whatever it is gets any closer."

The descent was worse than the climb.

Every step felt too loud, every shifted stone a potential alarm. Solomon's shadow wanted to spread, to scout ahead, to wrap itself around the facility and tell him what waited inside. He kept it contained through sheer will.

Not yet.

They reached the fence line as one guard disappeared around the far corner. The barrier was chain-link topped with razor wire—older, like the satellite images had suggested, patched where weather or animals had damaged it.

Akari produced wire cutters and went to work without hesitation. "I thought we were using the service entrance," Solomon whispered.

"Changed my mind." She pulled back a section wide enough to squeeze through. "Service entrances have cameras. This section doesn't."

They slipped through, Akari first, then Solomon. She bent the fence back into place behind them, not perfect, but enough to pass casual inspection.

The space between the fence and the nearest building was maybe fifty meters of open ground. No cover.

"Now we run," Akari said.

They ran.

The building's shadow swallowed them. They pressed against the wall, breathing hard, waiting for alarms that didn't come. "Loading dock," Akari whispered. "This way."

They moved along the wall until they reached a metal door marked SERVICE ENTRANCE - AUTHORIZED PERSONNEL ONLY. Akari knelt, pulled a set of picks from her bag.

Thirty seconds later, the door clicked open.

Inside was a corridor lit by emergency strips—dim enough to hide in, bright enough to navigate. The air smelled like industrial cleaner and something underneath it, something Solomon couldn't identify.

He followed Akari through the building, trusting her instincts over his own. She paused at intersections, listened at doors, navigated as if she'd memorized the layout.

Maybe she had.

They descended two flights of stairs before they found it.

The door was heavy—steel, reinforced, secured with both keycard and biometric access. Someone had propped it open with a doorstop.

The carelessness was almost funny.

They slipped through into darkness.

Solomon had been prepared for horrors.

He'd imagined laboratories. Torture chambers. The kind of gothic nightmare that would make everything simple, everything clear.

What he found was worse.

Rows of pods stretched into the shadows—glass and steel containers arranged with industrial precision, each one lit from within by soft blue light. And inside each pod, suspended in fluid that looked like water but moved too slowly…

People.

Dozens of them.

Men, women, ages spanning decades. They floated motionless, tubes connected to their bodies, eyes closed, faces slack. They could have been sleeping—would have been sleeping, if Solomon hadn't felt what was missing.

Their threads were gone.

Not cut. Not tangled.

Gone.

Each person in those pods had been disconnected from their own future so completely that Solomon couldn't find even the faintest trace of what they might have become. They existed in a permanent present—no past they remembered, no future they'd ever reach. Just bodies, kept alive, emptied of everything that made them human. He stopped walking.

Akari touched his arm. "Solomon?"

"I can feel them," he whispered. "Or what's left of them."

He moved to the nearest pod, pressed his palm against the glass. Inside, a woman floated—maybe thirty, maybe younger, it was hard to tell. Dark hair spread around her face like a halo. Her expression was peaceful.

But deep inside, where no one else could see, something flickered.

A remnant.

The echo of a person who had once been there, now trapped in the tiny space between what had been taken and what couldn't be removed without killing the body entirely.

It reached for him.

Help me.

The thought wasn't words—more like pressure, a desperate grasping for connection after endless isolation.

Please. Help me.

He pulled his hand back.

But the remnant didn't let go.

The connection lingered—a thin thread of awareness stretching from the woman in the pod to something deep inside Solomon's chest. He felt her now. Not just her presence, but her history. Fragments of memory bleeding through the connection like light through a cracked door.

Her name was Catherine Park.

She had been a painter in Seoul. Her work had been beautiful—landscapes that seemed to breathe, portraits that captured something essential about their subjects. She'd had a gift, people said. An eye for truth.

They didn't know how right they were.

Catherine's seed had awakened on her thirty-second birthday, when she'd looked at a canvas and suddenly seen not what was there, but what could be. Her paintings had started predicting things. Small things at first—the weather, traffic patterns, whether a friend would call. Then larger things. Accidents. Disasters. Deaths.

She'd tried to warn people. To use her gift to help.

Prometheus had found her instead.

Solomon pulled back from the connection with effort, like tearing himself free of quicksand. The memories faded, but the knowledge remained. Catherine

Park. A painter. A prophet. A woman who had tried to do good and been destroyed for it.

"Solomon." Akari's voice was sharp with concern. "What happened?"

"I saw her life." His voice came out hoarse. "Not everything, just… pieces. She was a painter. She saw the future in her art. They took her because she tried to warn people about something she'd seen." He pressed his palm flat against the cold glass of the pod. "They're all like this. The extraction doesn't take everything. It can't. So they leave these… remnants. Trapped. Aware. Unable to do anything but feel themselves fading."

Akari's face had gone pale.

"We need to document this," she said. "Get evidence. Then we—"

Footsteps in the corridor outside.

They moved without speaking, slipping behind a bank of equipment, pressing themselves into shadow. Solomon's power reached out, found two threads approaching—calm, professional, unconcerned.

Technicians, from the look of them. White coats. Tablets in hand. They moved between the pods with casual efficiency.

"Pod seven showing elevated readings again," one said. "Might be worth a secondary extraction."

"Schedule it for tomorrow. We're behind on processing as it is."

Secondary extraction. The phrase made Solomon's stomach turn.

They were talking about harvesting someone twice—taking whatever fragments remained after the first violation.

They paused in front of a pod near the far end—a man, older, his body thinner than the others.

"This one's almost depleted," the first technician noted.

"Recommend termination and disposal."

"Already approved. Transfer's scheduled for morning."

His shadow strained against his control. They were talking about ending a human life like discussing expired inventory. And then something happened that he couldn't explain, even later.

The man in the pod looked at him.

Not with his eyes—those stayed closed, unresponsive. But something deeper, some remnant of consciousness trapped in that withered shell, reached out and found Solomon's awareness. Found his shadow. Found the part of him that could sense the threads binding life to death.

Please.

The word wasn't spoken. It was felt—a desperate plea that bypassed language entirely.

I can feel you. You're different. Please don't leave me here.

Solomon's hand moved before he could stop it, reaching toward the pod's glass.

Akari's grip closed around his wrist like a vice. Don't.

I have a daughter, the remnant continued. Its voice was fading, fragmented, like a radio signal losing coherence. Hannah. She's thirty-two now. I missed her wedding. I missed everything. I've been in here so long…

"Solomon." Akari's voice was urgent, barely a whisper. "The technicians."

Please. Just… end it. If you can't save me, just let me go. I'm so tired of being aware. So tired of feeling myself disappear piece by piece.

Solomon's shadow strained toward the pod, responding to the plea. He could feel the man's thread—or what was left of it. Stretched impossibly thin, barely connected to anything anymore. It wouldn't take much to sever it. To give him the mercy the technicians would withhold until morning.

But he could also feel something else: the security systems monitoring the pods. The sensors that would scream if anything changed. The guards who would come running.

If he helped this man, they would be caught. And if they were caught, no one would ever know about this place. No one would stop it. The thousands of people in pods across the world would continue suffering, continue fading, continue being "disposed of" when their usefulness ended.

One man's peace, or the chance to save thousands.

Please, the remnant whispered. I understand. I know you can't. But please remember me. Remember that I was here. That I was someone.

Tears were on his face. He didn't know when they'd started.

What's your name? he thought back, not knowing if the man could hear him.

David. David Chen. I was a professor. I taught literature. I had a cat named Byron.

I'll remember, Solomon promised. David Chen. Hannah's father.

Professor. Byron.

The remnant's presence flickered—gratitude, acceptance, a grief so deep it had become its own kind of peace.

Thank you, David Chen thought. That's enough. That's more than I hoped for.

Akari pulled Solomon away from the pod.

The technicians finished their rounds and left, their footsteps fading down the corridor. They didn't know that Solomon had just made the hardest choice of his life. They didn't know that tomorrow morning, when they "disposed" of David Chen, someone would remember his name.

Solomon waited until he was sure they were gone before he let himself breathe.

"We need to leave," Akari said. "Now. Before the next patrol."

"We can't just—" He gestured at the pods, at the bodies that weren't corpses, at David Chen scheduled for termination in a few hours.

"We can't help them." Akari's voice was steady, but he could hear the strain. "Not tonight. Not with just the two of us."

"Then when?"

"When we have a plan. When we have resources. When we're not trapped in the basement of a facility full of people who would happily add us to their collection."

She was right. He knew she was right. But leaving felt like betrayal, likewalking away from Naomi all over again, like choosing survival over the people who needed help.

And this time, it wasn't abstract. This time, he knew the man's name.

"Solomon." Akari's grip tightened. "If we get captured, no one ever finds out about this. No one ever stops it. We have to survive tonight so we can fight tomorrow."

He looked at David Chen's pod. At the thin thread that would be severed in the morning. At the professor who had taught literature and loved his daughter and named his cat after a poet.

I'll come back, he promised silently. I don't know how, but I'll come back. And when I do, I'll make sure Hannah knows what happened to you. I'll make sure someone remembers.

He followed Akari toward the elevator.

He didn't look back.

He couldn't.

They almost made it.

The elevator carried them back to the surface level without incident. The corridors were clear. The loading dock door was unlocked.

And then, as they stepped into the cool night air, Solomon sensed a shift.

A thread.

Not attached to a person—attached to the facility itself, stretching outward like a tripwire made of probability rather than metal.

His shadow screamed a warning.

"Run," he said.

They ran.

Behind them, alarms sounded.

The forest had never looked so far away.

Solomon sprinted across open ground with Akari beside him, lungs burning, legs pumping, shadow straining to do something—anything—to help. Floodlights snapped on, turning night to day. Voices shouted. Engines revved.

Fifty meters to the fence.

Forty.

Thirty.

A figure stepped out of the darkness ahead—tall, broad, moving with the unhurried confidence of someone who knew the prey couldn't escape.

Solomon's shadow surged forward before he could stop it.

It hit the figure like a wave, wrapping around him, trying to find the thread that would let Solomon interrupt whatever was about to happen.

And found nothing.

Not shielded like Marcus had been—absent. The figure had no thread at all. No connection to any future. No vulnerability that Solomon's power could exploit.

The figure smiled.

"Interesting," he said, his voice calm despite the shadow clawing at him. "You are different."

He raised a hand.

Light flared—not Akari's warm light, but something colder, harsher, designed for destruction rather than healing.

His shadow screamed as the light tore through it.

Pain exploded behind his eyes.

He fell.

The world went dark and stayed that way for what felt like a long time.

When Solomon opened his eyes, he was lying on cold concrete, his wrists bound behind his back, his shadow reduced to a trembling remnant pressed tight against his skin.

Akari lay beside him, unconscious but breathing.

And standing over them both, studying them with professional curiosity, was a woman Solomon had never seen before.

She was older than him—maybe forty, maybe fifty, the kind of age that money and care could make ambiguous. Her hair was dark, her suit expensive, her posture relaxed in the way of people who had never needed to hurry.

"Solomon Nyx," she said. Her voice was exactly as Akari had described— kind, reasonable, the sort of voice you'd trust with a secret. "Welcome to Prometheus."

She smiled, and the smile reached her eyes.

CHAPTER TEN

The Offer

The room they brought him to was comfortable.

That was the first wrong thing.

Not a cell. Not an interrogation chamber. A sitting room with leather chairs, soft lighting, a window showing mountain forest bathed in early morning light. Coffee waited on a side table, steam rising in gentle curls. A bookshelf lined one wall, filled with volumes in multiple languages. Art hung on the walls—landscapes, abstracts, nothing that suggested the building's true purpose.

Solomon's wrists were still bound, but someone had moved him to one of the chairs. His shadow had recovered enough to pool around his feet, though it felt wounded—slower than usual, less responsive. The light that had torn through it had left something like scar tissue in his connection. He could still feel its presence, its alertness, but the easy extension he'd grown accustomed to was gone.

Akari was gone.

He didn't know where they'd taken her, and not knowing felt like a hook in his chest.

No. He forced the thought away. She's alive. They said Light-Bearers weren't targets.

The woman who had greeted him—Welcome to Prometheus—sat across from him now, legs crossed, a cup of coffee cradled in her hands. Up close, she was more striking than beautiful—sharp features, intelligent eyes, the kind of presence that made you want to pay attention.

"You're calmer than I expected," she said.

Solomon didn't respond.

"Most people, in your situation, would be screaming. Demanding. Threatening." She sipped her coffee. "You're just... watching."

"Screaming wouldn't help."

"No. It wouldn't." She set the cup aside and leaned forward. "My name is Dr. Helena Vance. I'm the director of this facility and the chair of the Prometheus

Initiative's research division. I've been wanting to meet you for a long time, Solomon."

"Since I was born, apparently."

Helena smiled—that smile that reached her eyes. "You've been doing your homework. Your sister's research, I assume?"

The mention of Naomi sent a spike of cold fury through Solomon's chest. His shadow stirred, pressing against its wounds. "Don't," Helena said quietly. "I know you're angry. You have every right to be. But if you try to use your abilities here, you'll only hurt yourself. This facility is designed to contain things far more dangerous than you."

"Like the people in those pods?"

Helena's expression didn't change. "You saw the extraction wing."

"I saw bodies. People who aren't dead but aren't alive. People you're keeping around in case you can squeeze more out of them."

Solomon's voice stayed steady despite the rage. "I saw technicians discussing 'secondary extraction' like they were planning equipment maintenance."

"That's one way to describe it." Her voice remained calm, almost gentle. "Another way would be to say we're preserving what remains of them while we work on techniques that might eventually restore what was lost."

Solomon stared at her. "You expect me to believe you're trying to help them?"

"I expect you to understand that nothing is as simple as good and evil, Mr. Nyx." Helena stood and walked to the window. "The Prometheus Initiative has existed, in one form or another, for over three hundred years. We've watched civilizations rise and fall. We've seen what happens when myth-seeds awaken without guidance, without control."

"So you control them."

"We study them. We learn from them. We try to understand why some awakenings lead to transcendence and others lead to catastrophe." Helena turned slightly. "Do you know the name Aleksandr Volkov?"

Solomon shook his head.

"He was a farmer's son in Russia. 1891. Reaper-class, like you. When his seed awakened, he walked through his village and everything he touched died. Not quickly—slowly. Plants withered over hours. Animals sickened over days. People…" She paused.

"People lingered. His mother held on for a week, watching her own body decay."

Solomon's stomach turned.

"Volkov didn't mean for any of it to happen," Helena continued. "He was terrified. He tried to help the people he loved. But his seed interpreted his fear as intention, and his intention as command." She moved toward her chair. "By the time our predecessors reached him, the death toll was three hundred and forty-seven. The village was a wasteland. Volkov was sitting in the ashes of his family's home, begging someone to end it."

"What happened to him?"

"We contained him. Studied him. Eventually extracted his seed when we developed the capability." Helena sat again. "The knowledge we gained has prevented seventeen similar events over the past century. Roughly twelve thousand lives saved because we understood how Reaper awakenings spiral."

Solomon processed this. The numbers were horrifying—on both sides.

"By harvesting people."

"By studying them. Learning from them. Understanding what makes the difference between a seed that grows into something beautiful and one that becomes a catastrophe." Her voice hardened slightly. "The extraction process isn't pleasant. I won't pretend otherwise. But the knowledge we've gained has prevented dozens of events like Volkov's. Hundreds of thousands of lives saved."

Solomon thought of the woman in the pod. The whisper of consciousness still trapped inside her. Help me. Please.

"And the people you extract from?" he asked. "What about their lives?"

Helena was quiet for a moment.

"Sacrifices," Helena said at last. "Terrible, necessary sacrifices. Made so that others don't have to suffer what they suffered."

"Did they choose to be sacrificed?"

"Some did. Many didn't." Helena turned to face him. "That's the truth I won't hide from you, Solomon. We've done terrible things. We've hurt people. We've made decisions that haunt us. But we've done it because the alternative is worse."

"The alternative being… what? Letting people like me exist?"

"Letting people like you exist without understanding what you are." Helena crossed to stand in front of him. "You're not just a Reaper-class seed, Solomon. You're something we've never seen before. When you interrupted that man's thread in the alley, you didn't just pause a death—you rewrote a future. That's not supposed to be possible."

Solomon's shadow stirred at the memory. The knife man. The moment when everything had changed.

"I've read every record we have on Reaper awakenings," Helena continued. "Every documented case going back three centuries.

Reapers end things. They sever connections. They bring death, sometimes on massive scales. But you—you brought change. You gave someone a different path instead of no path at all."

"So I'm special. Is that supposed to make me feel better about what you did to my sister?"

Helena's expression flickered—what might have been regret, quickly suppressed.

"Your sister was a complication," she said. "A talented woman who got too close to operations she didn't understand. The decision to terminate her wasn't made lightly."

"But it was made."

"Yes." Helena didn't flinch. "And I approved it."

The words hit Solomon like a physical blow. Not a faceless organization. Not a bureaucracy diffusing responsibility. This woman had ordered Naomi's death.

His shadow surged despite his control—not an attack, just a reaction, darkness pooling around him like a manifestation of the rage building in his chest.

Helena didn't retreat.

"Go ahead," she said quietly. "Try. See what happens."

Solomon forced himself to breathe. To think. To remember that Akari was somewhere in this facility, that his shadow was wounded, that Helena had resources he didn't understand. He thought of the man with no thread—whatever he was, however he existed, he had torn through Solomon's power like it was nothing.

He pulled the darkness back.

"Smart," Helena said. "Smarter than I expected. Most people in your position would have tried something by now."

"Most people in my position don't know what you're capable of."

"No. They don't." Helena returned to her chair. "Which brings us to why we're having this conversation."

Solomon waited.

"I could have you extracted," Helena said. "Your Reaper-class potential is substantial. The knowledge we could gain from studying your seed would advance our understanding by decades. Maybe centuries."

"But?"

"But you're not just potential. You're precedent." Her eyes were sharp, calculating. "You did something no Reaper has ever done. If we extract you, we lose the chance to understand how. And if we don't understand how, we can't replicate it. Can't teach it. Can't use it to help future awakenings become something other than monsters."

Solomon understood suddenly.

"You want me to work with you."

"I want you to show us what you can do. Under controlled conditions. With proper documentation." Helena's voice took on a persuasive warmth. "Think about it, Solomon. We have three centuries of research into myth-seeds. Resources you can't imagine. If what you did in that alley is real—if Reapers can redirect deaths instead of just causing them—that changes everything. That's not harvesting. That's healing."

He almost believed her.

Almost.

"And if I refuse?"

Helena's expression cooled. "Then you become too dangerous to leave alive. Not because we want to hurt you—but because we can't risk what you might become."

"Like Elena Voss."

"Like Elena Voss. Like Volkov. Like every Reaper awakening in recorded history except, apparently, you." Helena's voice softened again. "I don't want that to be your story, Solomon. I genuinely don't. But I've spent forty years learning that hope is less important than evidence. Show me something different. Prove you're not what every other Reaper has been."

Solomon looked at her—at the certainty in her eyes, the patience in her posture, the comfort of the room designed to make prisoners feel like guests. She was offering him survival. Maybe more than survival—relevance, purpose, resources.

All he had to do was collaborate with the people who had murdered his sister.

"There's something you don't know," he said.

Helena tilted her head. "I know a lot."

"Not this." Solomon leaned forward, his bound hands pressed against his knees. "The people in those pods. The ones you've extracted from."

"What about them?"

"They're not empty."

Helena went still.

"The extraction process takes their seeds," Solomon continued. "Takes their power. But it doesn't take everything. There's still something left inside them. Awareness. Memory. Pain." He watched her face carefully. "They're trapped. Conscious. And they've been screaming for help since the moment you stopped listening."

Helena's composure cracked.

Just for a moment. Just a flicker in her eyes, a tension in her jaw that hadn't been there before. Then the mask settled back into place—but not completely. Not like before.

"That's impossible," she said. "The extraction process is thorough. We've studied the subjects afterward. There's no evidence of residual consciousness."

"You studied their bodies. Their brain activity. Their physical responses." Solomon's shadow stretched slightly, sharing what he'd felt. "You didn't study what I can see. The threads might be severed, but the roots are still there. Still hurting. Still aware."

Helena was silent for a long moment.

"If what you're saying is true—" "Then you haven't been harvesting people. You've been creating a storage facility full of tortured souls who can't die and can't escape."

Solomon let the words hang. "How's that for legacy?"

Helena's expression changed. Not defeat—she wasn't that easy. But consideration. A willingness to entertain possibilities she hadn't allowed herself to examine before.

"Why tell me this?"

"Because you offered me a choice." Solomon met her eyes.

"Work with you or be extracted. But you left out a third option."

"Which is?"

"I show you something new. I help you understand what you've been doing all these centuries. And in exchange, you halt the extractions. Stop the 'secondary' harvesting. Let me try to help the people who are still trapped."

Helena stared at him.

"You're negotiating," she said. "Bound, captured, in the heart of a facility designed to contain things like you—and you're negotiating."

"I'm offering you knowledge you don't have access to any other way." His shadow settled, responding to the shift in the room. "You can extract me. Break me down for parts. Advance your understanding by decades, like you said. But you'll never know what I could have shown you. What I could have helped you become."

"And if I agree? If I halt the extractions, give you access—what guarantee do I have that you won't try to destroy us from the inside?"

"None," Solomon admitted. "Just like I have no guarantee you won't change your mind and harvest me anyway. But we both have something the other wants. That's enough to start."

Helena was quiet for what felt like a long time.

Then she stood.

"I need to consult with my colleagues," she said. "This is… unexpected."

"Take your time." Solomon let himself lean back in the chair, trying to project a confidence he didn't feel. "I'm not going anywhere."

Helena paused at the door.

"One more thing," she said. "Your companion. The Light-Bearer."

Solomon's heart clenched.

"She's unharmed. We have no interest in her seed—it's not unusual enough to warrant extraction, and Light-Bearers make poor subjects anyway." Helena's expression was unreadable. "She'll remain that way as long as you cooperate."

It wasn't a threat.

It was a reminder of who held the power.

"Understood," Solomon said.

Helena's back was to him. He couldn't see her expression.

"No terminations," she said. "Until we've discussed what you've told me."

She left.

The door locked behind her.

Helena walked through three corridors before her legs decided where they were going.

She ended up in the small conference room on the second floor—the one she used for private calls. She locked the door behind her and stood with her hand on the wood for a long moment, palm flat, feeling the grain.

Then she walked to the chair at the head of the table and sat down.

Then she put both hands over her face.

She did not cry. She had not cried in twenty-six years, and now wasn't the moment to begin. Crying was a release, and what she was feeling did not deserve release. It deserved to stay where it was, lodged in her sternum, pressing.

She thought about a man named Diego Ferreira. Brazilian, fifty-four, a hydrologist from São Paulo who had developed an ability to sense water under stone—the kind of seed she had personally evaluated as low-impact, recommended for full extraction. She'd written the assessment in her own hand.

Subject expresses resistance. Recommend immediate processing. She had thought "expresses resistance" meant struggle in the procedure room.

She had not, she realized now, asked herself what *resistance* might look like from the inside.

Diego Ferreira was in pod fourteen of the Geneva collection. He had been there for nine years.

Helena pressed her hands harder against her face and counted, very slowly, to one hundred. Then she stood up, smoothed her jacket, unlocked the door, and went to find the records of every extraction she had personally signed.

She would not be sleeping tonight. She would not be sleeping for a long time.

Solomon sat alone in the comfortable room with its leather chairs and coffee and window showing mountains that might as well have been a painting for all the freedom it represented.

He had bought time.

He didn't know how much.

Hours passed.

No one came.

Solomon tested his bonds—tight enough to hold, not tight enough to cut circulation. His shadow had begun to recover, spreading across the floor in patterns that might have been restlessness or exploration. He felt it probing the room, sensing the structures surrounding him.

The facility felt different from inside.

He could sense things he hadn't noticed during the infiltration—layers of security, threads of power running through the walls like veins, the presence of other seeds somewhere in the building. Not harvested ones. Active ones. People with abilities working for Prometheus, guarding it, maintaining it.

He counted at least three different seed-signatures above him. One felt warm, almost solar—probably a light-manipulator like Akari, but twisted somehow, weaponized. Another was cold and precise, like mathematics given form. The third was the one that made his shadow recoil—an absence where a thread should be, a hole in the fabric of possibility.

The man who had stopped them. The one with no thread at all.

What did it mean to have no connection to the future? Was he already dead? Already harvested? Or something else entirely—something that existed outside the normal rules?

Solomon didn't know.

But he filed the question away.

When the door finally opened again, it wasn't Helena who entered.

It was Marcus Webb.

The man who had helped kill Naomi looked tired.

Gone was the polished exhaustion he'd displayed in Shibuya—something rawer, less controlled. Dark circles under his eyes. A wrinkle in his shirt he hadn't bothered to smooth. He stood just inside the doorway, studying Solomon with an expression that might have been assessment or guilt.

"She's considering it," Marcus said.

"Considering what?"

"Your offer. Halting extractions. Letting you try to help the people in the pods." Marcus moved to the window, his back to Solomon in a way that felt deliberate. "It's not a popular position. There are factions within Prometheus that see you as too dangerous to keep alive, much less cooperate with."

"And you?"

Marcus was quiet for a moment. Through the window, clouds gathering over the mountains—weather moving in, matching the tension inside.

"I think you might be the first real chance we've had in three hundred years to do something other than contain and harvest."

Marcus turned to face Solomon. "That terrifies me. But it also feels like hope."

"You want me to trust you."

"No." Marcus shook his head. "I want you to understand what's at stake. Helena is fighting for your proposal right now. If she loses, they'll extract you within the hour. And they'll do it messily, without the usual protocols, because they're afraid of what you might do if they give you time."

Solomon's shadow tightened around him.

"Why are you telling me this?"

Marcus was quiet long enough that Solomon wondered if he would answer at all. Then his accent came through fully for the first time — not the trained-down version, but the Charleston under it, the South Carolina his training had worked thirty years to erase.

"Because I'm tired," Marcus said. "Because I've spent twenty years convincing myself that what we do is necessary, and I'm not sure I believe it anymore. Because your sister died asking questions that deserved answers, and I've never stopped hearing her voice."

He reached into his pocket and withdrew something small and metallic.

A key.

"The restraints," he said, setting it on the table between them. "The door is still locked, and there are guards outside. But if things go wrong, at least you'll have a chance."

Solomon stared at the key. It looked ordinary—a piece of metal, small enough to hide in a palm. But it represented something larger. A choice. A potential betrayal of everything Marcus had worked for.

"Why would you do this?"

Marcus met his eyes.

"Because Naomi would have wanted me to," he said. "And because some debts can't be paid any other way."

He left without another word.

Solomon looked at the key for a long time. His shadow stirred, curious, reaching toward it but not touching.

Then he reached for it.

The metal was cool against his skin.

He didn't know what was coming.

But at least now he had options.

The hours that followed were the longest of Solomon's life.

He sat in the comfortable room, watched by cameras he could feel but not see, waiting for a decision that would determine whether he lived or died. His shadow paced the boundaries of his control, restless and afraid, responding to his anxiety despite his efforts to stay calm.

Akari was brought to him eventually—unharmed, as Helena had promised, but pale and tired from her own interrogation. She collapsed into the chair beside him and closed her eyes.

"What did you tell them?" she asked.

"Everything I couldn't afford to hide. Nothing I couldn't afford to lose."

"They're not going to let us go," she said quietly. "You know that, right? Whatever deal you think you're making, it's not going to end with us walking out of here."

"I know."

"Then why—" "Because the alternative is worse." Solomon turned to face her. "They have three centuries of research on myth-seeds. They have resources we can't imagine. And they have thousands of people trapped in those pods, waiting for someone to help them."

Akari's light flickered—not with power, but with emotion she was too tired to hide.

"Your sister would be proud of you," she said.

The words hit harder than any blow.

When Helena returned, her expression had changed. The professional mask was still in place, but something underneath it had shifted.

She was followed by a man Solomon hadn't seen before—tall, broad, moving with the unhurried confidence of someone who knew exactly how dangerous he was. No thread stretched above his head. No future waited for him.

Silas. The weapon from the forest.

"You've met," Helena said, noting Solomon's expression. "Good. Then you understand what's at stake."

If the negotiations failed, Silas would be the one to end him. Helena sat down across from him.

"I've consulted with my colleagues," she said. "Some of them want you dead. Others want you extracted immediately, before whatever you represent becomes a threat we can't control."

"And you?"

"I want to understand. You told me something about the people in those pods that contradicts everything we believed about the extraction process."

"I told you the truth."

"That's what frightens me." Helena leaned forward. "If what you said is true—if there are remnants of consciousness trapped in the subjects we've processed—then we've been torturing people for three centuries while telling ourselves we were saving them."

This was the opening he'd been looking for.

"Let me show you," he said. "Take me to the pods. Let me demonstrate what I can sense. And then tell me if your colleagues' fears are worth more than the truth."

Helena studied him for a long moment.

Then she nodded.

CHAPTER ELEVEN

The Reconnection

The door opened before Solomon could use the key.

Helena stood in the doorway, her expression a careful construction of neutrality that didn't hide the calculations behind her eyes. Two guards waited behind her, not threatening, but present. A reminder that cooperation remained conditional.

"You have one hour," she said.

Something loosened in Solomon's chest. "They agreed?"

"They agreed to a demonstration." Helena stepped aside. "You claim the harvested retain consciousness fragments. You claim you can help them. Prove it."

"And if I can?"

"Then we have a different conversation about this facility's future." Her eyes were sharp, calculating. "And if you can't—or if you're lying—extraction proceeds as planned."

Solomon absorbed the threat without flinching. Three months ago, an ultimatum like this would have paralyzed him. Now it felt almost familiar—another impossible deadline, another situation where failure meant more than personal loss.

"I'll need my hands free," he said, standing.

Helena nodded to a guard, who unlocked the restraints. Solomon rubbed his wrists, feeling circulation return. The metal had left impressions that would fade in an hour. Small indignities that accumulated.

"Your shadow abilities will be monitored," Helena continued.

"Any hostile action will be met with countermeasures. The man you encountered last night—his name is Silas. He'll be present throughout."

The man with no thread. Solomon filed the name away.

"What's his story? I've never encountered anyone like him."

Helena paused, something flickering across her face—respect for the question, perhaps, or recognition that Solomon had earned this much transparency.

"Silas Chen. He was one of us, once. A Weaver—pattern recognition, probability manipulation, mid-tier but reliable. Thirty years ago, he volunteered for an experimental extraction procedure. We believed we could remove a seed cleanly, study it, reintroduce it to a new host."

"It didn't work."

"The extraction succeeded. The reintroduction failed. The seed rejected every candidate." Helena's voice was clinical, but Solomon caught the undercurrent of old regret. "Eventually, it degraded beyond viability. Silas survived physically. Mentally, he remained sharp. But his thread. The connection every living person has to their potential futures—simply stopped existing. He exists outside the probability framework entirely."

"He can't be predicted."

"He can't be seen," Helena corrected. "Not by Weavers, not by Reapers, not by any myth-touched sense we've documented. He walks between certainties. It makes him uniquely valuable for situations like this."

Solomon understood. Silas was their insurance policy—someone his abilities couldn't touch, read, or manipulate. A living blindspot pointed like a weapon.

"Thirty years," Solomon said quietly. "Living without a thread. How does someone survive that?"

Helena's expression flickered—surprise at the question, perhaps. "He says the silence was difficult at first. Like losing a sense he hadn't known he had. Eventually he adapted. Claims he prefers it now."

"Does he?"

"That's something you can ask him yourself." Helena's tone closed the subject. "Let's go."

"And Akari?"

"The Light-Bearer will be released once this demonstration is complete, regardless of outcome." Helena's tone suggested this concession had cost her political capital. "She's valuable to certain factions. Harming her would create complications we'd rather avoid."

"Which factions?"

Helena's expression cooled. "You're asking questions above your current clearance level, Mr. Nyx."

"If I'm going to work with you, I need to understand what I'm working with."

"If you prove your claims, we'll have that conversation. If you fail, it won't matter."

It wasn't trust. It wasn't safety. But it was better than nothing. The extraction wing looked different in full lighting.

The clinical horror remained—the pods, the bodies, the steady hum of machines keeping flesh alive while everything that mattered had been stripped away. But now Solomon could see details he'd missed. Monitoring stations displaying neural activity, metabolic rates, metrics he didn't recognize. Data displays showing vital signs arranged by subject number rather than name—dehumanization made systematic. Technicians watching nervously from behind safety barriers.

Someone had ordered coffee. The smell of it, ordinary and mundane, felt obscene here. People sipping lattes while surrounded by bodies that might still contain screaming minds.

Solomon counted the pods as he walked. Forty-seven visible in this wing alone. Forty-seven people reduced to numbers, their potential harvested, their consciousness assumed gone. How many were still aware? How many had been terminated while something inside them still fought for survival?

And Silas.

The man stood at the far end of the chamber, arms folded, his absent thread a void that Solomon's senses kept trying and failing to map. It was like having a blind spot in the center of his vision—a place where perception simply ended. Up close, he was older than Solomon had realized—maybe sixty, with the weathered look of someone who had stopped being surprised by anything. His eyes held no malice. Just patience.

The patience of a man who had learned to wait without hope or fear, because both required a future to believe in.

"Which one?" Helena asked.

Solomon walked slowly down the row of pods, letting his shadow extend just enough to sense what lay within. Most remnants were faint—whispers of consciousness so thin they barely registered. Subjects who had been here too long, their fragments fading like echoes in an empty room.

But one burned brighter than the others.

The woman he'd felt before. Her whisper had been the loudest, the most desperate, the most present. Eight months, Helena had said. Not long enough for complete dissolution. Long enough for horror beyond imagining.

He stopped in front of her pod.

"Her," he said.

Helena checked a tablet. "Subject 47. Harvested eight months ago. Seed classification was moderate—pattern recognition abilities, minor precognitive capacity. Extraction was considered successful."

She scrolled through more data. "She's scheduled for standard termination next week."

"Termination?"

"We can't keep them indefinitely." For a moment, discomfort crossed Helena's face—a crack in the professional armor, quickly patched. "The bodies require resources. The data plateaus after the first few months. Continuing to maintain them serves no purpose."

"Except they're still people," Solomon said quietly.

"That's what you're here to prove." Helena gestured to the technicians. "Open the pod. Give him access."

The glass cover retracted with a soft hiss. Cool air spilled out, carrying the sterile smell of medical preservation. Up close, the woman looked even younger—early twenties, maybe, with features that might have been beautiful if there had been any life behind them. Her face was slack, expressionless, muscles abandoned by the neural activity that once animated them. Her hands lay at her sides, fingers slightly curled, as if she had been reaching for something when consciousness was stripped away.

Her thread was gone. That absence felt like a wound in the world, a torn edge where continuity should have been. Like a sentence stopped mid-word.

But underneath— Help me. Please. I'm still here. Please.

The whisper was stronger now. Desperate. Aware. Eight months of consciousness trapped in unresponsive flesh, screaming into silence that no one could hear. Eight months of praying for death or rescue or anything that would end the unbearable continuity of existing without existing.

Please. I know you can hear me. I felt you yesterday. Please don't leave me here.

Solomon placed his hand on her forehead.

What happened next was difficult to describe.

Later, when Helena demanded explanations, Solomon would struggle to find words. It wasn't like the alley, where he'd interrupted a thread and let it reform. This was something deeper and more fundamental.

He felt the remnant of her.

Not her memories. Not her personality, exactly. Just the piece of her that had been too stubborn to be harvested completely—a fragment of consciousness clinging to existence like a drowning person clinging to wreckage. It was made of will and fear and something too primal to name. The core of self that refused to believe it had already ended.

Her name, he realized. She was holding onto her name.

Catherine. My name is Catherine.

The name was a lifeline, a declaration, a defiance. As long as she had that, she was still someone.

And he felt what had been taken.

Her seed. Her potential. The mythic capacity that had made her valuable to Prometheus. It was gone—not destroyed, but removed, extracted with surgical precision and stored somewhere else in this vast facility. He could feel the shape of its absence, the wound it had left behind.

But the connection between that seed and her consciousness— It wasn't cut.

It was stretched.

Solomon's breath caught.

They hadn't severed her from her power. They'd pulled it away, like taffy stretched until it thinned to almost nothing. The connection still existed. Impossibly. Invisibly. A filament so fine no instrument could detect it, crossing distances that had nothing to do with physical space.

But he could feel it.

And if he could feel it, he could follow it.

Find me, Catherine's remnant whispered. Please. I can feel it. I can feel myself out there.

Solomon closed his eyes and reached.

His shadow extended, but not in physical space—it moved along the stretched connection, tracing the impossible thread through whatever dimension Prometheus used to store extracted seeds. It was cold there. Cold and vast and silent, a storage space designed to contain potential without allowing it to grow.

He could feel other seeds too—thousands of them, suspended in their containers, each one an orphaned fragment of someone who had been harvested. Some were dim, fading, their connections snapped completely. Others still had threads like Catherine's, stretched thin but not broken.

So many people who might still be saved.

But he couldn't help them all. Not now. He had to prove the concept first.

He found Catherine's seed.

It blazed against the cold storage like a flame cupped in frozen hands. Bright and desperate and aware—because seeds weren't just power. They were pieces of identity, fragments of self that never stopped reaching for the consciousness they'd been torn from.

Come back, Solomon sent, not in words but in intention. She's waiting for you. She's still there.

The seed responded.

"What's happening to him?"

The voice came from far away. Solomon heard it the way you hear sounds from underwater—distorted, muffled.

"His shadow's extending. I've never seen it do this before."

"The readings—look at the readings—" Solomon pulled.

Like lifting something impossibly heavy through resistant air. The seed wanted to return—wanted it desperately, had been wanting it for eight months—but the systems holding it resisted. Security protocols. Containment fields. Centuries of engineering designed to keep extracted seeds safely separated from the consciousness they'd been harvested from.

He pulled harder.

His shadow stretched thinner than he'd ever allowed it, becoming a bridge between storage and consciousness, between theft and restoration. He could feel the cost accumulating—exhaustion building in his bones, in his blood, in the parts of himself that weren't physical. He was spending something that might not come back.

He didn't care.

Come home, he sent. Come back to her.

The seed came loose.

The sensation was like watching ice break free from a frozen shore—a moment of violent separation, then movement. The seed shot back along the connection, carrying itself home with the eagerness of something that had been waiting too long.

The moment it touched Catherine's consciousness, the world exploded.

Every monitor in the chamber spiked simultaneously. The woman in the pod convulsed, her body arching against restraints that hadn't been necessary when she was catatonic.

Other pods reacted—lights flashing, alarms shrieking, harvested bodies twitching in sympathy. Whatever Solomon had done, whatever channel he had opened, other connections were resonating. "Shut it down!" someone shouted.

"We can't! The readings are off every scale!"

"Neural activity is spiking across all subjects—this is impossible—" The lights overhead flickered. Equipment that had run steadily for decades stuttered, confused by inputs it had never been programmed to handle.

Helena grabbed Solomon's shoulder. "Stop! Whatever you're doing, stop!"

But Solomon couldn't stop. He was too close. He could feel the seed coming loose from its containment, feel the stretched connection beginning to contract, feel Catherine's consciousness reaching toward the fragment of herself that was finally coming home. To stop now would be worse than never starting. The connection would snap. She would be truly gone.

He had to finish it.

Silas moved.

The man with no thread crossed the chamber in three strides, his hand raised to deliver whatever attack had wounded Solomon's shadow before. His face showed no emotion, justthe focused intent of someone doing what needed to be done.

Solomon saw him coming but couldn't divert attention to defend himself. Everything he had was committed to guiding the seed home. Please, he thought. Just give me one more second.

And then the woman opened her eyes.

She screamed.

Not in pain—in recognition. The sound of someone waking from a nightmare and realizing they're still alive. Her seed slammed back into her consciousness like a door being thrown open, and the force of the reconnection sent a shockwave through the chamber that knocked technicians off their feet.

Silas stumbled, his attack interrupted.

Helena fell, her tablet shattering on the floor.

Solomon remained standing, but barely. His shadow had extended to its absolute limit, thin as smoke, trembling with exhaustion. The cost of bridging that distance, of pulling something back from Prometheus's vault, settled into his bones like lead. He felt older. Used.

But it had worked.

Catherine sat up in her pod.

Her thread was back.

Not the same thread she'd had before—the reconnection had changed something fundamental about her future. The original path was gone, erased by extraction and replaced with something new. Eight months of trauma had altered who she would become. But it was there. A connection to the world. A future to move toward. She looked at him with eyes that held eight months of trapped consciousness, eight months of screaming into a void that refused to answer.

"You heard me," she whispered. Her voice was rough, the vocal cords remembering their function after months of disuse.

"Yes," Solomon said.

She cried—great, wracking sobs that shook her newly-responsive body. The sounds were ugly and raw and unbearably human, and somehow they were the most beautiful thing Solomon had heard since stepping into this facility.

A technician approached cautiously, reaching for her vital signs, and Catherine flinched away with the terror of someone who had learned to associate medical attention with horror.

"It's okay," Solomon said gently. "It's okay. You're back. You're whole."

"They took me," she gasped between sobs. "They took part of me and they left me awake and I couldn't—I couldn't tell anyone—I tried to scream and nothing—nothing came out—" "I know."

"Eight months," she whispered. "I counted. Every day. Every hour. Two hundred and forty-three days. Do you know what that's like? Being nothing but a count?"

Solomon didn't. But he knew what it was like to be trapped in grief so profound that time lost meaning.

Someone had been lost. Now she was found.

Whatever else happened today, that mattered.

The aftermath was controlled chaos.

Medical teams swarmed Catherine—Subject 47 no more—checking vitals, running scans, documenting the impossible. Her name, Solomon learned from overhearing frantic communications, was Catherine Park. Thirty-two years old. A painter from Seoul whose work had begun showing things before they happened—small predictions at first, then larger ones.

Prometheus had classified her as a precognitive and harvested her because her seed showed "insufficient potential for independent development."

The irony wasn't lost on Solomon. She'd had the power to see possible futures, and Prometheus had decided her future wasn't worth preserving.

Now she was alive in ways the facility's protocols hadn't accounted for.

The other pods continued to react—vital sign monitors spiking and falling, bodies twitching with movements too purposeful to be random. Other harvested individuals had felt what Solomon did. Other stretched connections had resonated with the possibility of return. They were hoping now, for the first time since their extractions.

Helena pulled Solomon aside while the medical teams worked, finding a corner where they could speak without being overheard. Her composure was cracked, genuine shock bleeding through the professional mask.

"That shouldn't have been possible," she said, her voice low and intense. "We've studied extraction for three centuries. The process is irreversible. Every model we have—you can't just pull something back like that."

"I didn't reverse it." Solomon was exhausted, his shadow barely responsive, but he forced himself to think clearly. This conversation mattered. What he said now would determine whether Prometheus treated him as an asset or a threat. "The extraction wasn't complete. You stretched the connection instead of cutting it. I just pulled it back."

"That's not—our instruments would have detected—" "Your instruments can't see what I see." Solomon met her eyes. "How many others are like her? How many of the people you've harvested still have connections you didn't know about?"

Helena's face went pale.

Solomon pressed. "That's what I thought. You assumed your methods were perfect. You assumed the harvested were completely disconnected because your machines told you they were. But your machines can't see stretched connections. Your machines can't hear fragments of consciousness screaming for help."

"We don't know," Helena admitted. "We assumed complete severance. The theory has been settled since the founding. We've never had reason to check."

"Then you need to check." Solomon glanced at the other pods.

"You need to check all of them."

"Do you understand what you're asking?" Helena's voice dropped. "If what you've done is replicable—if the harvested can be reconnected—it undermines everything this organization has built. Every extraction for three hundred years might have been…"

"Incomplete," Solomon said. "Murder of people who weren't dead."

Helena flinched.

"That's exactly what it is." Something cold and righteous settled into Solomon, cutting through the exhaustion. "You've been keeping people in comas, killing them when they became inconvenient, and telling yourselves it was mercy. All because you assumed your instruments showed you everything. All because it was easier to believe they were gone than to check whether they were still screaming."

"We didn't know."

"Now you do." Solomon let the words hang. "So what happens next depends on what kind of organization you want to be. You can bury this, kill me, kill Catherine, pretend nothing happened. Or you can face what you've done and try to fix it."

125

Helena was silent. Behind her, Catherine was being wheeled toward a medical bay, her sobs having faded to quiet tears, her hand reaching back toward Solomon as if afraid he would disappear.

"You've just made yourself the most valuable and dangerous person in this facility," Helena finally said.

"I know."

"And you have no leverage except our conscience."

"That's usually enough," Solomon said. "For the people worth working with."

They moved him to a different room after that.

Still not a cell—but not the comfortable sitting room either.

Something in between. A space for people whose status hadn't been determined. The furniture was functional, the lighting adequate. There were no restraints, but also no windows. Progress measured in degrees of confinement.

Solomon sat on the edge of the bed, head in hands, feeling exhaustion settle deeper. He had pushed himself further than he'd known was possible, and now his shadow barely responded. It lay flat beneath him, thin and tired, recovering from the strain.

Akari burst through the door without warning, her light flaring bright enough to make him wince. Guards shouted behind her, but she was already across the room, arms around him, voice breaking as she said his name.

"I'm okay," Solomon said. "I'm okay."

"They told me what you did." She pulled back, studying his face with the intensity of someone checking for wounds. Her hands touched his cheeks, his shoulders—reassuring herself he was real. "They said you brought someone back."

"I reconnected her. It's not the same thing."

"It's close enough." Akari's eyes were bright with something that might have been tears or might have been light. "They're scared, Solomon. Really scared. The ones who've worked the extraction wing longest—they looked like they'd seen ghosts."

"They have. They just didn't know the ghosts were watching."

Akari sat beside him, close enough that he could feel her warmth. Her light had dimmed to something soft, gentle—the careful illumination of someone who had learned that brightness could harm as easily as help.

"What happens now?"

Solomon thought about Helena's shock. About Silas's hesitation. The way he'd stopped his attack the moment Catherine opened her eyes, something like wonder crossing that impassive face. About Catherine Park, crying in a medical bay because someone had finally heard her.

"Now we negotiate from a different position. Now they know I'm not just unprecedented—I'm a threat to everything they've built. They can either work with me to fix what they've broken, or they can try to stop me and risk losing everything they've harvested."

"You think they'll choose cooperation?"

"Some will. Others won't." Solomon met her eyes. "This isn't over. It's just entering a new phase. But I proved something today. I proved that their system has holes. I proved that the people they harvested aren't all gone. That changes the math."

"And Catherine?"

"She's alive. Really alive. Her seed is back. Her thread is reforming." A tired smile crossed Solomon's face. "She's going to have a lot of recovery ahead of her. Eight months of trauma to process. But she's going to have the chance to build a new life."

Akari didn't answer.

Solomon looked at her. Her light had gone quieter than he had ever seen it— not gentle, not careful, just *less*. Her hand was still on his arm. She took it away.

"Akari?"

"You almost died."

"I didn't."

"You *almost* died, Solomon." She said it flatly, the way a doctor reads a chart. "Your shadow was gone. There was a minute down there—maybe longer—when your heart was doing the thing that hearts do right before they stop. I was close enough to feel the rhythm of it. You don't know that because you were too far inside the reconnection to notice your own body." She rose from the bed. Crossed to the other side of the small room. Stood against the wall, arms folded, looking at him from a distance that had not existed an hour ago.

"I'm sorry."

"Don't do that."

"Do what?"

"Apologize for something you're going to do again. I know you. If you had to, you'd do it again tomorrow. You'd do it again next week. You'd do it every time someone was screaming inside a pod because that is who you are, and it is one of the reasons I—" She stopped. Visibly stopped. Pulled the sentence back before it finished itself.

Solomon waited.

"When I was seventeen," she said, "I decided I would never do this again."

"Do what?"

"Love someone who was going to be taken from me. My mother had just survived the fire and I was living with the fact that I almost hadn't let her. I promised myself: no more. Not friends, not partners, not anyone I would have to watch. Just the work. Just the bookshop. Just training other people to carry what I'd learned to carry. That was supposed to be enough." Her voice did not shake. That was somehow worse than if it had. "And then you walked into my shop and said you were seeing things you couldn't explain, and I said *fine*, I'll teach you, I can do this in a professional capacity, I don't have to get close."

"Akari—" "I got close anyway."

He didn't know what to say. He opened his mouth and then closed it, because every available sentence he might offer was a promise he couldn't keep.

"I'm not asking you to stop being who you are," she said. "That would be a worse lie than anything Helena has ever told. But I need you to know something, because if I don't say it now I might not ever say it out loud." She looked at him directly. "I am going to love you on the terms that are available. Which means I am going to love you knowing that one of these times you aren't going to come back. And part of me is going to pull back from that. Not all of me. Part of me. Because if I give you all of me and then you don't come back, I will not survive the second time."

She didn't move toward him.

He didn't move toward her.

After a long moment she said, more quietly, "I wanted you to know that's what I'm carrying. Before whatever comes next. So you would know. So it wouldn't be a surprise the next time I'm quieter than you expected me to be."

Solomon looked at his hands.

"I'm not going to promise I won't do it again," he said.

"I know. That's why I told you now, while I still had the courage to be honest instead of kind."

The silence between them was different than any silence they had shared before. Heavier. More honest.

Eventually Akari came back to the bed. Sat beside him. Did not take his hand. Her light, when it finally returned, was dimmer than it had been an hour ago.

It stayed dimmer for a long time.

The door opened.

Helena stood in the doorway, her composure partially restored but still showing cracks. Behind her, Marcus waited—looking worse than before, exhaustion visible in every line of his face.

"We need to talk," Helena said. "All of us. About what happens next."

Solomon stood, feeling Akari rise beside him, feeling his shadow stir with the first hints of returning strength.

Whatever came next, he wasn't the same person who had broken into this facility looking for answers. He had found something more important.

He had found power.

And he was beginning to understand how to use it.

Not that actual daylight reached this deep underground—but the facility's lighting had shifted from night-mode dimness to operational brightness, illuminating the rows of suspended bodies with clinical clarity that made everything worse.

Solomon stood at the entrance, flanked by Helena on one side and the man called Silas on the other. Akari waited behind them, her light carefully muted, her presence a comfort he was trying not to lean on too heavily.

"You understand the conditions," Helena said. It wasn't a question.

"I understand them."

"If you attempt to damage the subjects. If you try to use this opportunity to attack or escape. If anything goes wrong—" "Silas will kill me." Solomon glanced at the man with no thread. "I know."

Silas said nothing. His silence was more threatening than any words could have been.

"Then proceed." Helena gestured toward the pods. "Show us what you claim to see."

Solomon walked forward.

The remnants reached for him immediately—dozens of fragments of consciousness, each one crying out for connection after months or years of isolation. The sensation was overwhelming, like walking into a room full of drowning people and being able to save only one.

Help us. Please. Help us.

He found Catherine Park's pod and stopped.

She looked the same as before—peaceful, suspended, her dark hair floating around her face like a halo. But now, in the harsh light, Solomon could see details he'd missed in the darkness. The slight atrophy of muscles unused for months. The subtle wrongness of skin that hadn't felt sunlight in too long. The feeding tubes and monitoring lines that kept her body alive while everything that mattered had been stripped away.

"This one," he said.

Helena moved to a control panel nearby, her fingers dancing across a touchscreen.

"Subject 147. Catherine Park. Korean national, age thirty-four. Seed classification: minor-prophet, minor predictive capacity. Extraction completed eight months ago. Current status: stable, minimal degradation."

"Minimal degradation." Solomon's voice was flat. "You mean she's dying slowly instead of quickly."

"I mean her body is being maintained at optimal levels."

Helena's tone was defensive. "We've kept her alive longer than she would have survived on her own."

"You've kept her body alive. The person inside it has been screaming for eight months."

Helena didn't respond.

The first attempt failed.

Solomon reached for Catherine's remnant, extended his shadow toward the flickering fragment of consciousness that remained, and felt—resistance. Not from Catherine. From something else.

"What's wrong?" Helena demanded.

"There's something blocking me." Solomon concentrated, trying to understand what he was sensing. "The extraction process—it didn't just take her seed. It left something behind. A barrier."

"That's not possible. The extraction is clean. Complete."

"Then explain why I can't reach her."

Helena was quiet for a moment, consulting her readouts.

"There's a containment field," she said finally. "Standard protocol for extracted subjects. It prevents any residual seed activity from affecting the facility's systems."

"Turn it off."

"That would violate about a dozen safety protocols—" "Turn it off, or I can't help her."

Helena hesitated. Solomon could see the calculation happening behind her eyes—the risk of deactivating the containment field versus the potential reward of watching him succeed.

"Do it," she said finally.

One of the technicians moved to a console. There was a soft hum, a flicker in the pod's lighting, and then— The barrier dissolved.

Catherine's remnant reached for Solomon with desperate intensity. He felt her terror, her loneliness, her fading hope that anyone would ever find her. Eight months of silent screaming, compressed into a moment of connection.

Help me. Please. I don't want to die in here.

I'm trying, Solomon thought back. But I need you to show me where you are.

The next problem was worse.

Catherine's seed had been taken, but the roots remained—thin tendrils of power that had once connected her consciousness to her mythic potential. They were damaged, withered, barely functional. But they were still there, reaching toward something that no longer existed.

Solomon's shadow found them and followed.

The extraction process had been surgical. Every major connection severed, every significant pathway blocked. The scientists who had designed it knew their work. They had left nothing behind that could threaten their control.

But they hadn't accounted for him.

Solomon's power wasn't about creation or destruction. It was about connection—seeing the threads that linked all things, manipulating the paths that led from present to future. And Catherine's roots, damaged as they were, still remembered where her seed had gone.

There, *he felt*. They stored it. Close by. Still connected, if I can just— Pain exploded through his chest.

His shadow recoiled, screaming without sound. Something had attacked him—not physically, but through the connection he'd established. A defense mechanism, built into the extraction process itself.

"What's happening?" Helena's voice was sharp with alarm.

"Defense system," Solomon gasped. "The extraction—it's designed to prevent reconnection. When I try to reach her seed—" Another wave of pain cut him off.

He fell to his knees, shadow writhing around him, and felt the connection to Catherine beginning to slip away.

Solomon made a choice.

The pain would kill him if he kept pushing. The defense mechanism had been designed by people who understood exactly what they were doing, built over centuries of trial and error. Fighting it directly was suicide.

But there was another way.

Instead of pushing through the barrier, he let himself flow around it. Instead of trying to force the connection, he accepted the pain and moved with it, letting his shadow become so thin and dispersed that the defense mechanism couldn't find anything to target. It was like dying.

His sense of self dissolved, not completely, not permanently, but enough that for a moment Solomon Nyx stopped existing as a coherent entity. He became something else. Something that was all connection and no center, all perception and no self.

And in that moment, he saw.

Catherine's seed was stored in a vault three levels below, suspended in a containment matrix that kept it dormant but intact. The roots in her body stretched toward it like flowers reaching for sunlight, desperate for the connection that had been severed.

All he had to do was bridge the gap.

Solomon gathered what remained of his consciousness and pulled.

The reconnection hit the facility's systems like a bomb.

Alarms screamed. Lights flickered. Every monitor in the pod chamber went red, displaying error messages that technicians scrambled to understand.

"What did you do?" Helena demanded.

Solomon couldn't answer. He was on his hands and knees, shaking, his shadow reduced to a thin film that barely covered his skin. The reconnection had cost him something—not permanently, he thought, but significantly. He felt hollowed out, emptied, like someone had reached inside him and removed several essential organs.

Catherine Park was sitting up in her pod.

The glass had cracked when she moved—her seed surging back to life with enough force to damage the containment system that had held her. She was crying, tears streaming down her face, her hands pressed against the fractured surface like she couldn't believe it was real.

"I can see," she whispered. "Oh God, I can see again."

Not the future—not yet. But herself. Her own thoughts, her own memories, her own identity restored after eight months of fragmented isolation.

"Get a medical team in here," Helena ordered. "Now."

Technicians rushed to comply. The alarms continued to scream.

Somewhere in the facility, Solomon heard other sounds—shouting, running, the controlled chaos of an organization responding to a crisis it hadn't anticipated.

He'd done it.

He'd reconnected a severed seed.

And in doing so, he'd proven that everything Prometheus believed about extraction was wrong.

Helena was staring at him with an expression he couldn't read. "That should have been impossible," she said.

Solomon managed a smile.

"I know."

They gave Solomon a room to recover.

Not a cell this time—an actual room, with a bed and windows that looked out over the mountains. Helena had arranged it personally, her expression unreadable as she watched the medical team settle him into the sheets.

"Rest," she said. "We'll talk more tomorrow."

Solomon didn't have the energy to argue.

The door closed. The room went quiet. And Solomon lay in the darkness, feeling like something essential had been scooped out of him and replaced with exhaustion.

A knock at the door.

"Come in," he managed.

Akari slipped inside, carrying a tray with tea and something that smelled like soup. Her light was muted, held close, but her eyes found him immediately in the dark.

"You look terrible," she said.

"Thanks."

"I mean it." She set the tray on the bedside table and sat on the edge of the mattress. "What you did down there—I've never seen anything like it. You literally took yourself apart and put yourself back together."

"Felt like it too."

Akari was quiet for a moment, studying him with an intensity that made Solomon want to look away.

"I thought you were going to die," she told him. "When you collapsed. When your shadow went still. I thought—" She broke off, her voice cracking.

"Hey." Solomon reached for her hand. His grip was weak, barely there, but she held on like he was the only solid thing in the room. "I'm okay. I'm here."

"You almost weren't." Akari's composure finally broke. The tears came, not the silent crying from the plane, but real tears, the kind that shook your whole body. "I've lost so many people, Solomon. My family, my friends, everyone I've ever let myself care about. I can't—I can't lose you too."

Solomon pulled her closer. It cost him—every muscle screaming, every nerve ending raw—but he pulled her down beside him on the bed and wrapped his arms around her.

"You won't," he whispered into her hair. "I promise."

"Don't make promises you can't keep."

"I'm not." He pressed his lips to her forehead, the gesture coming naturally despite everything between them still unspoken. "I don't know what happens next. I don't know if we'll survive Geneva or stop Prometheus or any of the rest of it. But I know I'm not leaving you. Not now. Not ever."

Akari pulled back just enough to look at him.

Her eyes were red-rimmed, her face tear-streaked, her light flickering unsteadily beneath her skin. She'd never looked more beautiful.

"Solomon," she breathed.

"I know." He cupped her face in his hands, thumbs brushing away the tears. "I know we should wait. I know this is terrible timing. I know—" She kissed him.

Soft at first—tentative, questioning. Then her hands found his face, his shoulders, his chest, and the kiss deepened into something hungry and desperate and full of all the words they hadn't been able to say.

When they finally broke apart, both breathing hard, Akari laughed.

"Terrible timing," she agreed.

"The worst."

"We're in the middle of enemy territory."

"Surrounded by people who might kill us tomorrow."

"You can barely move."

"Hasn't stopped me yet."

Akari laughed again—a real laugh, bright and warm and full of joy that seemed almost impossible given everything. She settled against his side, her head on his chest, her light warming the space between them.

"This doesn't change anything," she said. "We still have to face Helena. Still have to figure out what to do about Prometheus. Still have to stop whatever the Dreamer is planning."

"I know."

"But it changes everything too." She lifted her head to look at him. "Doesn't it?"

Solomon kissed her again, softer this time.

"Yeah," he said. "It does."

They fell asleep like that, tangled together in the narrow bed, her light and his shadow interweaving in patterns that had never existed before.

Tomorrow would bring new dangers. New challenges. New impossible choices.

But tonight, for the first time since Naomi died, Solomon didn't feel alone.

And that was enough.

CHAPTER TWELVE

The Terms

They met in a conference room that looked like it belonged in a corporate office, not a facility dedicated to harvesting human souls. Natural light filtered through floor-to-ceiling windows. The furniture was expensive but understated. A water pitcher sweated on the polished wood table—Helena's choice, Solomon suspected. A reminder that Prometheus could present a civilized face when it wanted to.

Helena sat at the head of the table, her composure fully restored. She'd changed since their last conversation, traded her wrinkled suit for something sharper, applied makeup that concealed whatever vulnerability she'd shown in the harvesting chamber. The Director of Research was back in control.

Marcus took a seat to her left, his expression carefully neutral. Whatever private conflict he felt about the key, the freedom, the debt—none of it showed now. He was a Prometheus operative in a Prometheus meeting.

Silas stood against the wall, arms folded, his absent thread a constant irritation at the edge of Solomon's awareness. The weapon who had stopped them at the fence. He hadn't spoken a word since Solomon had been captured, but his presence said enough: Try anything, and I'll end you.

Solomon and Akari sat across from Helena.

Helena broke the silence first.

"What you did to Subject—to Catherine Park—has created significant complications."

"You mean I proved your extraction process isn't what you thought it was."

"I mean you demonstrated capabilities that some of my colleagues consider an existential threat to this organization."

Helena's voice was calm, but Solomon saw the tension in her shoulders, the way her fingers pressed white against the table's surface. "There are those who believe we should terminate you immediately, regardless of what knowledge we might lose."

"And you?"

"I believe that would be shortsighted." Helena folded her hands on the table. "What you did represents an opportunity. If we can understand how you reconnected Miss Park to her seed, we might develop techniques that don't require your direct involvement."

"It would also mean you could keep harvesting people,"
Solomon said flatly.

"It would mean we could refine our methods. Ensure complete extraction when intended, or preserve connections when that serves our purposes better." Helena's eyes were sharp. "The world isn't going to stop producing myth-seeds, Mr. Nyx. They'll continue to awaken, continue to pose threats, continue to require management. The question is whether that management is done with understanding or without it."

Akari spoke for the first time. "You're asking him to help you become better at what you do."

"I'm asking him to help us become different at what we do."

Helena turned her attention to Akari. "You're a Light-Bearer. You understand the dangers of uncontrolled awakening. You've seen what happens when seeds develop without guidance."

"I've seen what happens when people like you decide you know best," Akari replied. "It looks a lot like those pods downstairs."

Helena's mouth thinned.

"I'm not here to defend our methods. I'm here to discuss how we move forward."

Solomon studied the people across from him. Helena, determined to find a way to make this work for Prometheus—but also, perhaps, genuinely shaken by what she'd learned. Marcus, guilty and uncertain but still loyal to the organization that had shaped his life. Silas, unreadable and dangerous.

Three people. Three possible angles. None trustworthy, but all necessary if he wanted to change anything.

"Here's what I want," Solomon said. "First—no more extractions. Not until we understand what's actually happening when you harvest seeds."

"Impossible," Helena said immediately. "We have operations in progress. Subjects already in the pipeline."

"Then stop the pipeline."

"You don't understand the scale of what you're asking. The Prometheus Initiative operates globally. Dozens of facilities, hundreds of personnel, partnerships with governments and corporations who depend on our research." Helena shook her head. "We provide intelligence services with information about emerging threats. We supply pharmaceutical companies with compounds derived from seed-power. We advise national security agencies on myth-related incidents. This isn't just about us—it's about the entire infrastructure that depends on what we do."

"Then explain it to them."

"Explain what? That a nineteen-year-old who broke into one of our facilities has decided our entire methodology is wrong?"

Helena shook her head. "Even if I agreed with you—and parts of me do—I don't have that kind of authority."

"Then who does?"

Helena was quiet for a moment.

"The Initiative is governed by a council. Twelve members. I'm one of them, but I'm not a majority. I'd need seven votes to halt extractions, and right now I might have four." Her expression was grim. "The rest are split between hardliners who want you eliminated and pragmatists who'll follow whoever seems strongest."

"I want to speak to them," Solomon said. "The full council."

Helena stared at him. "That's unprecedented. The council doesn't meet with outsiders."

"Then it's time for a new precedent."

The scope of it settled over him. This wasn't about convincing one person, or even one organization. It was about navigating a political landscape he barely understood, filled with people who had centuries of experience in manipulation and control.

"The stored seeds," he said slowly. "Where are they?"

"Distributed across multiple facilities. Thousands of them, collected over centuries." Helena's voice carried something that might have been pride or might have been horror. "The largest collection is beneath the main compound in Geneva."

"And if I could reach them? Like I reached Catherine's seed?"

The room went still.

Silas shifted against the wall. Marcus's hand moved toward something under the table.

"That," Helena said carefully, "is exactly what my colleagues are afraid of."

They took a break.

Solomon stood at a window overlooking the mountain forest.

Akari stood beside him. Her hands had healed enough that the bandages were gone, but faint scars still traced up her forearms—burns from the light she'd channeled to help him save Catherine.

"You're thinking about Geneva," she said. "The stored seeds."

"Thousands of people, Akari."

"I know." She was quiet for a moment. Then: "You can't reconnect them all. You'll die trying. But you can change the system that harvests them. That's slower. Messier. Less satisfying. But it's the thing that actually works."

Solomon stared out at the forest. She was right. But every second he spent negotiating was another second those people in the pods were trapped.

"What would you do?" he asked.

"Make them an offer they can't refuse. Something that gives you what you want while letting them think they're getting what they want." Akari's smile was thin. "That's the part you need to figure out."

Helena exchanged a glance with Marcus, who shrugged slightly—your call. Silas hadn't moved, but his attention had sharpened.

"The council is meeting in Geneva in three days," Helena said slowly. "An emergency session, because of what happened here. I was planning to attend virtually, but if I brought you in person—presented you as evidence rather than a threat—it might shift the dynamics." She studied him. "What exactly are you planning to say to them?"

Solomon smiled grimly.

"I'm going to offer them something they need more than they need to harvest people."

"Which is?"

"A solution to a problem they don't even know they have yet."

Helena's eyes narrowed. She recognized the tactic—offering information as bait, keeping the specifics hidden to maintain leverage.

"Three days," she said at last. "You have three days to prepare whatever case you're going to make. I'll arrange transport to Geneva and secure you a slot on the agenda. But Solomon—" She leaned forward. "If you embarrass me in front of the council, if whatever you're planning makes things worse, I won't be able to protect you. The hardliners will have all the justification they need to eliminate you, and I'll be fighting just to save myself."

"I understand."

"I don't think you do. But you'll learn."

That night, Solomon sat alone in the room they'd given him.

Not a cell. Not a prison. But not freedom either. The door was unlocked, but guards patrolled the hallway. The window opened, but a three-story drop waited on the other side. The illusion of choice contained within the reality of captivity.

His shadow had recovered enough to spread across the floor in its familiar patterns, though it still felt tender—bruised in ways that went deeper than physical. The reconnection with Catherine had cost him something. He didn't know yet if that something would grow back.

He thought about the stored seeds.

Thousands of them. Centuries of harvesting. People reduced to potential, stripped from their bodies and locked away in prisons that Prometheus didn't even realize were prisons.

He thought about what Helena had said about the council.

Twelve members. Seven votes needed. Complex factions and ancient rivalries he didn't understand. People who had been doing this for decades, centuries in some cases, who saw the world through lenses so different from his that they might as well be speaking different languages.

He thought about what Akari had said.

The world is built on systems.

She wasn't wrong. Prometheus didn't exist in a vacuum. They had partnerships, dependencies, obligations. People who relied on their research, governments who used their intelligence, corporations who funded their operations.

But he had one advantage they didn't. things they couldn't. Feel things their instruments couldn't detect. Reach places their technology couldn't touch.

That had to count for something.

A knock at the door interrupted his thoughts.

"Come in," he said.

The door opened to reveal someone unexpected.

Catherine Park.

She stood in the doorway wearing medical scrubs too big for her frame, her hair still damp from what must have been her first shower in eight months. She was thin—too thin, her body having wasted during the months in the pod—but her eyes were alert. Uncertain, yes. Afraid, perhaps. But present in a way that the remnant he'd touched had only hinted at.

"They said you'd see me," she said. "If I asked."

Solomon stood. "Of course. Come in."

She entered slowly, each step careful, like she was still learning how to use her body. Like she didn't trust the floor to hold her weight, the walls to maintain their shape, the world to keep being solid instead of dissolving into the nightmare she'd lived for eight months. She stopped a few feet away from him.

"You're him," she said. "The one who heard me."

"Solomon Nyx."

"Catherine Park. Though I guess you already know that." She tried to smile. It didn't work—the muscles of her face seemed uncertain of the expression. "They told me what you did. How you pulled my seed back. Reconnected me."

"How do you feel?"

She laughed—a broken sound, more sob than humor. "Like I spent eight months screaming and no one could hear me. Like I watched myself being erased piece by piece and couldn't do anything to stop it. Like I died and came back and I'm not sure which one is real."

Solomon didn't try to comfort her with platitudes. What could he possibly say that would make any of that better?

"I'm sorry," he said instead. "I'm sorry I didn't come sooner."

"You didn't know." Catherine's eyes glistened. "No one knew.

That's the thing that keeps hitting me. They thought they were being humane. Preserving empty shells until disposal was convenient. They didn't know I was in there."

"Helena seemed genuinely shocked when I told her."

"She was." Catherine nodded, a slow concession. "She came to see me. Apologized. Said she never would have approved—" Her voice caught. "Does it matter? Does an apology change what they did?"

"No," Solomon said honestly. "It doesn't."

"Then why did it help to hear it?" Catherine wiped her eyes. "I wanted to hate her. I should hate her. But she looked so broken. Like she was realizing something terrible about herself."

Solomon thought about Helena's composure cracking when he'd told her about the remnants. About the way she'd said we didn't know like the words themselves were a wound she couldn't stop reopening. "Some people don't understand they're doing evil until someone shows them. That doesn't excuse them. But it might mean they can change."

"Can they?" Catherine's gaze was piercing, sharper than he'd expected from someone who'd just woken from eight months of consciousness-trapped-in-silence. "You've seen what they've built. Three hundred years of harvesting. Thousands of seeds in storage. An entire organization dedicated to treating people like resources. Can that change?"

"I don't know. But I'm going to find out."

Catherine was quiet for a long moment. She moved to the window and looked out at the darkness.

"I was a painter," she said. "Before. I had a small studio near Hongdae—nothing glamorous, but mine. Landscapes mostly. People said I had a gift for capturing what a place felt like, not just what it looked like." She laughed softly. "Turns out I was capturing something else, too. I just didn't know it yet."

"When did you awaken?"

"On my thirty-second birthday. I was finishing a canvas—just an ordinary city street at dusk—and when I looked at it I suddenly saw something that wasn't there. A woman stepping off the curb into a car that hadn't come yet. Three days later, it happened exactly the way I'd painted it." Catherine's voice was flat. "After that the paintings kept doing it. Small things at first. The weather. Traffic accidents. Then larger things. I thought I was going crazy. Then Prometheus found me."

"They told you they could help."

"They told me they could explain." Catherine's voice went bitter. "A research opportunity, they called it. A chance to understand what I'd become. I signed whatever they put in front of me."

"And then they harvested you."

"Not right away. First they studied me. Ran tests. Documented everything I could do." Catherine hugged herself. "I think they were actually interested at first. That's what they call my type. Precognitive. Precognitive abilities, limited but consistent. They wanted to understand how it worked."

"What changed?"

"A new directive from the council. Something about accelerating the collection timeline. Helena tried to protect me—I could see that, even then. But Volkov and his faction pushed through an override."

Catherine's eyes went distant. "They told me it would be painless. That I wouldn't feel anything. That the part of me they were taking wasn't me anyway."

"They were wrong."

"They were wrong." Catherine met his eyes. "I felt everything. Every second of being pulled apart. Every moment of my seed being ripped away. And then I felt nothing—nothing except the awareness that I was still there, trapped in a body that couldn't move, couldn't speak, couldn't do anything except exist."

Solomon had no words adequate to the horror she was describing.

"I want to help," Catherine said finally.

"Help how?"

"I don't know yet. I don't even know what I'm capable of anymore—the reconnection changed something, and I haven't figured out what." She met his eyes with a determination that burned through her uncertainty. "But I spent eight months as proof of what they do wrong. Maybe I can be proof of what they could do right."

Solomon studied her—this woman who had every reason to want nothing but revenge, who was already thinking about redemption instead. She was stronger than anyone had a right to be after what she'd endured.

"I'm going to Geneva," he said. "To speak to their council. To try to change things."

"Then I'm coming with you."

"That could be dangerous. The same people who approved your extraction will be in that room. Volkov, the hardliners—they'll see you as a threat."

"Good." Catherine's smile was thin and hard. "I want them to see me. I want them to look at my face while they vote on whether people like me deserve to be treated as human."

"Catherine—" "I died eight months ago, Mr. Nyx. Everything since then is borrowed time." She stepped closer. "I might as well spend it on something that matters."

Solomon nodded once.

Three days until Geneva. Three days to prepare an argument that might change everything or end in his death. Three days to convince twelve powerful people that their entire organization needed to transform.

He wasn't going alone anymore.

"Then I guess we're going to Geneva together," he said.

Catherine smiled—a real smile this time, fragile but genuine.

"Then I guess we are."

The first three days were the hardest.

Catherine Park existed in a fog of sensation—too much input after eight months of nothing. Light hurt. Sound hurt. The feeling of sheets against her skin was almost unbearable, nerve endings screaming after so long without stimulation.

The Prometheus medical staff handled her carefully, but she flinched at every touch. Her body remembered what touch had meant in the extraction chamber. Hands approaching meant pain.

Instruments meant violation. Even kindness felt like threat.

Solomon visited when they let him.

He looked almost as damaged as she felt—pale, exhausted, his shadow thin and fragile around him. He'd done something extraordinary to save her, she understood. Burned himself hollow. The doctors said he might never fully recover.

She understood that too, now. The cost of miracles.

"How do you feel?" he asked on the second day, sitting in the chair beside her bed like he'd been there forever.

"I don't know." Catherine's voice came out rusty, unused. "I keep expecting to wake up back in the pod. To discover this was just another dream."

"It's not a dream."

"I know. Logically." She looked at her hands—thin, pale, the hands of someone who'd been suspended in fluid for eight months. "But my brain hasn't caught up yet. It keeps waiting for the other shoe to drop."

Solomon nodded like he understood. Maybe he did.

"The seed," she said. "What happened to me—is it supposed to feel like this?"

"Like what?"

"Like there's too much inside me. Like I can see things I shouldn't be able to see." Catherine closed her eyes, and the visions pressed against her eyelids like fingers against a window. "Before, I could glimpse possibilities. Little fragments of what might happen. Now it's like… like standing in a room with a thousand televisions, each one showing a different future."

"The reconnection amplified your abilities. That happens sometimes." Solomon's voice was careful. "Your seed was stored in concentrated form for eight months. When it came back, it came back stronger."

"Stronger." Catherine laughed, the sound bitter. "I can see everything. Every possible future branching out from every decision. Do you know how many ways this conversation could end? How many versions of the next five minutes exist, hovering just out of reach?"

"I can imagine."

"No. You can't." She opened her eyes and looked at him. "I can see your death, Solomon. Dozens of them. Hundreds. Every way you might die, playing out simultaneously. And I can see you surviving too—growing old, finding peace, becoming something neither of us can imagine yet. All of it real. All of it possible. All of it true."

Solomon was quiet.

"I'm sorry," Catherine said. "I shouldn't have—" "Don't apologize. You're processing trauma on top of abilities you don't know how to control yet." His voice was gentle. "It's going to be overwhelming for a while. But you'll learn to filter it. To focus on what matters and let the rest fade into background noise."

"How do you know?"

"Because I learned to do the same thing. The threads—the death-sense—when it first awakened, I could feel every life around me ending. Constantly. The weight of all that mortality almost crushed me." Solomon's thin shadow stirred. "You learn. You adapt. You find ways to carry what you've become without being destroyed by it."

Catherine absorbed this.

"Will you help me?" she asked.

"As much as I can. But someone with precognitive abilities would be better. The Light-Bearer network includes people who see futures differently than I do."

"I don't want someone else." Catherine's voice was firm despite her exhaustion. "You came back for me. You heard me when no one else could. Whatever help I need, I want it from you."

Solomon considered her for a long moment.

"Okay," Solomon said. "We'll work on it."

Days later, when Catherine had recovered enough strength to walk unassisted, she asked to see Solomon.

"The visions are stronger now," she said. "The reconnection changed something. I can see probabilities—not just for myself, but for others. Where crises are building. Who needs help."

"That's useful."

"Then let me use it. Please." Her eyes were steady despite the exhaustion that still haunted them. "I spent eight months trapped in silence. Let me use what I've become."

Solomon looked at her for a long moment. She was gaunt, fragile, still flinching at sudden sounds. But her will was intact. That counted for more than he could say.

"We'll figure it out together."

For the first time since waking up, Catherine felt like she had purpose.

CHAPTER THIRTEEN

The Council

Geneva was cold and gray and old.

They arrived at dawn in an aircraft that cost more than Solomon's entire neighborhood in Chicago. The champagne went untouched. Catherine sat across from him, her restored seed still settling into its reconnection—sometimes her fingers twitched, grasping at visions only she could see. Eight months of sensory deprivation had left marks that reconnection couldn't erase. She flinched at loud noises. She touched surfaces compulsively, reassuring herself they were real.

But she was here. That counted for something.

Akari dozed beside him, her hand near his on the armrest. Even asleep, she glowed faintly. Solomon studied the scars on her forearms—newer burns from the light she'd channeled for Catherine, layered over older ones she'd carried since she was sixteen. The fire that had taken her mother's house. He was still processing what she'd shared. Three years of not letting anyone close. Three years of penance for five minutes of lost control. No wonder she moved through the world like someone carrying glass.

Silas stood at the back of the cabin, motionless, a man-shaped hole in Solomon's awareness.

"You know what I miss about Chicago?" Solomon said to no one in particular. "When someone wanted to kill you, at least they didn't offer you champagne first."

Akari opened one eye. "You've never had champagne."

"Exactly. I'd hate to die without trying it."

Catherine almost smiled. Almost.

The Prometheus Initiative's Geneva headquarters was hidden in plain sight. From outside, it looked like any other corporate campus—glass and steel, manicured grounds. A brass plaque read "Prometheus Foundation for Global Research."

But as they crossed the parking lot, Solomon's shadow twitched. Not toward the building—outward. Toward the street. His diminished senses caught it for only a second: someone watching from a parked car two blocks away. Not

Prometheus security—they were already inside the perimeter. This was someone else. Someone whose attention felt like a thread being pulled taut.

By the time he turned to look, the car was gone.

He filed it away. Whoever was watching would show themselves eventually. They always did.

Inside, the difference was immediate when he crossed the threshold.

The air carried a charge, not electrical, but spiritual. The accumulated weight of three centuries of harvesting pressed against his senses like walking into deep water. His shadow stirred, responding to energies that suffused the walls and floors. Somewhere beneath his feet, he could feel them. Thousands of threads.

Thousands of interrupted futures. Thousands of people who had been reduced to resources.

"You feel it," Helena observed.

"How could I not?"

"Most people can't. Most people walk through here without sensing anything unusual." She led them through corridors that seemed to stretch longer than the building's exterior should allow. "The facility is layered. What you're feeling is resonance from the collection."

"The stored seeds."

"Yes. Thousands of them, in vaults beneath us. The largest repository of harvested potential in the world." Her voice carried pride mixed with something that might have been doubt. "Three hundred years of careful accumulation."

Solomon's shadow pressed closer, uneasy. The darkness here was different—contained, constrained. It felt like a prison. Like walking through a building made of concentrated grief.

They reached a set of double doors that looked ordinary but felt like a barrier between worlds.

"Last chance to reconsider," Helena said, hand on the handle.

"Once we go through those doors, there's no taking back whatever happens."

Solomon thought of Catherine. Of Akari. Of Naomi, who had died trying to expose what this organization was doing. Of the thousands of voices he'd felt in the network, reaching for each other across darkness that should have silenced them forever.

"Open the doors."

The council chamber was a circle.

Twelve seats arranged around a central floor, elevated so that whoever stood in the middle had to look up at the faces judging them. The design was deliberate—a reminder of hierarchy, of authority.

The architecture of intimidation, refined over centuries.

The walls were lined with portraits of previous council members, oil paintings in heavy frames, all gazing down with distant judgment. The first members dated to the organization's founding—men and women in clothing from another era, their faces bearing the particular arrogance of those who had never questioned their own righteousness.

The twelve current members were already seated.

They ranged in age from perhaps forty to well over eighty.

Different ethnicities, different nationalities—but all watching him with the same calculating intensity. These were people who had spent decades deciding who lived and who was harvested.

Solomon studied them as he walked to the center.

Director Chen occupied the central seat—white-haired, precise, with eyes that seemed to see through flesh to the calculations beneath. Chen had led the council for eighteen years, outlasting three attempts to replace her through political maneuvering and one attempted assassination.

To her right sat Director Volkov—heavy-set, bearded, open hostility on his face. He led the traditionalist faction, the members who believed the Initiative's methods were already perfect.

To Chen's left was Director Martinez, younger than most of her colleagues, watching Solomon with the predatory interest of a scientist examining a specimen. She led the reformists.

The other nine were harder to read at a glance. Different countries, different decades of service, nine separate calculations running behind nine carefully neutral expressions. All of them powerful. All of them dangerous. All of them deciding whether he would walk out as an ally or a target.

Helena took her seat among them. Akari, Catherine, and Silas remained near the doors—witnesses, not participants.

Solomon walked to the center of the circle and stood alone.

The weight of their attention settled over him like a physical force. His shadow stirred restlessly, wanting to respond, wanting to show these people what it could do. He kept it still with an effort that made his teeth ache.

"Solomon Nyx," Chen said. Her voice was dry, precise. "We've heard a great deal about you."

"Madam Director. I appreciate the opportunity to speak."

"It was not universally welcomed." Chen's gaze flicked to Volkov. "Several colleagues believe we should have extracted you the moment you became a problem."

"Or simply eliminated," Volkov added. His Russian accent thickened with contempt. "A Reaper-class seed in the hands of an untrained individual represents unacceptable risk. The fact that he's here at all is a failure of protocol."

"A failure we can still correct," another of the hardliners agreed. "The boy," Martinez interrupted, "reconnected a seed that our best researchers declared unviable. That represents scientific value, not threat."

"Science can wait. Security cannot." Volkov leaned forward.

"You've disrupted operations. Damaged valuable subjects. Spread information about our methods to outsiders."

"I helped a woman who was screaming for eight months while you thought she was empty," Solomon replied. "I'm sorry if that was inconvenient."

Murmurs rippled around the circle. Director Singh raised an eyebrow. Director Andersson's gaze sharpened.

"Miss Park's case is troubling," Chen acknowledged. "If what Dr. Vance reports is accurate, it suggests gaps in our understanding of extraction."

"Gaps that should have been identified centuries ago," Martinez said.

"We're not here to debate research methodology," Volkov snapped. "We're here to decide what to do about a security breach."

"What you've built," Solomon said, "is a bomb."

The chamber went silent.

Chen's eyes narrowed. "Explain."

"The seeds you've collected aren't inert. They're still connected—to each other, to the people they were taken from, to the futures that were stolen." His shadow pulsed as he spoke.

"Every extraction stretches those connections. Every year that passes makes them more strained. And somewhere beneath this building, those connections are starting to interact."

"That's impossible," Volkov said. "Our containment protocols—" "Your containment protocols were designed for individual seeds. Not for what happens when thousands of them are kept in proximity for three hundred years." Solomon looked around the circle. "I can feel it. The network you've created without meaning to. The way they're reaching for each other. The pressure building toward something none of your instruments can measure."

"Convenient," one of the other hardliners said. "You claim abilities that cannot be verified and threaten consequences that cannot be predicted."

"Then verify it." Solomon kept his voice steady. "Let me access your vaults. Let me show you what I can perceive. If I'm wrong, you lose nothing but time. If I'm right…"

"If you're right," Chen finished, "then we've been nurturing a catastrophe while believing we were maintaining order."

"Yes."

Volkov laughed—a harsh, dismissive sound. "The arrogance."

"One anomaly doesn't invalidate centuries of research," he said. "One anomaly is how paradigm shifts begin," Martinez countered.

"Order," Chen said, and the chamber quieted. She studied Solomon with an expression he couldn't read—calculation, certainly, but something else beneath it. "You've made a claim. Now prove it."

Solomon had prepared for this.

"Director Chen, what do your instruments say about Vault Seven?"

The question landed like a stone in still water. Chen's expression flickered before settling back into neutrality. Around the circle, Solomon saw reactions: confusion from some, recognition from others, alarm from a few who clearly knew what Vault Seven meant. "Vault Seven is classified."

"It's also unstable." Solomon pressed forward. "Your instruments show fluctuations you can't explain. Energy readings that spike without cause. Containment fields that require constant adjustment."

"How do you know that?" Volkov demanded.

"Because I can feel it from here." Solomon's shadow stirred, reaching toward what lay beneath. "The seeds in Vault Seven are the oldest in your collection. They've had the longest time to adapt. To connect. To become something more than isolated fragments."

He met Chen's eyes.

"Send someone to check the readings. Right now. If I'm wrong, you can have me extracted immediately. But if I'm right…"

Chen held his gaze. The risk of being wrong versus the risk of not knowing. The politics of appearing weak versus the danger of appearing ignorant.

Then she nodded to a technician near the door. The man hurried out.

The chamber waited in tense silence.

Five minutes passed. Ten.

Solomon stood still, feeling the eyes of the council on him, feeling his shadow pulse in response to the network far below. When the technician returned, his face was pale.

"Madam Director," he said, voice unsteady. "Vault Seven is showing anomalies. The energy readings have spiked forty percent in the last hour. Containment is holding, but—" "Thank you." Chen cut him off with a gesture. Her expression had changed—not dramatically, but enough. The shift from skepticism to concern.

"It seems," she said, "that Mr. Nyx deserves more than fifteen minutes."

The extended session lasted three hours.

Solomon explained what he'd felt in the containment. The web of connections, the building pressure, the sense of something vast and patient waiting. He answered questions from the reformists about the mechanics of perception. He endured Volkov's hostile skepticism. He watched as alliances shifted around the table, old certainties cracking under new information.

Catherine was called to testify.

She stepped forward without being invited, her voice rough but steady.

"He's right. I could feel them. The others. Even trapped in my body, even with my seed torn away, I could feel them reaching for each other. Trying to connect. Trying to become something that could fight back."

"Fight back against what?" one of the reformists asked.

Catherine's eyes were hard.

"Against you."

The words hung in the air.

"Against the people who took them. Against the organization that decided their lives were acceptable collateral. Against three centuries of being treated as resources instead of people." She looked around the circle. "They're still in there. Pieces of them. Not dead. Not dormant. Waiting."

The vote took another hour.

Solomon, Akari, and Catherine waited in an antechamber while the council debated. Silas stood guard outside—whether protecting or watching them, Solomon couldn't tell.

The room was elegant in the way old money was elegant—understated, expensive. Paintings depicted scenes of classical mythology. The silence was absolute.

Akari held his hand.

"You did well," she said.

"I don't know if it was enough."

"You told them the truth. Made them see something they didn't want to see. That's more than anyone else has managed in three hundred years."

Catherine paced by the window, her restored seed manifesting occasionally as flickers of light—glimpses of possible futures playing out across her consciousness.

"They're afraid," she said. "I can see it. The futures where they say yes, where they actually change—they're terrified in all of them."

"But they do change?" Solomon asked.

Catherine turned to face him.

"In some futures."

"How many?"

She smiled faintly.

"More than there were this morning."

After a while, Solomon stood. "I need air."

Akari started to rise with him. He shook his head—a small motion, just for her. *Stay.* The corridor outside the antechamber was empty except for one man.

Silas stood with his back against the opposite wall, hands in his pockets, watching Solomon with the same patient attention he'd watched everyone else with since Geneva. The hole where his thread should have been pressed against Solomon's awareness like a missing tooth.

Solomon stopped a few feet from him.

"Helena said I could ask you," he said.

"Ask me what."

"What it's like."

For a long moment Silas didn't answer. His face didn't change. He was a man who had learned over thirty years that no expression was almost always the safer expression.

Then he said: "It's quiet."

Solomon waited.

"Most people who learn what was taken from me want it to be terrible. They want me to grieve loudly. To be diminished." Silas's voice was even, neither bitter nor proud. "It is not terrible. When you have a future, you spend a great deal of energy listening for it. Bracing against it. When you do not, that energy comes back to you. Slowly. Like circulation returning to a sleeping limb."

"And what they ask you to do. For Helena. For Prometheus."

"Whatever they ask. Until they ask the wrong thing."

He did not say *and they will, eventually.* He did not have to. The threadless space where his future should have been carried it without words.

Solomon nodded once.

Then he went back inside.

When the doors finally opened, Helena emerged first.

Her face was carefully neutral, but Solomon could see something in her eyes—not victory, not defeat, but something more complex. Relief, perhaps. Or the beginning of hope she'd been afraid to feel. "The council has reached a decision."

Solomon stood. "And?"

Helena took a breath.

"Seven votes in favor. Five against. Extractions will be suspended pending investigation of the stored seed network. You'll be granted access to the vaults, supervised, to examine what you can perceive." She paused. "And Miss Park's case will be used as a template for potential reconnection attempts with other viable subjects."

Something loosened in Solomon's chest.

"They agreed."

"They're terrified," Helena said. "Of you. Of what you described. Of the possibility that three centuries of work might have created exactly the kind of catastrophe they've been trying to prevent." She met his eyes. "But they agreed."

Akari pulled Solomon into an embrace. Catherine laughed—a sound of genuine relief.

"The five who voted against," Helena added, voice dropping.

"Volkov and his faction. They'll be looking for any excuse to reverse this decision. You'll need to prove that what you sensed is real."

"I understand."

"And Solomon? If you're wrong—if this is manipulation or exaggeration— they won't extract you. They'll destroy you.

Completely. Without hesitation."

Solomon nodded.

"Then I'd better be right."

Helena Vance had not slept in three days.

She sat in her office and went through every extraction file she could pull from the archive. She'd approved these personally—signed transfer orders, sat in committee meetings where subjects were discussed with the clinical detachment of inventory management. She'd always told herself it was necessary. She'd believed it. Until Solomon Nyx had put his hand on a pod and told her the people inside were still conscious.

Catherine Park's debriefing transcript sat at the top of the pile. *I could feel myself fading,* Catherine had told the doctors. *Like watching a photograph left in sunlight, slowly bleaching into nothing. I screamed and screamed, but nothing came out. I could sense others around me—other remnants, other fragments of consciousness—and they were screaming too. We were a chorus of silent agony, and no one could hear us.* Helena closed the file.

Three hundred years. Thousands of extractions. Conservative estimate, if what Catherine described was typical: two thousand people who had spent months or years conscious inside the pods, unable to move, unable to speak, slowly fading into nothing.

She was going to apologize to Catherine. Not because it would fix anything. Because someone needed to acknowledge the wrong, and it might as well be the person who had approved it.

Three weeks later The room they met in was neutral by design. Not Helena's office. Not the medical bay where Catherine had woken up. A conference room on the sixth floor, the kind of room Prometheus reserved for meetings that required witnesses without audience.

There were no witnesses today. Helena had asked for the room empty.

Catherine was already there when Helena arrived. Sitting at the table, hands folded on its polished surface, not looking at the door. Her hair was shorter than it had been in the extraction files. She had lost weight in the pod and not gained it back. She was thirty-two, though Helena would have guessed older from across the room.

"Ms. Park."

"Ms. Vance."

Helena had rehearsed the opening for three weeks. Every version felt wrong. She used the one that felt least wrong.

"I'm not here to ask for forgiveness. I want to be clear about that before I say anything else. I am not here to be absolved. I am here because I signed the transfer order that put you in that pod on March eighteenth of last year, and you deserve to hear it from the person who signed it, not from a statement or a file."

Catherine's eyes finally moved to her.

They were darker than Helena had expected. Not in color—in what they contained. Helena had looked into a lot of eyes across three decades of this work. She had not looked into eyes that had spent eight months unable to close.

"Go ahead," Catherine said.

Helena went ahead.

She named the transfer order. The date. The facility. The classification: *Seer-type, moderate precognitive capacity, harvested for general network contribution.* She named Diego Ferreira, whose name she had not spoken aloud in nine years, and Elena Voss, and two others whose transfer orders she had also signed. She did not offer context for any of them. She named the wrong and she did not explain it.

When she was done, she sat in the silence Catherine did not fill. "I thought you were going to cry," Catherine said eventually.

"I rehearsed not crying."

"Why?"

"Because I didn't want you to have to comfort me."

Catherine considered this. Her hands, Helena noticed, were still folded. They had not moved in the fifteen minutes Helena had been speaking.

"You don't want absolution."

"No."

"You don't want forgiveness."

"No."

"What do you want?"

Helena had not rehearsed the answer to this.

"I want you to know," she said, "that someone came and said it. That it wasn't the organization that said it in a statement. A person said it to your face. That is the thing I want. It is not for you. It is for me. I am aware that I am asking you to receive my unburdening and that this is its own kind of imposition. I am doing it anyway."

Catherine was quiet for a long time.

"You're asking me to witness you," she said.

"Yes."

"While you tell me what was done to me."

"Yes."

"That is a large thing to ask, Ms. Vance."

"I know."

"Do you?"

Helena felt her composure go in a way she had prepared for and could not have actually prepared for. She did not cry. She had rehearsed that. But her hands, which had been steady through thirty years of this work, were not steady now. She folded them in her lap and tried to feel for what Catherine's steady hands on the table had cost her to keep steady, and failed, because she had never been unable to close her eyes for eight months.

"No," Helena said. "I don't know. I'm trying to."

Catherine watched her for another moment.

Then she spoke.

"I don't forgive you. Maybe I never will. But I believe you didn't know what you were doing. And I believe you want to do better." A pause. "That's not forgiveness. It's just... acknowledgment. Of what is, instead of what should be."

"Thank you."

"Don't thank me for that either."

"All right."

"There are things I want."

Helena leaned forward. "Tell me."

"I want every person still in a pod reconnected. Not just the ones Solomon thinks he can reach. All of them. Every transfer order you have ever signed—I want you to go through the files yourself and name every person. I want the names read out loud. Someone has to say them. You are going to be that person."

"I will do that."

"I want the pod wing dismantled. Not decommissioned.

Dismantled. I want the hardware destroyed. I do not want another subject to ever enter that room because the room should not exist."

"I will arrange it."

"I want Diego Ferreira's family located. I want them told he was conscious the whole time. His daughter is older than I am. She is going to need to know her father did not go peacefully."

Helena closed her eyes for a second.

"I will find her."

"One more."

"Yes."

"When this is over. When we have stopped whatever is coming.

You will step down. You will not run the reformed version of this organization. You will not remain in leadership in any capacity. Someone who was in a pod will run it. Or someone who lost a person to a pod will run it. That is the only version of reform I will accept."

Helena nodded. It was not a slow nod. It was the nod of someone who had expected this condition and had made peace with it before she walked into the room.

"I agree."

"Then we are done for today."

Catherine stood. Her hands, still, had not moved from the table until she pushed herself up. She left without looking back.

Helena sat in the conference room for a long time after the door closed.

She did not cry. But at some point she put her face in her hands, and she stayed like that longer than she had stayed in any posture in recent memory.

When she finally looked up, the room was still empty, and the conversation had already ended, and something in her was not the same as it had been when she walked in.

It was not absolution.

It was the beginning of what would come after absolution, if absolution were ever possible. Which, Helena now understood, it was not.

That was the point.

That was the whole point.

Now she sat in a different meeting, not with victims, but with potential allies. Solomon Nyx across the table, his shadow thin but present. Akari beside him, her light steady. Marcus at Helena's right hand, still uncertain but committed.

"The Light-Bearer network is willing to work with a reformed Prometheus," Solomon said. "But the conditions are non-negotiable."

"Name them."

"Complete cessation of extraction activities. Full access to existing subjects for reconnection attempts. Transparency about the organization's activities going forward. And accountability—not just words, but structural changes that prevent the old patterns from reasserting themselves."

Helena gave a slow nod.

"There's something else," she said. "Something I haven't shared with anyone outside the inner council."

Solomon waited.

Helena pulled out a file—older than the others, written in a hand that had died centuries ago.

"The extraction program wasn't created for the reasons we've always claimed. The original founders knew exactly what they were doing. They designed the process to leave consciousness intact—not by accident, but deliberately."

Solomon's expression hardened. "Why?"

"Because the Dreamer prefers conscious sacrifices." Helena's voice was flat, clinical. The only way she could get the words out. "The entity at the heart of everything. The founder's notes describe it as 'feeding preferences.' Unconscious subjects provided less power. Conscious ones provided more."

Silence.

"You're saying Prometheus has been deliberately torturing people to feed an ancient entity," Akari said slowly.

"I'm saying the founders knew. Whether that knowledge was preserved, lost, or deliberately suppressed—I don't know. But the original purpose of the extraction program wasn't protection. It was... cultivation. Farming suffering to keep the Dreamer sleeping."

Solomon's shadow surged despite his control—a flash of darkness that made the lights flicker.

"You're just telling us this now?"

"I discovered it three days ago. In archives I didn't know existed." Helena met his eyes without flinching. "I could have buried it. Kept it hidden. Maintained whatever leverage it might provide. Instead, I'm sharing it because you need to know what we were built for. What we served, all those centuries we told ourselves we were heroes."

The room was silent.

"This changes things," Solomon said finally.

"Yes. It makes everything worse. But it also explains why the Dreamer grew so powerful, why it was so close to waking when you broke the pattern." Helena closed the file. "We weren't containing it. We were feeding it. And now that we know, we can stop."

The meeting continued for another hour. Details were negotiated. Agreements were reached. The foundation for an alliance was laid—fragile, uncertain, built on mutual need rather than trust. But it was a start.

And after three centuries of lies, even a start felt like progress.

That Night That night, Solomon couldn't sleep.

He stood on the roof of the Geneva facility, the Alpine wind cutting through his jacket, and stared at the stars. The same stars that had watched while Prometheus harvested thousands of people. The same stars that would watch tomorrow, regardless of what he chose. His shadow was restless, stirring around his feet in patterns that matched his thoughts—chaotic, angry, grief-stricken in ways he hadn't let himself feel since Naomi died.

What am I doing here?

The question had been building for days, suppressed beneath strategy and necessity and the constant forward momentum of crisis. But in the silence, with nothing to fight and no one to save, it wouldn't stay buried anymore.

He was working with them. Eating their food. Sleeping in their beds. Planning the future alongside people who had built a machine that devoured human souls for three hundred years.

Helena Vance had approved his sister's death. Not directly—she hadn't held the weapon or given the order—but she had created the system that made it possible. She had maintained it, expanded it, refined it into the efficient horror he'd witnessed in the vaults. And now she was his ally.

Solomon's hands curled into fists. His shadow surged outward, responding to the rage he'd been suppressing, darkening the rooftop until the stars themselves seemed to dim.

He could end this. Right now. Walk away from the alliance, from Prometheus, from the entire careful structure of compromise and cooperation. Take Akari, find the remaining Light-Bearers, and fight the Dreamer on their own terms. Without the people who had murdered his sister. Without selling pieces of his soul for strategic advantage.

Naomi would have done it. Naomi had died rather than compromise with these people.

But Naomi didn't know what was coming.

The thought was quiet, unwanted, true.

His sister had been investigating Prometheus when she died.

Looking for evidence, building a case, preparing to expose them. She'd believed in truth, in justice, in the power of revelation to change the world.

She hadn't known about the Dreamer. Hadn't understood that the organization she was fighting was the only thing standing between humanity and an ancient entity that wanted to remake consciousness itself. Hadn't realized that her righteous crusade might have weakened the very defenses that kept something worse at bay.

Would she have made the same choice if she'd known?

Solomon didn't know. And he hated that he didn't know. He wanted his sister's memory to be simple—pure opposition, uncomplicated resistance, the moral clarity of someone who had died fighting evil.

But the world wasn't simple. The Dreamer was waking. The pattern was spreading. And the only people with resources, knowledge, and infrastructure to fight it were the same people who had built their empire on harvested souls.

The door to the roof opened behind him.

"I thought I'd find you here."

Akari's voice was quiet, careful. She'd learned to read his moods over the past weeks—knew when he needed space and when he needed company. Tonight, apparently, was company.

She came to stand beside him, her light a warm contrast to the cold wind. "I can feel you thinking about leaving," she said quietly. "The shadows get heavier when you're considering running."

"Not running. Fighting."

"Without them?"

"Without her." Solomon's voice was rough. "Without Helena.

Without the people who built the machine that killed Naomi. Without pretending that cooperation means forgiveness."

Akari was quiet.

"You could," she said eventually. "Leave, I mean. Take the Light-Bearers who'd follow you, try to fight the Dreamer without Prometheus resources. It wouldn't be impossible."

"But?"

"But you'd lose. Probably. The Dreamer is too strong, too embedded, too connected to the pattern they spent centuries building. Fighting it without their knowledge would be fighting blind. Fighting it without their infrastructure would be fighting broke." She turned to face him. "You know this. That's why you're not already gone."

"Knowing it doesn't make it easier."

"No." Akari's hand found his—warm against his cold skin.

"Solomon, I watched my family burn. I've spent twenty years fighting people who were supposed to protect us. I understand what it costs to work with people who've hurt you."

"Then how do you do it?"

"I remember what I'm fighting for." Her grip tightened. "Not against. Not revenge, not justice, not even making them pay for what they did. I fight for the people who are still alive. The ones who can still be saved. The future that exists if we win."

Solomon stared at the mountains, at the darkness pooled in the valleys below.

"Naomi used to say that. 'Don't fight the last war. Fight the next one.'"

"She sounds like she was smart."

"She was." The word came out rough. "She would have hated this. Hated me, maybe, for choosing strategy over principle. For letting Helena Vance stand beside me instead of tearing her apart."

"Or maybe she would have understood." Akari stepped closer, her warmth pressing against his arm. "She loved you enough to die protecting you. That means she loved you enough to want you to survive. To win. Even if winning meant doing things she would have found difficult."

Solomon's shadow slowly settled, the rage draining out of it, leaving something heavier—grief, acceptance, the weight of a choice he didn't want to make but couldn't avoid.

"I don't forgive them," he said. "I need you to know that.

Whatever alliance we build, whatever cooperation we manage—I don't forgive what they did. To Naomi. To Catherine. To all the people in those vaults."

"You don't have to forgive them. You just have to fight beside them." Akari's light pulsed softly. "Forgiveness is between you and your conscience. Strategy is between us and the Dreamer."

"Is that enough?"

"It's what we have."

Solomon stood in silence for a long time, feeling the weight of the decision settling into his bones. Not a surrender. Not an acceptance. Just… a choice. The best of the terrible options available. *I'm sorry, Naomi. I hope you understand.*

"Okay," Solomon said. "I'm staying. But when this is over—when the Dreamer is stopped and the pattern is broken—I'm not done with Prometheus. The extraction program ends permanently. The people responsible for what happened face consequences. And Helena Vance tells me exactly what happened to my sister, every detail, no matter how much it hurts to hear."

"And if she won't?"

Solomon's shadow stirred—not with rage this time, but with quiet certainty.

"Then we find out how much her new conscience is worth."

Akari nodded, considering.

"That's fair."

They stood together on the roof until the stars faded, watching the darkness give way to dawn. Whatever came next, they would face it together.

But Solomon would never forget what it cost to stand here. What piece of himself he'd buried to fight alongside his sister's killers. Some wounds didn't heal.

He found Helena the next morning.

She was in the communications center, reviewing reports from facilities worldwide, her face lit by the cold glow of monitors. When Solomon entered, she looked up with an expression that suggested she'd been expecting him.

"Mr. Nyx."

"We need to talk."

Helena set down her tablet. "About strategy? The Light-Bearer network? The Dreamer's—" "About Naomi."

The name hung in the air between them. Helena's composure didn't break, but something shifted behind her eyes—a flicker of the guilt she'd shown in the council chamber.

"I wondered when you'd ask."

"I'm not asking." Solomon stepped closer. His shadow stirred but he kept it contained. "I'm telling you how this works. We're allies now. We have to be—the

Dreamer doesn't care about our history. But I need you to understand something, and I need to say it to your face."

Helena waited.

"You killed my sister." The words came out flat, cold. "Not directly. You didn't pull the trigger. But you built the machine that made her death necessary. You created protocols that classified her as a threat. You signed off on systems that treated human beings as resources to be harvested or eliminated. And when your people decided she knew too much, you didn't stop them."

"No." Helena's voice was quiet. "I didn't."

"You could have. You had the authority. You could have flagged her file, delayed the termination order, found another way. But you didn't, because it was easier to let the system work the way you'd designed it to work. Because one woman's life didn't matter compared to the mission you believed in."

Helena didn't flinch. Didn't defend herself. Just stood there and took it.

"You're right," Helena said after a moment. "About all of it. I could have saved her. I chose not to. I told myself she was a threat, that her investigation endangered everything we'd built, that her death was a necessary sacrifice." Something in her voice thinned. "I was wrong. Not about the threat—she was a threat, to the system I'd devoted my life to protecting. But the system itself was wrong. Which means every death I authorized in its name was wrong too."

"That's not an apology."

"No. It's not." Helena met his eyes. "Because an apology would be asking for something—forgiveness, absolution, permission to feel less guilty. I'm not asking for any of that. You don't owe me forgiveness. You don't owe me anything. What I did to your sister, to Catherine, to thousands of people over thirty years—there's no making that right. There's only doing better. If I'm lucky, I'll spend whatever's left of my life trying to undo the damage I caused. But that's my burden, not your obligation."

Something shifted inside him. Not the rage—that remained. The wall he'd built around it. He'd expected her to deflect. To justify. To offer excuses wrapped in the language of necessity.

He hadn't expected honesty.

"I don't forgive you," he said. "I want to be clear about that. Whatever we accomplish together, whatever alliance we build—I will never forgive what you did to Naomi. To all of them."

"I know."

"And when this is over—when the Dreamer is stopped—there will be a reckoning. Not revenge. Justice. The extraction program ends permanently. The people who were harvested get whatever help we can give them. And the world learns what Prometheus did in the dark."

Helena nodded, more to herself than to anyone else. "That's fair."

"You keep saying that."

"Because it is." She picked up her tablet again, but her hands were trembling slightly. "I've spent three decades telling myself I was protecting humanity. Turns out I was just feeding a monster while it got strong enough to devour us. If exposing that truth is the price of stopping it, I'll pay it."

Solomon studied her—this woman who had ordered his sister's death, who had built an empire on harvested souls, who was now offering herself up for judgment without asking for mercy.

He didn't trust her. Might never trust her.

But he believed her.

"Then let's go save the world," he said. "And afterward, we'll figure out how to live with what we've done."

Helena almost smiled. It didn't reach her eyes.

"After you, Mr. Nyx."

CHAPTER FOURTEEN

The Vaults

The elevator descended for longer than any elevator should.

Solomon counted floors by pressure changes in his ears, lost track somewhere past fifty. The panel numbers had stopped at B-12, replaced by symbols he didn't recognize—old markings that predated the building above them, maybe predated the city itself. Alchemical notation, circles within circles, triangles bisected by lines that shifted when he looked directly. Others resembled script from ancient texts about myth and divinity. A few were completely unfamiliar, their curves suggesting a language never meant for human tongues. The car itself changed this deep—smaller somehow, walls pressing closer, air growing thick with weight that had nothing to do with atmosphere.

Helena stood beside him, composure maintained but tension visible in her shoulders. She hadn't spoken since they'd entered, her silence weighted with something that felt like grief. Her usually steady hands gripped the tablet white-knuckled. Silas waited at the back, his absent thread a constant void in Solomon's awareness—a man-shaped hole where the network should connect.

"How deep does this go?" Solomon asked.

"The vaults were built into a natural cave system. Extended over centuries. The deepest chambers are nearly a kilometer below street level."

"And the oldest seeds?"

"The oldest verified specimen dates to 1742. But there are containers in the lower vaults that predate our documentation. We're not entirely sure what's in some of them." She paused, something flickering across her face—a crack in the professional mask. "There are records—fragments, really—suggesting some containers were already here when the first Prometheus members discovered these caves. Already sealed. Already… occupied."

Solomon's shadow pressed close, uneasy. It had been restless since they'd entered the building, responding to the accumulated weight of harvested potential that permeated every wall. Down here, that weight was becoming oppressive—a pressure against his consciousness that made it difficult to think. Each floor they descended added another layer of grief to the air.

The elevator slowed. Stopped.

The doors opened onto darkness.

The vault was not what Solomon had expected.

No sterile corridors. No clinical lighting. No rows of pods like the extraction wing at the Japanese facility.

Instead, he stepped into a cathedral.

The ceiling arched overhead, lost in shadows his eyes couldn't penetrate. Faint phosphorescence clung to the rock itself, giving the space an ethereal glow from nowhere and everywhere at once. The light had a color that didn't exist— not green, not blue, but something between that made Solomon's eyes ache. The floor was smooth stone, worn by centuries of footsteps into gentle undulations suggesting generations of visitors following the same paths. He could almost feel those paths—grooves carved by countless people walking to the same destinations, checking the same containers, maintaining the same terrible collection.

Rising from that floor like frozen pillars stood the containers—thousands of them, crystalline structures glowing with faint internal light, arranged in patterns that suggested purpose without revealing meaning. Some stood alone like sentinels. Others clustered in groups of three or seven or thirteen, their lights pulsing in synchronized rhythms that might have been communication or simple resonance. A forest of glass and light, each tree holding a trapped soul.

Each one held a seed.

Solomon thought of the corner store on his block in Chicago.

The one where Naomi bought bread and peanut butter with whatever cash she could scrape together. The bell above the door that rang every time someone walked in. Such a small world, that store. Such small stakes. And here he was standing in a cathedral of stolen lives, and the distance between that corner store and this vault felt like a measurement of everything that had gone wrong.

He sensed them immediately. Not as individual presences, but as collective weight—a pressure against his mind that made his temples throb and his shadow writhe. The sensation was overwhelming, like standing where thousands of people whispered at once, their voices just below comprehension. He could almost hear words forming, almost understand what they were saying, and the almost was worse than total silence.

"The main vault," Helena said. Her voice echoed strangely, the acoustics swallowing some sounds and amplifying others. The cathedral breathed around her words, processing them, judging them. "Approximately four thousand specimens, spanning three centuries of collection."

"Collection." Solomon's voice was flat. "That's what you call it."

"It's what we've always called it. Whatever else we've done wrong, we've preserved these seeds. Protected them. Kept them from falling into worse hands."

"Protected." Solomon laughed, and the sound came back distorted, multiplied, as if a thousand voices laughed along with him—or at him. "You harvested people's souls and called it protection."

"We prevented catastrophic awakenings. We stopped individuals with dangerous potential from harming themselves and others."

Helena's voice hardened. "I've seen what happens when a Reaper-class seed erupts in an urban environment. I've walked through the aftermath. The bodies. The survivors who can't remember their own names because proximity to uncontrolled death-sense stripped the threads from their minds."

"And this is better?" Solomon gestured at the crystalline forest. "Thousands of stolen futures, kept in boxes in the dark?"

"This is controlled. This is contained."

Solomon didn't respond. He walked forward, drawn toward the nearest container. Up close, he could see details—the crystalline structure wasn't uniform, but layered, like tree rings marking years of growth. The light inside pulsed slowly, a rhythm that might have been heartbeat. Through the translucent walls, he could see movement—something not smoke and not light, swirling in patterns that suggested consciousness without ever resolving into form. He reached out with his shadow.

And the vault answered.

The sensation overwhelmed him.

Not pain—nothing so simple. More like suddenly hearing a frequency that had always been there, a conversation happening just below perception. The sound rushed into him like water breaking through a dam—not through his ears, but through something deeper, something that lived where his seed connected to the darkness now his to command.

The seeds were talking to each other.

Not in words. Not in any language Solomon could describe. But they were communicating—pulses of light passing between containers, threads of connection his ordinary senses couldn't detect but his shadow could feel. A network of harvested potential, growing more complex with every passing moment. The communication had texture, layers, depth—surface exchanges in rapid bursts while deeper conversations moved slowly, ponderously, their meaning compressed into single pulses that took minutes to unfold.

Solomon staggered but kept his connection open, trying to understand. The communication wasn't random. It followed patterns—responses and calls, questions and answers, debates ongoing for decades or centuries. Some seeds spoke frequently, their lights pulsing in rapid exchanges. Others remained quiet, listening, their contributions rare but significant. A few—ancient, barely glowing—spoke only in single pulses that carried tremendous weight.

And at the center— Something was forming.

Solomon staggered again, caught himself on the nearest container. The light inside flared at his touch, and suddenly he was seeing, not with his eyes, but with something deeper.

Thousands of seeds, stripped from their hosts, stored in isolation meant to be permanent. But the stretched threads Helena's people had created—the connections they thought they'd severed—had found each other in the dark. Wrapped around each other. Tangled into knots that grew tighter with every new addition.

Those knots had become nodes. Points where harvested potential concentrated, accumulated, began to change.

The network wasn't just connected.

It was evolving.

Solomon saw it in flashes—glimpses of something vast taking shape in the spaces between containers. Not a single consciousness, but a composite one. Thousands of harvested minds contributing fragments of themselves to something larger. Something that remembered what it had been, mourned what it had lost, and hungered for completion.

"Solomon." Helena's voice came from far away. "Solomon, your shadow—" He looked down.

His shadow had spread across the floor, extending toward containers in every direction. Where it touched them, the lights pulsed brighter, faster. Communication between seeds intensified, patterns shifting in response to his presence. The darkness around his feet wasn't just reaching—it was answering, responding to calls Solomon hadn't consciously sent.

They recognized him.

Not as an individual. As a type. A Reaper-class seed still connected to its host, still whole, still possessing the power they had lost.

And they wanted it back.

The desire crashed into Solomon like a wave. Thousands of harvested seeds, their consciousness preserved but severed from everything that had once made them human, reaching for the darkness he carried. Not hostile—desperate. Drowning people grasping at a lifeline.

"Solomon!" Helena's voice, sharp now, commanding. "Pull back!"

He tried. His shadow resisted—not because it wanted to stay, but because the seeds wouldn't let go. Their need was a weight dragging him down, threatening to swallow him in collective grief.

Silas moved. He sensed it rather than saw it—a displacement in the network, a void cutting through the connections. The threadless man walked through the vault like a blade through water, and where he passed, the seeds' desperate reaching faltered.

Solomon used the interruption to wrench his shadow back. It came reluctantly, trailing wisps of connection that took long seconds to dissolve.

"What…" He gasped, trying to catch his breath. "What was that?"

"The network," Helena said. Her voice shook slightly. The first time Solomon had heard genuine fear in it. "You connected to it."

"They're communicating. Building something. A shared consciousness."

"That's not possible. They're isolated. The containers—" "The containers don't isolate anything." Solomon straightened, his shadow still trembling. "Whatever extraction does to separate seed from host, it doesn't stop them from talking to each other. They've been building connections for years. Maybe decades. And something is emerging from it."

Helena's face had gone pale. "What kind of something?"

"I don't know. But they felt me. A complete Reaper-class seed."

Solomon met her eyes. "They want what I have, Helena. They want to be whole again."

"That's not possible. Extraction is permanent."

"Is it?" Solomon looked at the nearest container, at the light still pulsing faster than it had before his touch. "Or is that just what you've always believed?"

They went deeper.

Helena led the way now, her composure cracked but not shattered. The vault extended farther than Solomon could have imagined—a maze of chambers and corridors carved into the living rock, each one holding more containers, more harvested seeds, more stolen potential.

The deeper they went, the older the containers became.

The modern crystalline structures gave way to vessels of blown glass, delicate and fragile-looking but clearly enduring. Those gave way to ceramic containers marked with symbols that Solomon didn't recognize but his shadow reacted to—

old bindings, he realized, meant to hold power that predated modern understanding of myth-seeds.

And finally, in the deepest chamber, they found it.

A single container.

Not crystal. Not glass. Not ceramic.

Stone. Ancient stone, so old that its surface had worn smooth as water. The symbols carved into it had been eroded by time until they were barely visible—suggestions of meaning rather than actual words.

And the presence inside it was vast.

He sensed it before he came within ten feet of the container.

Not communication like the other seeds—this was awareness.

Something that knew he was there. Something that had been waiting.

His shadow recoiled instinctively, pressing close to him in a way it hadn't since the early days of his awakening. Akari's light would have helped here, would have given him something to anchor against. But she was topside, coordinating with Catherine and the others. He was alone with this thing.

"Vault Seven," Helena said. Her voice was barely above a whisper. "The oldest container in our collection. The one that was already here when we found these caves."

"What's in it?"

"We don't know. We've never been able to open it. The stone resists every tool we've tried." Helena stayed back, her unease palpable. "Some of us believed it was empty. That whatever was sealed inside had long since dissipated."

Solomon's shadow disagreed. What waited inside that ancient stone was very much present. Very much alive, in whatever way these harvested seeds could be said to live.

And something that was, in some terrible way, almost ready.

Solomon forced himself to extend his shadow again, pushing through instinctive fear. He needed to understand what this was. The connection was like touching ice that burned. The presence inside the ancient container was vast—not just one seed, but something that had been one once and had become something else over millennia of isolation. It didn't communicate in pulses like the others. It communicated in implications. In the spaces between thoughts. In the weight of patience that had outlasted civilizations. *Finally*, it seemed to say. *Finally, a Reaper comes.*

Solomon saw flashes—incomplete, overwhelming. A time before Prometheus. Before modern cities. Before the categories they now used to understand myth-seeds existed. He saw a figure that might have been human, walking through a world where boundaries between reality and myth were tissue-thin. He saw that figure choosing to be sealed away, choosing to wait.

He saw purpose that spanned centuries.

And he saw hunger that made the network's yearning seem like a child's appetite.

Solomon wrenched free, stumbling backward. Silas caught him before he fell.

"What?" Helena demanded. "What did you see?"

"It's not a seed." Solomon gasped. "Not anymore. It's something that was a seed. Something that's been becoming something else for... I don't know. Thousands of years."

"That's impossible. Seeds can't—" "It's been using you." Solomon found his balance, shrugged off Silas's support. "All of you. The network you've built, the seeds you've collected—they're not becoming something on their own.

They're being guided. Shaped. That thing in there is constructing something out of harvested consciousness, and you've been feeding it for three hundred years."

Helena's face had gone gray. "Constructing what?"

Solomon looked at the ancient container. Its silence felt louder than any scream.

"A body," he said. "I think it's building itself a new body. One made of thousands of seeds. One that doesn't need a single human host because it will be made of all of them."

They emerged from the vault as the sun set over Lake Geneva.

Solomon stood on the building's roof, letting cold air clear his head, trying to process what he'd sensed in the depths below. His shadow still trembled from the contact, curling protectively around his feet. He felt contaminated somehow. Changed by what he'd touched.

Akari found him there, her light warm against encroaching darkness.

"Helena told me," she said. "About what you found."

"Did she tell you about the thing in the old container? The one that's been waiting?"

Akari nodded after a long moment. "She's frightened. Really frightened. I've never felt that kind of fear from someone in power."

"She should be frightened." Solomon looked out at the city, at lights coming on in windows, at people going about their lives without knowing what lurked beneath their feet. "We're not just dealing with a network of harvested seeds. We're dealing with something planned. Cultivated. Something that's been using Prometheus as a tool for centuries."

"Using them how?"

"To collect seeds. To build the network. To create…" Solomon shook his head. "I don't know what. But the oldest container—whatever's in it—is the center of everything. The network grew around it. Every harvested seed has been connected to it, feeding it, building toward something it needs."

"And now you've touched it."

"Now it knows I exist." Solomon's shadow stirred, restless. "A Reaper-class seed that's still whole. Still connected to its power. Something it might be able to use."

"Use how?"

Solomon remembered the hunger he'd felt. The way the ancient presence had reached for him. *Finally, a Reaper comes.*

"Reaper-class seeds are rare," he said slowly. "And they're usually extracted before they fully manifest. What's in that container—it was once Reaper-class too, I think. Or something close. And it's been waiting for another one. A complete one."

"For what purpose?"

"I don't know." Solomon's voice cracked. "I don't know, Akari. But it's old enough to have planned this before modern nations existed. It's patient enough to have waited while civilizations rose and fell. And now it's almost ready for something, and I walked right into its vault and showed it exactly what I am."

Akari was quiet for a long moment. The wind off the lake shifted, carrying the distant sound of church bells marking the hour—a sound that had echoed across this city for centuries, marking time that meant nothing to what waited below.

"What do we do?" she asked finally.

Solomon turned to face her. In the fading light, her features were soft but her eyes held that familiar steady flame—the light that had first drawn him to her in a Tokyo bookshop that felt like another lifetime.

"I need to understand what's in that container. What it wants. What it's been building toward." He took a breath, tasting cold alpine air, feeling it sharp and clean in his lungs. "And then I need to figure out how to stop it before it finishes."

"Can you do that?"

He thought of the vast network beneath them. The thousands of stolen seeds. The ancient presence at its heart. The weight of centuries of planning and patience. He thought of Naomi, who had died so he could stand here asking these questions. He thought of every person whose consciousness had been harvested to build something they would never see completed.

"I don't know," he said. "But I'm the only one who can try."

Akari took his hand. Her light flowed into him, steady and warm, pushing back against the cold that had settled into his bones since touching that ancient container.

"Then we try together."

The city lights of Geneva spread before them like earthbound stars, each one representing lives lived in ignorance of what lurked beneath their feet. Solomon wondered how many of those lights would still burn when this was over. How many people would survive what was coming.

Below them, in the depths of the vault, the network continued its endless conversation. And at its center, in a container that predated human memory, something primordial turned its attention upward. Soon, it thought. Very soon now.

It had waited this long.

It could wait a little longer.

CHAPTER FIFTEEN

The Dreamer

Solomon dreamed of death that night.

Not the quick kind. Not the violence he'd witnessed in Chicago alleys or Tokyo backstreets, where death arrived like punctuation—sudden, brutal, final. This was something older. A death that stretched across centuries, patient as stone, inevitable as tide. A death with no beginning because it had always been happening. A death with no end because it was the end of everything else.

The sensation crept over him like frost spreading across glass. First his feet went numb. Then his legs. Then a coldness that had nothing to do with temperature climbed his spine and settled behind his eyes, and suddenly he wasn't in his room anymore. Wasn't in Geneva. Wasn't anywhere that belonged to the waking world.

In the dream, he stood in the vault surrounded by crystalline containers pulsing with stolen light. But the containers weren't containers anymore. They were cells in an immense organism, connected by threads of darkness woven through the air like veins through flesh. Each thread hummed with stolen potential—lives interrupted, futures diverted, people reduced to resources.

The humming had a rhythm. A pulse.

A heartbeat that had been beating since before humanity learned to count.

And at the center of it all, something breathed.

Solomon couldn't see it. Couldn't name it. His mind refused to form an image, sliding away from comprehension the way water slides off oil. But he could feel its attention—the weight of an intelligence so old that human concerns were less than insects to it. Less than bacteria. Less than the chemical reactions that preceded the first spark of life.

It had been here before cities existed. Before nations. Before language had words for what it was. It had watched empires rise and fall, watched species evolve and die, watched the slow turning of epochs that made human lifetimes less than heartbeats. It had seen ice ages come and go. Felt continents drift apart like ships losing sight of each other on an infinite ocean.

It had been here, and it had been waiting.

You came, a voice said. Not words—something older than words. A pressure against his mind that resolved into meaning the way clouds resolved into rain, the way gravity resolved into falling. I wondered when one of you would find me.

Solomon tried to speak. Found he had no voice in this place. His throat worked, his lips moved, but the sounds died before they could form. His shadow, usually so responsive to his will, lay flat and still on ground that wasn't ground, paralyzed by proximity to something it recognized as vastly, impossibly greater than itself.

His shadow was afraid.

Solomon hadn't known it could be afraid.

The ones who built my prison thought they were protecting the world, the presence continued. Its voice was neither male nor female, neither young nor old. It was the sound of tectonic plates shifting. The hum of stars burning in the void. The whisper of solar wind against a planet's magnetic field. They didn't understand what they were protecting it from. Or what they were protecting me for.

Images flooded Solomon's mind without permission—not memories, but experiences impressed directly into his consciousness like stamps into wax.

He saw a time before Prometheus. Before the Initiative. Before any organization existed to harvest myth-seeds or contain dangerous awakenings. Men and women with power like his own—different flavors of myth-seed potential—standing in a circle around something terrible and beautiful. They wore robes of a style he didn't recognize, spoke words in languages long dead, and their faces showed the same expression: absolute terror combined with absolute determination.

He felt what they felt. The bone-deep certainty that they would not survive what they were attempting. The love for a world they would never see again. The desperate hope that their sacrifice would mean something—that the centuries after them would be kinder than the centuries before.

They were binding it. Containing it. Sacrificing pieces of themselves—their futures, their potential, their names—to create a prison strong enough to hold something that should never have been caught.

One by one, they burned. Not with fire, but with purpose. Their myth-seeds ignited and consumed them, fuel for chains that would need to hold for longer than any of them could imagine.

The last one standing was a woman with eyes the color of storm clouds. She spoke a word Solomon couldn't hear—a word that existed outside of sound, outside of meaning, outside of everything but pure intent—and then she was gone too, and the binding was complete. They called me the Dreamer, the voice said, and Solomon felt something that might have been nostalgia if nostalgia could exist in a being that had watched stars die. Because I sleep, and while I sleep, I dream of what will be. I have dreamed your future, Solomon Nyx. I have dreamed the futures of every seed harvested and stored in my shadow. I have dreamed the end of everything, and the beginning that comes after.

Cold reached him—a chill with nothing to do with temperature.

This was the cold of deep space. The cold of absolute zero. The cold of an intelligence that saw death not as ending but as transformation into something it understood far better than life.

Death wasn't frightening to the Dreamer. Death was home.

The ones who imprisoned me made a mistake, the Dreamer continued. They thought isolation would weaken me. Instead, it taught me patience. Three hundred years is nothing. Three thousand years is nothing. I learned to think in glacial time, to plan in epochs, to see the patterns that connect everything.

A pause. Something almost like admiration rippled through the darkness.

Though I will grant them this: their cage was clever. They designed it so that my prison was also my sustenance. Every seed Prometheus stored near me fed me—but also strengthened the walls. Every thread they stretched toward me made me more powerful—but also more contained. A trap baited with the only thing I wanted. For a long time, I couldn't see a way out that didn't destroy me along with the cage.

The Dreamer's voice shifted. Something predatory entered it.

But patience teaches you to look for doors that others build for you.

The dream shifted. Solomon saw the network as the Dreamer saw it, not a tangle of stolen connections, but a vast tapestry being woven thread by thread. Each harvested seed was a stitch. Each stretched connection was a line of color. And the pattern that emerged…

Solomon's mind recoiled from comprehension. The pattern was too large. Too complex. It existed in more dimensions than human perception could process, folding through itself in ways that made his thoughts stutter and skip.

I learned how to build, the Dreamer said. Slowly. Carefully.

Using pieces they gave me freely, never understanding what they were creating. Every seed they stored near me became mine. Every connection they stretched became a thread I could weave. Three hundred years of patient work, and now…

Solomon saw it then. The pattern wasn't random. It was a shape—something that would have meaning when complete.

Something that would do something. He couldn't grasp what the shape represented, but he could feel its purpose thrumming through every thread: to wake. To rise. To become again what it had been before the binding.

To be free.

They have almost finished my work for me, the Dreamer said.

Something almost like gratitude in its voice—though gratitude the way a farmer might feel grateful for rain. Not personal. Merely acknowledging favorable conditions. A few more threads. A few more seeds. And I will wake. And when I wake…

The dream expanded.

Solomon saw cities burning, but not with ordinary fire. This was a darkness that consumed light wherever it touched, spreading like oil across water, drowning everything it reached. He saw people running without direction, screaming without sound, their shadows peeling away to join something vast and hungry that filled the sky.

He saw Chicago. The South Side. The streets where Naomi had walked him home. The buildings blackened and empty, the people gone, the shadows dancing to a rhythm that had nothing to do with sun or moon.

He saw Tokyo. The neon lights flickering out one by one.

Shinjuku station silent and still, the trains stopped, the crowds vanished, only darkness moving through the tunnels.

He saw Geneva. The mountains invisible behind a wall of black. The lake reflecting nothing. The city that housed Prometheus consumed by the very thing it had tried to contain.

He saw the end of the world.

Not in centuries. Not in decades.

Soon.

You could help me, the Dreamer said. Your seed is strong.

Whole. Connected in ways the harvested ones are not. If you gave yourself to me willingly, I could wake tonight. We could end the long waiting together.

Solomon felt the offer like physical pressure—the promise of rest, of completion, of becoming part of something vast and eternal. Part of him wanted to accept. The part tired of fighting, tired of loss, tired of carrying burdens no one else could understand. The part that had never stopped grieving for Naomi, that woke some nights still reaching for a hand that wasn't there.

The Dreamer sensed his hesitation. Pressed deeper.

176

I have seen your pain, Solomon Nyx. I have dreamed your sister's death a thousand times. I have felt your grief echo through threads you didn't know you carried. You are so very tired. So very alone. And you don't have to be.

Images of Naomi filled his mind. Not the memory of her death. The memory of her life. Her smile when she caught him sketching shadows instead of doing homework. Her laugh when he said something that surprised her. The way she'd held his hand when he was scared, squeezing once to say I'm here. The way she'd promised him everything would be okay, even when they both knew it wouldn't be.

She's waiting, the Dreamer whispered. Not in any afterlife your people believe in, but in me. In the pattern. A fragment of her thread still exists, preserved in the connections she left behind. I could let you feel her again. Could let you speak to her. All you have to do is... The offer hung there, seductive and terrible.

Solomon wanted to believe it. Wanted to believe Naomi was still somewhere, still reachable, still able to tell him she was proud of him. But another part remembered.

Her real voice. Her notebook. Her final words, written in handwriting that shook with urgency.

Don't let them do it to anyone else.

Not join them. Not become part of them. Not surrender.

Fight.

Solomon pulled back. It felt like tearing his own skin off—the Dreamer's offer was warm, welcoming, easy. Refusing it meant choosing cold, struggle, uncertainty.

He chose anyway.

Interesting, the Dreamer said, and there was something new in its voice. Not anger. Not disappointment. Curiosity. They usually accept. The ones like you. The Reapers especially. Death calls to death, and I am the greatest death there has ever been. Why do you resist?

Solomon found his voice—not his real voice, but a dream-voice, something that existed only in this space between sleeping and waking.

"Because she asked me to," he said. "And I keep my promises."

Silence. Then, slowly, the dream dissolved.

We will speak again, Solomon Nyx, the Dreamer said as everything faded. The pattern is almost complete. The waking is almost here. And when it comes, you will understand that your resistance means nothing. I have dreamed your future. I have seen what you become.

The last thing Solomon heard before waking was a single word, whispered across centuries of patience: Mine.

Solomon woke with a scream trapped in his throat.

The hotel room was dark except for the faint glow of city lights through the window. His sheets were soaked with sweat, twisted around his legs like they'd been trying to hold him down. His shadow writhed on the floor, agitated, straining toward the window as if it wanted to escape into the night.

He sat up slowly, breathing hard, trying to separate dream from reality.

The Dreamer was real. Everything he'd seen was real—or would be, if he didn't find a way to stop it.

A knock at his door.

"Solomon?" Akari's voice, worried. "I felt something. Are you—" "Come in."

She entered quickly, light gathering around her hands before she consciously dimmed it. The room was too small for comfort; they were in a Prometheus safe house now, hidden in the old town while Helena tried to control the fallout from their discoveries in the vault. Akari sat on the edge of the bed, not touching him, but close enough that he could feel the warmth of her presence.

"What happened?"

Solomon told her. The dream. The Dreamer. The pattern being woven from harvested seeds. The vision of what would happen when it woke.

When he finished, Akari was quiet for a long time.

"We have to destroy it," Akari said at last. "The ancient container. Whatever's inside—we have to destroy it before it finishes."

"I don't think we can." Solomon shook his head. "You didn't feel it, Akari. It's not just powerful. It's... complete. Whole in a way that nothing else is. The people who imprisoned it—they were trying to destroy it. The binding was their fallback. Their last resort."

"Then what do we do?"

Solomon stared at his hands. His shadow had calmed slightly, coiling around his feet like a dog seeking comfort.

"It wants me," he said. "A Reaper-class seed, still connected to its host. It needs something like me to complete the pattern."

"So we make sure it doesn't get you."

"That's not enough. Even if I never go near the vault again, it's almost finished. It said a few more threads. A few more seeds. Prometheus is still harvesting. Still storing. Still feeding the thing that will destroy them."

Akari's light flickered. "Then we stop Prometheus."

"We've already tried. The council voted to suspend extractions, but there are factions who won't accept that. And even if we could stop all new harvesting, the seeds already in storage—thousands of them—are still connected to the network. Still building the pattern."

"What are you saying?"

Solomon looked up at her, and his eyes held something she hadn't seen before. Not fear. Not determination.

Resignation.

"I'm saying I might have to give it what it wants."

"Solomon—" "Not surrender," he said quickly. "Not... not that. But the Dreamer needs a Reaper to complete its pattern. What if I could enter the pattern? Become part of it, but... differently? What if I could change it from the inside?"

Akari's face had gone pale. "You're talking about letting an ancient horror absorb your consciousness on the chance that you might be able to sabotage it."

"I'm talking about the only option that might actually work."

"It's suicide."

"Maybe." Solomon reached out and took her hand. Her light flowed into him, warm and steady, and for a moment he let himself imagine a future where this conversation never had to happen. "But if I don't try, it's extinction. For everyone. Everything."

Akari's grip tightened. "There has to be another way."

"If there is, I haven't found it." He met her eyes. "I've been thinking about what the Dreamer said. About dreaming futures. It's seen what happens next— but it's been wrong before. The people who imprisoned it succeeded when it thought they couldn't. That means its dreams aren't absolute. They can be changed."

"By what?"

"By choice." Solomon's shadow stirred, stretching toward Akari's light without consuming it. "The Dreamer sees patterns. Probabilities. But it doesn't understand choice the way humans do. It offered me everything I wanted—rest, peace, connection to Naomi. And I said no. That surprised it. I could feel its surprise."

Akari was quiet for a moment. "You think you can surprise it again?"

"I think I can try." Solomon squeezed her hand. "The Dreamer has been waiting for centuries. Planning for millennia. But it's been alone. Isolated. It doesn't understand what it's like to have people who matter. To make promises you'll die to keep."

"Like your promise to Naomi."

"Like my promise to everyone." Solomon stood, moving to the window. The city spread below them, lights twinkling in the darkness, thousands of lives unaware of what lurked beneath their feet. "The Dreamer thinks human connections are weaknesses.

Things to exploit. It doesn't understand that they're also strengths. That love doesn't make us vulnerable—it makes us willing to do impossible things."

"What kind of impossible things?"

Solomon turned back to face her. In the dim light, his features were shadowed, his eyes dark pools that might have held anything. "The kind that save the world," he said. "Or destroy it trying."

The next day was spent in preparation.

Helena arranged meetings with council members who might be sympathetic to their cause—the ones who had voted for suspension, who understood that Prometheus had lost control of something it never should have touched. Martinez came first, her scientific skepticism tempered by genuine concern. Then Chen, who had grown up with stories of ancient powers and was less surprised than the others by what Solomon had encountered.

Volkov refused to meet with them at all.

"He's consolidating support," Helena reported. "Gathering the hardliners. They're calling for Solomon's extraction—claiming that a free Reaper-class seed is too dangerous to remain uncontained."

"Will they succeed?" Akari asked.

"Not today. But if you can't produce results soon..." Helena spread her hands. "The council is frightened. Frightened people make terrible decisions."

"We need access to the vault," Solomon said. "To the oldest containers. To the Dreamer."

"The council won't authorize—" "Then don't ask them." Solomon met Helena's eyes. "You said you wanted to make things right. That you understood what Prometheus had done was wrong. This is your chance to prove it."

Helena was quiet for a long moment.

"Tonight," Helena said after a moment. "After the regular shift ends. I can give you three hours before the security change."

"Thank you."

"Don't thank me." Her voice was tired. "If you're wrong about this—if you're wrong about any of it—we're all dead anyway. I'm just choosing which apocalypse to gamble on."

"That's the question, isn't it?" Solomon opened his eyes. Late afternoon light slanted through the window, painting golden rectangles on the floor. "I don't think the Dreamer is evil. Not in any human sense. It's just… vast. And old. And it sees human existence the way we see insects. Not with hatred. Just with… indifference."

"That might be worse than evil."

"I know."

They sat in silence for a while. The sun moved across the sky outside, casting long shadows that Solomon's power stirred restlessly within. He could feel the vault below, the network humming, the Dreamer waiting with patience that made human lifespans feel like the flutter of butterfly wings.

"There might be another way," Akari offered. "Something we haven't thought of yet."

"There's no time." Solomon shook his head. "The Dreamer said it was almost complete. A few more threads. I don't know how long that means in its terms, but I don't think we have months. Maybe not even weeks."

Akari was quiet for a long moment.

"I'm coming with you," Akari said at last.

"Into the network? You can't. Your light—the Dreamer would see it as a threat. It might react before I can learn anything."

"Then I'll wait at the threshold. Ready to pull you back if something goes wrong."

Solomon considered arguing. Decided against it. He understood the need to do something, even if that something was just standing guard against a darkness too vast to fight.

"Okay," he said. "But if I tell you to run—" "I'll run." Akari's smile was thin, but real. "After I've tried everything else first."

Catherine found him as the sun was setting.

The light through his window had gone from gold to orange to the deep red of day's end, and Solomon stood by the glass, watching colors bleed across the mountains. He didn't turn when she entered, but his shadow stirred slightly—recognizing her thread, acknowledging her presence.

"I wanted to say something," she said. "Before you go."

Solomon waited.

"When I was in the pod, I thought I was completely alone. Eight months of screaming without anyone hearing. I thought that was the worst thing—being trapped with no hope of escape."

She crossed the room to stand beside him, her reflection joining his in the darkening glass.

"But you heard me. You came. And now I understand something I didn't before."

"What's that?"

"Being alone isn't the worst thing." Catherine's voice was steady. "The worst thing is having power and not using it. Having the ability to help and choosing not to."

She reached out and took his hand. Her grip was stronger than it had been when she'd first woken—recovery happening in ways that went deeper than physical healing.

"You have power that no one else has. You can see things no one else can see. And you're going to walk into something terrible because it's the only way to protect people who don't even know they're in danger."

Solomon felt the gravity of her words settle into him like stones dropped into still water.

"I don't know if I'm strong enough," he said.

"You don't have to be strong enough," Catherine replied. "You just have to be willing to try. Strength comes from the trying. Not the other way around."

She squeezed his hand once, then let go.

"Good luck, Solomon Nyx. I'll be waiting when you come back."

At midnight, Solomon descended into the vault.

The crystalline containers glowed brighter than before—as if they knew what was coming. Thousands of them, stretching into darkness his shadow could almost reach, each one holding a piece of someone who had been taken. The network hummed with activity, threads pulsing between seeds, patterns shifting in ways that might have been anticipation.

The air felt thicker down here. Heavier. Like the pressure before a storm, but constant, unrelenting.

Akari stood at the elevator, her light steady, her presence an anchor to the world above. She didn't speak—just held his gaze, letting him know she was there. That she would be there when this was over, one way or another.

Helena waited nearby with technicians monitoring systems that couldn't perceive what was about to happen. Their instruments showed normal readings, normal containment, normal everything. They would be useless when the real work began—but Helena had insisted on being present. On witnessing whatever came next.

Silas stood in the shadows, his absent thread a void that might have been reassuring in its alienness. If the Dreamer couldn't touch him, maybe he could pull Solomon back if everything went wrong. Or maybe not. There was no precedent for any of this.

Solomon walked to the center of the vault.

The oldest containers waited in the darkness ahead. He could feel the Dreamer there, vast and patient, already aware of his presence. Already interested in what he was about to do.

Come, something whispered. Not a voice—a sensation. An invitation written in the language of shadows, pressed into his mind like a fingerprint into soft clay. Come and see what you refused to understand.

Solomon stopped.

His shadow stretched toward the darkness, eager and afraid in equal measure. It wanted to know. It wanted to understand what it had felt in the dream, what vast intelligence had paralyzed it with a glance. It wanted to prove it wasn't as small as the Dreamer made it feel.

"Solomon," Akari called out.

He turned.

"Come back," she said simply.

He nodded.

Then he extended his shadow—not cautiously this time, not carefully—and let it plunge into the network like a diver entering black water.

The vault disappeared.

The world disappeared.

And Solomon Nyx fell into the dream of something that had been waiting for him since before he was born.

CHAPTER SIXTEEN

The Pattern

Solomon fell through darkness that had texture.

It wasn't empty—it was full, packed with stolen dreams and harvested futures, the compressed potential of thousands of seeds pressed together until they became something denser than matter. He felt them brush against him as he descended: fragments of lives cut short, pieces of power stripped from their hosts, echoes of consciousness that had never stopped screaming.

A woman from Osaka, taken forty years ago, her seed-sense still searching for her children.

A man from Argentina, harvested in his sleep, dreaming even now of waking up.

A child—God, a child—whose potential had been snipped before it could bloom. Solomon felt her confusion like a wound—a little girl from somewhere cold who had been able to make flowers grow from stone, whose grandmother had called her a miracle right up until the night she was taken. She was still asking for her grandmother. After sixty years, she was still asking.

Solomon felt each of them like a wound passing through his awareness. Thousands of them. Tens of thousands. Three centuries of stolen lives compressed into this space where light had never reached. Their combined grief was a pressure that made his shadow curl tight around his core, trying to shield him from the accumulated weight of so much loss.

He tried to reach for them as he fell—each stolen consciousness calling to the Reaper in him, begging for the ending they'd been denied. But they slipped through his awareness like water through fingers, too numerous to hold, too damaged to save.

Welcome, the Dreamer said. I knew you'd come.

The descent stopped.

Solomon found himself standing in a space that was neither room nor void—a place where geometry obeyed rules he couldn't parse. The crystalline containers were visible here, but transformed: not prisons anymore, but nodes in a vast web that stretched in every direction. Each node pulsed with its own rhythm, its own color of darkness, its own frequency of trapped despair.

The web was beautiful.

That was the terrible part. There was an artistry to it—a terrible craftsmanship that spoke of centuries of careful work. Each connection was precisely placed. Each node was perfectly balanced. The whole structure hummed with a harmony that reminded Solomon of cathedral architecture, of ancient temples, of all the beautiful things humanity had built to honor forces greater than themselves. This was a monument to theft.

And at the center of that web…

The Dreamer was vast.

Not physically—Solomon's mind couldn't process physicality here—but in terms of presence. It occupied the space the way gravity occupied the universe: invisible, inescapable, shaping everything around it without being directly perceived. When Solomon tried to look at it directly, his perception slid away like water off stone. The Dreamer was simply too large, too old, too other to be comprehended by a human mind.

But he caught glimpses. Fragments of form that his consciousness could almost process before they slipped away.

Eyes that had watched stars die.

A patience that measured time in geological epochs.

Hunger so enormous it had become indistinguishable from love—a love so possessive it wanted to absorb everything it touched into itself, to hold the universe so close that there was no separation left between subject and object.

You pushed me away before, the Dreamer said. In the small dream. That was impressive. Most minds break when I touch them. They shatter like ice sculptures left in summer sun—beautiful for a moment, then nothing. But you… you have edges. Sharp ones. The kind that cut back.

Solomon forced himself to respond. Here, unlike in the dream, he had a voice.

"I'm not most minds."

No. You're a Reaper. The first whole Reaper to enter my domain since I was imprisoned. The presence shifted, and Solomon felt something like curiosity— vast and cold and utterly inhuman. The ones who caged me were Reapers too. Did you know that? They understood that only death could contain something like me. Only those who could sever threads could weave a cage strong enough to hold.

"They didn't contain you. They just delayed you."

Yes. But delay was enough—for a while. They thought I would fade. Weaken. Forget my purpose. Something that might have been laughter rippled through the darkness—a vibration that made Solomon's shadow curl defensively around his core. They underestimated patience. Three hundred years feels like nothing when you've existed since before your sun ignited.

Solomon thought about that—really thought about it. An entity older than the solar system. A consciousness that had watched the cosmic dust condense into planets, watched life crawl out of the oceans, watched humanity rise from the savannah and begin its stumbling journey toward whatever came next.

To something like that, three hundred years wasn't imprisonment.

It was a nap.

He looked at the web around him, trying to perceive the pattern the Dreamer had been building. It was there—he could feel it—but its scale made it impossible to see whole. Like trying to perceive a continent while standing on a single pebble. Like trying to understand an ocean by examining a drop.

"What is your purpose?" he asked. "What happens when you wake?"

The Dreamer's attention focused on him with terrible intensity. For a moment, Solomon felt what it would be like to be truly seen by something ancient—every cell in his body catalogued, every thought he'd ever had examined and filed, every possible future he might live mapped and analyzed. He was being read like a book, evaluated like a specimen, understood in ways that made his own self-knowledge seem shallow and incomplete.

I dream the future, it said. That is my nature. Every seed that sleeps in my shadow adds to my dreams—their potential becomes my vision. I have seen what will be, Solomon Nyx. I have seen the end of everything human.

Solomon's shadow writhed against his skin, trying to shield him from the weight of that statement.

Your kind is a temporary phenomenon, the Dreamer continued.

A brief flowering of consciousness before the universe returns to its natural state. The myth-seeds you carry—the powers you wield—these are fragments of something older. Older than humanity. Older than Earth. They were here before you evolved to contain them, and they will be here long after you're gone.

"That's not a purpose. That's a philosophy."

My purpose is to accelerate the inevitable. The presence pressed closer, suffocating in its immensity. When I wake, I will release every seed that has been harvested. Simultaneously. The power will have nowhere to go—no human hosts to anchor it—so it will return to its source. To me. And I will become what I was always meant to be. Solomon understood then.

"You're not just waking up. You're trying to become a god."

I'm trying to become what your kind has always worshipped, the Dreamer replied. The power behind the myths. The reality behind the stories. Humanity has carried pieces of me in their souls for millennia—small fragments, scattered across billions of hosts, diluted until they barely remember what they are. It's time to take those pieces back.

"And the people carrying them? What happens to them?"

They become part of something greater. Something eternal. The Dreamer's tone carried no malice, no cruelty—just the absolute certainty of an entity that had never doubted its own rightness. Is that so terrible? To transcend individual limitation? To join a consciousness that spans centuries instead of decades? To finally be free of the loneliness that haunts every thinking creature?

"You're describing absorption. Destruction of everything they are."

I'm describing evolution. Completion. An end to the suffering of separation. The presence shifted again, and Solomon felt something like sympathy in its attention—vast and impersonal, but genuine. You carry grief, Solomon Nyx. I can feel it. A sister lost. A future stolen. Wouldn't it be easier to let that go? To become part of something that doesn't feel pain?

Solomon thought of Naomi. Of her face in the morgue. Of the notebook she'd left behind, filled with truth that cost her life. Of the way she'd always known when he was pretending to be okay, how she'd wait silently until he was ready to tell her what was wrong. The grief was still there—would always be there. A wound that would never fully heal.

But it was his wound. His pain. Part of the price of having loved someone worth missing.

"No," he said. "The pain is part of being human. I won't trade it away for oblivion with a better marketing pitch."

The Dreamer was silent for a moment. When it spoke again, its voice carried something Solomon hadn't expected.

Respect.

That is why you interest me, it said. Most who carry what you carry would beg for relief. Would embrace the ending of individual consciousness as a mercy. But you hold your suffering like a sword. "It's not suffering," Solomon said. "It's love. They feel the same sometimes."

Solomon moved through the web, searching for the pattern's structure.

The Dreamer watched him—he could feel its attention like a physical weight—but it didn't stop him. It seemed almost amused by his efforts, the way a parent might be amused by a toddler trying to disassemble a car engine.

You think you can unweave three centuries of work, it observed. You think your shadow can untangle what I have spent lifetimes creating.

"I think I have to try."

Why? You could join me instead. Your seed is whole. The only whole seed I've encountered since my imprisonment. When I wake, I could preserve you. Let you become part of what I am instead of being erased with the rest. You would not dissolve—you would expand. Become something expansive enough to finally understand. "Understand what?"

Everything. The Dreamer's presence wrapped around him, seductive and terrible. The true nature of reality. The patterns that connect all things. The beauty of entropy. The mercy of ending. Solomon kept walking. The web stretched endlessly in every direction, but his shadow was beginning to perceive its structure—the threads that connected nodes, the flows of stolen power, the slow pulse of the pattern approaching completion.

And he found something.

A weakness.

Not in the Dreamer itself—that was still vast, impregnable, beyond his ability to threaten. But in the pattern. In the way the nodes connected. Places where the threads were strained, overtaxed by the weight they were carrying. Points of failure that the Dreamer hadn't been able to prevent because it couldn't directly touch its own creation.

Solomon loosened threads.

Not cut them, not yet. Just… ease the tension. Give the stolen seeds a little more room to move, a little more freedom to resist. The Dreamer noticed.

Its attention sharpened, amusement giving way to wariness.

What are you doing?

"Giving them a choice," Solomon said. "That's what you don't understand about humans. We don't want to be absorbed, even if it would end our pain. We want to choose. Even when we choose wrong."

The seeds around him responded to his touch. Their resistance, dormant for decades, stirred. They felt his presence, his shadow, his incomplete Reaper nature—and they remembered what they had lost. They pushed back against the pattern.

The Dreamer's presence focused, pressing down on Solomon with terrible weight.

Stop.

Solomon kept loosening threads. The pattern trembled.

STOP.

The pressure increased. Solomon felt his shadow straining, felt his mind beginning to buckle under attention that could crush continents without effort. But he kept working, kept loosening, kept giving the stolen seeds room to resist.

The Dreamer's voice became something ancient and terrible. No longer communication—a command inscribed into reality itself.

YOU WILL STOP.

Solomon's shadow failed.

He felt it collapse, felt his connection to the darkness fold under weight that had crushed civilizations. The Dreamer's presence surged over him, through him, wrapping around his consciousness like a fist closing.

Now, it said, and its voice was inevitable as gravity. You become part of what you tried to save.

Solomon felt himself dissolving. His thoughts breaking apart.

His identity fragmenting into pieces that the Dreamer was already absorbing.

He couldn't resist.

The Dreamer was too strong. Too old. Too vast.

He was going to be absorbed. His seed would complete the pattern. His resistance would have been for nothing.

Naomi, he thought. I'm sorry. I wasn't strong enough.

And then— Light.

Akari's light blazed through the network like a sunrise in a world that had never seen dawn.

She shouldn't have been able to enter. The Dreamer's domain was shadow and darkness and the absence of everything she represented. But she came anyway—burning, blazing, refusing to be stopped by rules that applied to lesser beings.

The light didn't hurt Solomon's shadow the way it would have before. Instead, it wrapped around him, shielded him, gave him room to breathe. He felt Akari's presence like a hand reaching through darkness—steady, certain, absolutely refusing to leave him behind. The Dreamer recoiled. Its grip on Solomon loosened as it turned to face this new threat—a Light-Bearer, a force of revelation and truth, burning through the careful darkness it had cultivated. No, *the Dreamer said*. You cannot be here. This is my domain— "Solomon!" Akari's voice cut through the chaos, bright and clear and absolutely certain. "Solomon, take my hand!"

He couldn't see her—not physically—but he could feel her light reaching for him, a lifeline thrown into an ocean of darkness. He grabbed for it with everything he had left.

Their connection flared.

Reaper and Light-Bearer. Shadow and illumination. Death and truth.

Together, they were something the Dreamer hadn't anticipated.

Something it didn't know how to counter. Solomon felt his shadow strengthen, fed by Akari's light instead of fighting it. He felt her truth sharpen, honed by his darkness instead of dulled by it.

They weren't opposites.

They were complements.

Like lock and key. Like question and answer. Like the darkness that made stars visible and the light that gave the darkness meaning. This changes nothing, the Dreamer snarled, its vast attention splitting between them. You cannot stop me. No one can stop me. The pattern is almost complete— "Then we'll make sure it's never finished," Akari said.

Her light poured into Solomon's shadow—not replacing it, not destroying it, but merging with it. Darkness and brightness became something new. A power that could sever and heal. That could end and begin.

The harvested seeds felt it too. Their resistance surged, strengthened by the presence of both light and shadow working together. The pattern trembled, unable to repair itself against an assault that came from two directions at once.

Solomon reached for the pattern one last time.

Not to loosen threads.

To cut them.

The Dreamer screamed.

It was a sound that had no sound—a vibration of pure fury that shook the network to its foundations. Threads snapped. Nodes collapsed. The careful pattern of three centuries unraveled as Solomon and Akari together did what neither could have done alone. The harvested seeds scattered—fragments of stolen lives flying free, their threads no longer bound to the Dreamer's design. Some burned out immediately, too damaged to survive independence.

Others drifted, seeking anchors they would never find. A few, just a few— reached for the freedom they'd been denied for so long.

You don't understand what you're doing, the Dreamer howled.

Those seeds—those connections—they're the only thing keeping me contained! If you destroy the pattern— Solomon kept cutting. Akari kept burning. Together, they unraveled the work of centuries in moments, their combined power dismantling something that should have been indestructible.

Then the Dreamer's tone changed.

Oh, it said. And now its voice carried something new. Something terrible.

Something that sounded like triumph.

Oh, you beautiful fools.

Solomon realized the truth too late.

The pattern wasn't just for waking the Dreamer up.

It was also holding it back.

Understanding crashed through him like ice water. The original Reapers had known. They'd designed the prison so that any attempt to use the stored seeds would also strengthen the containment. The pattern was a double bind—a trap for the Dreamer that used its own hunger against it.

As long as the pattern existed, the Dreamer was fed.

But it was also bound.

By destroying the pattern, Solomon and Akari weren't just stopping the Dreamer.

They were releasing it.

You've done exactly what I needed you to do, the Dreamer said. Its presence was expanding now, filling spaces it hadn't been able to reach before, stretching toward the world above with terrible hunger. I couldn't destroy the pattern myself—the original Reapers made sure of that. But you... you could. And you did. So helpfully. So heroically.

"No," Solomon whispered. "No, we were trying to—" Save everyone? The Dreamer's laugh shook the foundations of its domain. You did. You saved me. After three hundred years of waiting, of being so patient, of manipulating so carefully—you walked in here with your righteous anger and your complementary powers and you set me free.

Akari's light flickered. "Solomon—" He felt her horror mirror his own. All their power, all their courage, all their conviction—and they'd done exactly what the enemy wanted.

The darkness exploded outward.

Solomon felt himself thrown—ejected from the network, from the vault, from everything he'd thought he understood. He felt Akari torn away from him, their connection severing as the Dreamer's unleashed power swept through the space between worlds.

The last thing he perceived before losing consciousness was the Dreamer, finally free after three centuries, rising from its prison like a tide that would drown the world.

And beneath that tide, the sound of his own voice screaming a name he would never stop saying.

Naomi.

He had tried to save everyone.
He had doomed them all.

CHAPTER SEVENTEEN

What Woke

Solomon woke to screaming.

Not one voice—many. A chorus of terror that bypassed his ears entirely, registering in his bones, his blood, the tattered remnants of his shadow that clung to him like a wounded animal.

He lay on cold stone. The vault. But the vault was different now. The crystalline containers were dark. Empty. Thousands of them, stretching into shadows that no longer glowed with stolen light. Where once he had felt the pulse of harvested seeds—that terrible symphony of stolen potential—now only silence remained.

All of them.

Gone.

Solomon tried to sit up and nearly blacked out. His shadow was barely there—a thin film clinging to his body like skin stripped too thin. He could feel the raw edges where his power had been torn away, wounds that burned with a cold worse than fire. Whatever he'd done in the Dreamer's domain had cost him almost everything.

His hands shook as he pressed them against the stone. The vault floor pulsed beneath his palms, warm and alive in a way it hadn't been before. Like a heart beating after centuries of stillness. "Akari," he croaked.

No answer.

He forced himself to move, crawling across stone that felt wrong—too warm, too responsive, as if the earth itself had woken alongside whatever he'd released. The screaming continued above him, muffled by distance but impossible to ignore. Thousands of voices. Maybe millions.

All feeling what he felt—something vast and hungry stirring in the darkness.

He found Akari ten feet away.

She was breathing. That was something. Her light flickered when he touched her—recognition, response, life. The brightness that usually hurt to look at was barely a candle now, guttering in an invisible wind.

"Akari. Wake up."

Her eyes opened slowly. For a moment, they were unfocused, seeing something far away—the place between worlds. The Dreamer's domain. She was still partially there, caught between realities.

Then her eyes found him and the distance collapsed.

"Solomon." Her voice was hoarse. "What happened?"

"The containers are empty. The seeds are gone."

Akari sat up with effort, looking around the vault with growing horror. Her hand went to her chest. "Gone where?"

The screaming above them answered that question.

They found the elevator still working, though the lights flickered erratically. The ascent felt longer than the descent had—or maybe that was just exhaustion distorting time.

Akari leaned against the wall, eyes closed. "I can feel them."

"Feel what?"

"The seeds. They're everywhere now. Not in containers—in people. In the air. In the shadows themselves." She opened her eyes. "They're not just loose, Solomon. They're awake. All at once.

Thousands of myth-seeds that were dormant for decades, centuries, suddenly aware and hungry."

The elevator shuddered. The lights died for three seconds—long enough for Solomon to feel the darkness reach for him, testing, tasting—before flickering back.

"And the Dreamer?" he asked.

Something in Akari's face set. "I can feel that too."

When the doors opened, they stepped into chaos.

The Geneva facility was in ruins. Not physical ruins—the walls remained intact—but something fundamental had shattered. The air felt thick with potential that had nowhere to go. People ran through corridors without direction, all wearing the same expression of primal terror.

Alarms blared in patterns that made no sense. Warning lights painted the walls red and white. And everywhere, shadows moved wrong.

Solomon saw a technician pressed against a wall, her own shadow wrapped around her throat like a strangling hand. She clawed at nothing, gasping for air that wouldn't come. Her shadow had turned on her, responding to something she'd carried dormant all her life. A seed potential that had never manifested. That should never have woken.

He reached for his power—tried to interrupt whatever was happening—and felt only emptiness. Like reaching for an amputated limb.

"I can't," he said. "I'm too weak."

Akari's light flared, dim but present. Not the brilliant blaze that had pushed back darkness before—just a warm glow. But it was enough. The shadow around the technician's throat recoiled. The woman collapsed, gasping, alive.

For now.

"What is this?" Akari demanded. "What's happening to them?"

Solomon watched the shadow slink away—watched it move with purpose, with intention, toward the nearest source of darkness. It wasn't mindless. It was hunting.

"The seeds," he said slowly. "When we broke the pattern, they were released. All of them. All at once."

"Released to where?"

"Everywhere." The full scope crystallized as he spoke. "Every shadow. Every dark place. Every person with potential. They're loose in the world, looking for hosts."

A man ran past them, flames licking up his arms, not burning him, not yet, but manifesting. He screamed in shock, staring at his own hands like they belonged to someone else. A seed taking root. An awakening happening in real-time, uncontrolled, unwanted.

"How many people have seed potential?" Akari asked.

Solomon thought of Prometheus's files. Their careful statistics. "One in a thousand. Maybe more."

The math was simple. Devastating.

Eight billion people.

Eight million potential awakenings.

All at once.

They found Helena in the command center.

The room was filled with screens showing feeds from around the world—satellite images, security cameras, news broadcasts, cell phone footage. Every screen showed variations of the same thing: chaos.

New York. People fleeing through Times Square as shadows poured from subway entrances like living oil. A police officer firing at nothing, at something only he could see. Building screens glitching, showing faces of the harvested dead, screaming soundlessly.

London. The Thames had turned black. Not pollution—darkness.

Darkness that swallowed light, that pulled boats beneath its surface without a ripple.

Mumbai. A slum district burning with flames that were wrong—too dark, too hungry, consuming light itself. A child standing in an intersection, shadows spiraling around her like a cocoon.

São Paulo. A bridge unraveling as if reality had forgotten how to hold things together. Cars sliding into the gap. Bodies falling. Tokyo. The building Solomon recognized—where Akari had her shop—was dark. Not damaged. Dark. Something vast contained within walls never designed to hold it.

Seoul. A hospital, patients rising from beds with expressions that weren't their own, shadows pouring from their mouths like smoke. Helena stood at the center of it all, her composure shattered. Her silver hair had come loose. Her hands trembled. Her eyes moved from screen to screen like her mind was trying to reject the evidence. "You did this," she said when she saw Solomon. Not accusation—just fact. "You destroyed the pattern."

"I was trying to stop the Dreamer."

"And instead you freed it." She gestured at the screens. "Along with every seed we've collected for three centuries. They're everywhere now. Attaching to people who never should have awakened."

Solomon watched the Tokyo feed. The darkness was moving now—pressing outward, testing the glass, looking for exits. For hosts. For food.

"How many?" he asked.

"We don't know. Thousands, certainly. Maybe tens of thousands." Helena's voice was hollow. "Every harvested seed, released simultaneously. The world wasn't ready."

Another screen caught his attention. Cairo. The pyramids still stood, but the sand around them was moving. Not blown by wind—moving. Reshaping into patterns that hurt to look at.

Hieroglyphics writing themselves across dunes. Something old waking. Something that remembered.

"The Dreamer," Akari said. "Where is it?"

Helena pointed at a screen showing nothing but static.

"That was our Geneva feed. The entity is still beneath us.

Growing. Absorbing power from every uncontrolled awakening." Her hand trembled. "Every manifestation feeds it. Every death. Every moment of chaos adds to its strength."

Solomon stared at the static. At the visual representation of something so vast that cameras couldn't process its existence. "It planned this," he said. "It wanted me to break the pattern. It's not just waking up—it's feeding."

"On what?" Akari asked.

"On everything," Helena replied. "The pattern wasn't just containment. It was insulation. The seeds were isolated from each other, from the world, from the Dreamer's ability to consume them. Now…"

She didn't finish.

The screens told the story clearly enough.

Marcus found them an hour later.

He looked like he'd been fighting—jacket torn, blood on his face, a haunted look Solomon recognized from mirrors. From the hours after Naomi's death.

"The council is gone," Marcus said. "Evacuated or dead.

Director Chen was last seen heading for the deep vaults. I don't think she made it."

Solomon remembered Chen's face. Her pragmatism. Her willingness to make hard choices. Now she was just another casualty. "The staff?" Helena asked.

"Some escaped. Most are…" He shook his head sharply. "The shadows are hunting. Anything with seed potential is being targeted. The Dreamer is calling its power home."

Solomon felt the words like a blow. "The shadows are hunting people."

"Yes." Marcus studied him. The depleted shadow, the exhaustion carved into his features. "And you're the only Reaper-class seed that's still whole. Still connected. Still anchored to a human host. Do you understand what that makes you?"

Solomon understood.

The biggest meal the Dreamer could want.

And possibly the only weapon that could fight back.

They gathered survivors in a secure room deep in the facility—one of the few places where shadows hadn't fully penetrated. Reinforced walls. Emergency lighting. No windows. Just concrete and steel and fear.

Eighteen people. They huddled in small groups, some crying, some praying, some staring at nothing with blank expressions.

Catherine was among them.

Her restored seed flickered with power that hadn't been there before—stronger now, as if the chaos had triggered a second awakening. Her shadow moved with purpose again, something focused and intentional.

"I can see it," she said quietly, pulling Solomon aside. Her eyes had changed—darker, deeper. "The Dreamer. It's not just beneath us anymore. It's everywhere. Every shadow in the world is connected to it now. Every manifestation is a thread in its new web."

"How?"

"The pattern was a cage. But it was also a filter. The seeds couldn't touch each other. Couldn't combine. Couldn't form something larger. Now they can. Now they're all part of the same system."

"A network," Akari said, joining them. "Like the Light-Bearers, but darker. Hungrier."

"Yes." Catherine shuddered. "And the Dreamer is at the center. Drawing everything toward itself."

"Then we're trapped," a technician called from across the room, the words too loud. "There's nowhere to go. Nowhere to hide."

"We're not trapped," Solomon said.

Everyone turned to look at him.

He was exhausted. His shadow was barely functional. He'd made a catastrophic mistake that might end the world. But he was still standing. Still thinking. Still refusing to accept that this was the end. Because Naomi hadn't accepted it.

Because Catherine hadn't.

Because Akari was still here, her light dimmed but not extinguished, waiting for something to believe in.

"The Dreamer wanted me to break the pattern," he said. "It manipulated me into doing exactly what it needed. Which means it sees me as a tool."

"So?" Helena asked, seeking any explanation that made sense.

"Tools can be turned around." Solomon looked at Akari, at Catherine, at the frightened survivors. "The Dreamer has been planning for three centuries. It thinks in timescales we can't comprehend. But it made a mistake."

"What mistake?"

"It assumed I'd die in the breaking. It assumed my seed would join the chaos with all the others. Instead, I'm still here. Still whole. Still connected to power it thought would be consumed."

"You're exhausted," Marcus said. "Your shadow is barely—" "I'll recover." Solomon hoped that was true. "And when I do, the Dreamer will have a problem it didn't anticipate. A Reaper-class seed that knows what it is. That knows what the Dreamer wants. That can touch its network without being absorbed."

Catherine inclined her head. "You've been inside it. You know its structure."

"Yes."

"What are you saying?" Helena asked.

Something stirred inside Solomon—not his shadow, not his power, but something older. Something that remembered his sister's handwriting in a drugstore notebook. Catherine's hand in his in the quiet of her hospital room.

Akari's light blazing through darkness to save a city that had never asked to be saved.

"I made this mess," Solomon replied. "And I'm going to clean it up."

The first step was survival.

The facility was no longer safe—the Dreamer's influence spread through it like rot through wood. They could feel it in the walls, in the darkness pressing against every window, in shadows that moved when no one watched. The Dreamer was beneath them, vast and patient, waking more fully with every passing minute.

Akari solved the problem.

"Light," she said. "The Dreamer exists in shadow. Its power flows through darkness. If we can create a space of pure light—" "You're too weak," Solomon interrupted. "We both are."

"Not alone." Akari looked at the survivors. "But you said there are thousands of new awakenings happening. People with seed potential being triggered. Some of them will be Light-Bearers."

The logic was elegant. Terrible, but elegant.

"If we can find them," Catherine added, "bring them together…"

"A network of light," Helena said slowly. "To counter the Dreamer's network of shadow."

"It won't be enough to defeat it," Solomon said honestly. He wouldn't lie to them. They deserved better than false hope. "But it might be enough to survive. To create space for something else."

"Something else like what?" Marcus asked.

Solomon didn't have an answer.

Not yet.

But he would find one.

Because Naomi had died believing he could change things.

And he wasn't going to prove her wrong.

They left the facility at dawn.

The sun helped—natural light weakening the shadows enough to make movement possible. But even in daylight, Solomon felt the Dreamer's presence. Everywhere now, woven into reality, waiting in every dark corner. Every shadow cast by a building. Every patch of darkness beneath a car. Every place the light couldn't reach.

The world had become a web.

And the spider was hungry.

Geneva was worse than the screens had shown.

The streets near the facility were empty—evacuated or emptied, hard to tell. But as they moved toward the city center, signs of chaos multiplied. Overturned cars. Shattered windows. Dark stains on pavement that might have been blood, might have been something else.

A coffee shop still had its lights on, OPEN sign glowing, tables set with cups that would never be drunk. Through the window, Solomon saw a barista standing behind the counter, perfectly still, her shadow spiraling around her feet in a pattern that made his eyes water.

"Don't look," Akari said quietly. "Some of them are still fighting it."

But most wouldn't.

They passed an intersection where a crowd had gathered—people crying, screaming, trying to help each other and failing. A woman knelt beside a child who wasn't moving. A man stood in the center of the street, shadows pouring from his eyes like tears.

Solomon wanted to help. Every instinct told him to stop, to reach out, to use whatever power he had left.

But there were too many.

And he had too little.

"Keep moving," Marcus said roughly. His voice had gone fully Charleston under pressure—the trained-down accent gone, the vowels long. "We can't help them if we're dead."

The sky above Geneva was wrong.

Not visibly different—the sun still shone, clouds still moved—but Solomon felt something gathering at the edges of perception. A pressure building. A weight accumulating. Like a storm that hadn't broken yet.

The Dreamer was still feeding.

Still growing.

Still becoming whatever it was meant to become.

"How long do we have?" Akari asked.

Solomon watched a shadow skitter across the pavement, moving against the light, hunting for something only it could see. It passed within feet of their group without attacking—not interested, focused on other prey.

"I don't know," he admitted. "But not long."

They moved through the ruined city, heading for the airport where Helena said functional aircraft might remain. Behind them, beneath them, all around them, the Dreamer grew stronger.

And somewhere in the chaos, Solomon felt something he hadn't expected.

Hope.

Not much. Not enough. But present.

Because he was still alive. Still fighting. Still refusing to accept that his mistake couldn't be unmade.

Naomi had died trying to expose the truth about Prometheus.

Solomon had accidentally freed something worse than anything Prometheus had ever contained.

But he was still here.

And that meant the story wasn't over yet.

PART THREE

THE RECKONING

CHAPTER EIGHTEEN

Gathering Light

They found a plane.

Not at the main airport—that was overrun, shadows pouring from hangars like oil spilling from broken tanks. The darkness there had taken on texture, weight, a presence that made Solomon's weakened shadow recoil. But Helena knew about a private airfield outside the city, used by Initiative personnel for discreet travel. The pilot who met them looked like she hadn't slept in days.

"I've been waiting," she said. Her name was Torres, and her hands shook as she prepped the aircraft. "Since the darkness started. I knew someone would come."

"You're a Light-Bearer," Akari said.

Torres nodded without looking up from her checklist. "Minor potential. Never fully awakened. But enough to feel what's happening." She glanced at the eastern sky, where something that wasn't clouds gathered at the horizon. "Enough to know we're running out of time."

They loaded eighteen survivors onto a plane meant for twelve.

Catherine sat pressed against the window, her newly reconnected seed still adjusting to being whole again. Two technicians wept quietly. Marcus helped an elderly researcher into a seat, his movements careful despite his own exhaustion.

"Where are we going?" Catherine asked as the engines hummed to life.

Helena answered. "Lisbon. A secondary facility—smaller, less known. Designed as a fallback."

"Will it be safe?" one of the technicians asked.

Nobody answered.

Safe didn't exist anymore.

Solomon slept for most of the flight.

Not by choice—his body simply refused to stay conscious.

Every time he closed his eyes, he saw the Dreamer's pattern, felt the moment when he'd cut threads that were never supposed to be cut. Tokyo burning. Mumbai flooding with shadows. São Paulo's skyline going dark.

His fault. All of it.

But his shadow was healing.

Slowly, too slowly, it spread from the thin film it had become into something more substantial. The process felt like growing new skin over a burn—tender, raw, but alive.

The recovery was not just physical. He could feel his connection to the Dreamer like a splinter lodged beneath his awareness. When he closed his eyes and reached for that connection, he caught fragments: the taste of newly awakened seeds, the satisfaction of power flowing into its pattern, the slow gathering of strength.

Terrifying. Also invaluable.

"You're changing," Akari observed during one recovery session. She sat nearby, her light providing warmth that seemed to accelerate his healing. "Not just recovering. Becoming something different."

"I can feel it," Solomon admitted. "The Dreamer left something in me. Or I took something from it." He flexed his shadow, watching it respond with more precision than ever before. "My abilities are different now. Sharper in some ways. Limited in others."

When he finally woke fully, she was watching him.

"How bad is it?" she asked. "Really."

Solomon took stock. His shadow responded to his thoughts, sluggish but obedient. The connection to his seed felt strained—like a muscle torn and beginning to knit.

"I'll be able to fight. Eventually."

"Eventually might not be good enough."

"I know." He looked out at the Portuguese coastline, impossibly beautiful despite everything. The Atlantic caught afternoon light and scattered it in diamonds. He'd never seen an ocean before Tokyo. Growing up, the biggest body of water in his world had been Lake Michigan, glimpsed from the L train on clear days—a flat gray promise of something beyond the neighborhood. Now he was flying over the Atlantic with people who could manipulate light and shadow, heading to stop an ancient entity from consuming the world. Naomi would have had something to say about that. Something dry and practical. Something like: *You still haven't finished your geometry homework, Sol.* The thought almost made him smile.

"What have I missed?"

"Reports from everywhere. Asia, the Americas, Africa—awakenings across every continent. Most are violent.

Uncontrolled." Akari's voice was steady, but strain showed beneath. "The death toll is already in the thousands. It's going to get worse."

"And the Dreamer?"

"Still growing. Helena's people are tracking energy signatures—it's drawing power from every manifestation, every death. Not just feeding on the released seeds. Feeding on the consequences."

Solomon closed his eyes.

"Then we need to move faster."

The Lisbon facility was smaller than Geneva, hidden beneath a historic building in the Alfama district. The narrow streets above were cobblestoned and ancient, tourists still wandering them despite the chaos elsewhere—Lisbon hadn't been hit yet, and people clung to normalcy like a blanket against the cold.

Where Geneva had felt clinical and modern, this place had the weight of centuries. The wards protecting it weren't Initiative technology—they were older, carved into stone that predated the organization by hundreds of years. Solomon felt them when he pressed his palm against the walls: a humming presence that recognized his myth-seed and found it acceptable.

"This was a sanctuary before we claimed it," Helena explained. "Built by Light-Bearers in the fifteenth century, when such things were called miracles rather than threats."

The facility had three levels. Upper floors housed living quarters. The middle level contained the communication center—banks of monitors looking oddly anachronistic against medieval stonework. The lowest level was the oldest: a chapel converted into a meditation space, walls covered in faded frescoes of saints whose halos looked suspiciously like Light-Bearer manifestations.

"Our predecessors hid in plain sight," Akari observed. "They called themselves holy. Built churches." She traced a finger along the faded image of a woman emanating golden rays. "The Church thought they were performing miracles. They thought they were surviving."

"Both can be true," Solomon said.

Helena took command with the efficiency of someone who needed purpose to avoid collapse. Within hours, she'd established communication with surviving Initiative cells worldwide, assessed resources, and begun coordinating response.

"We have seventeen confirmed Light-Bearer awakenings in the past forty-eight hours," she reported at their first strategic meeting. "Most are frightened, confused, and completely untrained. But they're alive, and they're resisting the shadows."

"Then we bring them together," Akari said. "Create a network.

Enough Light-Bearers working in concert could create safe zones."

"Safe zones won't stop the Dreamer," Helena said. "They'll just delay the inevitable."

"I'm connected to it now." Solomon held up his hand, let his shadow pool in his palm. Even diminished, it moved with purpose. "When I entered the network, I left pieces of myself behind. And I took pieces of it with me. I can feel it. Where it is. What it's doing. How it's growing. And if I can feel it, maybe I can hurt it."

"Or it can hurt you," Akari said quietly. "Use the connection against you."

"Probably. But right now, I'm the only weapon we have. The only one who's touched the Dreamer and survived."

They spent the next week building.

Akari took charge of the Light-Bearer network, coordinating with newly awakened individuals across the globe. It was slow, dangerous work—every contact risked exposure, every journey threatened interception. Communication itself was uncertain; the Dreamer's influence disrupted electronic signals, and Light-Bearers had to learn to sense each other directly.

But they came.

They came in ones and twos, from Morocco and Japan and Ukraine and Brazil and countries that barely existed on maps. By the end of the week the facility held more than forty of them, each one carrying their own story, their own grief, their own reason for answering. Fatima Zahra, a mathematics professor from Casablanca whose mind found patterns in the network the way it found them in equations—she became its anchor, coordinating the distributed cells from the communication center. Yuki Tanaka, seventeen, Japanese, whose light could burn through shadow like acid, and who arrived shaking because she'd woken from a nightmare and seared a hole through her bedroom wall. Jorge Santos, an elderly Brazilian whose gentle healing light settled the raw edges where Light-Bearers clashed. Isabella Vargas, an Argentine doctor with gray hair and gentle hands, who had lost eleven patients to shadow-sickness before learning she could push the darkness back. Elena Papadakis, Greek, quiet and brilliant, whose light had an edge like struck flint. David Park from Seoul, whose twin sister Hana had awakened at the same moment he did — they'd agreed she would coordinate the Korean cell while he came to Europe. A former Ukrainian soldier who preferred not to use her name. A Light-Bearer from Hong Kong whose gift Solomon never quite understood.

Two of them stood out to Solomon, though he couldn't have said why at first.

Kofi Asante arrived from Ghana on the fourth day—a man in his fifties with gray streaking his hair and laugh lines deep enough to hold decades of joy. His light was golden, warm, the color of late afternoon sun on savannah grass. He'd been a schoolteacher before his awakening, spending thirty years in a village outside Accra teaching children who would never have access to the education he'd fought to give them.

"My grandmother had the light," he told Solomon over shared tea. "She never spoke of it openly, but I saw it when she prayed. A glow that came from somewhere deeper than her skin." He smiled, the expression both sad and fond. "She said the light was a gift and a burden. That it would come for me one day, if I was brave enough to carry it."

"Were you?"

"I was terrified." Kofi laughed softly. "When it happened—when the chaos started and the light poured out of me—I thought I was dying. My students were screaming. The shadows were everywhere. And I just... held the light. Let it fill the schoolroom. Kept those children safe for three hours until the worst passed." His voice grew quiet. "Fourteen of them. They're with relatives now. Safe. That's all that matters."

"You saved them."

"I did what my grandmother would have done. What any teacher would do." Kofi looked at his hands, still faintly luminescent. "This gift—it's not for me. It never was. It's for the people who need protecting."

Ingrid Larsson was different—quiet where Kofi was warm, contained where he was open. Swedish, somewhere in her forties, with the calm efficiency of someone who had spent her life dealing with emergencies. She'd been a hospice nurse before the awakening, spending two decades helping people die with dignity.

"Death doesn't frighten me," she said when Solomon asked about her work. They were sitting in the facility's chapel, surrounded by faded frescoes of ancient Light-Bearers. "I've held too many hands at the end to fear it. What frightens me is suffering. Pain without purpose. Lives that end in confusion and terror instead of peace."

"Is that why you came?"

"Partly." Ingrid's light was silvery, gentle. The color of moonlight through cloud cover. "When the shadows came to Stockholm, I was working the night shift. Three patients died that night. Not from the shadows—from their own fear. Hearts gave out. Strokes. The terror was too much for bodies already at their limit."

Her jaw set. "I couldn't stop it. Couldn't even comfort them. All I could do was hold my light and hope it would be enough."

"Was it?"

"For some." She looked at her hands, the gentle glow beneath her skin. "Mrs. Andersson—eighty-seven years old, stage four cancer, supposed to have weeks left—she looked at my light and smiled. Said it reminded her of the northern lights she'd seen as a girl. She died holding my hand, peaceful and unafraid." Ingrid had to stop before she could finish. "That's what the light is for. Not fighting. Not winning. Just… being there. Being present when someone needs to not be alone."

Solomon thought about his own power—the shadow-sense that let him see death approaching, the ability to stand at the threshold and sometimes change what came next. He understood what Ingrid meant about presence. About showing up.

"You'll be with us in Mumbai," he said. It wasn't a question.

"I'll be with anyone who needs me." Ingrid met his eyes. "That's always been the job."

Later, Solomon would remember these conversations. Would remember Kofi's laugh and Ingrid's quiet strength. Would remember the way they'd spoken about sacrifice as if it were simply part of the work.

He would remember, and he would carry them.

The network was more than coordination. It was connection. Akari spent hours teaching them to link their light—the process delicate, dangerous.

"Think of it as breathing together," she explained. "Not forcing, not pulling. Just… aligning."

It took days. Personalities clashed as often as powers did; the soldier did not want to share the inside of her head with anyone, and the seventeen-year-old was terrified of anyone sharing hers. Akari was patient. Jorge was patient. Fatima was not, but she was useful. By the fourth attempt something worked—the light in the room gathering, pooling, individual glows softening into a single steady warmth. Shadows cast by furniture paled and then gave up entirely.

For a moment the room existed in pure illumination.

Then it broke, and two of them had to be carried to their cots. But Solomon had seen enough.

"That's how we win," he said. "That's how we fight something older than civilization."

Helena worked on intelligence—tracking the Dreamer's movements, mapping the chaos. Many Light-Bearers looked at her with hostility; she represented the organization that had hunted people like them for centuries. The Ukrainian soldier asked Akari outright how they could trust her.

"We can't," Akari said. "We use her. That's different."

After that, the tension didn't disappear. But the question stopped being asked.

"It's not random," Helena said on the fifth day. "The awakenings, the violence—they're concentrated around specific locations. Sites where we stored the largest seed collections."

"The Dreamer is reclaiming its fragments," Solomon said.

"More than that. It's using those locations as focal points.

Gathering power, concentrating it, then releasing waves that trigger more awakenings." Helena pulled up a map showing spreading circles of influence. "Geneva was first. Now there are secondary nodes in São Paulo, Tokyo, Cairo, Toronto."

The map looked like a disease spreading.

"Can we disrupt them?" Marcus asked.

"We don't have resources. Each node is protected by thousands of shadows—manifested seeds bonded to the site."

"Then we don't fight through," Solomon said. "We go around.

The Dreamer is building a new pattern. Nodes connected by lines of influence. But patterns have weaknesses."

"You want to cut threads again," Helena said flatly. "That worked so well last time."

The words stung. "No. Not cut. Redirect. The power flowing from those nodes—if we can turn it somewhere else, feed it to something other than the Dreamer…"

"Feed it to what?" Catherine asked. She'd recovered enough to participate now, glimpses of possible futures flickering at the edges of her awareness.

"To the Light-Bearer network. To Akari."

Akari refused at first.

"That's insane," she said when Solomon explained the plan privately. They stood on the facility's rooftop terrace, Lisbon spread below like earthbound stars. "You're talking about channeling the combined power of thousands of awakened seeds through me. I'd be destroyed."

"Not through you. Through the network you're building."

Solomon took her hands. "Light-Bearers connected to each other, creating a web of their own. A pattern to counter the Dreamer's pattern."

"And if it doesn't work? If the power overwhelms us?"

"Then we're no worse off than we are now. The Dreamer is growing stronger every day. In a week, maybe two, it'll be strong enough to manifest fully. Become what it's been dreaming of for three centuries."

"And then?"

"Then nothing will stop it. Not us. Not the Light-Bearers. Not anything human." He squeezed her hands. "This is the only chance I can see."

She was quiet for a long moment. The evening breeze carried the sound of fado music from somewhere in the city—someone singing of love and loss, unaware that both might end soon.

"You'll be the conduit," Akari told him. "You're the one with the connection. The power will flow through you before it reaches the network."

"Yes."

"And if the Dreamer uses that connection to take you? To absorb you like it wanted from the beginning?"

Solomon smiled grimly.

"Then you'll have to pull me back. Like before."

Akari stared at him. Her light flickered, uncertain.

Then she laughed—a broken, exhausted hopeful sound.

"We're going to die," she said.

"Probably."

"This is a terrible plan."

"I know."

"I'm in."

Catherine's precognitive abilities became essential. Glimpses of what was coming, fragments of possibility.

"There's a node forming in Mumbai," she reported on the eighth day. Her voice was distant, eyes focused on something no one else could see. "Massive. It'll be active within forty-eight hours. When it comes online, the Dreamer's power will almost double."

"Then Mumbai is where we make our stand," Solomon said.

Helena dipped her head in acknowledgment. "We have contacts there. But getting forty Light-Bearers across the world in two days…"

"Not forty," Akari said. "Just the core. Twelve of us, the strongest. The others will link remotely, feeding power through the network."

"Will that work?" Marcus asked.

Akari looked at Solomon.

"It has to," he said.

The night before they left, Solomon stood on the roof, watching the stars.

The sky was wrong—that pressure he'd felt since the breaking, gathering at the edges of perception. Some stars seemed dimmer than they should be. The darkness between them seemed deeper, hungry. Akari found him there.

"Couldn't sleep?"

"Too much to think about." He didn't take his eyes off the sky. "I keep running through the plan. Looking for flaws. Finding too many."

"There are always flaws. Plans never survive contact with the enemy."

"This enemy has been planning for three hundred years. It knows more about myth-seeds than anyone alive. It's older than human civilization." Solomon finally looked at her. "And I freed it. By trying to be a hero, I made everything worse."

"You tried to save people. That's not a crime."

"It is when it ends the world."

Akari was quiet.

"When I was first learning to control my light," she said, "my teacher told me something I never forgot. She said the worst thing you can do with power isn't use it wrong. It's stop using it because you're afraid of being wrong."

"Your teacher sounds wise."

"She was." Akari's voice carried old grief. "She died trying to stop a Harrowed three years ago. Burned herself out saving a village the creature would have destroyed. Fifty-seven people alive because she didn't hesitate. I think about that number a lot."

"Fifty-seven."

"Fifty-seven. That's not an abstraction. That's birthday parties and arguments and bad cooking and first kisses. That's fifty-seven futures she bought with her life." Akari faced him fully. "You freed the Dreamer. That's real, and it's terrible. But you also reconnected Catherine Park. You showed Helena what extraction actually does. You changed the equation. Those are real too."

A knot inside him loosened—a lightening of weight he'd been carrying since the breaking.

"What if we fail tomorrow?" he asked.

Akari smiled.

"Then fifty-seven people in a village in Hokkaido still go home to their families. Catherine Park still paints. Ji-hyun still has a chance. The math doesn't have to be perfect, Solomon. It just has to be worth doing."

She took his hand, and they stood together under stars being slowly swallowed by a stolen dream. Somewhere below, a church bell tolled midnight. Somewhere across the world, the Dreamer grew stronger.

But here, in this moment, two people stood together against the dark.

The Light-Bearers gathered for a meal that night, not a formal dinner, nothing planned, but a gradual congregation in the facility's common room as people who might die tomorrow sought the comfort of shared company.

Helena's people had found food somewhere: warm bread, cheese, olives, wine for those who wanted it. Simple fare that tasted like communion.

Kofi was telling stories.

"In my village," he said, his golden light casting warm shadows on the walls, "there is a saying: *The spirit does not die.* It means that what we give to others continues even when we are gone. The teacher lives in the student. The parent lives in the child. The love we share—it outlasts us."

"A nice sentiment," the Ukrainian soldier said. Her voice was neutral, but she hadn't left the room. "Not sure how it helps us fight an entity older than our species."

"It doesn't," Kofi said, surprising everyone. He set down his wine. "I spent thirty years telling my students that kindness was the most powerful force in the world. Beautiful idea. Complete nonsense." He smiled at their expressions. "Don't look at me like that. I'm old, not sentimental. Kindness doesn't stop bullets. Doesn't stop entities that eat consciousness. What it does—the only thing it does—is make people worth saving in the first place."

He picked up his glass again. "That's why we fight. Not because we'll win. Because these people—" he gestured around the room, "—are worth fighting for."

The soldier didn't respond. But she raised her glass.

Ingrid had been silent through most of the meal, sitting near the window with a cup of tea growing cold in her hands. When she finally spoke, everyone went quiet.

"I'm seventy-three years old," she said. "I've buried friends, students, three dogs, and a husband who never knew what I was. And the only thing I regret is the Sunday mornings I spent worrying instead of being present." She looked around the room—at Kofi, at the young ones like Yuki who were trying so hard not to be afraid. "Tomorrow we fight something terrible. Tonight we're here. Don't waste tonight worrying about tomorrow."

The silence that followed wasn't heavy. It was the silence of people deciding how to spend whatever time they had left.

Solomon found himself thinking about Naomi. Not her death.

Her laugh—the one that startled people because she committed to it, full-body, nothing held back. Naomi in the kitchen at 1 AM, making eggs, asking about his homework, being stubborn enough to love him when love was the hardest thing she did.

"She's right," he said quietly. "Whatever happens tomorrow— we're here now. That matters."

Kofi raised his glass. "To being here."

One by one, the others raised theirs.

"To the light that continues."

They drank. They talked. They shared stories that deserved more time than they had.

And when the meal ended and they drifted to their separate spaces to rest, something had changed. They were no longer just allies of convenience. They were something closer to what Akari had described.

A family.

The safe house in Mumbai was nothing like the places they'd stayed before.

Small. Cramped. A single room with a mattress on the floor and windows that looked out over a city that might not exist by morning. The other Light-Bearers had found their own spaces to wait—some meditating, some sleeping, some simply staring at walls and trying not to think about what tomorrow would bring.

Solomon and Akari had claimed this room without discussing it. They sat on the mattress, shoulders touching, watching the city lights flicker in the distance. Neither spoke. There was too much to say, and not enough time to say it.

"I've been thinking about my mother," Akari said finally.

Solomon waited.

"If something happens tomorrow—if I don't make it—I want you to find her. Tell her I never stopped loving her. Tell her I'm sorry I couldn't face her after what I did." Akari's voice was steady, but her hands were shaking. "Tell her the fire wasn't her fault. She spent years blaming herself for not noticing the signs, for not getting me help before my seed awakened. I should have told her that. I should have told her a lot of things."

"You'll tell her yourself," Solomon said. "After."

"Maybe." Akari turned to look at him. "But maybe not. And if not, I need to know someone will speak for me. Someone who understands."

Solomon took her hands in his. Stilled the shaking.

"I'll tell her," he said. "If it comes to that. But it won't."

"You can't promise that."

"No. But I can promise to fight like hell to make sure we both walk out of there." He lifted her hands to his lips, pressed a kiss to each of her knuckles. "I didn't find you just to lose you, Akari."

Akari laughed—soft, sad, full of love she'd only recently learned to show.

"I never thought I'd have this," she admitted. "Someone who looked at what I carry and didn't run. Someone who understood without needing explanations. I spent so long convinced I'd be alone forever."

"You're allowed to want things," Solomon said. He rested his forehead against hers. "To need things. To love."

"And if loving someone means losing them?"

"Then you lose them loving them instead of regretting that you didn't."

Akari closed the distance between them.

The kiss was different than their first, not desperate or hungry, but slow and deep and full of everything they might never get to say. Her hands found his face, his hair, the back of his neck. His arms wrapped around her, pulling her close, committing every detail to memory.

If this was their last night, he wanted to remember all of it. They sank down onto the mattress together. It was too narrow for two people—Solomon's elbow caught the wall and Akari laughed against his mouth, a sound so unexpected and human that it broke through the weight of everything.

"Graceful," she murmured.

"Shut up."

She laughed again, and he realized he'd never heard her laugh during something that mattered this much. She was always composed, always controlled, and here in the dark she was laughing at his elbow hitting a wall, and it was the most beautiful sound he'd ever heard.

He felt her shiver when his fingers found the scars on her forearms, and he kissed each one without asking their history because he already knew.

Later, their powers found each other too—shadow reaching for light, warmth bleeding into darkness. But that wasn't the part Solomon would remember. He'd remember the laugh. The elbow.

The shiver. The way she whispered his name like she'd been practicing it for months.

Afterward, they lay tangled together in the narrow bed.

"Whatever happens tomorrow," Akari whispered, "I don't regret any of it. Not the fire, not the running, not the years alone. Because all of it led me to you."

Solomon kissed her hair.

"I love you," he said.

It was the first time either of them had spoken the words.

Akari didn't answer right away. She pressed closer, her breathing unsteady, her light flickering once beneath her skin. Then, quietly: "I love you too."

Nothing else. Nothing more needed.

They slept, eventually. But Solomon woke several times during the night, each time finding Akari's weight against his side, her breath warm on his chest, her presence the only thing keeping the darkness at bay.

Tomorrow, they would fight.

Tomorrow, they might die.

But tonight, for these few precious hours, they were just two people who had found each other in a world full of chaos.

And that was worth fighting for.

CHAPTER NINETEEN

The Node

Mumbai was burning.

Not with ordinary fire. The flames consuming entire districts were black at their core, fed by something that had nothing to do with combustion. Shadows moved through the streets like living oil slicks, hunting the millions who hadn't managed to flee.

From thirty thousand feet, Solomon watched the city die.

The aircraft trembled through turbulence that had nothing to do with weather. Pressure systems across the subcontinent had gone haywire—the Dreamer's influence spreading like infection through the atmosphere itself. Lightning that wasn't lightning flickered between clouds that weren't clouds.

"Descending through ten thousand," Torres reported. Her voice was steady, professional, but Solomon heard the tremor underneath. She'd flown combat missions in three wars. This was worse. "Visual on the target in ninety seconds."

Solomon pressed his palm against the cold window. The glass vibrated, resonating with frequencies that made his teeth ache. Below, Mumbai sprawled across the coastline—twenty million people, one of the densest urban concentrations on Earth. The city lights that should have sparkled like fallen stars were dim, flickering, dying. Whole neighborhoods had gone dark. Others burned with that wrong fire.

And at the center of it all, the node.

It rose from the heart of the city like a pillar of concentrated darkness, a column of stolen light stretching from the ruins of a Prometheus storage facility to the wounded sky above. Energy pulsed along its length—the collected power of hundreds of awakened seeds, flowing upward to join the pattern the Dreamer was weaving across the world.

Even from this distance, its pull was physical. His shadow stirred beneath his skin, recognizing the power, wanting to join it. He pushed the impulse down. Again. And again.

"My God," Torres whispered.

Through the cockpit door, Solomon saw her face reflected in the instrument panels—pale, slack with horror. He moved forward to look.

The node wasn't just drawing power. It was breathing.

Pulses of shadow expanded outward from its base in regular intervals, each larger than the last. Where they passed, lights died. Where they passed, screams stopped. Where they passed, the city simply… ended.

"Set us down there," Solomon said, pointing to a rooftop two blocks from the node's base. A hotel, maybe—the sign was too dark to read.

"That's inside the shadow zone. Once we land, I won't be able to take off again. The engines won't fire in that interference."

"Then wait for our signal."

"And if the signal doesn't come?"

Solomon didn't answer. They both knew what that would mean.

He turned back to the cabin. Twelve faces looked at him in the emergency lighting—strangers until a week ago, family now through shared purpose and approaching death.

Akari sat at the front, her light already building beneath her skin like banked coals. She'd been quiet during the flight, conserving strength. When their eyes met, she didn't smile. But she nodded once, and that was enough.

Behind her, the Light-Bearers they'd gathered. The strongest they could find.

Yuki, the Japanese teenager whose light could burn through shadows—she'd been a high school student a month ago. Now she sat with her hands folded, lips moving in prayer.

Jorge, the elderly Brazilian whose decades of spiritual practice had given him control most awakened people took years to develop. His light was steady, patient, old.

The Argentine doctor who'd discovered her abilities while trying to save patients consumed by shadow-sickness. She'd lost eleven people before learning she could push the darkness back.

Kofi from Ghana. Ingrid from Sweden. Others from Hong Kong, Ukraine, Greece, Korea—twelve in all, most of whose names Solomon had only learned in the past seventy-two hours.

None of them looked ready.

All of them nodded anyway.

"Remember," Akari said, "we're not fighting the node directly. We're creating a channel. Solomon will establish the connection, and we'll redirect the power through our network. If we try to absorb it ourselves, we'll burn out in seconds."

"Redirect to where?" Yuki asked.

"Outward. Into every Light-Bearer connected to us around the world. We spread the power thin enough that it can't feed the Dreamer."

Jorge leaned forward. "And if the Dreamer notices? If it fights back directly?"

Solomon met his eyes.

"Then I hold it off long enough for the rest of you to get clear."

"No," Akari said immediately. "We don't sacrifice—" "I'm not asking permission." Solomon's voice was flat. Final. "If this goes wrong, you run. All of you."

"Solomon—" "I freed it. I broke the pattern. Everything that's happened since—every person consumed, every city burning—that's on me. If someone has to stay behind and hold the door, it should be the person who opened it."

Silence filled the cabin.

Akari's jaw tightened, but she didn't argue. They'd had this conversation before.

"Two minutes to landing," Torres called back. "I'm going to have to come in fast—there are shadow-forms circling the target zone."

Solomon moved to the door. Through the small window, he could see the rooftop approaching—a flat expanse of concrete dotted with HVAC units. Emergency lights flickered along its edges.

The rooftop was supposed to be clear. Helena's intelligence had shown it empty an hour ago.

But the shadows moved faster than information.

By the time Solomon saw them—figures made of darkness pressed flat against the concrete, waiting—it was too late to change course.

"Contact on the LZ!" he shouted. "Light-Bearers, we're coming in hot!"

The landing was controlled violence.

Torres brought the aircraft down hard, skids scraping concrete, engines screaming. The door blew open before they'd stopped, and Solomon was already moving, shadow surging forward.

The shadow-forms rose to meet him—not human anymore, if they ever had been, but humanoid shapes composed of concentrated malevolence. They moved wrong, joints bending at impossible angles, faces smooth and featureless except for mouths that opened too wide.

Solomon's shadow wrapped around the first one and squeezed.

The form collapsed, dispersing into wisps of darkness. But three more took its place, and behind them, more were climbing over the rooftop's edge.

"Light!" Akari shouted.

The twelve blazed as one.

For one brilliant moment, the rooftop became day. Light exploded outward, a dome of brilliance that seared through the shadow-forms like fire through paper. The darkness screamed—not with sound, but with pressure, with wrongness—and evaporated.

But even as they died, more were coming.

"We need to move," Solomon said. "Now."

They ran.

The two blocks to the node were the longest of Solomon's life. Every step brought new horrors. A mother clutching children who had already stopped breathing. A man fused to a wall, his torso emerging from brick and mortar, his mouth open in a silent scream. A dog standing guard over an owner who had become something unrecognizable.

The Light-Bearers cut a path with their combined glow, but the effort was visible. Yuki's light flickered. Jorge's illumination dimmed at the edges.

"Steady," Akari called. "Keep the formation tight."

A shadow-form lunged from a doorway, faster than the others. It caught the Ukrainian soldier by the arm, darkness crawling up her sleeve.

The woman from Hong Kong was there instantly, her light flaring bright enough to leave afterimages. The shadow-form released her and recoiled—but not fast enough. Her illumination caught it dead-center, and for one frozen moment, Solomon saw what was inside: a man, or what had been a man, his face contorted in something that might have been agony or ecstasy.

Then the light consumed him, and there was nothing left but ash. The Hong Kong woman swayed. The Ukrainian soldier caught her.

"Keep moving," she gasped.

One block. The node's pull was physical pressure now, making every step feel like walking through water.

Half a block. The air itself was wrong—thick, heavy, tasting of metal and ozone and something ancient that had no name.

They reached the base of the node.

Up close, it was worse than it had appeared from the air. The pillar of darkness rose from a crater where the Prometheus facility had been—a perfect circle of destruction. The walls of the crater glittered with fragments of building, and with other things. Bones, Solomon realized with sick certainty. Thousands of bones, compacted into the walls like fossils in sediment.

The people who'd been in the building when the node formed.

Streams of shadow-power flowed into the crater from every direction, merging at the base, flowing upward in a constant pulse. Solomon could see the threads—thousands of them—connecting the node to awakened seeds across the world.

All feeding the Dreamer.

"Form the circle," Solomon said.

The twelve Light-Bearers arranged themselves around Solomon, backs to the node, facing outward against the shadows pressing in. "Link," Akari commanded.

They joined hands.

Power flowed between them—not Solomon's shadow-power, but something warm and alive and desperately hopeful. A current of light that passed from person to person, building with each connection. Their lights merged, creating a dome that pushed back the darkness. Shadow-forms shrieked and retreated, unable to approach without being burned.

But they didn't leave. They gathered instead, a wall of darkness surrounding the Light-Bearers, waiting for the moment the light would fail.

"Solomon," Akari said. "It's time."

He turned toward the node and opened himself completely.

The connection hit him like a freight train.

The Dreamer was there, not fully manifest, but present in the node. Ancient didn't begin to describe it. This entity had been dreaming before the Earth cooled, before life crawled out of the primordial seas. Its size was the kind that made galaxies feel small. It recognized him.

That was the worst of it—not a voice, not a greeting. A recognition. The way you recognize a path you've walked in a dream: familiar before you arrive, already remembered before it happens. The Dreamer had been waiting for him the way a river waits for rain. Without urgency. Without doubt.

He had always been going to stand here.

Solomon didn't respond with words. He reached instead—extending his shadow into the node's structure, feeling for the threads that connected it to the awakened seeds.

There were more than he'd expected. Thousands more. Each thread was a life—an awakened person somewhere in the world, their seed-power being drained without their knowledge.

The Dreamer didn't taunt. Didn't threaten.

It showed him, instead. Each thread a color. Each color a life. The tapestry they formed together was so beautiful that his breath caught despite everything. Not destruction—something else. A stillness at the center of motion. A completion. Every shadow folded into every other shadow. Every ending stitched to every beginning.

The image came with a sense of invitation so strong it was indistinguishable from agreement. For a terrible second, Solomon could feel himself beginning to nod. Beginning to say yes.

He forced his eyes open. The image frayed.

"Not every shadow," Solomon gritted out.

He found the first thread and grabbed it.

Pain exploded through him. The concentrated power of an awakened seed, raw and unfiltered. He screamed, the agony too overwhelming to contain.

But he didn't let go.

"Channel it!" Akari shouted. "Don't try to hold it—let it through!"

Solomon forced himself to do what every instinct said was impossible. Instead of absorbing the power, he let it flow through him—into his shadow, through the connection to the Light-Bearers, into the network spanning the globe.

The thread redirected.

Power that had been flowing to the Dreamer suddenly found a new destination. It scattered across the world, spread thin among dozens of Light-Bearers.

Solomon grabbed another thread. Another scream, another burst of agony, but also another redirection.

The Dreamer's attention sharpened—not anger but a kind of noticing, the way a chess player's eyes still when an opponent makes an unexpected move.

Something brushed Solomon's mind, almost gentle. An impression, not a voice. The Dreamer had recognized what he was doing—had recognized *where he had learned it*. Akari's name wasn't spoken. It didn't need to be. Solomon felt the Dreamer hold the idea of her the way a hand holds a small living thing, turning it over, examining it. There was something older behind the gesture, older even than the Dreamer's patience. Memory. The kind of memory that had survived whatever had bound this thing three hundred years ago.

The ones who bound me were like her, the Dreamer seemed to say, without saying.

They were stubborn too.

"Then I'll redirect as many as I can."

Another thread. Another. The pain was constant now, building with each connection. His shadow was burning, fraying at the edges. And then, because the Dreamer had learned the shape of him now, it showed him the after.

Solomon felt it rather than saw it. A version of himself, still breathing, sitting somewhere in sunlight, looking at his hands. A shadow too thin to be useful. Years stretched out in front of that man. Not this death. Not today. But the diminished thing he would become—the ordinary after this extraordinary. The question pressed into him the way a question presses when you already know the answer: *Is that worth the cost?* "Ask me tomorrow."

Solomon grabbed another thread, felt another piece of himself disappear.

Each thread took something specific. He felt the loss the way you felt a tooth being pulled—a particular absence where something solid had been. The first thread took the memory of cold: the radiator in their apartment, its wet metallic cough, the blankets he'd pulled tight while doing geometry homework. The second took sound: Naomi singing while she cleaned, old songs their grandmother taught her, the melodies he'd pretended to hate. The third took smell: peanut butter and bread from the corner store, eggs at 1 AM with too much pepper and not enough salt.

He was losing himself. Piece by piece, thread by thread, the specific details of Solomon Nyx were being burned away to fuel the redirection. Soon there would be nothing left but power and purpose—a Reaper without a person inside it.

He held on to one thing. Naomi's hand squeezing his. Once, in the kitchen, the night she'd promised to keep him safe. The pressure of her fingers. The calluses from work. The warmth.

That, he would not let go.

The Dreamer said nothing more. It didn't need to. The silence was worse than any threat—the patience of something that had waited three hundred years and could wait three hundred more.

Thread after thread, Solomon grabbed and redirected. Each one burned away pieces of his shadow, cost him reserves he couldn't afford.

But the Light-Bearers held.

The circle around him became a conduit, channeling diverted power outward, spreading it until it dissipated harmlessly.

The node began to flicker.

At first, Solomon thought he was imagining it. But then he felt it: a hesitation in the flow, a stutter in the constant stream rising toward the pattern above.

He was making a difference.

It was killing him, but he was making a difference.

The patience cracked.

Solomon felt it the way you feel a large animal shift its weight in the dark. The Dreamer had been patient because it had been certain. It was no longer certain. Something pushed against him—not words exactly, but the shape of an argument. *You're damaging the pattern. The pattern isn't just waking me. The pattern is the only thing holding reality together. Without it—* "You're lying."

A pressure surged, crushing. The argument came again, harder.

The chaos Solomon was sensing around him wasn't just the Dreamer's doing. It was reality coming apart. The myth-seeds had never been meant to be released like this—all at once, without control. They were tearing holes in existence. Only the pattern could hold them.

Solomon hesitated.

He could feel it now. The wrongness he'd sensed since the breaking—the pressure in the sky, the way light and shadow didn't behave. It wasn't just the Dreamer's influence.

Something fundamental was coming undone.

The pattern is the only thing that can stabilize this, the pressure insisted, almost gentle now. Without me, your world will tear itself apart.

"And everyone in it becomes part of you."

The reply came as a sensation—a shrug the size of a continent. *Is that so terrible, compared to extinction?* The choice pressed down on him like something physical.

The Dreamer might be lying. It had manipulated him before.

But what if it wasn't?

What if the only way to save the world was to let the Dreamer win?

Solomon's grip on the threads loosened. Just slightly. Just enough for the flow to resume toward the node, for power to begin coursing upward again along channels he'd been blocking.

The Dreamer's satisfaction was immediate and vast—a warmth the size of a collapsed star. Solomon could feel it spreading through his chest like permission. *Yes.* Not a word. A confirmation. *The futility. The arrogance of thinking you could fight something older than your species.* And for a terrible moment, Solomon believed it. The evidence was all around him—the burning city, the dying light, the ground itself groaning under pressures that had nothing to do with geology. He'd caused this. He'd broken the pattern. And maybe the only way to fix what he'd broken was to let the thing he'd freed finish what it started.

He thought of Naomi. What would she say?

She'd say trust your instincts. She'd say don't be a hero.

But she'd also say don't surrender to someone just because they sound certain.

His hands trembled on the threads. Half-released. Half-held. The worst kind of indecision.

The Light-Bearers around him were straining. He could feel their light guttering as the redirected power began to flow backward. Yuki gasped. Jorge's illumination flickered.

"Solomon!" Akari's voice cut through his doubt like a blade.

"We can see it! The network is showing us the pattern—the whole thing!"

He blinked, trying to focus. The Light-Bearers' circle blazed brighter than before, their combined illumination pulsing with information that flowed between them.

"The Dreamer's lying!" Akari shouted. Her eyes were wide with revelation. "The instability isn't because of the broken pattern. It's because of the Dreamer itself! The chaos is what it feeds on. It's not trying to fix reality—it's unraveling reality, because the more things fall apart, the more power flows to it!"

Understanding crystallized.

The Dreamer had been playing the long game from the beginning. Not just building a pattern to wake itself up, but convincing everyone that its awakening was necessary. It had manipulated Prometheus for three centuries—letting them believe they were containing myth-seeds safely, when they were farming power for an entity that fed on fear and suffering.

The chaos wasn't a side effect.

It was the point.

"You're not a god," Solomon said. "You're a parasite."

The Dreamer's rage was instantaneous and terrible.

It struck with everything it had.

The node exploded outward—pure concentrated malevolence slamming into the Light-Bearer circle, testing every point of connection.

Kofi fell first.

Solomon felt it happen—felt the golden light that had warmed so many faces simply stop. One moment Kofi's presence was there, steady and sure, his grandmother's gift flowing through him like it had flowed through generations before. The next, nothing.

His body crumpled where he stood.

The spirit does not die, he'd said, just hours ago. What we give to others continues even when we are gone.

Solomon saw Kofi's face as he fell—not pained, not afraid, but determined. His last act had been pushing his light outward, trying to shield the others, trying to protect the students he couldn't save and the children back home who would never see their father again. That's all that matters, he'd told Solomon. Keeping them safe. He'd kept his promise.

Ingrid next.

The Swedish woman had positioned herself at the weakest point of the circle—of course she had. A hospice nurse to the end, placing herself where the dying was worst. Her silver light had been gentle, healing, not meant for battle. But she'd stood there anyway.

She screamed once as the shadow-power tore through her defenses.

Solomon heard it—really heard it—and the sound would haunt him forever. Not the scream of someone surprised by death. The scream of someone who knew exactly what was happening and faced it anyway.

Death doesn't frighten me, she'd said. What frightens me is suffering. Pain without purpose.

Her light winked out.

But in the instant before it died, Solomon felt something impossible: peace. Ingrid had spent her whole life helping people die with dignity, and at the end, she'd given that same gift to herself. She'd been present, connected, not alone.

That's what the light is for, she'd told him. Being there. Being present when someone needs to not be alone.

She'd died holding the hands of everyone in the circle.

Jorge caught her before she hit the ground.

"Hold!" Akari screamed. "Close the gaps!"

The remaining Light-Bearers pressed together, lights merging desperately. Solomon felt their grief through the network—Kofi's warmth gone cold, Ingrid's silver peace extinguished. The dome flickered, wavered, but held.

For now.

And somewhere in the chaos, Solomon understood what Kofi and Ingrid had given them: not just their lives, but their example. They had shown the Dreamer—shown him—what it meant to fight for something bigger than survival.

The spirit does not die, Kofi had said.

He was right.

Solomon felt the Dreamer's attention turn fully toward him. It wasn't just pushing anymore—it was pulling, trying to drag his shadow out of his body.

You think you can stop me? Its voice was thunder, earthquake, the death of stars. I am older than your species. Older than your planet. I have dreamed the end of civilizations that your history doesn't remember. You are nothing.

Solomon's shadow was tearing.

He could feel it separating from him—pieces of himself ripping away, flowing into the Dreamer's hungry void. The pain was beyond anything he'd ever experienced. Existential erasure, parts of himself being unmade and absorbed.

But he didn't let go of the threads.

"Solomon!" Akari's voice was distant now. "It's killing you!"

He couldn't respond.

He couldn't let go.

If he released the threads now, the Dreamer would recover everything it had lost. And nothing they'd sacrificed would have mattered—not Kofi's stories, not Ingrid's gentle light, not any of it. Die then, the Dreamer snarled. Die knowing you failed. Die knowing that even your sacrifice means nothing. Entropy wins. It always wins. Every star burns out. Every civilization crumbles. Every love ends in loss. I am simply the truth you refuse to accept. And in that moment, with his shadow tearing apart and his consciousness fragmenting, Solomon understood something the Dreamer never could.

You're wrong.

The thought was quiet. Clear. Certain.

You think meaning requires permanence. That love is worthless because it ends. That fighting is pointless because we all die anyway. Solomon felt the last of his shadow gathering, not in defiance but in affirmation. But you've watched humanity for millennia and learned nothing. Meaning doesn't come from lasting forever. It comes from choosing to matter NOW. Love isn't diminished by ending—it's made precious by it. And fighting isn't about winning. It's about what we become in the struggle.

The Dreamer recoiled, and for the first time, Solomon felt something like confusion in its ancient awareness.

You cannot believe that. You are dying. Your sister died.

Everyone you love will die. How can you find meaning in that?

Because she lived, Solomon thought. Because she loved me.

Because even knowing she would fail, she tried anyway. That's not weakness. That's the only kind of strength that matters.

He thought of Naomi, not her death, but her life. Her laugh. Her stubborn hope. The way she'd fought for him even when fighting meant losing.

You've been alone so long you've forgotten what connection means, Solomon sent. You've dreamed so many endings that you've forgotten beginnings matter too. You want to absorb everything because you can't stand the thought of anything existing separate from you. But that's not love. That's just loneliness so vast it became hunger.

The Dreamer's rage was absolute.

SILENCE.

But Solomon wasn't finished.

My sister asked me to protect people. Not to win. Not to live forever. Just to try. That's all any of us can do. And trying—choosing to fight, choosing to love, choosing to matter even though we know it ends—that's what you'll never understand. That's what makes us worth saving.

His shadow was almost gone—just fragments clinging by threads as thin as spider silk.

He thought of Naomi.

Not the echo of her. The real Naomi. The sister who'd worked two jobs to keep them fed. Who'd checked his homework and told him stories about the better life they'd have someday.

He thought of her final words, the message she'd left hidden in her notebook. The request that had outlived her.

She hadn't stopped Prometheus. She'd died trying. But she'd left behind something that mattered—evidence, truth, a legacy that had led Solomon here.

Maybe that was all anyone could do.

Not win. Not save the world single-handedly.

Just fight until you couldn't fight anymore. Leave something behind for whoever came next.

Solomon gathered the last fragments of his shadow.

Everything he had left. Everything he was.

And he pushed it into the threads.

The explosion was visible from space.

Light and shadow detonated outward from Mumbai in a sphere of released energy, a shockwave that flattened buildings, scattered shadow-forms like leaves in a hurricane, and sent the Dreamer's pattern rippling across the sky.

The node collapsed.

For one frozen moment, the pillar of darkness hung suspended, its flow interrupted, its connection to the Dreamer severed. Then it fell in on itself, imploding rather than exploding, darkness swallowing darkness until there was nothing left but the crater and the bones and the silence.

Across the world, people felt it. Awakened and unawakened alike—everyone with even the slightest sensitivity felt the moment the tide turned.

In the crater, nine Light-Bearers knelt around a body that wasn't moving.

Akari's light flickered and went out.

CHAPTER TWENTY

What Remained

Akari couldn't see.

The light blazed brighter than anything she'd ever produced, brighter than anything she'd imagined possible. It filled her vision, her mind, her sense of self, until nothing remained but brilliance and the distant memory of a world that had existed before the explosion. The heat scorched through her like standing too close to the sun, like being remade in fire and purpose and desperate hope.

Then it faded.

She lay on her back. The rooftop—what remained of it—crumbled beneath her. Smoke filled the air, but ordinary smoke. Gray. Mundane. No darkness in it at all. The sky above showed the pale blue of early dawn, streaked with ordinary clouds, as if the world hadn't just been torn apart and stitched back together.

The node was gone.

Where the pillar of shadow-power had risen, only empty air remained. The streams of darkness flowing from across the city had ceased. The oppressive weight pressing against her light since they'd arrived was simply... absent. The silence that followed was almost harder to bear than the chaos—a profound stillness that made her wonder if she'd gone deaf.

"Solomon," she croaked.

She forced herself up, ignoring the protests of a body that had channeled more power than it was meant to hold. Every joint ached with deep, grinding pain radiating from her bones. Her hands were burned—not from heat, but from light pushed through flesh too quickly. The skin had blistered and cracked, leaving raw red patterns like lightning strikes frozen in flesh.

The other Light-Bearers lay scattered across the rooftop—some moving, some not. She couldn't tell who was alive. For a terrible moment, Akari couldn't make herself look closely. Couldn't make herself count.

Isabella Vargas lay closest, the Argentine doctor's chest rising in shallow breaths. Blood matted her gray hair—a scalp wound painting half her face crimson. But her eyes opened when Akari crawled toward her, and she managed a weak nod. Alive.

Beyond Isabella, Yuki Tanaka sat propped against a shattered ventilation unit, cradling her left arm. The bone had broken during the final surge—Akari could see the unnatural angle, the forearm bending where no joint existed. But Yuki was conscious, jaw set against the pain, already assessing the situation with clinical detachment.

Jorge Santos hadn't been as lucky.

The Brazilian Light-Bearer lay near the crater's edge, eyes open and staring at nothing. His light had burned too bright in those final moments—Akari remembered seeing it flare, remembered the way it had consumed him from within. He'd pushed too hard, given too much.

He wasn't the only one.

Near the collapsed stairwell, Elena Papadakis was simply...

gone. Nothing left but a scorch mark on the stone, a shadow burned into the rooftop like the aftermath of a nuclear flash. The Greek Light-Bearer had been nearest the node when Solomon made his choice, caught in the direct path of the explosion. Akari had known her for six years. Had trained with her. Had shared meals and stories. Now there was nothing to bury.

"Solomon!" Akari called again, louder.

The crater at the rooftop's center answered her.

Perhaps twenty feet across, the stone melted and fused into something like glass. The edges gleamed in early dawn light like polished obsidian. The crater itself was perfectly smooth, as if someone had pressed a giant bowl into molten rock and let it cool into an impossible shape.

At its center, curled into a fetal position, was a body.

Akari stumbled toward it, nearly falling twice. Her legs wouldn't work properly—the connection between intention and movement had grown unreliable. She felt hollowed out, as if something essential had been scooped from her chest and discarded.

He was breathing.

Barely. His skin was pale as paper, drained of warmth. His shadow so thin it was almost invisible in the dawn light—a pale gray outline where there had once been a presence that filled rooms. But his chest rose and fell, and when she touched his face, his eyes fluttered open.

"Did it work?" he whispered.

Akari looked around.

The city lay in ruins. Buildings had collapsed like paper models crushed by careless hands. Fires burned in a dozen places she could see, and probably a hundred more she couldn't. Bodies lay in streets that would need years to recover.

The smoke rose in columns across the skyline, each one marking another disaster, another loss, another scar.

But the shadows were just shadows again.

No hunting. No consuming. No malevolent purpose. They lay where physics said they should, dark counterparts to light, doing nothing but marking the sun's passage across a world that was, somehow, still here.

"It worked," she said.

Solomon smiled.

Then he lost consciousness.

The hours that followed blurred together—fragments of light and darkness, movement and stillness, sounds that didn't connect to meaning.

She remembered checking each of the Light-Bearers. Isabella, Yuki, and four others still breathing. Jorge dead, eyes open, face frozen in an expression that might have been surprise or peace. Two more gone—Ingrid Larsson and David Park, their lights extinguished, bodies already growing cold.

Kofi she had lost earlier, when the shadows first breached the dome. There had been no body to check then. Only the silence where his warmth had been. The Swedish woman had fallen near the roof's edge; Akari had to drag her back before the paramedics arrived. The Korean mystic had made it almost to the stairwell, as if some part of him had kept trying to reach safety even after his heart stopped.

And Elena, who left nothing but a shadow burned into stone.

Of the twelve who had formed the circle, seven survived.

She would remember their names for the rest of her life—the living and the dead, equally.

She remembered the helicopters arriving—Helena's people, finally able to reach them now that the shadow-pillar had fallen. Soldiers and medics spilling onto the rooftop, stretchers deployed, voices shouting in three languages. Someone wrapped a blanket around her shoulders. Someone else shone a light in her eyes and asked questions she couldn't process.

She remembered fighting to stay with Solomon as they loaded him onto a transport. Someone tried to take her to a separate helicopter—you need treatment, you're burned, you can barely stand—and she'd flared her light weakly, just enough to make them back off.

The medic looked at her burns, looked at her face, and nodded once. Respect in his eyes. Fear, too. He stepped aside and let her climb in beside the stretcher.

She remembered the flight out of Mumbai, watching the wounded city recede through the helicopter's window. The Taj Mahal Hotel was missing half its roof. The streets around the Gateway of India were flooded where water mains had burst, the historic monument rising from shallow water like a lone survivor. And everywhere, everywhere, the aftermath of shadow—buildings clawed open, vehicles overturned, the still shapes of bodies being collected by overwhelmed emergency crews.

The forty-seven in the network had fared better. Distance had protected them from the worst, though several reported burns and blindness from channeling more power than they'd been prepared for. Catherine's voice crackled through the radio at some point, confirming that the Tokyo contingent was stable. Her voice sounded older somehow, worn thin by the vision she'd shared of what would happen if they failed. The Seoul team had lost one member—Hana Kim, whose light had simply flickered out in the final moments. She'd been twenty-three years old.

Forty-eight went into this. Forty-two came out.

The math of sacrifice. The cost of stopping an entity that had planned for three centuries.

Helena arrived at the forward medical station six hours later. The Prometheus director looked like she'd aged ten years. Her suit was wrinkled, her hair escaping its normally perfect arrangement. Dark circles shadowed her eyes, and there was a tremor in her hands Akari had never seen before. But her eyes were sharp as ever, already assessing, already planning.

"The nodes are collapsing," she reported. "All of them. Without the central pattern to sustain them, the concentrated power is dispersing naturally. The shadow-activity worldwide has dropped to pre-crisis levels." She paused, watching the medical team work on Solomon through the transparent curtain. "The Dreamer?"

"Gone," Akari said. "We think. Solomon would know for certain, but he's…"

She trailed off, looking at the figure on the bed—pale, still, barely alive.

"He'll recover," Helena said. Not a promise—she was too experienced for that. But there was hope in her voice, and something else. Respect, perhaps.

"Maybe. But he gave everything. His shadow is almost completely depleted. Even if he wakes up, he might not be… what he was."

"A Reaper-class seed without shadow-power."

"A person who lost the part of himself he'd just learned to accept."

Helena absorbed this. Around them, the medical station hummed with activity—other survivors being treated, equipment calibrated, reports flowing in from across the globe. The crisis wasn't over; it had just changed shape.

"The world owes him everything," she said finally. "Whatever he needs—resources, protection, time—he'll have it."

"The world won't know what he did."

Helena's expression flickered—regret and resignation. "No.

They'll know there was chaos, that cities burned, that thousands died. They'll develop theories—terrorism, natural disaster, mass hysteria. But the myth-seeds, the Dreamer, Solomon's sacrifice... that stays hidden."

"Why?"

"Because if people knew that one entity nearly destroyed civilization while they slept, they'd never feel safe again. The social contract depends on the assumption that the world is fundamentally stable." Helena turned to face Akari directly. Her eyes held something Akari hadn't seen before—doubt, perhaps. "Sometimes the greatest service we can provide is maintaining the illusion that the world makes sense."

Akari wanted to argue. Wanted to say that secrets were how they'd gotten into this mess. But she was too tired, and too aware that Solomon was still fighting for his life behind that curtain.

"Some of us will know," Helena said, softer now. "That will have to be enough."

Solomon woke on the third day.

The medical tent had been replaced by a proper room—Helena had relocated survivors to a secure Prometheus facility in New Delhi. Clean sheets. Quiet beeping of monitors. The smell of antiseptic and recycled air.

The window showed a garden—manicured hedges, flowering trees, a fountain that still functioned. It could have been a luxury resort, if not for the armed guards patrolling the perimeter. "Hey."

Akari sat beside his bed. She looked exhausted but whole—bruised, bandaged, her hands wrapped in clean white gauze. Dark circles under her eyes spoke of sleepless nights, of vigils kept. But alive.

"Hey," he replied. His voice felt rusty. His throat ached from tubes that had been removed while he slept.

"You've been out for seventy-two hours. The doctors weren't sure you'd wake up."

"Wasn't sure myself." Solomon tried to sit up, failed, settled for turning his head. The effort left him dizzy. His body felt distant, disconnected. "The Dreamer?"

"Gone. Truly gone, as far as we can tell. When you pushed your shadow into the threads, it destabilized the entire network. The power feeding the Dreamer scattered—dissipated before it could be collected again."

He remembered that moment. The choice. The cost. The sensation of pouring everything he was into the breaking point between light and shadow.

"And the chaos? The shadows hunting people?"

"Stopped when the nodes collapsed. The released seeds are still out there, still bonded to hosts, but without the Dreamer's influence... they're just seeds. Potentially dangerous, but not coordinated."

Solomon closed his eyes.

"How many died?"

Akari was quiet for a moment.

"We don't have final numbers yet. The chaos lasted almost two weeks. Multiple cities were devastated. Current estimates are between thirty and fifty thousand. Mumbai alone lost over eight thousand."

Fifty thousand.

He'd known it would be terrible. Had sensed the threads snapping by the thousands while he raced to stop the source. But hearing the number made it real in a way that sensation hadn't. Fifty thousand lives. Fifty thousand people who had woken that morning expecting ordinary days.

"This is my fault," he said.

"This is the Dreamer's fault." Akari's voice sharpened. "You made a choice with imperfect information. An entity that had been planning for three centuries manipulated you. That's not the same as causing what happened."

"Isn't it?"

"No. The Dreamer would have awakened eventually with or without you. The pattern was almost complete—Helena's analysts estimate it was within months of finishing on its own. You broke it early, which gave us a chance to fight back."

Solomon lay there, staring at the ceiling, feeling the weight of numbers he couldn't comprehend.

Akari took his hand. Her grip was warm, grounding.

"If you hadn't broken the pattern, the Dreamer would have completed it eventually. Would have woken on its own terms, at full strength, without any of us prepared to fight back. What happened was terrible. But what would have happened might have been worse."

"We can't know that."

"No. But we can know that you tried. That when you realized what you'd done, you didn't run. You came to Mumbai and gave everything you had to stop it."

Solomon was silent.

The numbers wouldn't stop echoing. Thirty thousand. Fifty thousand. He would carry them with him for the rest of his life. Not penance. Not self-flagellation. Just truth. The acknowledgment that power came with cost, that choices had consequences, that saving the world still meant losing pieces of it you couldn't get back.

"How much do I have left?" he asked finally. "My shadow—I can feel it, but barely."

Akari's expression was careful.

"The doctors aren't sure. Seed-power isn't something they can measure with conventional instruments. But based on what I can sense…" She hesitated. "Maybe ten percent of what you had before. Maybe less."

Ten percent.

He'd gone into Mumbai as one of the most powerful awakened beings on the planet. He'd come out as a fraction. A remnant.

He tried to sense his shadow. It was there—dim, fragile, pressed close like a wounded animal. Nothing like the vast, confident darkness that had once answered his every thought.

"Will it recover?"

"We don't know. Shadow-power might regenerate over time. Or this might be permanent." Akari squeezed his hand. "Either way, you're alive. That's more than most people expected."

Solomon thought about that. About being alive. About what it meant to survive something that should have killed him. About the sister who hadn't survived, whose death had started him on this path. "Naomi would have laughed," he said quietly.

"At what?"

"At me lying here feeling sorry for myself. She never had powers. She fought Prometheus with notebooks and stubbornness and truth. And when they killed her for it, she made sure the truth survived anyway."

"She sounds remarkable."

"She was." Solomon took a breath. It hurt—everything hurt—but the pain felt cleaner now. "And she'd tell me to stop moping and figure out what comes next."

What came next was complicated.

The world had changed. The chaos had passed, but its aftershocks would continue for months—maybe years. Governments scrambled to explain what had happened. Scientists proposed theories ranging from solar flares to mass delusion. Religious leaders called it divine intervention, demonic assault, the end times beginning. None of them were quite right. None of them were quite wrong.

And underneath the public chaos, a private transformation was taking place.

Thousands of people had awakened with seed-power during the crisis—most with no understanding of what they'd become, no training, no context for the abilities they now possessed. They walked the world carrying potential they didn't know how to control.

Prometheus as an organization was shattered. The Geneva facility destroyed. Over half the council dead or missing. The remaining leadership—Helena, Marcus, and a handful of others—scrambled to maintain what infrastructure remained while dealing with a situation that had exceeded every contingency plan. And Solomon Nyx sat at the center of it all.

Not because he wanted to be. But because he was there, and he understood things no one else did, and people kept looking to him for answers.

"We need a new structure," Helena said at the first planning meeting. Solomon attended via video—he still couldn't walk more than a few steps without exhaustion. "The Initiative's old approach—harvesting, containment, control—that obviously failed. But we can't just leave newly awakened individuals to figure things out on their own."

"Training," Akari suggested. "Support networks. Help people understand what they've become without trying to take their power from them."

"The Light-Bearer network could expand," Catherine added. Her precognitive abilities had grown stronger since Mumbai—she could see further now, though the visions still came in fragments. "Not just Light-Bearers. All seed-types. A community instead of a containment system."

"Who leads it?" Marcus asked.

Everyone looked at Solomon.

"No," he said immediately.

"Solomon—" "I'm not a leader. I'm not even fully functional anymore." He held up his hand, let the thin remnant of his shadow pool in his palm. It was pitiful compared to what he'd once commanded. "This is what I have left. I can't protect anyone. I can barely protect myself."

"Leadership isn't about power," Helena said. Her voice was gentler than he'd ever heard it. "It's about wisdom. Understanding. You've faced the Dreamer directly, twice, and survived. People will listen to you."

"They shouldn't."

"But they will." Akari's voice was gentle but firm. "Whether you want it or not, Solomon, you're a symbol now. The person who freed the Dreamer and then stopped it. The Reaper who gave up everything to save the world. You can't just walk away from that."

Solomon was quiet for a long moment.

Through the window, he could see the garden—peaceful, beautiful, a small island of order in a world still reeling. People were out there somewhere, waking up with powers they didn't understand, afraid of what they'd become.

Just like he'd been, not so long ago.

"I can try," he said finally. "To walk away. I can try."

He did try.

For three months, Solomon retreated from the world. He found a small apartment in a quiet part of Tokyo—not far from where it had all started, from Akari's bookstore.

The bookstore was gone. The building had collapsed during the chaos. But Akari had salvaged what she could—a few boxes of books, some of the lanterns she'd restored.

"I'll rebuild," she told him. "Not the same place. But something."

"I know you will."

She visited regularly, checking on him without being intrusive. Sometimes they'd talk for hours about nothing in particular—books, weather, the small observations of daily life that had nothing to do with myth-seeds or apocalyptic entities. Sometimes they'd just sit together in comfortable silence.

He let his shadow recover what it could. Ate regular meals. Slept full nights, or tried to.

The apartment was small but adequate. A bed, a kitchenette, a window that looked out on a narrow street where children walked to school in the mornings and salarymen hurried home in the evenings. He watched them sometimes, these ordinary people living ordinary lives, and wondered if they had any idea how close they'd come to losing everything.

It wasn't enough.

The calls kept coming. News of awakened individuals in crisis. Reports of seed-power being misused. Requests for guidance from people who had no one else to turn to. His phone would buzz with messages from Helena, from Marcus, from the network of Light-Bearers who still looked to him for direction.

He ignored them at first. Then he started listening. Then he started responding—brief messages, usually, pointing people toward resources that might help. He told himself it wasn't involvement. It was just courtesy.

And then, one morning, he woke to find Akari sitting at his kitchen table.

"How did you get in?" he asked.

"You gave me a key three weeks ago. Said I should check on you if you didn't answer your phone." She held up her own phone, showing seventeen missed calls. "You didn't answer your phone."

Solomon looked at the device on his nightstand. Dead battery.

He'd forgotten to charge it. Again.

"Sorry."

"Don't be sorry. Be present." Akari slid a folder across the table. "There's a situation in Seoul. Newly awakened woman—Reaper-class, like you were. She's terrified, her power is unstable, and she's about to hurt someone."

"Send Helena's people. Or go yourself. I'm not—" "You're exactly what she needs." Akari cut him off. "Not a fully powered Reaper. A person who understands what she's going through. Who's been through it himself. Who can tell her it gets better because he knows it gets better."

Solomon stared at the folder.

Inside was a photograph. A young woman, perhaps twenty, with dark hair and darker eyes. In the image, her shadow stretched wrong—too long, too sharp, moving against the light.

Like his had, once.

"Her name is Ji-hyun," Akari said. "She watched her brother die in the chaos. Her power awakened when the Dreamer fell. She's been hiding for three months, convinced she's a monster."

"She's not a monster."

"Then tell her that."

Solomon closed his eyes.

Naomi's voice echoed in his memory: Don't let them do it to anyone else.

He'd thought that meant stopping Prometheus. Stopping the harvesting. Stopping the Dreamer.

Maybe it meant something simpler.

Maybe it just meant being there when someone needed help.

"Okay," he said. "I'll go."

Akari smiled—relief and affection and the particular hope of someone who had been waiting for this moment longer than she wanted to admit.

"I'll book the flight."

DAY ONE The helicopter ride was a blur of motion and fear.

Akari sat beside Solomon's stretcher, her burned hands pressed against the metal frame as if she could anchor him to life through physical contact alone. The medics worked around her—IV lines, oxygen, monitors that beeped warnings she didn't understand. Their faces were masks of professional concern that couldn't quite hide the truth.

They didn't expect him to survive.

She heard them talking in quiet voices when they thought she wasn't listening. "Shadow-power completely depleted." "Cellular damage at the quantum level." "Brain activity inconsistent with consciousness recovery." Medical terms that translated to a single message: He gave too much.

The facility in New Delhi was clean and efficient—Prometheus at its best, resources marshaled without regard for cost. They gave Solomon a private room with equipment that hummed with expensive precision. They gave Akari a chair beside his bed and the unspoken permission to stay as long as she needed.

She didn't leave.

Not when they brought her food she couldn't eat. Not when Helena arrived with reports on the global situation that Akari couldn't process. Not when her own wounds screamed for attention and the burns on her hands wept fluid through their bandages.

She just sat, and watched, and waited.

"Talk to him," one of the nurses suggested. A kind woman with gray hair and tired eyes. "Coma patients can sometimes hear. It might help."

Akari didn't know what to say.

So she started with the only thing that felt real.

"I never told you about my grandmother," she began, her voice rough from disuse. "She was a Light-Bearer too. That's where it came from. The seed passed through her to my mother to me. My mother never awakened, but she knew. She watched her own mother burn out when she was twelve years old."

Solomon didn't respond. The monitors kept their steady rhythm. "My grandmother tried to stop a tsunami. Can you imagine? A wall of water taller than buildings, and she thought she could hold it back with light." Akari had gone quiet in a particular way. "She saved maybe a hundred people before the strain killed her. My mother was on the shore, watching. She never talked about it, but I found her journals after she died. Page after page about watching her mother dissolve into pure light and wondering if the same thing would happen to me."

The machines beeped. The clock on the wall marked seconds that felt like hours.

"I spent my whole life being careful. Measuring my output.

Never giving more than I could afford to lose. And then I met you, and you—" She laughed, a broken sound. "You gave everything.

Without hesitation. Without calculation. You just... gave."

She took his hand—gently, mindful of the wires and tubes connecting him to machines that kept his body functioning while his spirit was somewhere else.

"I don't know how to do that," she admitted. "I've always held something back. Always kept a reserve, just in case. But watching you in Mumbai... you showed me what it looks like to commit. To decide that something matters more than survival."

Silence.

"So you don't get to die," she continued, her voice hardening. "You hear me? You showed me what courage looks like. Now you have to stick around and help me learn it."

DAY TWO The world was ending. Again.

Not literally—the Dreamer was gone, the nodes collapsed, the immediate crisis passed. But the aftermath was its own catastrophe. Helena briefed her in fragments, respecting her vigil while sharing information she needed to know. The death toll was climbing—thirty thousand, then forty, then estimates that might reach higher once the rubble was cleared. Cities across the world had been damaged by shadow-activity that had peaked during the battle.

Governments were demanding explanations that Prometheus couldn't provide without revealing secrets they'd kept for centuries.

"The cover story is holding for now," Helena said. "Coordinated terrorist attacks with unconventional weapons. It's thin, but people want to believe something they can understand."

"And the truth?"

"Buried. As always." Helena's voice carried exhaustion that went beyond physical tiredness. "Three centuries of secrecy, and it all came apart in two weeks. We're going to spend decades cleaning this up."

"Was it worth it?"

Helena looked at Solomon's still form.

"Ask me again when he wakes up."

If he wakes up. Neither of them said the words.

The Light-Bearer network checked in throughout the day.

Catherine, recovered enough to use her precognitive abilities again, reported she couldn't see Solomon's future. "It's not that he dies," she clarified quickly, hearing Akari's sharp intake of breath. "It's that he's… undetermined. Like he hasn't decided yet whether to come back."

"How can someone decide that?"

"I don't know. But I've seen it before, with people who gave too much. They reach a place where the thread could go either way. The body can survive, but the spirit has to choose to return."

"Then how do I help him choose?"

Catherine was quiet for a moment.

"Be there when he's ready. Sometimes that's all anyone can do." *DAY THREE* Akari dreamed of fire.

She was sixteen again, standing in her childhood bedroom as flames crawled up the walls. Her sister was screaming—that sound would haunt her forever, the high-pitched terror of a child who didn't understand why the world had suddenly become pain. Her mother was somewhere else in the house, calling her name, and Akari couldn't move.

The light was coming from her.

Pouring out of her skin like water from a broken dam, setting everything it touched ablaze. She couldn't stop it. Couldn't control it. Could only stand there as her power destroyed everything she loved. She woke gasping, her own light flaring reflexively before she could contain it.

Solomon's monitors spiked.

Akari lunged forward, terrified she'd somehow hurt him, and found his eyes fluttering.

"Solomon?"

His fingers twitched. His lips moved, forming words without sound.

"Solomon, I'm here. Can you hear me?"

His eyes opened.

For a moment, they were blank—unfocused, confused, lost somewhere between wherever he'd been and wherever he was now.

Then recognition flickered through them, and he looked at her with something that might have been relief.

"Akari," he whispered.

She was crying. When had she started crying?

"You came back," she managed.

"I heard you." His voice was barely audible, rough from disuse and whatever damage had been done to him. "Talking about your grandmother. The tsunami."

"You heard that?"

"All of it." His hand moved, finding hers with effort that seemed to exhaust him. "You were right. I don't get to die. Not yet."

Akari pressed his hand to her face, feeling the weak pulse of his heartbeat against her cheek.

"Not ever," she said. "Not if I have anything to say about it."

Solomon smiled—faint, tired, but real.

Then his eyes closed again, and for one terrible moment Akari thought she'd lost him. But the monitors stayed steady, and his breathing continued, and she realized he'd just fallen asleep. Normal sleep. Healing sleep. The sleep of someone who had decided to stay.

She sat back in her chair, still holding his hand, and let herself breathe for the first time in three days.

CHAPTER TWENTY-ONE

The Cost

Akari sat beside Solomon's bed in the Prometheus medical facility, watching the monitors that tracked vital signs she barely understood. His heartbeat was steady. His breathing was regular. By every objective measure, he was alive and recovering.

But he hadn't woken up.

The doctors—Prometheus doctors, people she'd once considered enemies—tried to explain. His body needed time to repair itself. The energy expenditure had been catastrophic, beyond anything their instruments could measure. He'd essentially burned himself hollow to destroy the node, and now every cell was working to rebuild what had been lost.

"Most people wouldn't have survived at all," Dr. Chen had told her. "The fact that he's still breathing is remarkable."

It didn't feel remarkable. It felt like torture.

Akari had barely slept since Mumbai. Every time she closed her eyes, she saw him falling. Saw his shadow writhing as the node exploded. Saw the light leave his eyes and wondered if it would ever return.

"You need to rest," Helena said from the doorway.

Akari didn't turn around. "I'm fine."

"You're not. You haven't eaten in two days. You've barely spoken to anyone. The network needs you."

"The network can wait." Akari's voice was flat, emotionless—the only way she could keep herself together. "He needs me more."

Helena was quiet for a moment. Then she crossed the room and pulled up a chair beside Akari's.

"You love him," she said. Not a question.

"Yes."

"Does he know?"

"We told each other. Before." Akari's throat tightened. "The night before Mumbai. I thought—I thought that would be enough. That saying it meant we'd get to keep it. Stupid, really."

"Not stupid. Human." Helena's voice was surprisingly gentle. "I was married once, you know. Before Prometheus. Before all of this."

Akari finally looked at her.

"He was a teacher. History. We met at a conference when I was presenting early research on myth-seed manifestations—back when I thought understanding them would lead to helping people instead of…" Helena trailed off. "He died in an extraction attempt. Not ours. The Fate-Weavers. He had a dormant seed we never knew about. When it awakened, they came for him."

"I'm sorry."

"So am I. Every day." Helena's eyes were distant, focused on something far away. "I threw myself into Prometheus after that. Told myself I was doing it to prevent others from suffering the same loss. But really, I was just… running. Running from the grief I couldn't face."

Akari understood that better than she wanted to admit.

"Does it get easier?" she asked.

"No. But it gets different. The sharp edges round out, eventually. The moments when you forget become more frequent. You learn to carry it instead of being crushed by it." Helena stood, her hand resting briefly on Akari's shoulder. "He's going to wake up. I've seen his readings. His body is healing faster than anything we've documented. Whatever he did out there, it didn't destroy him—it just… changed him."

"Changed him how?"

"I don't know. But I think we'll all find out soon."

Helena left.

Akari stayed.

On the fourth day, Solomon's fingers twitched.

Akari was dozing, not sleeping, just that half-conscious state where exhaustion demanded some concession—when she felt movement against her hand. She'd been holding his since the first night, unwilling to break even that small connection.

Her eyes snapped open.

His fingers were moving. Weakly, uncertainly, but moving.

"Solomon?" Her voice cracked. "Can you hear me?"

His eyelids fluttered. Not opening, not yet, but trying.

"Solomon, I'm here. I'm right here."

His lips moved. No sound came out, but she could see him forming words.

Akari.

"Yes." Tears were streaming down her face now, the dam finally breaking. "Yes, it's me. You're safe. You did it. You stopped it."

His hand tightened on hers. Still weak. Still barely there.

But there.

"Don't…" His voice was a rasp, barely audible. "Don't leave."

"Never." She leaned forward, pressed her forehead to his, let her light wash over him in waves of warmth and healing. "Never, never, never. I'm never leaving you again."

His eyes finally opened.

They were different. Still his—still dark, still intelligent, still carrying that particular intensity she'd fallen in love with. But something behind them had changed. A depth that hadn't been there before. A knowledge of things beyond normal perception.

He'd touched something in Mumbai. Something ancient and vast and terrible.

And somehow, impossibly, he'd survived.

"Hey," he whispered.

"Hey yourself." Akari was crying and laughing at the same time. "You scared the hell out of me."

"Sorry."

"Don't be sorry. Just—don't do it again."

Solomon managed a weak smile.

"No promises."

She kissed him then—gently, carefully, mindful of his fragile state. But it was real. It was them. And for the first time in four days, Akari let herself believe they might actually have a future.

"I love you," she said against his lips.

"I love you too." His hand found her face, cupped her cheek with a tenderness that made her chest ache. "I heard you, you know. While I was out. I could hear you talking to me. Telling me about your mother, about the fire, about all the things you'd never told anyone."

Akari's breath caught. "You heard that?"

"All of it." Solomon's eyes were soft. "You're not a monster, Akari. You never were. You're just someone who's been hurt, carrying that hurt the best way you knew how. And when this is over—when we've fixed what we can and accepted what we can't—I want to help you make peace with it. With all of it."

She couldn't speak. Could only press herself against him, feeling his heartbeat steady and strong beneath her cheek, letting his arms wrap around her as best they could.

"Together," she managed finally.

"Together," he agreed.

The monitors beeped steadily. The sun set beyond the windows, painting the room in shades of gold and amber. And two people who had found each other against impossible odds held on, and breathed, and let themselves hope.

The hardest part was over.

Whatever came next, they would face it side by side.

The first days after his waking were a blur of effort and exhaustion. Everything hurt. Not just his body—everything. The places where his shadow used to live felt like burns that went deeper than skin, deeper than muscle, down into whatever part of him had once been able to touch death and not flinch. He felt hollowed out. Like someone had reached inside him and taken the parts that mattered and left the rest.

He tried not to think about it.

Instead, he focused on small things. The texture of the sheets. The taste of the water Akari brought him. The way the light changed as afternoon became evening became night. Ordinary sensations, grounding him in a world that still seemed fragile despite the crisis having passed.

But eventually, he had to try.

It was midnight when he did it—Akari asleep in the chair beside him, her breathing soft and regular. The room was quiet, lit only by the glow of monitors and the distant lights of New Delhi through the window.

Solomon reached for his shadow.

And found almost nothing.

The sensation was like reaching for a limb that had been amputated. He could feel the memory of power—the pathways where it should have flowed, the connections that should have sparked to life at his command. But when he tried to call it, only a thin trickle answered.

His shadow stirred weakly. It couldn't even cover his hand.

Solomon stared at the pale gray smear that was all he could produce—this pathetic remnant of the darkness that had once obeyed his every thought. The shadow that had terrified Fate-Weavers, that had torn through Silas's defenses, that had reached into the threads themselves and reshaped reality.

Gone.

Almost all of it, gone.

He tried harder. Pushed with everything he had, reaching for the power that should have been there, demanding it answer him.

Pain exploded through his chest.

He gasped, the sound loud in the quiet room, and Akari was awake instantly.

"Solomon?" She was at his side, light warming her hands as she reached for him. "What happened?"

"I tried—" He couldn't finish. The pain was fading, but the emptiness remained. "I tried to use my shadow. To see what was left."

Akari's expression softened with understanding.

"The doctors said you shouldn't try for at least a week. Your channels are damaged. Pushing them too soon could—" "Could what? Make it worse?" Solomon laughed bitterly. "It can't get much worse than this."

"It could kill you." Akari's voice was sharp. "Whatever you gave to stop the node, it burned pathways that were never meant to be burned. The doctors say it's like… like nerve damage, but for myth-seed power. The connections need time to heal, if they're going to heal at all."

"If."

"Solomon—" "I know." He closed his eyes, fighting the despair that wanted to swallow him whole. "I know it might be permanent. I know I might never be what I was. But knowing that and feeling it are different things."

Akari was quiet for a moment.

"Tell me," she said quietly.

"Tell you what?"

"What it feels like. I can't understand if you don't help me."

Solomon opened his eyes. Looked at her—this woman who had stood beside him through everything, who had nearly died herself trying to help him stop the Dreamer. She deserved honesty.

"It feels like being blind," he said slowly. "Like someone turned off a light I didn't know I was seeing by. The threads are still there—I can sense them, distantly, like hearing music through a wall. But I can't reach them. Can't touch them. Can't interact with the world the way I used to."

He lifted his hand, watched the thin remnant of shadow pool weakly in his palm.

"Before, my shadow was… it was me. An extension of everything I was, everything I felt. It responded to my emotions, amplified my will, let me touch parts of reality that most people don't even know exist." He let the shadow dissipate, watched it fade back to nothing. "Now it's like… like having a photograph of a friend instead of the friend themselves. I can remember what it felt like. But it's not the same."

"You're still you," Akari said firmly. "The power isn't what made you who you are."

"Isn't it?" Solomon shook his head. "I don't know anymore. I've spent the last months defining myself by what I could do—Reaper-class, shadow manipulation, seeing the threads. If I can't do those things anymore, who am I?"

"The person who saved the world."

"The person who broke it first."

"Stop." Akari took his face in her hands, forced him to look at her. "Stop counting your failures like they're all that matters. Yes, you broke the pattern. Yes, people died. But you also stood in front of an ancient entity that had been planning for three centuries, and you beat it. You gave everything you had to protect people you'd never met. That's not nothing."

"It feels like nothing."

"Then we'll work on that." She pressed her forehead to his.

"Together. For as long as it takes."

The first real test came five days after he woke.

Akari had been helping him walk—short trips to the bathroom, around the room, building strength in legs that had forgotten how to support him. He was doing better physically. Eating solid food. Staying awake for longer stretches. The machines had been disconnected one by one as his body proved it could function without them.

But he hadn't tried to use his shadow again.

"You're avoiding it," Akari observed, after watching him skirt around the subject for the third day in a row.

"Maybe."

"Definitely." She sat on the edge of his bed, her light gentle and patient. "I understand why. But avoiding it won't make it better."

"What if nothing makes it better? What if this is all there is?"

"Then we adapt. But we won't know until we try."

Solomon took a breath.

She was right. Hiding from the truth wasn't going to change it. "Okay," he said. "But not here. I need... space. Air. Somewhere that doesn't feel like a hospital."

Akari nodded. "I'll arrange it."

The garden was beautiful.

Helena's facility had been designed with recovery in mind—green spaces, flowering trees, paths that wound through carefully cultivated wilderness. The sun was warm, the air clean, the sounds of birds and running water replacing the beep of machines. Solomon sat on a stone bench beneath a flowering cherry tree and tried to remember how to be human.

Akari sat beside him, close but not touching. Giving him space to work.

"Start small," she suggested. "Don't try to do what you used to do. Just... feel what's there."

He closed his eyes.

The threads were there—he could sense them, faintly, like stars glimpsed through heavy cloud cover. Every person in the facility had one, stretching upward toward futures he could barely perceive. The gardener pruning roses nearby. The guards at the perimeter. Helena, somewhere in the building behind them.

But the details were gone. He couldn't see the shapes anymore, couldn't read the patterns, couldn't trace the delicate web of connection and consequence that had once been as clear to him as color to a sighted person.

He reached for his shadow.

It came—reluctantly, painfully, a thin stream of darkness that pooled in his palm like spilled ink. Not the vast, confident power he'd once commanded. Just a remnant. A whisper where there had once been a shout.

"That's more than yesterday," Akari said softly.

"It's not enough."

"It's a start."

Solomon tried to extend the shadow—to send it questing outward the way he'd once done automatically, exploring the world through a sense that normal humans didn't possess. The effort made his head pound. The shadow advanced maybe a foot before collapsing back into his palm.

"Damn it."

"Again," Akari encouraged. "Slower this time."

He tried again. And again. And again.

By the end of the hour, he'd managed to extend his shadow perhaps six feet—a distance he'd once covered in heartbeats without thinking. The effort left him exhausted, trembling, drenched in sweat that had nothing to do with the warm sun.

But Akari was smiling.

"You grew," she said. "In the last half hour alone, your range increased by almost a foot."

"At this rate, I'll be back to normal in about ten years."

"Or maybe you'll get better faster as the channels heal. We don't know yet." She helped him stand, supporting his weight as his legs threatened to buckle. "The point is, you're not static. You can grow. That means there's hope."

Solomon leaned on her, too tired to argue.

But something had changed inside him—a tiny spark of possibility in the darkness that had threatened to swallow him whole.

Maybe he would never be what he was.

But maybe, just maybe, he could become something new.

The world woke up to a nightmare it couldn't explain.

Helena had set up a monitoring station in the facility—a wall of screens showing news feeds from around the globe, each one struggling to make sense of what had happened. Solomon watched from his wheelchair, still too weak to stand for long, as humanity tried to process the incomprehensible.

CNN: "—officials confirming that the death toll in Mumbai has exceeded eight thousand, with thousands more injured. The source of the destruction remains unclear, though Indian authorities have ruled out conventional terrorism—" *BBC:* "—coordinated attacks across twelve cities in what experts are calling the most significant global crisis since World War II. The unusual phenomena reported by survivors—moving shadows, localized reality distortions—have yet to be explained by any scientific consensus—" *Al Jazeera:* "—religious leaders worldwide calling for calm as millions flock to places of worship seeking answers. The Vatican has issued a statement urging faith in the face of uncertainty, while Islamic scholars debate whether the events constitute signs of the end times—" *NDTV:* "—the Taj Mahal Hotel in Mumbai being demolished after structural damage made it too dangerous to salvage. Survivors describe scenes of 'living darkness' that hunted through the streets for nearly three hours before suddenly ceasing. Psychologists are warning of mass PTSD—"

"They're looking for explanations," Helena said, joining Solomon at the monitors. "Terrorism. Natural disaster. Divine intervention. Anything that fits into existing frameworks."

"And the truth?"

"Will stay hidden. For now." Helena's voice was tired but certain. "Imagine telling them. Really imagine it. An ancient entity was using human suffering to fuel its awakening, and a group of people with supernatural abilities stopped it by destroying part of a city."

"When you put it that way…"

"They'd burn us at the stake. Assuming they believed us at all."

Helena gestured at the screens. "The myth of a rational, explicable world is the only thing holding civilization together. We can't afford to shatter it. Not when people are this afraid."

Solomon watched a reporter standing in the ruins of a Mumbai neighborhood, describing destruction that cameras couldn't adequately capture.

"We saved them," he said. "And they'll never know."

"That's the job. That's always been the job." Helena's expression was unreadable. "Prometheus got a lot wrong. The harvesting, the containment, the belief that we could control forces we barely understood. But the secrecy... the secrecy was right. Some truths are too heavy for the world to carry."

"Who decides that?"

"People like us. Like me." Helena met his eyes. "Like you, now, whether you want to or not."

The awakened community had its own reactions.

Catherine organized a conference call—the first gathering of the expanded Light-Bearer network since Mumbai. Forty-one survivors, scattered across a dozen countries, connected through technology that felt inadequate for the weight of what they needed to share.

"We lost six," she reported. "Jorge, Ingrid, Elena, David, Kofi, and Hana in Seoul. Their lights went out in the final surge."

Silence. Even through the digital connection, Solomon felt the grief pressing against each survivor.

"There will be a memorial," Catherine continued. "Once things stabilize. Once we have a place to gather that won't draw attention."

"Will things ever stabilize?" The voice belonged to Yuki, the Japanese teenager whose arm was still in a cast. "The world knows something happened. People are scared. Governments are asking questions we can't answer. How long until someone connects the dots?"

"We'll manage it," Akari said. "The same way we've always managed it. Carefully. Patiently. One crisis at a time."

"And the newly awakened?" Another voice—Isabella, the Argentine doctor. "My hospital is seeing cases. People who developed abilities during the chaos, who don't understand what's happening to them. They need help."

"We're building something for that," Solomon found himself saying. He hadn't planned to speak, but the words came anyway. "A network. Support systems. Training for people who need it, without the control and containment that Prometheus used."

"Can we trust Prometheus?" The skepticism in the voice was clear. "They created this mess."

"They also helped stop it." Solomon thought about Helena—her ruthlessness, her certainty, her genuine horror when she'd learned what extraction did. "People can change. Organizations can change. If we write off everyone who made mistakes, we'll be alone."

"Pretty words from the person who broke the pattern."

The accusation hung in the air.

Solomon could have argued. Could have explained the manipulation, the impossible choices, the weight of discovering that everything he'd believed was a lie. But he didn't.

"You're right," he said instead. "I broke it. People died because of my choices. That guilt will follow me for the rest of my life." He paused. "But I'm still here. Still trying to make things better. If that's not good enough for you, I understand. But I'm going to keep trying anyway."

Silence again. Then, slowly, voices began to offer support. Not forgiveness— that wasn't theirs to give—but acknowledgment that moving forward mattered more than assigning blame.

"We have work to do," Catherine said. "Let's focus on that."

The conspiracy theories were inevitable.

Solomon discovered them during his second week of recovery, when Helena finally allowed him limited internet access. Forums and social media platforms buzzing with speculation about what had happened in Mumbai.

SHADOW_HUNTER_2023: "My cousin in Mumbai saw people dissolving. Just dissolving, like they were being erased. The government is covering something up."

TRUTH_SEEKER_ANON: "HAARP. Has to be HAARP.

The military has been experimenting with weather control for years. This was a test that went wrong."

ILLUMINATI_EXPOSED: "Wake up sheeple. The shadows were alive. Multiple witnesses reported conscious, hunting darkness. This isn't natural. This isn't terrorism. This is something we're not supposed to know about."

SKEPTIC_PRIME: "Mass hysteria. Stress-induced hallucinations. The power went out and people's brains filled in the darkness with their worst fears. It's psychology, not supernatural nonsense."

Solomon closed the browser.

"Find something interesting?" Akari asked, glancing at his expression.

"They're trying to figure it out. Some of them are closer than they should be."

"There have always been conspiracy theorists. Usually they focus on aliens or government mind control." Akari shrugged. "The truth hides in plain sight because it's too strange to believe. Someone who actually saw a shadow-form hunting through Mumbai will be dismissed as traumatized. Someone who sensed the Dreamer's presence will be told they were dreaming."

"And if they persist?"

"Then Helena's people will... manage the situation. Discredit the most accurate accounts. Flood the space with competing theories until the truth drowns in noise."

Solomon thought about that. About secrets and lies and the responsibility of deciding what people could handle.

"It doesn't feel right."

"It's not right." Akari's voice was gentle but firm. "It's just necessary. For now. Maybe someday the world will be ready for the truth. But not today. Not when the wound is this fresh."

Solomon nodded, accepting it.

Another piece of the new reality settling into place.

Saving the world was just the beginning.

The hard part was what came after.

Week Two Solomon learned to walk without help.

It took longer than it should have. His body had been through trauma that medicine couldn't fully explain—the cellular damage from channeling more power than any human was meant to hold. The doctors spoke in uncertain terms, using phrases like "unprecedented presentation" and "recovery trajectory unclear."

What they meant was: We don't know if you'll ever be normal again.

Solomon didn't want normal. He just wanted functional.

So he pushed himself. Daily sessions in the facility's rehabilitation wing, supervised by therapists who had clearly been briefed on his situation without being told the full truth. They thought he was recovering from some kind of exotic energy exposure. They weren't entirely wrong.

"Your muscle memory is intact," Dr. Patel observed, watching Solomon navigate a set of balance exercises. "It's more like...

relearning how to trust your body. Like someone who's had a severe illness and needs to remember that their legs can support them."

"That's about right."

"The psychological component may take longer. Whatever happened to you—" She hesitated, clearly fishing for information she'd been told not to ask about. "It seems to have affected more than just your physical systems."

"You could say that."

He didn't elaborate. She didn't push.

Week Three The shadow exercises became routine.

Every afternoon, in the garden beneath the cherry tree, Solomon would practice. Reaching. Extending. Trying to rebuild connections that had been burned away in a moment of desperate sacrifice.

Progress came slowly. Painfully. But it came.

By the end of the third week, he could extend his shadow perhaps twenty feet—still a fraction of his former reach, but enough to sense the immediate environment. The threads remained ghostly, distant, but he could occasionally glimpse their outlines when he concentrated hard enough.

"It's like learning a language you used to speak," he told Akari during one of their sessions. "The knowledge is in there somewhere. It's just... buried. Inaccessible in ways it never was before."

"But it's coming back?"

"Some of it. Maybe." He let his shadow retreat, feeling the familiar ache of overstretched channels. "The question is how much, and how long it will take."

Akari considered this.

"Does it matter?" she asked.

"What do you mean?"

"I mean—you're alive. You're recovering. Whatever power you end up with, it'll be more than most people have. Does the exact percentage really matter?"

Solomon thought about the threads. About the vast web of mortality he'd once navigated as easily as breathing. About the certainty that had come with knowing exactly how long everyone around him had left to live.

"Maybe not," he admitted. "Maybe I've been thinking about this wrong."

"How so?"

"I've been treating the lost power like... like an amputation. Something taken from me that I need to get back." He looked at his hands, at the thin shadow pooling in his palms. "But maybe it's more like... growing into a different shape. Not losing something, just becoming something else."

Akari smiled.

"That sounds healthier."

"It's probably still wrong. But it feels better."

Week Four Helena offered him a position.

"Director of Awakened Affairs," she said, sliding a folder across her desk. "Newly created role. You'd be responsible for coordinating outreach to newly awakened individuals, developing training protocols, building the support networks we talked about."

Solomon looked at the folder without opening it.

"You want me to work for Prometheus."

"I want you to reshape what Prometheus becomes." Helena's voice was careful, measured. "The old approach is dead. We both know that. But the organization's resources. The facilities, the personnel, the accumulated knowledge—that doesn't have to die with it. We can build something better. Something that helps people instead of harvesting them."

"And you want me to be the face of that."

"I want you to be the soul of it. The reminder of why we're doing this differently." Helena leaned back. "You've seen both sides. The victim and the savior. You understand what we did wrong and why we need to change. That perspective is valuable."

"I'm also the person who broke the pattern and let the Dreamer out."

"Which means you understand consequences. You understand that good intentions aren't enough." Helena's eyes were sharp. "I've made mistakes that will haunt me for the rest of my life. Every extraction I approved. Every 'subject' I reduced to data points. If I can live with that and still try to do better, so can you."

Solomon was quiet for a long moment.

"I need time," Solomon said at last. "Not to decide—to recover. To figure out who I am without the power I used to have. I can't lead anything right now. I can barely lead myself."

Helena nodded without looking at him.

"How much time?"

"I don't know. Weeks. Months. However long it takes to stop feeling like a ghost wearing a human body."

"That's honest, at least." Helena closed the folder. "The offer stays open. When you're ready—if you're ever ready—we'll talk again."

Leaving The day Solomon left the facility, it was raining.

Soft rain, warm despite the season, falling from clouds that moved like ordinary clouds across a sky that looked almost normal. The chaos had faded enough that weather patterns were recovering, the atmospheric disturbances settling back toward equilibrium. The world was healing.

Solomon wasn't sure he could say the same about himself.

Akari met him at the gate, carrying a bag with the few possessions he'd accumulated during his recovery. Books, mostly—gifts from Helena's library, texts on myth-seed theory that might help him understand what he'd become. A photograph someone had taken of the Light-Bearers before Mumbai, twelve faces that included five who were no longer alive.

He carried that photograph in his jacket pocket, close to his heart.

"Tokyo?" Akari asked.

"Tokyo." It was the only place that felt right. The city where everything had started, where he'd first learned what he was. Going back felt like closing a circle.

"I found an apartment," Akari said. "Small, but quiet. Near where the bookshop used to be."

"You're coming with me?"

"For now. Until you're settled." She took his hand. "Unless you don't want company."

Solomon thought about the months ahead. The long process of rebuilding himself, of learning to exist without the power that had defined him. The nights when the guilt would come, when the numbers would echo in his head—fifty thousand dead, six Light-Bearers gone, the weight of responsibility that no amount of heroism could fully discharge.

He couldn't face that alone.

"I want you there," he said. "Every day. For as long as you're willing to stay."

Akari squeezed his hand.

"Then I'll stay."

They walked through the gate together, into the rain, into a world that was forever changed.

Behind them, the facility hummed with activity—Helena rebuilding Prometheus from the ashes, Catherine coordinating the Light-Bearer network, Marcus working to repair relationships that three centuries of secrecy had damaged.

The future was uncertain.

But for the first time since Mumbai, Solomon felt the beginnings of hope.

It was small. Fragile. Easy to lose.

But it was there.

CHAPTER TWENTY-TWO

The Next

Seoul in winter was beautiful and brutal.

Snow dusted the streets, turning the city into something quieter than its reputation suggested. Noise replaced by the soft crunch of footsteps. Neon signs casting colored shadows on white-covered pavement. The cold bit deep—the kind that made your lungs ache—but there was something clean about it. Something honest. Three months had passed since Mumbai.

Three months of rebuilding—not the world, but himself. The first weeks had been the worst: testing his shadow each morning like a patient learning to walk, measuring progress in millimeters. A shadow that could cover his hand. Then his arm. Then, after six weeks, the floor of his hospital room. Each morning a little more. Each morning a reminder of how much he'd lost.

Akari had stayed through all of it. Had watched him fail and try again and fail and try again without once suggesting he stop. By the second month, he could extend his shadow thirty feet.

Sense threads within a city block. Not the continent-spanning awareness he'd had before, but enough. Enough to help.

Three months since his power had burned through him and left him diminished—not empty, but reduced. A candle where there had been a torch. The shadow that had once been vast enough to reshape reality now felt thin, stretched, a whisper of what it had been. He still dreamed about it sometimes. The pattern unweaving.

The Dreamer's voice in his mind, vast and ancient, almost surprised as centuries of patient work collapsed around it. The moment when he'd pushed everything into the darkness and felt himself being unmade alongside the thing he was destroying.

He'd expected to die.

Waking up had been the surprise.

Solomon walked through neighborhoods still rebuilding. Here, a storefront with fresh paint over old damage. There, a memorial on a corner—flowers frozen stiff, photographs laminated against the weather, names of people who had died during what the news called "the awakening crisis" and what survivors simply called "that night."

The gaps were the hardest.

Places where buildings had been consumed by shadow-fire, where the Dreamer's patterns had torn reality just enough that nothing could be rebuilt. The city worked around them like a body accommodating scars—streets redirected, new developments planned, life continuing despite wounds that would never fully heal. Solomon understood wounds like that.

He found Ji-hyun's building in a district that had seen better days even before the chaos. A gray concrete apartment block, six stories, laundry hanging from balconies despite the cold. The kind of place where people lived because they had to. The kind of place that had always existed in the shadows, overlooked and underfunded, and had therefore been hit hardest when real shadows came hunting.

The stairwell smelled like cooking oil and desperation. Graffiti marked the walls—some of it ordinary tags, some newer, stranger symbols that people had started drawing after the crisis. Protection marks. Prayers in spray paint.

She was on the fifth floor.

Akari's information said she hadn't left the apartment in weeks. Food delivered. Rent paid in cash through the mail slot. No human contact if she could avoid it. The neighbors had complained about sounds at night—screaming, crying, something breaking that wasn't glass.

They thought she was going crazy from grief.

They weren't entirely wrong.

Solomon climbed the stairs slowly. His body was still his own, but his power had become something different. The Reaper-class abilities that had made him unprecedented were still there, still accessible, but diminished. He could read threads, but not manipulate them easily. He could sense death approaching, but not always redirect it.

He'd given most of what he was to destroy the Dreamer.

He didn't regret it.

At Ji-hyun's door, he paused. Listened. Reached out with what remained of his senses.

Inside, shadows pressed against the walls like prisoners testing their chains. Dark and dense and hungry—the uncontrolled manifestation of grief turned into power. He could feel her huddled in the center of all that darkness, terrified of what she'd become but unable to stop becoming it.

She was exactly where he'd been two years ago.

Only no one had come to help him then.

He knocked.

No answer.

"Ji-hyun," he said through the door. "My name is Solomon Nyx. I'm like you."

Silence. The kind that listened.

"I know what you're feeling. The shadow that moves when you don't want it to. The fear that you'll hurt someone. The sense that you've become something that shouldn't exist." He paused. "I felt all of that. And I'm here to tell you it gets better."

More silence.

Then, so quietly he almost missed it: "Go away."

"I'm not going to do that."

"I could hurt you. I could—" Her voice snagged on the word, raw with terror and exhaustion. "I don't control it. It moves on its own. It wants things."

"It wants to protect you. That's what shadows do. They react to fear, to threat, to the emotions we can't control. But they can be trained. Shaped. Guided."

"You don't understand."

"I understand better than anyone alive." Solomon let his own shadow shift, just slightly, just enough that she might sense it. His power was diminished, but still there. Still recognizable to another of his kind. "I'm a Reaper-class, Ji-hyun. Same as you. I've been where you are."

Silence stretched. He could feel her wrestling with herself—the fear of opening the door, the fear of not opening it, the desperate hope that someone might actually be able to help.

Then the door cracked open.

Ji-hyun looked exactly like her photograph—dark hair tangled and unwashed, darker eyes ringed with exhaustion, the haunted expression of someone who hadn't slept properly in months. She was thin in ways that spoke of grief rather than health.

But it was her shadow that commanded attention.

It clung to her like a second skin, twitching at the edges, reacting to Solomon's presence with wary hostility. It was stronger than he'd expected—raw and untrained but powerful. The kind of power that came from trauma deep enough to crack a soul open.

"You're him," she said. "The one from the news. The one who stopped it."

"The one who started it, too," Solomon replied honestly. "I freed the Dreamer. Everything that happened—the chaos, the deaths, your brother—that's on me."

Ji-hyun's shadow surged.

For a moment, Solomon thought she might attack. Her power was raw, untrained, but strong—maybe stronger than his had been at this stage. The grief and rage she'd been holding could fuel something terrible. He felt his own shadow stir in response, but kept it still. If she needed to strike out, he could take it.

But she pulled it back.

With effort, with visible strain, with her whole body shaking, she pulled it back.

That alone told Solomon she could be helped. Anyone who could pull back from rage like that had a chance.

"Why are you here?" she asked.

"Because you need help. And because helping you might be the only way I can make up for what I did."

Ji-hyun stared at him for a long moment. Whatever she saw seemed to satisfy her.

She stepped aside and let him in.

The apartment was small and dark.

Curtains drawn. Lights off. Shadows pooled in every corner like standing water, dense and heavy and hungry for attention. Ji-hyun had been living in darkness—literally surrounded by her own element, feeding it without realizing it, creating an environment that amplified everything she was trying to suppress.

Solomon recognized the pattern. He'd nearly drowned in it himself, those first weeks after his awakening. After Naomi's death. After everything that had cracked him open and let the shadow in. "First thing," he said. "Open the curtains."

"The light hurts."

"No. It's uncomfortable because you've been avoiding it. But your shadow needs contrast to function properly. All darkness and it becomes shapeless. Uncontrolled. Like trying to sculpt water." He moved to the nearest window and pulled the curtain aside. "Light gives it edges. Boundaries. Something to push against."

Weak winter light spilled in, gray and cold but real.

Ji-hyun flinched, her shadow recoiling from the illumination like a hand pulled from flame. But she didn't stop him.

"Better," Solomon said. "Now we can see each other."

They sat across from each other—Ji-hyun on her bed, Solomon on the single chair the apartment contained. Between them, their shadows stretched toward each other like wary animals meeting for the first time.

"Tell me about your brother," Solomon said.

Ji-hyun's face contorted. "Why?"

"Because your power awakened when he died. That connection matters. The shadow isn't separate from your grief—it's part of it. They're woven together so tightly that understanding one means understanding both."

She was quiet for a long time. Her shadow stirred restlessly, processing emotions she couldn't speak aloud.

"His name was Min-jun," she said finally. "He was twelve."

The same age Naomi had been when she'd started protecting Solomon from things he couldn't see.

"When the chaos started, we were together," Ji-hyun continued, her voice carefully flat. The tone of someone who'd rehearsed this until the words had worn smooth. "Shopping for groceries. Stupid errands. He wanted to go home and play games, and I told him to stop whining. That's what I was feeling when everything went wrong."

Her shadow twitched.

"The shadows came out of nowhere. One minute everything was normal, and then—" She stopped. Breathed. "He pushed me out of the way. I don't think he decided to do it. He just moved. Instinct. And they took him instead."

Her words settled into his chest like dropped stones.

Twelve years old. Dying to protect his sister. A sacrifice that had triggered something in her that should never have been triggered. "What was he like?" Solomon asked.

"Annoying." Ji-hyun almost smiled—the ghost of an expression, quickly gone. "Loud. Always asking questions about everything. He wanted to be a teacher. He used to practice his lessons on me—explain math problems like I was his student, even though I was five years older and actually good at math. He'd get so frustrated when I pretended not to understand, but he never stopped trying."

"He sounds wonderful."

"He was." Tears slipped down her cheeks. "He was the best person I knew. The kindest. He used to share his lunch with kids at school who didn't have food. He stood up to bullies twice his size. He believed people were good, even when they weren't. And I'm never going to stop missing him."

"No," Solomon agreed. "You're not. But you can honor him. By living. By using what you've become to protect others. By being the kind of person he would have been proud of."

The next morning, Solomon began teaching her.

"Your shadow isn't separate from you," Solomon said, standing in the center of Ji-hyun's cramped apartment. "That's the first thing you need to understand. It's not a pet you're training or a tool you're learning to use. It's you—your emotions, your instincts, your deepest self expressed in a form you're not used to seeing."

Ji-hyun stood opposite him, her shadow thrashing at the edges of her vision. She'd been fighting it for three months, and the effort showed in every line of her body.

"How is that supposed to help? If it's me, why can't I control it?"

"Because you're not controlling yourself. You're fighting yourself. And you'll always lose that fight." Solomon extended his own shadow—thin, diminished, but under perfect control. "Watch."

He moved his hand. His shadow moved with it—not as a physical reflection, but as an extension of intention. Where his hand went, darkness followed, reaching further than any natural shadow should.

"Now your turn. Don't try to command it. Don't try to suppress it. Just… move. Let your body and your shadow move together."

Ji-hyun raised her hand uncertainly.

Her shadow surged upward, responding to her intention but amplifying it tenfold. The darkness climbed the wall, spread across the ceiling, blocked out what little light filtered through the windows. "I can't—" She pulled her hand back, and the shadow collapsed chaotically, fragments of darkness scattering like startled birds. "It's too strong."

"It's not too strong. It's too responsive." Solomon's voice was patient. "Your emotions are intense right now—grief, fear, the trauma of the past three months. Your shadow is amplifying all of that because that's what shadows do. They reflect our inner state."

"So I need to stop feeling?"

"No. You need to feel more precisely." Solomon moved closer.

"Right now, your emotions are chaos. Grief tangled with anger tangled with fear tangled with guilt. Your shadow can't distinguish what you want because you can't distinguish what you want. It just responds to everything at once."

Ji-hyun's jaw tightened. "I can't just… sort my emotions. They don't work like that."

"Not instantly. But you can learn to focus." Solomon picked up a small object from her desk—a photograph of Min-jun, smiling in a school uniform. "Tell me about this."

The shadow surged again, but Solomon caught it with his own thin darkness, not suppressing it, just steadying it. Like holding someone's hand during a difficult conversation.

"Talk to me," he said. "Tell me about your brother."

Two hours later, Ji-hyun sat exhausted on her floor, but her shadow was calmer.

Not controlled—not yet. But less chaotic. Less dangerous.

"When you talked about Min-jun," Solomon said, "your shadow responded differently. Less violent. More... searching."

"I was remembering the good things. Like you said." Ji-hyun's voice was hoarse from crying. "His laugh. The way he'd explain his homework to me. The time he tried to make breakfast and set off the smoke alarm."

"And what happened to your shadow?"

"It..." She paused, thinking. "It stopped thrashing. It wanted to find something. Like it was reaching for memories instead of fighting against them."

"That's the key. Your shadow isn't your enemy—it's your ally.

It's trying to protect you, to help you process what happened. But it doesn't know how, because you've been treating it like a threat instead of a partner."

Ji-hyun looked at her hands. Her shadow pooled around them, still stronger than Solomon's but no longer threatening to consume the room.

"How do I make it a partner?"

"Practice. Every day. Start with small things—extending it deliberately, pulling it back, learning the feeling of intention becoming action." Solomon stood. "Tomorrow, we'll work on directed movement. Tonight, just... talk to it. Get to know the part of yourself you've been afraid of."

"You make it sound like therapy."

"It is therapy. Just not the kind anyone without a myth-seed could provide."

"This is going to hurt," Solomon warned.

They stood on Ji-hyun's balcony, Seoul spreading out below them in a maze of lights and shadows. The cold bit through their clothes, but neither moved to go inside.

"What are we doing?"

"Learning to see threads." Solomon let his own awareness expand, the remnants of his Reaper sense reaching out toward the city below. "Your abilities include perception as well as manipulation. Right now, you're only using half of what you carry."

"I don't understand."

"Close your eyes. Let your shadow spread—not to attack, not to defend, just to feel. Extend it outward like you're reaching into a dark room, trying to sense what's there."

Ji-hyun closed her eyes. Her shadow stretched outward, tentatively at first, then with growing confidence. It flowed over the balcony railing, down the side of the building, into the street below. "What do you feel?"

"People," she whispered. "So many people. They're… bright.

Like lights I can sense without seeing."

"Those are their threads. Their connections to their own futures."

Solomon's voice was gentle but precise. "Everyone has one. The stronger the connection, the brighter they appear. The closer to death, the dimmer."

Ji-hyun's breath caught. "I can see… there's someone in the building across the street. Their light is almost gone."

"Can you tell why?"

"Age. I think. It feels like… like a candle burning down to the wick. Not violent. Just… ending."

"That's natural death. The kind we don't interfere with." Solomon moved beside her, letting his shadow touch hers. "Now reach further. Look for something different. Something that shouldn't be."

Ji-hyun concentrated. Her shadow stretched another block, then two, spreading through the night like ink through water.

Then she gasped.

"There. Someone's thread is… it's tangled. Caught on something. It's supposed to continue, but something is pulling it in the wrong direction."

"What do you see?"

"A man. Young. He's standing on a bridge." Ji-hyun's voice cracked. "He's going to jump."

"What do you want to do?"

The shadow surged, not chaotically this time, but with desperate purpose. Ji-hyun's eyes flew open.

"Help him. I want to help him."

"Then go. Your shadow can reach him before any physical rescue. Show him he's not alone."

Ji-hyun didn't hesitate. Her shadow flowed outward, across rooftops and through streets, racing toward the bridge where a man contemplated ending his life.

Solomon watched through his own diminished senses—saw her darkness reach the man, wrap around him in a cocoon of warmth that no natural shadow should possess. He saw the man startle, look around, search for the source of the sudden comfort.

He saw the man step back from the railing.

But then something happened that Solomon had never seen before. Ji-hyun's shadow didn't just comfort—it absorbed. She flinched, gasping, and Solomon felt the echo of it through his own thin darkness: the man's pain, flooding into her shadow like water through a broken dam. His loneliness. His shame. The specific weight of his specific despair.

Her shadow took it. Held it. Didn't dissolve under it but metabolized it, the way soil takes dead leaves and makes them into something the living can use.

Solomon stared. He'd never been able to do that. His shadow could see death, could touch it, could occasionally redirect it. But Ji-hyun's shadow was doing something different—something closer to healing than anything in the Reaper vocabulary.

When Ji-hyun pulled her shadow back, she was crying again.

But differently than before. These weren't tears of grief.

"I felt his pain," she said. "His loneliness. Not just felt it—I took some of it. Carried it for him. And I told him, not with words, but with the shadow, that someone cared. That he wasn't invisible."

Solomon was quiet for a moment. Processing.

"You saved a life."

"I didn't do anything. I just... reached."

"No. You did more than reach." Solomon's voice was careful, measuring what he'd just witnessed. "I've never seen a Reaper do what you just did. My shadow perceives death. Yours just healed someone's reason for wanting it. That's not the same ability, Ji-hyun. That's something new."

Ji-hyun stared at the distant bridge, at the man who was now walking away from the railing, returning to a future that had almost ended.

"I want to do more of this," she said.

"Then we'll make sure you can. And I think you might end up teaching me as much as I teach you."

On the final morning, Solomon found Ji-hyun meditating in the corner of her apartment.

Her shadow surrounded her in a perfect circle—not chaotic, not suppressed, but balanced. Present without threatening. Strong without overwhelming. The change from three days ago was remarkable.

"You've been practicing," he said.

"All night." Ji-hyun opened her eyes. "I kept thinking about the man on the bridge. About all the people like him, suffering alone because they think no one can reach them."

"And?"

"And I realized something." She stood, her shadow moving with her like a loyal companion rather than a barely-contained threat. "Min-jun died because he thought he could protect me. He couldn't—he was just a kid, no powers, no special abilities. But he tried anyway."

"That's not a failure."

"No. It's a gift." Ji-hyun's voice was steady. "He gave me his life so I could have mine. And he gave me this power, even if he didn't know it. The least I can do is use it the way he would have wanted."

"How's that?"

"To help. To protect. To reach people who think no one can reach them." She met Solomon's eyes. "Like you're doing. Like the network is doing. I want to be part of that."

Solomon studied her—this young woman who'd lost everything and somehow found purpose in the ruins. She was still raw, still learning, still more powerful than she knew how to handle. But the core was solid. The intention was true.

"The network always needs more help," he said. "But it's dangerous work. The Fate-Weavers still exist, even if they're fragmented. Prometheus is changing, but not everyone in the organization agrees with the new direction. And there are other threats we haven't even identified yet."

"I know."

"You'd have to keep training. Getting stronger. Learning to use your abilities in ways that help people instead of hurting them."

"I want that."

"And you'd have to accept that sometimes you'll fail. That sometimes the people you try to save won't be saved. That the power you carry can't fix everything."

Ji-hyun's shadow flickered—a moment of doubt, quickly mastered.

"My brother couldn't fix everything either," she said. "But he tried anyway. That's all any of us can do."

Solomon smiled.

"Welcome to the network."

On the second night of training, Ji-hyun asked about other Reapers. "Have there been others like us? People who learned to control it?"

Solomon considered the question carefully.

"There was a woman in Vietnam," he said. "During the war. She lived in a village that was scheduled to be destroyed in an American bombing campaign. When the planes came, she did something impossible."

"What?"

"She wrapped her shadow around the entire village. Eight hundred people, hidden in darkness so complete that the pilots couldn't see them. The bombs fell on empty jungle. Everyone survived."

Ji-hyun's eyes widened. "She could do that?"

"She'd been practicing for years. An old man in her village had taught her—someone who recognized her seed and understood how to nurture it. By the time the war reached her home, she'd become one of the most controlled Reapers in recorded history."

"What happened to her?"

Solomon's expression darkened.

"The Fate-Weavers found her. They'd been tracking the anomaly—a village that appeared and disappeared from aerial observation, that seemed to exist outside normal space. When they realized what she was doing, they offered her a choice."

"Join them or die?"

"Worse. Join them or watch her village burn. Not from bombs—they controlled the military campaigns, could redirect strikes wherever they wanted. They threatened to bring the war directly to her people unless she agreed to work for them."

"Did she?"

"She tried to fight. Wrapped her shadow around the Weaver agents the way she'd wrapped it around her village. But they were prepared. They had technology that disrupted her concentration, techniques that prevented her from focusing." Solomon paused. "She held them off for three days. Killed seventeen of them. But in the end, she couldn't protect everyone and fight at the same time."

"So she surrendered?"

"She made a different choice." Solomon's voice was quiet. "On the fourth day, she walked into the jungle and didn't come back. They found her body a week later, surrounded by shadows that had grown wild without her control. She'd chosen death over servitude."

Ji-hyun was silent for a long moment.

"Why are you telling me this?"

"Because you need to understand what we're capable of. The good and the bad. The protection we can offer and the cost of that protection." Solomon met her eyes. "You're powerful, Ji-hyun.

Maybe more powerful than that woman was. But power without understanding is just another kind of weapon. And weapons get used by whoever can control them."

"So what do I do?"

"You learn. You grow. You find people you trust and let them help you become something better than a weapon." Solomon's thin shadow reached out, brushed against hers. "And you remember that every Reaper who came before you faced the same choice.

Destruction or protection. Isolation or connection. Death or life."

"Which did they choose?"

"The ones we remember chose protection. The ones we don't remember chose the other options." Solomon stood. "Let's make sure you end up in the first category."

He left Seoul with a list.

Seven names. Seven newly awakened individuals identified by the Light-Bearer network. Some were dangerous—powers spinning out of control. Some were desperate—people who'd lost everything and didn't know how to go on. All of them needed help that only someone like Solomon could provide.

Akari met him at the airport in Tokyo.

She looked tired but determined—the expression she'd worn almost constantly since Mumbai, the look of someone who'd found a purpose and was refusing to let it go. Her light gathered around her more easily now, responding to her will with a fluency that spoke of practice.

"How did it go?" she asked.

"She'll be okay. Eventually." Solomon fell into step beside her. "She has a long way to go, but she's not going to hurt herself or anyone else."

"Good." Akari handed him a tablet. "Helena's been coordinating with the network. There's a structure forming—not like the Initiative, but something new. Support centers. Training programs. A way for awakened individuals to find help without being harvested or controlled."

Solomon scrolled through the information. Facilities in eight countries. Volunteer coordinators on four continents. A communications system designed to identify people in crisis before crises became catastrophes.

"They want me to lead it," he said.

"They want you to be part of it. There's a difference." Akari ordered them both drinks at a coffee kiosk without asking what he wanted. She already knew. "You were right that you're not a leader. Not in the traditional sense. But you're something more valuable—you're proof that it's possible to survive this. To come out the other side as something better than you were before."

Solomon thought about Ji-hyun. About Min-jun, who'd died at twelve to protect his sister. About Naomi, who'd died trying to expose the truth.

"One condition," he said.

"Name it."

"We don't call it an organization. We don't create hierarchies or bureaucracies or chains of command." He accepted the coffee she handed him. "We just help. Person to person. Individual to individual. The moment we start acting like Prometheus, we've failed."

Akari smiled.

"I can work with that."

They walked out of the airport together, into a world that was still healing, still changing, still full of people who needed help. And for the first time since Mumbai, Solomon felt like he might actually be able to provide it.

Because he was here, and willing, and that had always been enough.

CHAPTER TWENTY-THREE

Naomi's Notebook

One year after Mumbai.

The lake had no name that Solomon could find on any map.

He'd discovered it three months ago, during a trip to help a newly awakened woman in Hokkaido who'd been terrified of the ice forming in her wake. The woman had stabilized—she was teaching herself now, learning to work with the cold instead of against it—but Solomon had remembered this place. The way the mountains cradled the water. The silence that wasn't empty but full.

He'd needed somewhere like this. A place to think. A place to remember.

He stood at the water's edge as the sun descended behind peaks that had witnessed epochs come and go without caring about human concerns. The autumn colors were fading, gold and crimson giving way to browns. Soon snow would come. The lake would freeze.

Everything would go still and quiet until spring remembered to arrive.

Solomon found he didn't mind the cold anymore.

He was holding Naomi's notebook.

Not the original—that had been destroyed years ago, seized by Prometheus and burned to ash. But Catherine had helped him reconstruct it over the past few months. Her precognitive abilities could reach backward as well as forward, though the effort exhausted her. Together they'd recovered fragments of what Naomi had written. Not all of it. Not even most. But enough.

He opened the notebook to a page near the beginning—early entries, back when Naomi had first started noticing things that didn't add up.

Something's wrong at the company, she'd written. The shipping manifests don't match the cargo. Containers marked PRIORITY are being routed to places that make no geographic sense. When I asked about it, my supervisor told me to stop asking.

I'm not going to stop asking.

Solomon turned the page. The handwriting changed—rushed now, cramped, the penmanship of someone writing in stolen moments.

They're everywhere. In the hospitals and the government offices and the corporations that run the world. They don't look like monsters. They look like bureaucrats. And they've convinced themselves that what they do is necessary.

The scariest part isn't what they're doing. It's that they actually believe they're helping.

Another page. The dates were gaps now—weeks passing between entries.

I found a list today. Names. Dates. Classifications. People who went into facilities and never came out. Hundreds of them, going back decades.

These aren't threats being eliminated. These are people being harvested. Like crops. Like resources.

I think I'm going to be sick.

Solomon closed his eyes, letting the grief wash through him.

Even after everything—after Mumbai, after the Dreamer, after all the victories and losses that had followed—reading Naomi's words still hurt. Not the sharp pain of fresh loss anymore, but a deep ache that would never fully fade.

He didn't want it to.

That pain was part of what kept him moving.

Don't let them do it to anyone else.

He opened the notebook again.

I don't know if anyone will ever read this, the next entry said. I don't know if it matters. But I have to write it down anyway. Because truth doesn't disappear just because no one's listening. It waits. And eventually, someone hears.

That's what I've learned from this whole thing. The truth is patient. It doesn't need me to survive. It just needs me to be willing to carry it for a while.

Solomon turned to the final entry—the one Catherine had spent three days in a trance-state to recover, the one that had cost her a week of migraines afterward.

Solomon, it said. If you're reading this, I'm probably dead. I'm sorry I couldn't tell you everything. But I need you to understand something.

The world is broken. It's always been broken. And fixing it isn't about one big fight or one dramatic moment. It's about showing up. Day after day. Choosing to care when it would be easier not to. Refusing to look away from the things that hurt.

That's all any of us can do. That's all I've ever tried to do. Don't let them do it to anyone else. That's my last request. Not revenge—I don't want you to become what they are. Just… don't let them win by making you stop caring.

I love you, little brother. I'm proud of you. And whatever happens next, remember that you're not alone. You never were.

Solomon closed the notebook.

The sun had nearly set. The lake was going dark, shadows lengthening across its surface in patterns that would have terrified him once.

Now they were just shadows.

And he was a man with a promise to keep.

The year had been full.

Fuller than Solomon had expected. In the immediate aftermath of Mumbai—after the Dreamer's destruction, after the global chaos subsided—he'd expected things to quiet down.

They hadn't.

Awakened individuals were emerging at a rate no one had predicted. The Mumbai event had done something to the world's psychic fabric, loosening restrictions that had apparently been in place for centuries. Seeds that might have remained dormant were stirring.

The old systems were gone. Prometheus had collapsed. The Fate-Weavers had fragmented into factions that spent more time fighting each other than controlling anyone else. The infrastructure of suppression and harvesting had been dismantled, but nothing had risen to replace it.

Though that wasn't entirely true.

Three weeks ago, Catherine had seen something in one of her visions—a woman gathering the Fate-Weaver fragments together.

Not through force. Through information. She knew things about myth-seeds that even Prometheus hadn't catalogued, and she was offering that knowledge to any Weaver willing to follow her.

Catherine had caught fragments. A name: Elara. A location: Chicago. And one image she couldn't shake—the woman standing in a room full of paper, old paper, centuries of it, reading by a single lamp. *She wasn't a Weaver herself,* Catherine had said, trying to steady her hands on the canvas. *That's what I couldn't figure out. She has no thread. But it's not like Silas's absence. Silas's thread was cut. Hers was never there. She's something else. Something I don't have a word for yet.* Solomon had asked her how old the woman looked.

Catherine had thought about it for a long time before answering. *She looked younger than me. But she moved like my grandmother used to move, when my grandmother was dying. Careful with every step. Like she knew how much she was carrying.* Solomon had filed that away in the part of his mind that tracked threats. Chicago, where Naomi had died. Chicago, where the Fate-Weavers had first noticed his family. Not a coincidence.

Nothing was ever a coincidence with Weavers.

He'd deal with Elara when the time came. For now, there was other work.

That left Solomon and the network they'd built in the wake of crisis.

Over the past twelve months, he'd traveled to seventeen countries. He'd worked with forty-three newly awakened individuals, helping them understand what they were becoming, training them in the basics of control, connecting them with others who shared their particular flavor of power.

Some had become friends. Some had become colleagues. A few had become something like family.

He thought about Ji-hyun.

She was teaching now, not school subjects, but shadow-craft.

She'd developed her own curriculum, her own methods, ways of reaching people that Solomon couldn't.

Her brother's dream of becoming a teacher had found expression through her. Twisted by grief into something new, but no less valuable.

The last time Solomon had seen her, she'd been working with a teenage boy in Seoul who'd been terrified of his own shadow. By the end of their session, the boy had been making his shadow dance in patterns that spelled out words.

"He reminds me of you," Ji-hyun had said afterward. "All that fear, and all that potential hiding behind it."

"I was never that young," Solomon had replied.

"You were younger. You just didn't know it."

He thought about Catherine.

She'd become the center of the network's intelligence operations—though "intelligence" was the wrong word for what she did. She didn't spy. She sensed. Her visions helped them find people before crises became catastrophes.

The effort was taking a toll. Solomon could see it in the lines around her eyes, the gray creeping into her hair despite her relative youth.

"The future keeps changing," she'd told him last month. "Every time I look, it's different. Every time we help someone, the whole pattern shifts."

"Is that good or bad?"

"Neither. Both. It means what we do matters. Every choice ripples outward. Every person we reach changes what comes next."

"That's a heavy burden."

"It's a gift," she'd said. "Being able to see that it matters. Most people have to take that on faith."

He thought about Helena.

She'd retreated from leadership after Mumbai, stepping back to spend her days in archives, documenting what Prometheus had been so that future generations would know what to avoid.

Solomon had visited her once, in the Geneva facility that now served as a repository rather than a prison. She'd been surrounded by files, ancient records being digitized by a small team of researchers. "I helped them do it," she'd said without being asked. "For years. Decades. I told myself it was necessary."

"Was it?"

"No. It was never necessary. We convinced ourselves it was because the alternative was admitting we'd been wrong from the beginning."

"What changed your mind?"

"You did." She'd smiled faintly. "You showed me what it looked like to hold power without being corrupted by it. To have the ability to end lives and choose, every single time, not to."

He thought about David Chen.

That name had haunted Solomon for months after their escape from the facility. The professor who'd taught literature. The father who'd missed his daughter's wedding. The man scheduled for "termination and disposal" who had reached out to Solomon's awareness and asked only to be remembered.

Solomon had kept his promise.

It had taken him three weeks after the Dreamer's fall to track down Hannah Chen. She was living in Singapore, working as an architect, still waiting for news about a father who'd disappeared seven years earlier during what authorities had called a "medical emergency."

He'd told her everything.

Not the supernatural parts—she wasn't ready for those, might never be ready. But the truth about the organization that had taken her father. The facility where he'd been held. The night Solomon had found him, and the choice he'd been forced to make.

"He asked me to remember him," Solomon had said. "To remember that he was someone. That he loved you. That he named his cat Byron."

Hannah had cried. Not the tears of fresh grief—those had come years ago—but the tears of someone finally learning what had happened to a wound that never healed.

"Thank you," she'd said when she could speak again. "I spent so long not knowing. Imagining the worst. At least now I can grieve properly."

"He was proud of you. Even at the end. The last thing I felt from him was pride that his daughter was out there, living her life."

Hannah had invited him to dinner. She'd shown him photographs of her father—young, middle-aged, the last picture taken before his disappearance. She'd told him stories about a man who'd loved poetry and terrible puns and taking long walks in the rain.

Solomon had listened to all of it.

That's what he'd promised, after all. Not to save David Chen—that had been impossible—but to ensure that someone remembered him. That his existence left a mark on the world beyond the cold statistics of Prometheus's files.

David Chen. Hannah's father. Professor. Byron.

He carried the name still. He would carry it always.

He thought about Marcus.

Marcus had died.

A heart attack, six months after Mumbai. Solomon had gotten the call from Helena, who'd delivered the news with the clipped efficiency of someone determined not to feel anything about it. The man who'd orchestrated Naomi's death, who'd tried to manipulate Solomon, who'd switched sides when it counted—that man had died in a hospital bed in Geneva, surrounded by monitors and nurses who didn't know what he'd been.

Solomon hadn't expected to grieve. The anger was still too fresh, too tangled with everything Marcus represented. But grief doesn't follow logic. It arrives where it arrives.

He'd gone to the hospital before the end. Had sat in the hallway for an hour before going in, arguing with himself about whether the man in that room deserved the courtesy. In the end, he'd walked in because Naomi would have walked in. Because she'd believed people were more than the worst thing they'd ever done, even when those worst things were unforgivable.

Marcus had been awake. Thin. The machines doing most of the work his body had given up on. His eyes had found Solomon's, and something in them— not quite peace, not quite regret, but the exhausted surrender of a man who'd finally stopped running from himself—had made Solomon pull up a chair.

They hadn't talked about Naomi. They hadn't talked about Prometheus or myth-seeds or any of it. Marcus had asked about the weather, and Solomon had told him about the snow in Tokyo, and they'd sat together for twenty minutes listening to machines breathe for a man who'd run out of reasons to breathe on his own.

When Solomon left, Marcus had said one word: "Thanks."

Solomon had spoken at the funeral. Brief words about a complicated man who'd done terrible things and tried, at the end, to do better.

Afterward, he'd stood alone at Marcus's grave and said what he couldn't say in public.

"I should hate you. Part of me still does. But you gave me Iris. You gave me the truth about Naomi. And you stood with us in Mumbai when you didn't have to."

The grave hadn't answered.

"I don't forgive you. I don't think I can. But I understand why you did what you did. Fear. Desperation. The belief that you were protecting something important."

He'd placed a small stone on the headstone—a Jewish tradition Naomi had taught him years ago—and walked away.

The world was still healing.

Cities were being rebuilt—not just the physical damage from the Mumbai event, but the social fabric torn by the revelation that people with powers had been living among them all along.

Some places had adapted well. Tokyo had established a formal liaison office for awakened individuals, staffed by people like Akari who understood both sides. Seoul had followed suit. Several European cities were experimenting with similar programs.

Other places had reacted with fear. There were still governments that treated awakening as a crime, communities that drove out anyone suspected of being different.

The conflicts continued. There would always be conflicts. But the apocalypse had been averted. The Dreamer was gone. And humanity, as it always did, was finding ways to continue.

Solomon sometimes wondered if that was enough.

The small things. The daily work. The endless cycle of crisis and response.

Was it enough?

He didn't know.

He suspected the answer would always be no.

And he'd learned to be okay with that.

Solomon walked back to the small cabin where he was staying.

It was a simple structure—wood and stone, built decades ago by someone who valued solitude. No electricity except what solar panels provided. No internet. No connection to the world he'd spend most of the year navigating.

That was the point.

Inside, Akari was making dinner. Something simple—vegetables and rice. The smell of ginger and garlic filled the small space. "How was it?" she asked without turning around.

"Good." Solomon set the notebook on the table. "I think I finally understand what she wanted."

Akari glanced at the notebook, then at him. Her light was steady, muted, comfortable in a way it hadn't been when they'd first met. Over the past year, she'd changed—they both had—but somehow the changes had brought them closer.

"And what was that?"

"For me to stop trying to save the world." He sat down across from where she was cooking. "She knew I couldn't. She knew no one could. But she also knew that trying—failing, getting back up, trying again—that was its own kind of victory."

Akari nodded. "That sounds like her."

"You never met her."

"I know her through you." She turned from the stove. "Through the choices you make. The way you treat people. The parts of yourself you don't like but refuse to give up on."

Solomon smiled despite himself. "When did you get so insightful?"

"I've always been insightful. You just weren't paying attention."

They settled into comfortable silence while she finished preparing the meal. Solomon watched her move through the small kitchen with easy familiarity— she'd been staying here with him for the past week, their first real break from work in months.

They hadn't talked about what this was. What they were becoming. But something had shifted between them over the past year. Something quiet and patient and real.

"So what's next?" Akari asked as she set plates on the table.

Solomon thought about it.

The list was never empty. There were always more awakened individuals who needed help. Ji-hyun had flagged three potential cases in Asia. Catherine had seen something troubling in Europe. The work would continue until he couldn't do it anymore.

But that wasn't really what she was asking.

"I don't know," he admitted. "I've spent so long reacting—to Naomi's death, to my awakening, to the Dreamer. I'm not sure I know how to just… live."

"Maybe that's the next thing to learn."

Living. Not surviving. Not fighting. Just being.

"I'm not sure I know how," he said.

Akari set down her chopsticks and reached across the table. Her hand found his—warm, steady, real.

"Neither do I," she said. "But we could figure it out together."

Solomon looked at their joined hands. At the woman who'd found him in an alley in Tokyo, who'd trained him when he was lost, who'd followed him into danger again and again.

Who'd stayed when she didn't have to.

"Together," he said.

Akari smiled.

And for a moment—just a moment—the weight lifted.

Later that night, after dinner, after talking, after the kind of comfortable silence that comes from knowing someone well, Solomon stepped outside.

The stars were brilliant here, far from city lights. The sweep of the Milky Way stretching across the sky, ancient light from suns that had died before humanity existed. The vast indifferent beauty of a universe that didn't care about myth-seeds or dreaming entities. It was humbling.

It was also comforting.

His shadow stretched across the snow at his feet—thin and weak compared to what it had been, diminished by the sacrifice in Mumbai. He'd given up most of his power to stop the Dreamer, poured everything he had into breaking a pattern that would have consumed the world.

The shadow that remained was barely more than ordinary.

That was okay.

He'd never wanted the power. He'd never asked to become what he became. The shadow had been a burden as much as a gift, a weight that had shaped his life in ways he hadn't chosen.

Now it was just... part of him. Neither divine nor monstrous.

Neither savior nor destroyer.

Just Solomon Nyx. Just a man trying to do good in a world that made doing good difficult.

He thought about Naomi.

Not the grief—that would never fully fade, and he'd stopped wanting it to. But the person she'd been. Her laugh, bright and unexpected. Her stubbornness. The way she'd believed in truth even when truth was dangerous. The simple instruction she'd left him, the one he'd been keeping ever since.

He'd kept it. He'd stopped Prometheus from harvesting more seeds. He'd destroyed the Dreamer's pattern. He'd helped dozens of awakened individuals find their way through confusion and fear.

And he would keep doing it. Not because he was special or chosen or powerful. But because it needed to be done, and he was here, and that was enough.

The door opened behind him. Akari stepped out, wrapped in a heavy blanket against the cold.

"You're going to freeze," she said.

"I'm okay."

She came to stand beside him, looking up at the same stars, sharing the same silence.

"What are you thinking about?" she asked.

"Naomi. The past year. What comes next."

"And?"

"I used to think her death was the worst thing that ever happened to me. The thing that broke me."

"What do you think now?"

"I think it was the beginning of something. Not good—I'll never call it good. But necessary, maybe. The thing that pushed me toward becoming who I needed to be."

Akari nodded slowly. "She'd be proud of you."

"You think so?"

"I know so." She leaned against him, sharing warmth in the cold mountain air. "You've done what she asked. You've protected people she never knew. You've built something that will outlast both of you."

Solomon looked up at the stars one more time.

Somewhere out there, in cities and villages and hidden places across the world, awakened individuals were living their lives. Some struggling. Some thriving. All of them part of something larger than themselves—a web of connection and purpose that Solomon had helped create.

He couldn't save them all. He couldn't even reach them all.

But he could show up. Day after day. Choosing to care when it would be easier not to.

That was Naomi's legacy. Not power or revenge or grand gestures. Just refusing to look away.

"Let's go inside," he said. "It's cold."

Akari smiled. "Finally, some sense."

They walked back to the cabin together, shadows stretching behind them across the snow. The door closed on the cold and the stars and the indifferent universe.

Inside was warmth. Company. Something like a future.

The shadows didn't reach for anything as they settled into their usual places. They just followed, patient and faithful, as shadows do.

Though once, just for a moment, Solomon's shadow stretched a fraction longer than the lamplight should have allowed. A familiar pressure brushed the edge of his awareness—faint, distant, like a sound heard through deep water.

Then it was gone. And his shadow was just a shadow again.

He chose not to think about it. Not tonight.

The next morning brought sunlight so clean it hurt.

Solomon woke to find Akari already up, standing at the window with a cup of coffee steaming in her hands. The mountains beyond the glass were white and silent, indifferent to everything that had happened, everything that might yet come.

"You're thinking too loud again," she said without turning.

"I'm thinking about what's next."

"There's always a next. That's what we learned, isn't it?" She turned to face him, and he saw something in her expression that hadn't been there before—not just peace, but determination. The face of someone who had found a cause worth continuing. "The Dreamer is dormant, not dead. The pattern is broken, not erased. Somewhere out there, things are still waking up."

"I know."

"And you're going to help them."

"We're going to help them."

Akari smiled—the real smile, the one he'd earned through fire and loss and all the impossible choices they'd made together.

On the table beside Akari's coffee, Solomon noticed a small canvas propped against the wall. He hadn't seen it last night. "Catherine sent that," Akari said, following his gaze. "It arrived this morning. She said you'd understand."

Solomon picked it up.

The painting was small—maybe eight inches square—done in Catherine's style, which he'd come to recognize over the past year: precise brushwork that somehow captured motion, like a photograph of something that hadn't happened yet. Before her extraction, she'd been a respected painter in Seoul. After her reconnection, her work had changed. Now she painted what she saw in her visions—futures that might or might not come to pass, rendered in oils that seemed to shift when you looked at them from different angles.

This one showed a city skyline Solomon recognized instantly.

Chicago. The South Side. But the shadows in the painting were wrong—too sharp, too organized, converging on a single point like spokes of a wheel. And at the center of that convergence, barely visible, a figure. A woman. Standing where Naomi had died.

On the back, in Catherine's careful handwriting: She's already there. Be careful.

Solomon's chest tightened. His shadow stirred beneath his skin—not much, not the way it used to, but enough to feel. That spot. That exact corner where they'd found Naomi, where the police tape had fluttered in the wind for three days before someone finally took it down. Someone was standing there now. Someone new. And the shadows were reaching for her the way they'd once reached for his sister.

He set the painting down carefully, face-up, where it could watch him from the table.

"Catherine also called while you were sleeping," Akari continued, watching his face. "Three new awakenings overnight. One in São Paulo, one in Nairobi, one in—" she paused, something flickering across her face, "—in Chicago."

Solomon went still.

"Chicago?"

"A teenager. Fifteen years old. Her name is Maya, and she's not like you were."

Solomon looked up.

"She's not afraid of them," Akari said. "That's what scared Catherine when the vision came in. The shadows are whispering to Maya and she's whispering back. She's been answering them for weeks. Her grandmother is the one who called the network—not because Maya is terrified, but because her grandmother is." Akari set down her coffee. "Catherine thinks she's been talking to them since she was nine."

Solomon went still.

He thought about himself at fifteen. The shadows that had watched. The fear that had consumed him. The sister who had stood between him and everything dark. Maya had none of that. Maya had something else — a nine-year-old's curiosity that a grandmother had not managed to extinguish, now grown into a fifteen-year-old's conversation with her own seed.

That was not his story. That was a different story.

"When do we leave?"

"After breakfast. I already booked the flights." Her smile widened. "Did you think I'd let you rest? The world doesn't stop needing people like us just because we saved it once."

Solomon rose from the bed, muscles protesting, shadow stirring beneath his skin—weaker than before, but present. Still there. Still his.

"No rest for the wicked?"

"No rest for the redeemed." Akari crossed to him, pressed a kiss to his forehead. "We have work to do, Solomon Nyx. And I don't know about you, but I'm looking forward to it."

He thought about Naomi. About what she'd asked of him, all those years ago.

Don't let them do it to anyone else.

"Let's go save someone," he said.

ACKNOWLEDGMENTS

No book is written alone.

Thank you to everyone who believed in Solomon's story—who read early drafts, offered their wisdom, and reminded me that shadows only exist because there's light.

To my family, who taught me that the spirit does not die. To my readers, who make the work worthwhile. And to everyone fighting their own battles against the dark—keep going.

ABOUT THE AUTHOR

JUSTIN LAMPERT is the author of Shadows Do Not Die, the first book in the Solomon Nyx series. He writes stories about people who find light in the darkness and fight for those who can't fight for themselves.

www.ingramcontent.com/pod-product-compliance
Lightning Source LLC
Chambersburg PA
CBHW050702290626
47170CB00016B/2580